Prime Cut

Diane Mott
Davidson

Prime Cut

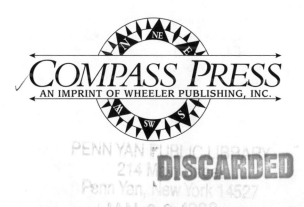

COMPASS PRESS

AN IMPRINT OF WHEELER PUBLISHING, INC.

Published in Large Print by arrangement with Bantam Books, a division of Bantam Doubleday Dell Publishing Group, Inc., in the United States and Canada

Compass Press Large Print book series;
an imprint of Wheeler Publishing Inc., USA

Set in 16 pt Plantin.

Library of Congress Cataloging-in-Publication Data

Davidson, Diane Mott.
  Prime cut / Diane Mott Davidson.
    p. (large print) cm.(Wheeler large print book series)
  ISBN 1-56895-588-X (hardcover)
  1.. Large type books. I. Title. II.
[PS3554.A925P75 1998b]
813'.54—dc21   98-47822
                                                          CIP

In loving memory of
Ann Ripley Blakeslee
1919-1998

Wonderful teacher, brilliant writer, unfailing
friend

They shall perish, but you [Lord] will endure;
they all shall wear out like a garment;
as clothing you will change them,
and they shall be changed;

But you are always the same,
and your years will never end.

PSALM 102: 26-27

Acknowledgments

The author wishes to acknowledge the help of the following people: Jim, Jeff, J.Z., and Joe Davidson; Kate Miciak, a fabulous editor; Sandra Dijkstra, a superb agent; Susan Corcoran, an outstanding publicist; Amanda Powers, a brilliant factotum; the great Lee Karr and the wonderful group that assembles at her home; John William Schenk, a wonderful chef and teacher; Karen Johnson, who fuels the author with truffles and culinary information; Thorenia West, who came up with the idea for this project and allowed the author to work in her domain; Meiko Catron, a phenomenal artistic director; all the talented people at Independence Pass Productions: Kit De Fever, Larraine Todd, Evan Waters, Errol Hamilton, Ludovic Chatelain, Levente, and Greg Griner; Aaron Bixby, for sharing insights; Katherine Goodwin Saideman, for her diligent reading of the manuscript; Ellen Shea, Schlesinger Library, Radcliffe College, Cambridge, Massachusetts; Richard Staller, D.O., Elk Ridge Family Physicians; Sergeant Robert Knuth; Carol Devine Rusley; Triena Harper, assistant deputy coroner, Jefferson County, Colorado; Jim Dullenty of the Rocky Mountain House in Hamilton, Montana;

Sybil Downing, and Richard "Pat" Patterson, for sharing their knowledge of the historic West; Brian Lang, curator, Hiwan Homestead Museum; Elaine Mongeau, King Soopers Pharmacy; and, of course, for continuing to be an unending source of patience and information, Sergeant Richard Millsapps, Jefferson County Sheriff's Department, Golden, Colorado.

"No woman can be too thin or too rich."

—ATTRIBUTED TO
THE DUCHESS OF WINDSOR

Buffet Lunch

◆

MERCIFUL MIGRATIONS CABIN
BLUE SPRUCE, COLORADO
MONDAY, AUGUST 18

◆

Models' Mushroom Soup

Asian Spring Rolls

Savory Florentine Cheesecake

*Endive, Radicchio, and Arugula with
Red Wine-Pear Vinaigrette*

Honeydew and Raspberries

*Parker House Rolls, Cornbread
Biscuits, Sourdough-Thyme Baguettes*

Burnt Sugar Cake, Whipped Cream

*Sparkling Water, Fruit Juices,
Coffee, Tea*

Chapter 1

Like a fudge soufflé, life can collapse. You think you have it all together—fine melted chocolate, clouds of egg white, hints of sugar and vanilla—and then *bam*. There's a reason things fall apart, my husband would say. But of course Tom would say that. He's a cop.

On the home front, things were not good. My kitchen was trashed, my catering business faced nasty competition, and my fourteen-year-old son Arch desperately missed our former boarder, twenty-year-old Julian Teller. For his part, Tom was embroiled in a feud with a new assistant district attorney who would plea-bargain Hermann Göring down to disturbing the peace. These days, I felt increasingly frantic—for work, for cooking space, for perspective.

Given such a litany of problems, life had brightened somewhat when my old cooking teacher, Chef André Hibbard, had offered me a one-day gig helping to cater a fashion shoot. My clients—the ones I still had—would have scoffed. *Catering to models? You must be desperate.*

Maybe I was. Desperate, that is. And maybe my clients would have been right to ridicule me, I reflected, as I pulled my van into the dirt lot at the edge of Sandbottom Creek. Across the water stood the Merciful Migrations cabin, where the first week of the photo shoot would take place. My clients would have cried: *Where are you going to hide your butter and cheese?* I didn't know.

The cloudless, stone-washed-denim sky overhead and remote-but-picturesque cabin seemed to echo: *You're darn right, you don't know.* I ignored a shudder of self-doubt, jumped out of my van, and breathed in air crisp with the high country's mid-August hint of fall. It was only ten A.M. Usually I didn't arrive two hours before a lunch, especially when the food already had been prepared. But show me a *remote historic home* and I'll show you a *dysfunctional cooking area.* Plus, I was worried about my old friend André. This was his first off-site catered meal since he'd retired four years ago, and he was a basket case.

I opened the van's side door and heaved up the box containing the Savory Florentine Cheesecakes I'd made for the buffet. I expertly slammed the door with my foot, crossed the rushing water, and carefully climbed the stone steps to the cabin. On the deck, I took another deep breath, rebalanced my load, then pushed through the massive wooden door.

Workers bustled about a brightly lit, log-lined, high-beamed great room. I rested my box on a bench and stood for a few minutes, ignored by the swirl of activity. Frowning, I found it challenging to comprehend my surroundings. Two workers called to each other about where to move the scrim, which I finally deduced was a mounted swath of fabric designed to diffuse the photographer's light. The two men moved on to clamping movable eight-foot-square wood screens—flats, I soon learned—into place. The flats formed a three-sided frame for "the set." Meanwhile, other folks rushed to and fro laden with hair dryers, notebooks, makeup trays, tripods, and camera equipment. Hoisting my box, I tried to figure out where André might be.

As I moved along, the models were easy to spot. Muscular young men and impossibly slender women, all with arrestingly sculpted faces, leaned against the log walls or slumped in the few stripped-bark bentwood chairs. The models' expressions were frozen in first-day-of-school apprehension. And no wonder: They were about to undergo the cattle call for the famed Prince & Grogan Christmas catalog. Prince & Grogan was an upscale Denver department store. Auditioning to model Santa-print pajamas for their ads *had* to be anxiety-creating.

I plowed a crooked path to what I hoped was the kitchen entrance. As I feared, the dark, cramped cooking space featured plywood glued along the one wall not covered by cupboards. Above the plywood, a dusty lamp hung to illuminate the battered sink. Next to the sink, buckled linoleum counters abutted a gas oven that didn't look much newer than a covered wagon's camp stove. In the center of the uneven wood floor, short, paunchy, white-haired André Hibbard surveyed the room with open dissatisfaction. As usual, my old friend and mentor, who had made a rare compromise when he'd immigrated, anglicizing his name from Hébert to Hibbard, sported a pristine white chef's jacket that hugged his potbelly. His black pants were knife-creased; his black shoes were shiny and spotless. When he saw me, his rosebud mouth puckered into a frown.

"Thank *goodness.*" His plum-colored cheeks shook; the silvery curls lining his neck trembled. "Are these people *pigs,* that I have to work in this *trough*? I may need money, but I have *standards!*"

I put down my box, gave him a quick hug, and sniffed a trace of his spicy cologne. "André! You're never happy. But I'm here, and I brought the nonmeat entrée you requested. Main-dish cheesecakes made with Gruyère and spinach."

He *tsk*ed while I checked the ancient oven's illegible thermostat. "The oven is hot. Whose recipe is it?"

"Julian Teller's. Now training to become a vegetarian chef." I lifted the cakes from the box and slid them into the oven to reheat. "Now, put me to work."

I helped André pour out the tangy sauces that would accompany the delicate spring rolls he'd stuffed with fat steamed shrimp, sprigs of cilantro, and lemongrass. Then we stirred chopped pears into the red-wine vinaigrette, counted cornbread biscuits, Parker House Rolls, and sourdough baguettes, and discussed the layout of the buffet. Prince & Grogan was the client of record. But

6

the fashion photography studio, Ian's Images, was running the show.

"Ian Hood does fashion photography for money," André announced as he checked his menu, "and nature photography for fun. You know this?"

In André's scratched, overloaded, red cooking equipment box—one I knew well from our days at his restaurant—I pushed aside his garlic press and salamander, and nabbed the old-fashioned scoop he used to make butter balls. "I know his pictures of elk. You can't live in Aspen Meadow and miss them."

André pursed his lips again and handed me the tub of chilled butter. "The helpers are day-contractors working for Prince & Grogan."

The word *contractor*, unfortunately, instantly brought my trashed kitchen to mind. *Forget it for now—you have work to do.* I scraped the butter into dense, creamy balls. I wrapped the breads in foil while André counted his platters. Because the cabin kitchen was not a commercially-approved space, he had done the bulk of the food preparation at his condo. While he gave me the background on the shoot, we used disposable thermometers to do the obligatory off-site food-service tests for temperature. Was the heated food hot enough? The chilled offerings cold enough? Yes. Finally, we checked the colorful arrangements of fruit and bowls of salad, and tucked the rolls into napkin-lined baskets.

When the cheesecakes emerged, golden brown and puffed, they filled the small kitchen with a heavenly aroma. André checked their temperature and asked me to take them out to the buffet. I stocked the first tray, lifted it up to my shoulder, and nudged through the kitchen door. When I entered the great room, a loudly barked order made me jump.

"Take off your shirt!"

I banged the tray onto the ruby-veined marble shelf that a note in André's familiar sloping hand had labeled *Buffet*. The shelf, cantilevered out of the massive log walls, creaked ominously. The tray of cheesecakes slid sideways.

"Your *shirt!*"

I grabbed the first springform pan to keep it from tipping. This was not what I was expecting. Because the noise outside the kitchen had abated, I'd thought the room was empty and that the models' auditions had been moved elsewhere. I was obviously wrong. But my immediate worry was the cheesecakes, now threatening to toboggan downward. If they landed on the floor, I would be assigned to cook a new main dish. This would not be fun.

With great care, I slid the steaming concoctions safely onto the counter. Arguing voices erupted from the far corner of the great room. I grabbed the leaning breadbasket. The floor's oak planks reverberated as someone stamped and hollered that the stylist was supposed to bring out the gold chains *right now!* I swallowed and stared at the disarray on the tray.

To make room on the counter, I skidded the cheesecakes down the marble. The enticing scents of tangy melted Gruyère and Parmesan swirled with hot scallions and cream cheese spiraled upward. The thick tortes' golden-brown topping looked gorgeous, fit for the centerfold of *Gourmet*.

Best to avoid thoughts of *gorgeous*, I reminded myself as I placed a crystal bowl of endive and radicchio on the marble. Truth to tell, for this booking I'd been a bit apprehensive in the appearance department. Foodie magazines these days eagerly screamed a new trend: *Today's caterer should offer pretty servers in addition to beautiful food! Submit head shots along with menus!*

I pushed the butter balls onto the counter, keenly aware of my unfashionably curly blond hair and plump thirty-three-year-old body beneath a white shirt, loose black skirt, and white apron. I hadn't submitted a photo.

Of course, neither had André, who was now fuming at a kitchen intruder. I sighed and moved the plate of juicy honeydew melon and luscious fat raspberries onto the counter. With one hand still gripping the tray, I inhaled uncertainly, then parted the cloth folds of the breadbasket. The tower of butter-flecked rolls, moist cornbread biscuits, and sourdough-thyme baguettes had not toppled, thank goodness. Self-doubt again reared its head. *Will the fashion folks eat this?*

"And while you're at it, take off your *pants*!" the same female voice barked.

"For sportswear?" a man squealed in dismay.

I turned and peered past the bentwood chairs

9

Savory Florentine Cheesecake

2 cups dry bread crumbs, preferably made from
   homemade brioche bread
8 tablespoons (1 stick) unsalted butter, melted
1 (10-ounce) package frozen chopped spinach
3 (8-ounce) packages cream cheese, softened
¼ cup whipping cream
½ teaspoon salt
½ teaspoon prepared Dijon mustard
4 eggs
1¼ cups freshly grated Gruyère cheese (about
   4 ounces)
¼ cup freshly grated imported Parmesan cheese
¼ teaspoon paprika
⅛ teaspoon cayenne
¼ cup chopped scallions

Preheat the oven to 350°F. Combine the bread
crumbs and melted butter and press on the bottom
and sides of a buttered 9-inch springform pan. Bake
for 8 to 12 minutes, or until very lightly browned.
Set aside to cool.

Cook the spinach according to package directions, place in a strainer, and press out all the liquid. In a large bowl, beat together the cream cheese, cream, salt, and mustard until smooth. Add the eggs, one at a time, and beat well after each addition. Add the spinach, grated cheeses, paprika, cayenne, and scallions. Beat on low speed until well combined.

Pour the mixture into the prepared crust and bake for approximately 1 hour and 5 minutes, or until the filling is set and browned. Cool for 15 minutes on a wire rack. Serve with sliced fresh fruit and a green salad with vinaigrette dressing.

Makes 12 servings.

and sleigh-bed frames the workers had piled higgledy-piggledy in the dusty, sun-steeped space. By the far bank of windows, a solitary, beautiful young man stood in front of a trio of judges. The judges—two women and a man, all of whom I knew—perched on a slatted bench. None of them looked happy.

Nearest was Hanna Klapper—dark-haired, wide-faced, fiftyish, recently and unhappily divorced. Hanna was familiar to me from my stint as a volunteer at Aspen Meadow's Homestead Museum. With her authoritarian voice and exacting ways, Hanna had designed exhibits installed by trembling docents, yours truly included. She had demanded that we put on surgical gloves before moving woven baskets or antique Indian pots even two inches. If we forgot, or, God forbid, dropped an item, she'd kick us out faster than you could say *Buffalo Bill's bloodstained holster*. According to André, Hanna had been appointed as the new artistic director at Prince & Grogan. I was amazed to see that she had shed her gingham-smock-and-sensible-shoes wardrobe for an elegant black silk shirt, tie, and pants. Her mahogany-colored hair, formerly pulled into a severe bun, was now shaped into a fashionably angled pageboy. This wasn't just a new job. It was a metamorphosis.

Hanna opened and closed her fists as she chided the male model. The gorgeous fellow, whose hair *might* have been a tad too black to be real, argued back. I wondered how Hanna's exhibits on *Cattle-Rustling Meets*

Cowboy Cooking and *Gunslingers: Their Gripes and Their Girls* had prepared her for ordering models to strip. In any event, I certainly wouldn't want her judging *my* body.

The woman next to her on the bench was a bit younger. Leah Smythe, small-boned and delicate-featured, wore her blond-streaked black hair in a shaggy pixie cut. She had jumped up and was now holding out her hands in a pleading gesture to the model. André had confided to me that Leah was the big cheese here today, the woman with the power: the casting director for Ian's Images. Leah also owned the cabin. When Ian's Images was not engaged in a shoot, Leah allowed Merciful Migrations to use the space for elk-tracking, fund-raising, and salt-lick distribution.

The beautiful young man who wouldn't take off his shirt looked as if *he* could use a lick of salt, especially on the side of a glass of tequila. My heart went out to him.

The man seated next to Hanna and Leah, photographer Ian Hood, had a handsome, fine-boned face, wavy salt-and-pepper hair, and a trim beard. Ian's photos of trotting elk, grazing elk, big-buck elk, and mom-and-baby elk graced the libraries, grocery stores, post offices, banks, and schools of Aspen Meadow and Blue Spruce. My best friend, Marla Korman—the other ex-wife of my ex-husband—had sent Ian a dozen elk burgers when he'd criticized her fund-raising abilities. He hadn't spoken to her since.

"Do you want this job or not?" Hanna brusquely asked the model. Seeming to take no notice, Ian squinted through the lens of a camera.

No, as a matter of fact, my inner voice replied. *I don't want this job.* No matter how much I tried to deny it, my heart was as blue as the gas flame on André's old restaurant stovetop. *Quit fretting,* I scolded myself as I counted out glasses and lined them up.

I sneaked another peek at the male model still being appraised by Ian, Hanna, and Leah. He was in his mid-twenties, indisputably from the Greek-god category of guys. His ultradark curly hair, olive complexion, and perfectly shaped aquiline features complemented wide shoulders above an expansive chest, only *slightly* paunchy waist, and long legs. But his handsome face was pinched in frustration. Worse, his tall, elegant body—clothed in fashionably wrinkled beige clothing—didn't seem too steady on its feet. Hands on hips, Hanna looked intensely annoyed. Leah sadly shook her head. Ian gestured angrily and squawked something along the lines of *You have to be able to compete. If you can't compete, get out of the business.*

"I hate competing," I muttered under my breath.

Apollo-in-khaki put his hands behind his head and scowled. He snarled, "We're having a few problems. So what? I'm the best guy for this job, and you know it."

I smiled in spite of myself. A *few* problems?

"Didn't your agent tell you about the cruise

section?" asked Leah Smythe, in a pleading tone. Ian Hood popped a flash, then stared quizzically at the camera, a Polaroid. When nothing happened, he lifted the apparatus and thwacked it loudly against the bench. I gasped.

"Spit out the picture!" Ian yelled at the camera, then lofted it back to his eye. Another flash sparked; no photograph emerged.

From the cabin's far door, footsteps and the clank of tools announced one of the workers who'd set up the scrim. Tall and gangly, this fellow traipsed into the great room hauling a load of bulging canvas bags. He writhed to get loose of his load, then dropped the sacks and thoughtfully rubbed a beard so uneven and scruffy it looked pasted on his ultrapale skin. After a moment, he picked up a framed picture and centered it on the wall. I broke out in a sweat and turned back to the buffet.

Please, I prayed, *no hammering.* Unfortunately, the crack of metal hitting log wall conjured up my commercial kitchen—retrofitted into our old house—as it was being destroyed by our general contractor, Gerald Eliot. One of the reasons I'd been interested in catering here at the cabin was that, apparently, Merciful Migrations had hired Gerald to do some remodeling, then fired him before paying him a cent. I wish I'd been that smart. I'd told André I didn't mind dealing with models; it was *remodelers* who'd made my life a living hell.

As the hammer banged methodically, I pictured Gerald Eliot, his yellow mane spilling to his shoulders, his muscled arms broadly gesturing, blithely promising he could *easily* install a new bay window—my ex-husband had destroyed the original—over my sink. *Won't take more than three days,* Eliot had vowed at the beginning of August, with a wide grin.

The pounding reverberated in my skull. Eliot had brandished his power saw, destroyed the window's casing and surrounding wall, then accidentally ripped through an adjoining cupboard. The entire cabinet, along with its load of dishes and glasses, had crashed to the floor. *Just an additional day of work to fix that,* he'd observed with a shrug. *No extra charge. Start first thing tomorrow.*

I groaned, checked my watch, and turned my attention back to the tray. Swiftly, I plugged in the electric warmer and moved the cheesecakes on top. I was here; I was working. I would even be paid. And I needed the money. Before Gerald Eliot had sliced into our kitchen wall, the new catering outfit in town had cut my business by thirty percent. And unfortunately, on Day One of the two days Gerald Eliot had actually worked for me, he'd pocketed the full seven-hundred-dollar down payment on the new window installation. On Day Two, he'd covered the gaping hole he'd made with plastic sheets, hopped into his pickup truck, and roared away.

I straightened the row of spring rolls bulging with pink shrimp. *Focus.* At least at this cabin there's a *kitchen*—although *it* wasn't in very good shape, either.

"What else?" I asked André cheerfully when I strode back into his domain. He was fingering the plywood on the wall beside the oven.

"Drinks, serving utensils, and ice." He looked up from the wall, his wide blue eyes merry. "Guess what I just found out? They fired Gerald Eliot for sleeping with a model!" I sighed; André loved gossip. It was one of the reasons he'd despised retirement.

I swung back out to the buffet with my newly loaded tray. Sleeping with a model, eh? At least he was getting some sleep. This was not the case with my friends the Burrs, whose house was to be the site for the second part of this fashion shoot. Neither one of *them* was getting much sleep at all these days, thanks—once again—to good old Gerald Eliot.

In April, Cameron and Barbara Burr had been convinced the sun room Gerald Eliot was adding onto their house would be completed by August. That was when Ian's Images was scheduled to set up the P & G catalog's outdoor shots, using as a backdrop the Burrs's spectacular view of the Continental Divide's snow-capped peaks. Gerald Eliot had already been working on the sun room for eleven months—admittedly, off and on—but what was left to be done?

Ah, but the windows had been delayed; for some reason, the drywall couldn't go up until the windows were in; Eliot had had a cash flow problem; he'd sailed off to his next job. Mountain breezes swirling through the house at night had forced Barbara Burr into the hospital—with pneumonia. Cameron Burr had moved into their guest house. The last I'd heard, Barbara's pulmonologist had put her on a ventilator.

Maybe when the P & G catalog was done, all of Gerald Eliot's former clients could have lunch and form a chiseled-by-a-contractor support group. But not today. Today, I was catering with André, watching models undress, taking food to malnourished, depressed Cameron Burr, trying to think of new ways to make money, worrying about my husband's conflicts with an arrogant prosecutor, and calling down to Lutheran Hospital to see if Barbara Burr had died.

I admired the beautiful dishes on the buffet. That was enough for one day, wasn't it? *Don't ask.*

Chapter 2

The angry voices on the far side of the room intensified; I glanced out the picture window above the counter. A hundred feet below the cabin, a crowd of young men and women streamed through a stand of white-skinned aspens profuse with lime-colored leaves. The waiting models had briefly taken their nervousness outside, apparently, but now they were coming back. Clouds of cigarette smoke obscured their faces as they ascended the stone steps. Behind them, the rippling creek glittered in the morning sun.

I hustled back to the kitchen. I was surprised that so many young people had even been able to find this turn-of-the-century cabin. The six-mile dirt road that led to it meandered beside a long-abandoned stagecoach trail. In summer, the narrow byway alternated between treacherous mud and sandstorm-thick dust. In winter, the road was closed.

When I returned with the knives and forks, the popping noise of a battery-operated screwdriver ceased abruptly. Hanna's enraged voice grated through the still air. "One last time, do you want to do swimwear or not? You know the rules! We have to see your *body*."

I glanced around to see the Greek god slowly unbuttoning his shirt. The faces of the three judges swiveled; their eyes drilled into me. Embarrassed, I whirled and clattered together a batch of serving spoons.

"Go away!" André's strained voice rose from the kitchen. "No food until later! Guard my buffet, Goldy!" A door slammed.

My palms itched. I glanced at the spread on the marble, then back out the window. Guard the buffet? How? The models, massed at the cabin door, were filtering inside. Beyond the aspens, a warm August breeze wrinkled the dark expanse of the creek, which bent in a ragged U-shape around the cabin. Sunlight played over a huge boulder abutting the creek. I smiled and briefly wished Arch were with me: My son would have instantly pointed out how much the enormous rock resembled an elephant. And it did.

I clattered the ice bath onto the marble shelf and topped it with the gold-rimmed china bowl of butter balls. Carefully, I smoothed plastic wrap over the bowl and unloaded the pewter bread-and-butter plates. Next to these I set the container of red wine-pear vinaigrette. I picked up the tray and tried to summon up some of the old resolve I felt so lacking these days.

"You know, Bobby, we don't really *care* that you were out partying last night," Hanna was saying earnestly to the Greek god. "We don't *care* why you've gained ten pounds. And we can't *care* that you drank a lot of coffee waiting for us. Your stomach's not flat and your eyes are bloodshot. Bloodshot and bloated don't sell swimwear."

"You're too damned hard to please!" Bobby-with-the-slight-paunch shrieked.

I sighed, checked all the foodstuffs one last time, and squared the cheesecakes between the spring rolls and breadbasket. With infinite care I turned back, determined to invite Bobby over for a bite to eat and a glass of sparkling water.

Too late. Bobby, his beige shirt open, was pulling up his trousers. Now his much-criticized stomach hung over his undies like a hot-water bottle; his thighs jiggled as he grappled with the pants waistband. Clasping his trousers closed with one hand and his unbuttoned shirt with the other, he pushed his way clumsily through the rustic furniture. Suddenly, he tripped and flailed wildly.

"What is this damn thing?" he yelled as he regained his balance and savagely kicked a piece of equipment resembling a cannister vacuum across the room.

"Sorry, sorry," muttered the screwdriver-wielding construction worker. He loped across the wooden floor and yanked at the cannister's cord. "It's not our air compressor," he apologized to Bobby, who ignored him. "It was left here by Gerald Eliot." As if on cue, everyone groaned at the mention of the infamous contractor.

Bobby's no-longer-handsome face was wracked with fury and humiliation. As he rushed across the room, his ebony curls whipped behind him and his khaki shirt flapped open. *What is the deal with this guy?* I wondered.

"Please—" I began, gesturing toward the array of food.

"Forget it!" Bobby barked as he swept past me.

Across the room, Leah, Hanna, and Ian conferred. Hanna bellowed, "Peter!"

Beside the windows, the scruffy-bearded handyman pushed the air compressor aside and plugged in an ornament-bedecked Christmas tree. Sparkly lights flashed as a breathtakingly tanned male model, the presumptive Peter, strode across to the bench and the trio seated there. He was dressed in a snowy-white shirt and blue jeans. His very straight, very shiny brown hair swung forward as he bent to say a few words. When the judges responded, Peter's plump lips curved into a confident smile. He flipped the glossy hair out of his eyes and

21

handed what looked like an oversized scrapbook to Leah. She leafed through it briefly while Hanna looked over her shoulder. Ian Hood murmured to Peter, who quickly started unbuttoning.

This time, the white shirt dropped swiftly past muscled shoulders, a well-built chest, and concave, washboard abs. While the shirt puddled noiselessly on the floor, Peter undid his pants and dropped them. He hooked a thumb around the side of dark, shiny bikini briefs and struck a pose. I hastened back to the kitchen.

"Did you keep the marauders away?" André regarded me impatiently, then turned back to the stove.

"I tried to, but nobody...They've started to..."

He grunted, shook his head, and whacked his wooden spoon on a plate. Then he gave me the full benefit of his heart-shaped face with its button nose and sharp, dimpled chin. "Do you think I came out of retirement to fail? Are you going to doom me to playing checkers and visiting the cardiologist? To making small talk with my wife's nurse?"

I sighed. "André, I'm sorry—"

"Close the door," he ordered sternly. "Four people have already interrupted me this morning. Looking for cups of soup!" His silver eyebrows climbed his forehead. "Does this look like a *deli*?" His forehead wrinkled in disgust as he lovingly swirled a spoon through the steaming pot of his thick, herb-scented mushroom soup. "Now. My cake. It needs to be served warm, with cream." He paused and considered the pan on the front burner. "Ah, Goldy, I'm not certain I taught you to make this syrup. You must be very quick...." André touched the scar on my arm where I'd accidentally burned myself years ago retrieving a batch of Cornish hens from his restaurant oven. He'd never forgiven himself for not showing me how to handle his oversized roasting pan.

"André, listen, you're not supposed to make a cake in an off-site kitchen—"

"Phh-t." His chin trembled dismissively. "This must be fresh. And do you want to hear about the first boy? A very juicy story—"

"Well—"

"I had to listen to him. He is extremely immature, cannot even cook for himself." He glanced at his row of utensils, then commanded: "Please put away the first stirrers and hand me my candy thermometer." I did as directed. "His name is Bobby Whitaker, and he is the young half-brother to Leah Smythe, who feels sorry for him. But not sorry enough to teach him to make low-fat turkey loaf." André dramatically poured sugar into a cast-iron pan and set it aside. "Bobby has started to peddle real estate. He must attend many fattening luncheons, he says. He finally had his first sale last night and celebrated. He was hung over, he wanted to go back to bed. But he claims his true love is modeling, not being the salesman." André checked his recipe in his notebook, then pushed his thumb into wrapped butter sticks to make sure they were soft. "All this I had to hear while Bobby drank cup after cup of my coffee. He asked me if I'd been to Milan. He said he did his book there. I told him I was the pastry chef for a huge celebration outside the cathedral. At another cathedral, I made my *crème brûlée* for a hundred clergy. Where was that, he asked. In my town of Clermont-Ferrand, I told him, where, when I was eleven, I helped smuggle a Milanese Jewish woman and her French husband, also Jewish, out of the town. They went to Switzerland and then America. Do you think Bobby cared about *my* stories? No. He asked me if it was hard to make pastry and custards for so many people, and had I ever catered a lunch for top producers. I said, what is that? A meal for hens?"

"I care." I smiled. "I love your stories." Early on, I had learned the habit of nodding seriously while appearing to listen to André's tales of his culinary history, his dessert-making ability, the many well-heeled clients he'd had, or even his childhood capers during the war. I was convinced these tales were all exaggerated. But if you ignored André, you had a short career in André's kitchen. I asked thoughtfully, "What *book* did Bobby have made in Milan?"

André sniffed. "His portfolio. All the models have them. Hanna and Leah have to look at it first to see if they like the look of the model in different clothes." I tapped the counter and shook my head. "Goldy. Remember when I taught you to inspect meat? It is the same."

Assessing cuts of steak was like judging people's bodies? Was that where they got the term *beefcake*? I asked, "If Bobby is Leah's half-brother, why didn't she stick up for him out there?"

He paused over a cardboard box of eggs and grinned. "She tries, I think. Leah is the long-time lover of Ian," André announced. This tidbit I already knew—from Marla, of course. "Although," André continued thoughtfully, "those two don't seem to be getting along very well." The kitchen door opened; he scowled. "What pig wants something now?"

"Help me," pleaded a female whisper from the doorway.

"Pah!" howled André, without pity. He slid the sugar-filled iron pan to an unlit burner. "Go away!"

"What do you need?" I said quietly to a russet-haired woman whose large brown eyes glowed from within a gaunt, high-cheekboned face. She was stunning as well as very thin and tall. Despite the season, she was dressed in an oak-brown cashmere sweater, a long clingy brown wool skirt, and gleaming brown leather boots. She teetered precariously on the boots' stiletto heels.

Her cocoa-colored lower lip trembled. She drew her haunting face into an expression of intense pain. "Please—"

I said, "Are you okay?"

"Coffee," she whispered. She grinned uncertainly, affording a glimpse of brilliant teeth. "I just need a tiny sip. If you don't mind," she added.

André *hrumph*ed and shrugged. I reached for the glass pot, but it held only an inch of metallic-

Models' Mushroom Soup

5 tablespoons butter, divided
1 large carrot, chopped
1 large onion, chopped
2 celery stalks, chopped
8 ounces fresh mushrooms, thinly sliced
4 tablespoons all-purpose flour
6 cups homemade chicken stock (preferably the
   low-fat chicken stock made from the recipe
   in *Killer Pancake*)
2 tablespoons chopped fresh thyme
1 tablespoon chopped fresh marjoram
2 tablespoons whipping cream
6 tablespoons dry white wine
salt and freshly ground black pepper

In a large skillet, melt 2 tablespoons of the butter
and cook the carrot, onion, and celery, covered, over
medium-low heat for 15 to 25 minutes, until the
vegetables soften. Set aside to cool.

In a small skillet, melt 1 tablespoon of butter and
sauté the mushrooms briefly until they are cooked

through and begin to yield some juice. This takes less than 5 minutes. Set the mushrooms aside.

In a blender, puree the carrot, onion, and celery. In a large skillet, melt the last 2 tablespoons of butter, stir in the flour, and cook this paste, stirring constantly, over low heat until the flour bubbles. Slowly whisk in the stock. Cook and stir over medium heat until hot and thickened, about 10 minutes. Stir in the thyme, marjoram, whipping cream, mushrooms, wine, and pureed vegetables until hot and bubbly, about 5 minutes. Salt and pepper to taste. Serve immediately.

Makes 6 servings.

smelling brew. My next job after heating the savory cheesecakes, laying out the spring rolls, mixing the vinaigrette, and arranging the buffet, would be to brew a fresh pot of coffee. I wondered vaguely how André would have managed if I hadn't agreed to help today.

"Do you have powdered nondairy? Nonfat, that is?" the young woman inquired. Under the thick makeup, I figured she was about nineteen.

"Well, André keeps cream in his cooler—"

"No! Just give me that." She wobbled across the uneven floor toward me, eyes fixed greedily on the coffeepot. I sighed and poured the viscous liquid into a foam cup, which the model immediately grabbed, along with a jar of powdered creamer from a wooden shelf abutting the plywood over the sink. André frowned. The model ignored him, shook a dusty layer of creamer across the surface of the murky liquid, swirled it with a polished green fingernail, and took a noisy slurp.

"I'm Goldy." I kept my voice low in the hope that André would go on with his work and ignore us. "And you're—?"

"Rustine," she whispered over her shoulder as she clutched her cup and swayed toward the wooden door. She turned and gave me a vaguely flirtatious look. "Goldy? You're the famous caterer, right?"

"Uh," I said, mindful of André's ego, "not exactly."

Rustine mock-kissed the air. "I can't *wait* for lunch." She raised the coffee cup in salute. The door swooshed shut behind her.

Great, I thought as I turned back to André. Instead of continuing with the burnt sugar cake, however, he was penning another sign: DO NOT DISTURB OR YOU WILL NOT EAT!

"Put this on the door!" He thrust the sign at me. "Then we will make our syrup!"

I reluctantly thumbtacked the sign to the outside of the heavy kitchen door. In the cabin's small foyer, a dozen handsome young people huddled mutely, waiting to be called. Rustine put her cup to her lips and avoided my eyes. In the bright sunlight, her hair shone like an orange-gold cloud around her face. I nodded at the models and quietly shut the door.

"All right, we are ready. You must watch." André moved the iron pan back to the burner and adjusted the flame. "Sugar can kill you," he warned in a low voice. His very blue eyes, slightly bulbous above reddening cheeks, concentrated on the heating pan. He clutched the padded handle in a death grip. I stepped up beside the cabin's ancient stove and dutifully watched. André's wooden spoon moved rhythmically through the white crystals as they turned to slush.

"The sugar melts." The red folds on his neck trembled. "It is molten lead. It is lava. The burns to the skin are deep. Instantaneous." He shook the pan and glanced again at my scar, then at the lid and towel that lay on the wooden countertop. There was a knock at the closed door.

"Not now!" I called, ignoring André's scowl. The knocker went away.

The thick mass of muddy brown crystals melted under André's determined stirring. He reached for the beaker of water he had poured before starting the caramel.

"Of course you must never use water from the hot water heater." His small nose wrinkled. "Minerals in the filtering process." He shuddered, as if the minerals were radioactive. His eyebrows quirked upward as he poured the water onto the pan's molten mass. A nimbus of mist erupted as the pan's contents hissed. "The steam, mind!" he cried, and I made a great show of pulling back. André's free hand slapped the lid onto the pan.

"Very impressive," I said, with genuine admiration.

"My *sirop caramel*," he announced triumphantly. The dimple in his chin deepened as he smiled. "Now I will make my burnt sugar cake." The beater on his electric mixer hummed and twirled through the softened butter. "You will tell me about your fight at the Soirée tasting party with this horrible competitor, Litchfield," he ordered. He pronounced it *leachfield*.

I sighed. For the last five years, my business—*Goldilocks' Catering, Where Everything Is Just Right!*—had been the only professional food service in the mountain area. And for each of those years, I'd been the caterer of record for the September Soirée, the annual fund-raiser for Ian Hood and Leah Smythe's charitable enterprise, Merciful Migrations. But now there was Upscale Appetite, and its proprietor,

Craig Litchfield, was working diligently to steal the Soirée from me. Worse yet, Litchfield was cute. He *always* submitted a head shot.

"Dark brown hair, drop-dead gorgeous. That's Craig Litchfield," I began, as André showered sugar into the bowl. "Women love him. He started the caterers' version of a food fight in June. Ads, promotions, underbidding. He went after my customers with a vengeance. How he got my client list with all my schedules and prices, I don't know."

André shook his head and dropped an egg into the batter. "I should have come to the tasting party at the Homestead. My doctor is an idiot." Another egg plopped beside the whirling beater.

"We were in the Homestead kitchen when Litchfield lost his temper with Arch."

André poured cake flour into his mixture. "How can a chef lose his temper with a four-teen-year-old while he's cooking?" Teenagers, in André's view, did not figure in the world of food preparation.

I shrugged. "Litchfield's no chef. He was heating frozen hors d'oeuvre when Arch asked who his supplier was for phyllo triangles. Litchfield said Arch was being disrespectful, implying the food wasn't fresh. Arch argued, Litchfield yelled at him, then grabbed his arm and yanked him out of the kitchen. I calmed Arch down, told him to wait in the van. Then I marched back and told Litchfield to back off. But when Arch came in later for a snack, Litchfield shoved him out the back door so hard that he actually fell to the ground. I was so mad I banged my marble cake plate over Litchfield's head. Didn't hurt him. Broke my plate."

I groaned, remembering. Craig Litchfield had been unharmed; my son had recovered; the tasting party had been postponed. Litchfield, calling me an "unattractive, overweight harpy," had reported the incident to the Furman County Sheriff's Department. The investigating officer had told me I'd used undue force, even if I had been concerned about my son. The cop said I was lucky Litchfield hadn't pressed charges.

"Poor Goldy," murmured André, as he dribbled the burnt sugar syrup into the batter. Tom, too, had sympathized with my plight. Even Arch had felt bad.

André poured the batter into parchment-lined pans. Another knock, this one sharper, reverberated through the decrepit kitchen. "No!" André roared.

The door banged open. I stepped back. André grimaced and thrust his pans into the oven.

"What in the world is going *on* in here?" Leah Smythe demanded, her voice managing to be hurt, upset, and indignant all at once. Her shredded black-and-gold hair quivered as she regarded us. Stunned, neither André nor I answered her. She blew the bangs off her forehead and crossed her arms. Short and slender, she was dressed in faded blue jeans and a black cotton sweater.

"Well—" I began.

Leah studied me with an up-and-down look. Recalling my work on last year's Soirée? No. She said flatly, "You're not looking to work as a model."

I blushed. "No, I'm helping André with the lunch—"

"Then *please* don't give any more models coffee! Then everybody wants some and everybody complains about unfairness and nothing gets accomplished. And you'd better move that food outside to the deck. Hanna and Ian are terrified the set will be covered with crumbs. By the way, people have already started eating those burritos. The break hasn't even been announced! Why did you put out the food?"

André's face wrinkled with rage. "My spring rolls," he retorted loudly, "are *not* burritos, Miss Smythe. Goldy! Rescue my dish."

"I'm sorry, truly I am," I murmured to Leah. "I'll get it right now." Conflict with competitors is one thing. But the first rule of food service is that you avoid fights with *clients*.

In the great room, I snatched the spring rolls and slid them onto a tray. One was missing; one had been dug into. I scanned the cabin's interior for the culprits, squinting suspiciously at the scruffy man in overalls who'd moved Gerald Eliot's air compressor. Still engaged in set construction, the fellow was hanging a snakeskin on the wall between the Christmas tree and the far windows. Next to the skin, he'd hung a weapon I recognized: It was a Winchester, just like Tom's. Rattlesnakes and rifles. Now *that's* what I called the spirit of the holidays.

Leah quick-stepped to rejoin the judges. She, Hanna, and Ian peered dubiously at a sharp-faced blond woman wearing white pedal pushers and a halter top. The woman's extreme thinness, her bony hips, her distinct rib cage, contrasted bizarrely with her high, full breasts. The other auditioning models were nowhere in sight. Still, the smell of cigarette smoke told me they weren't far off.

Clutching the tray, I hustled back to the kitchen. André was cleaning up his beaters and bowl. I grabbed a clean pair of tongs and removed the gutted spring roll. To my chagrin, the tongs snagged unexpectedly. I carefully pulled them up; between the tongs was the violated roll and a cilantro-tangled piece of...hair. With a silent curse and surreptitious haste, I opened the tongs over the trash. Then I quickly covered the dishes with foil and rewashed the tongs and my hands. I had never seen André make such an error of hygiene. My doubts about his ability to shift from retirement to catering went from sea-level to subterranean.

I scooped up the covered dishes, slipped into the foyer, and stepped briskly past the dozen young people who'd suddenly reappeared. Rustine held the front door of the cabin open for me.

"The blonde's had her breasts enlarged.

Plus she's wearing flesh-colored falsies," she whispered.

"I beg your pardon?" I whispered back, startled.

"And that photographer's a prick."

"*What?*"

She gave me a *Mona Lisa*-mysterious smile. "You're the caterer who figures things out, right?"

"I don't understand—" But the door was already closing. Figure out *what?* Gratefully, I stepped out into the pine-scented fresh air.

When I darted past racks of clothing, a sapphire-winged hummingbird swooped by. Sixty feet off the deck, the creek gurgled over a bed of rocks. Two mountain chickadees flirted on the elephant-shaped boulder. When a breeze tossed the aspens' lacy tops, movement caught my eye. Across the creek, a small herd of elk lowered their long necks to graze in a meadow that sloped to a broken wooden fence. Everything was serene and ordered: utterly unlike the contentious scene inside.

The redwood deck wrapped around the cabin. I made a path through the clothing racks and deck chairs, then arrived at another row of windows. I carefully placed the covered cheesecakes and spring rolls on a picnic table and checked my watch: ten more minutes. I trotted back to the front door.

Suddenly, the deafening noise of breaking glass split the air. Two feet in front of me, the picture window exploded. Shards burst over the deck. Across the creek, the elk bolted. I froze and waited for my heartbeat to slow. The projectile that had done the damage lay on its side among sparkling slivers of glass. It was Ian Hood's Polaroid.

I wondered if we'd ever get to lunch.

Chapter 3

Inside, all was chaos. The models whispered fearfully. The handyman, his hammer in his hand, gaped at Ian Hood. Ian was shaking his fist at the shattered window.

"How many times have I asked for *three* new Polaroid cameras?" he screeched. "And I go to look for one, and trip over that damn compressor! Rufus, get the hell over here!"

Leah Smythe made soothing noises while the scruffy construction worker dropped his hammer and trotted to Ian's side. Hanna Klapper stood with her hands on her hips, judging the scene. Her face was a mask of fury.

I looked in horror at the buffet. The camera had cut a straight path through the food. The salad lay upended on the floor. Vinaigrette had spilled down the row of napkins and now dripped on strands of endive. Liquid-soaked rolls had landed topsy-turvy on the marble shelf. I scooted toward the kitchen.

André was leaning against the doorjamb with his arms crossed. He gave me a dry, appraising look. "Eccentric diners always provide the best stories," he observed. "Is my lunch canceled?"

"Let me check."

Ian Hood stomped past me, headed for the cabin door. Leah Smythe followed at his heels, urging, "C'mon, baby, we'll get the compressor out of the way, you won't trip over it again, don't give up—"

"Any chance we're still going to try to—" I began. But Leah ignored me and raced down the steps after the seething Ian.

At the buffet, Hanna delicately picked up the ruined rolls and piled them back into the basket.

"Ah, Hanna?" I ventured. "Goldy Schulz. I worked on your museum exhibits. Congratulations on your new job with P & G."

"Thank you." She sniffed and smoothed her clipped hair behind her ears. Her dark eyes challenged mine. "Do you know what my duties are?" But before I could answer, she went on, "Choosing the clothing to be photographed. Arranging the catalog layout. Selecting models. Overseeing the shoot." *Not* temper-tantrum cleanup, in other words.

"Leave the pick-up to me," I exclaimed cheerfully, as if photographers flung cameras through windows and ruined my buffets all the time.

"We promised the models lunch." The authoritarian tone I knew so well was like a steel shaft through her voice. I nodded meekly, booted the metal housing that had come loose from the compressor back toward the rustic furniture, and leaned over to snatch a lettuce leaf from the floor. Hanna continued, "We must serve it."

Of course, I instantly recognized the clients'

universal *we,* which means *you, caterer.* "It won't take ten minutes to set up on the deck." I turned and winked at her. "André is incredibly versatile," I lied.

"That is certainly a good thing," Hanna muttered skeptically.

In the kitchen, André had flicked on the oven light and was peering at his cake. "Lunch or no?" he demanded impatiently.

"Yes." I dumped the garbage and washed my hands.

He grunted. "You should take the backup food, and leave."

Right, I thought as I set a kettle of water on to boil for the chafing dish, *and leave you with this mess.* Within two minutes I had checked on the soup, loaded another tray with the backup platters of salad, vinaigrette, rolls, and butter, and was whisking it out to the picnic tables. I checked my watch: five past twelve. We weren't doing too badly, considering. I filled the chafer's *bain-marie* with the boiling water. André poured in the mushroom soup, then retrieved the burnt sugar cake. The smell was divine and I told him so. A rap at the kitchen door preceded Hanna's entry. Imperiously, she tapped at her watch.

"Right now," I promised as André lofted the cake platter and I picked up the bowl of whipped cream.

I half expected the lunch to be rocky. The red-haired crew member with the thin beard introduced himself to me as Rufus Driggle, set-builder and still-life photographer. He told me to call him Rufus; he hated his last name. The work made him a hearty eater, Rufus went on to inform me, but he never gained any weight because he always had indigestion from dealing with Ian. He paused and stroked his beard. "I prefer working with the elk, actually." I nodded vaguely and replenished the buffet as the male models piled their plates high with cheesecake, salad, baguettes, and spring rolls.

The female models depressed me. Eschewing the cheesecake, breads, and salad dressing, they uniformly arranged a few greens on their plates next to one or two Asian spring rolls. Then, like bio-class dissectors, they pulled the rolls apart to extract the shrimp. I hoped André wasn't watching, but of course he was. He *hrumph*ed and concentrated on cutting the cake.

Hanna curtly announced that the cattle call for that day was over except for two more female models: Rustine and Yvonne. The agents of the remaining models would be called later about a resumption of auditions. A groan went up from the group. Then all the women except for Rustine and the sharp-faced blonde, who I assumed must be Yvonne, made a beeline for André's burnt sugar cake. They sliced themselves fat wedges, smothered them with whipped cream, then skulked to far-away chairs to eat in solitary silence. I started transporting dirty dishes back to the kitchen.

To my surprise, André stood waiting at the front door. He held a basket bulging with a zipped bag of salad, a plastic-wrapped platter of spring rolls, and a steam-clouded jar of soup.

"Take this to your friend whose wife has pneumonia," he told me. "Your check is inside. I know what it is to have a sick wife, Goldy. Cater to your friend, and forget these other men upsetting you." He waved his free hand and enumerated them. "That idiot builder. That conniving caterer, Litchfield."

"You're the best," I replied, and meant it. I took the basket and thought of the pork butt I'd already roasted and wrapped. Cameron Burr would have food for three days. If only food could make his wife well again...

André murmured, "Where is the much-praised Julian Teller? Can't he help you beat this monster Litchfield?"

I shook my head. Two months ago, Julian had finished his freshman year at Cornell. He'd considered himself lucky to land a summer kitchen job at a swank upstate New York hotel. "Julian was supposed to come visit, but he never showed up. And his classes start next week." We had all been disappointed not to see Julian this summer. Arch, though, had felt Julian's absence most acutely.

"Go see your friend, Goldy. Have him tell you one of his stories of Nazi treasure. And stop worrying so much."

Clasping the basket, I hugged André and hurried down the stone steps. Once across the creek, I trotted between the mud-blackened bank, the granite boulders, and a thickly packed heap of dry twigs, monument to the industry of beavers. A rising wind whistled through a nearby stand of yellow-tinged cottonwoods.

Most of the models had departed. The elk had returned to the meadow to graze. Beside my van, the breeze whiplashed a slew of white-faced daisies. Leggy thistle branches waved bright pink-purple tops and spilled hairy nests of silver seeds. The breeze shifted and wafted my scent toward the elk. They lifted their racks and trotted cautiously toward the safety of the trees. I unlocked the door, shoved the picnic basket onto the front seat, and thought of André's words. Forget the men who were bothering me? How?

I revved the van. What I really needed was help from the main man in my life—Tom. I was terrified the county health inspector would descend on our home at any moment and deem that the cabinet-window mess left by Gerald Eliot wasn't technically a commercial kitchen *repair,* but a *remodeling.* Remodeling was illegal without pulling a permit and closing the kitchen. Tom had promised to help. But Andy Fuller, the prosecutor who was such a thorn in Tom's side, had just plea-bargained down to reckless driving a drunk driver's killing of six people on I-70. Tom's long, tempestuous meetings with Fuller precluded home maintenance.

I carefully negotiated the rocky road leading back to Blue Spruce. At the intersection with the highway, preoccupied with thoughts of Tom's troubles with Andy Fuller, I gunned the van and nearly hit a paint-peeled board announcing *Swiss Inn Apartments—Seven Miles Ahead, West of Aspen Meadow,* next to a *Real Estate For Sale* sign plastered with an *Under Contract!!!* sticker. I slowed and sloshed through the mud. Worry muddled my brain. Where was I? Oh yes, taking food to Cameron Burr, president of the Furman County Historical Society, an old friend whom I loved dearly, especially for the many tales of Aspen Meadow he'd told my son Arch. And the story André had alluded to was Arch's favorite: the improbable myth that somewhere in the Colorado mountains, the Nazis had buried a stash of gold. Before Barbara got sick, she'd told me she and her husband were going to *have* to find that money, if they were ever going to pay off Gerald Eliot.

I turned at the road running by the You-Snag-Em, We-Bag-Em Trout Farm, drove another three miles, then rocked over the Burrs' puddle-pocked driveway. My apprehension grew. The last time I'd been to visit Cameron, he'd been home in the middle of the afternoon, battling anxiety with tranquilizers that he washed down with hot chocolate while listening to old Ravi Shankar tapes. He'd told me how he'd tried to help Gerald Eliot with his cash flow by getting him a job as a security guard at the Homestead Museum. *But he still didn't come back to finish our sun room,* Cameron had moaned. Join the club.

I pulled up in front of a contemporary-style, green-stained A-frame house. Its roof was pitched steeply to the ground, like an oversized tent. Jutting out the back was the unfinished sun room; the few panes of glass Gerald Eliot had left untouched winked in the sunlight. Across the driveway from the main dwelling was the guest house, a miniature replica of the green A-frame. Cameron's maroon pickup truck was parked at an angle in front of the guest house door.

Standing on the van's step, I could just see the panoramic view of the Continental Divide's icy peaks beyond the A-frame. *The photographer wants a view of snow*, André had asserted over the phone. *And I am to make a treat for the homeowner with the view of snow. Do you think he would like my strawberry tart?* Maybe with chocolate sauce and a Valium, I'd thought.

"Cam?" I called when there was no response to my knock at the guest house door. "You in there?" I listened for the twang of sitar music but heard none, thank goodness. Unfortunately, there was no hum and pop of Cameron's printer, either, which I found more worrisome. Cameron wrote articles on the historic West; according to Marla, who knew everything, he hadn't written a word or made a sale in the past sixteen months, not since Gerald Eliot had made such a mess of their home. That, combined with his mounting depression and Barbara's illness—she might not be able to return to her teaching job—were distressing. For politeness, I knocked again, although it was a point of pride for Cameron that he always kept his door unlocked. I turned the knob and the door opened.

One of the sloped, wood-paneled walls was given over to the TV, the computer-printer setup, a kitchenette, and a tiny bath. The other featured a long shelf chockablock with framed photographs of Cameron and Barbara visiting ghost towns, abandoned mines, and historic sites. In the pictures, stocky, jovial Cameron and blond, plump Barbara looked as excited as kids.

But these photos did not reflect the way Cameron looked now. Disheveled, grizzled, he was snoring loudly on an unmade sofabed pushed up against the wide part of the A. His gray hair, pushed askew like windblown barbecue ash, desperately needed cutting. Mouth open, his chunky body contorted, he looked more like a wrestler on the skids than a historian. One shoe lay on the floor; there was no sign of a second. He wore muddied socks, rumpled dark chinos, and a denim shirt. He'd wrenched a patchwork quilt around him so that it knotted his middle.

He snorted, then jerked violently awake. "What? Who's there?"

"I'm sorry, I'll leave. It's just Goldy Schulz."

He scratched his scalp, then sighed. "Come on in, Goldy." His leathery face was even more deeply furrowed than the last time I'd seen him; his red-rimmed eyes lingered on the kitchenette side of the room. "Checking on me again, eh?" With sudden decision, he yanked the quilt around him and stumped toward the tiny bathroom. "Be right back."

Shower water began to run. I unpacked the basket and checked the refrigerator. It smelled terrible and contained only a green-edged, muddy-brown package of ground beef. When had Cameron had his last meal? For that matter, when had he last had contact with the outside world? I checked the bottles of pills on his bedside table: Librium and Restoril—tranquilizers and sleeping pills. The message light on his phone was blinking. On the floor next to his discarded shoe lay a half-empty bottle of Bacardi, a nibbled bar of chocolate, and a box of crackers. Great. The man obviously needed coffee and decent food, in that order. I knew from my previous food-bearing trips that Cameron kept an old-fashioned chrome percolator beside the kitchenette's yellow ceramic cannisters. Unfortunately, it was nowhere to be seen.

"Where's your coffeepot?" I called.

"Oh, hell," he yelled over the spray. "The coffeepot? Let's see." For a moment all I heard was the hiss of shower water. "I was watching one of those home improvement shows. You know, where they teach you to glaze your own windows? So I thought, why not?" The valve squealed as he turned off the water. "See any aspirin out there?"

I scanned the counter, the tables, even the tops of the TV and computer: no aspirin. "Nope. I'll go get you some, if you want."

"Aspirin would be in the main house bathroom. The coffeepot's in the sun room." He grunted, undoubtedly pulling clothes on over damp skin. "I bought some old window frames and glass...thought I'd do the glazing myself. Made a pot of coffee, started working, broke two pieces of glass, got frustrated. Poured some rum into the coffee. Then I cracked a window frame. Went into town to buy more supplies, but the hardware store was closed."

So you got sloshed instead. I looked down at the blinking message machine. "How's Barbara?"

"Don't know, need to call the hospital. You making that coffee?"

I trotted out the guest house door. When I rounded the corner of the big A-frame, I heard what sounded like cars starting up Cameron's driveway. Visitors? I wondered how many cups Cameron's coffeepot made, and if it would be enough for a slew of guests.

An orange auxiliary power line snaked out of the concrete foundation for the sun room. On the near side, glass of different hues filled the completed windows: one was slightly pink, one gray, one blue. This, Cameron had told me, was the result of Gerald Eliot trying to get a better deal by ordering windows from three different places. On the far side of the sun room, the plastic-swathed framing looked more like a ruin than a building-in-progress.

I took hold of the orange cable and stepped onto the concrete floor. I hopped gingerly over another empty Bacardi bottle, pieces of broken window glass, and several open boxes of nails. The cord wormed over one sawhorse and under another, then disappeared beneath a pile of broken drywall. I yanked on the cord: Chunks of drywall skittered across the floor, as did a jagged piece of cornice molding, a nail gun, rope, measuring tape, boxes of tools, a cutting blade, and glazing material. I finally located the coffeepot and picked it up. Then I dropped it.

Hanging by his blond hair between a pair of studs was Gerald Eliot. His stiff body was clothed in filthy jeans and a bloodied white shirt. His face was dark. His tongue protruded from his mouth.

He was dead.

Chapter 4

I backed up and promptly tripped over a pile of two-by-fours. My hand came down hard on broken glass. Pain snaked up my arm. A fist seemed to be pushing my voice into my throat. From between the studs, Gerald Eliot's dreadful face and unseeing eyes looked at nothing. Bits of drywall clung to his hair, as if someone had broken a piece of it over his head. His forehead had dark, bloody marks on it and I involuntarily glanced at the nail gun. *Oh, God,* I prayed, *no.*

I leapt ungracefully off the subfloor and onto the ground, then cried out as I stumbled over a tree root and landed painfully against the house's foundation. Where was I going? What was I supposed to do? My rubbery legs would not move. Nor would my brain cooperate. Where was my cellular? I gained my balance and started to run back to the van. Then I stopped.

Two Furman County Sheriff's Department cars had pulled up beside Cameron Burr's maroon truck. Assistant District Attorney Andy Fuller and three uniformed deputies slammed out of the first vehicle. Out of the second came my husband, followed by Furman County coroner Dr. Sheila O'Connor and another deputy I did not recognize.

"Tom!" I yelled frantically, then waved my arms. "Here! Tom! It's Gerald...back there—" I pointed mutely in the direction of the sun room.

Andy Fuller barked an order at Tom: Tom shook his head. What is going on, I wondered. Did they know about Eliot already? With one of the deputies in tow, Andy Fuller strode toward the guest house door. Tom trotted in my direction. He motioned me away from the big house. Dr. O'Connor and another deputy followed Tom at a slower pace. The other two cops grimly surveyed the main house and surrounding property. One pointed toward the Burrs' garbage receptacle beside the driveway. As they walked toward the trash, the cop who had pointed talked into a radio.

"Goldy." Tom hugged me. I clasped him like a life preserver. "Goldy, what is it?"

So they didn't know yet. "Gerald Eliot...He's...he's...in the sun room.... He's..." I choked. "Dead."

"That's what we heard. A hiker called in a while ago from a pay phone at the parking lot by the boundary of Furman County Open Space. By the Smythe Peak trailhead." Tom took a deep breath, then added curtly, "Eliot worked at the museum, where there's been a break-in. Looks like a botched robbery. The hiker saw Eliot's body here...hanging up. Is it back there?" His head indicated the rear of the A-frame. I nodded and he frowned. "They're going to ask what *you* were doing out here."

"Bringing Cameron food, then getting his stupid coffeepot and some aspirin from the main house. He was fast asleep when I arrived, and he sent me to get his percolator—"

"We got a complaint that Gerald Eliot and Cameron Burr fought at the Grizzly Saloon last night." Tom fell silent as Sheila O'Connor, tall, oblong-faced, her black-and-gray hair pulled into a taut ponytail, walked by with the deputy, whom I did not know. We nodded to them. Then Tom continued: "It wasn't the first time that had happened, but this time Burr brought a window frame into the bar. Apparently he was half in the bag already. Yelled something at Eliot like, *Hey! I saw your pickup out front and wondered if you wanted to do a little glass work.* We've got guys talking to the bartender now. Anyway, Burr threatened Eliot, and Eliot left for his night-guard job at the museum. That was the last time anybody saw Eliot alive."

"*Cameron* didn't do this, Tom. His wife is

in the hospital. Please. He couldn't have. Are you listening to me?"

Tom chewed the inside of his cheek. His green eyes and handsome face filled with concern and worry. "Goldy, we need to get you taken care of. Somebody will ask you questions in a few minutes, then I'll take you home. I knew you were bringing Burr food today. But I thought you had another job—"

"I just...it was over early." A wave of shivers washed over me.

"Good God, Goldy, your hand is bleeding."

Blood dripped from my palm onto the ground. To my amazement, I saw that it had also splattered and smeared up my arm, probably from when I'd tripped over the tree root.

"I fell and hit some glass. I need to get Cameron that aspirin...." While Tom whipped a handkerchief out of his pocket to tie up my wound, my eyes traveled to where Andy Fuller and the remaining uniform were leading Cameron Burr out of the guest house. "Why is *Fuller* here? And how could a *hiker* have seen Gerald? *I* didn't even see him until I'd spent a few minutes poking around in that mess."

Tom put his arm around me. "Hold your hand up." I obeyed and he began to walk with me back to the van. "Fuller thinks he's going to be a hero in this case, make up for his past mistakes. The guy has political ambitions, Goldy. So he's got a case of—"

"Case? Case of what? He hasn't even talked to, to...Hold up." I fought dizziness. I turned my face toward the sun room: Dr. O'Connor and the deputy stood near Gerald Eliot's body. A late afternoon breeze swished through the pines near the house, and a pattern of shadows played over the pink window. My vision blurred. *I need to get away from here. I need to get Cameron that coffee.*

One of the uniforms called to Fuller from the Burrs' green trash receptacle, piled high with construction debris. A hundred feet from us, Andy Fuller, chin up, hands thrust deep into his trench coat, strode resolutely toward the cop. The thin, metallic blond hair over Andy Fuller's red scalp shone in the sunlight as he peered down at what the cop had found. Fuller nodded, checked a radio on his belt, then asked the cop for *his* radio. I knew that the frequency used by the district attorney's office was different from the one used by sheriff's department deputies. So Fuller was trying to call a cop. Tom's radio crackled on his belt. Shaking his head, Tom pulled away from me and tugged out his receiver.

"Looks like the item the curator reported missing from the museum is here." Fuller's nasal voice crackled. *"Schulz, I need you to come down here and arrest Burr."*

Tom pressed the radio button. "It's too soon," he replied calmly. "Let me talk to him first, see what his side of the story is."

"This is no time for your shilly-shallying, Schulz!" Andy Fuller's shriek was laced with static. *"Burr faked the museum robbery so he could kill Eliot. Get your fat ass down here and arrest this guy!"*

51

Tom's shoulders tensed. He said, "Fuller, wait. Think. Why would Burr bring Eliot back here, to his own home, if he'd gone to the trouble to fake the robbery? Don't you even want to ask him? Before you have to Mirandize him, risk he gets a lawyer?"

"He was going to get rid of the body later. Didn't you hear me the first time? Get down here and arrest this guy!"

With my good hand, I pressed Tom's handkerchief onto my throbbing palm.

"Take Burr in for questioning, Fuller," Tom argued. "Or you'll do something you'll regret."

"What's your wife doing here, Schulz? Burr says the victim worked for your wife, too. Did the two of them do him together? You want to arrest her, too? Or maybe you could get her down here to do your job for you, how about that?"

I pressed my lips together. I *hated* Andy Fuller.

Tom dropped the receiver to his side and muttered, "One thing *I* won't regret is when that dummy finally runs for Colorado Attorney General and quits this new tactic of his, trying to turn every case into a TV show." Too late, I saw his finger was still pressing the radio button. I grabbed Tom's wrist with my bloodied palm. He cursed silently and shook his head.

Down at the guest house, the other deputy read my old friend Cameron Burr his rights. Cameron's face was wan under the tan, his wide shoulders slumped. His eyes roved

52

frantically, like a startled wild animal's, as he was cuffed. Then he was led to the first police cruiser. Andy Fuller, his back to us, talked to the uniformed cops. One cop was holding a plastic evidence bag. Inside the bag was...a book? Something from the Homestead Museum robbery? I shuddered to think how Hanna Klapper would frown over the cops' handling of the museum's precious historic items, even if it wasn't her *job* to do that frowning anymore.

At the van, Dr. Sheila O'Connor joined us. In a low, crisp voice, she asked Tom, "Can you talk?" Tom glanced at me, then nodded. Both moved away from the van door.

Left alone, I frowned at the cop with the bag. Plastic bags mean the evidence is dry. Paper bags are used when evidence is wet. So Cameron Burr, a historian, masked his murder by stealing a valuable book from the museum and then putting it into his *garbage*? But he was careful enough not to get it soiled or wet? If you stole something to cover up a murder, why wouldn't you throw the evidence out onto the road? Nothing about what was going on here felt right to me.

One of the uniformed officers approached me. Andy Fuller turned to watch.

"Mrs. Schulz? I'm Sergeant Chambers." The officer was very young, with orange hair, a pie-shaped face, and a complexion like dough. His pale, nail-bitten fingers clutched a notebook and department-issue ballpoint. "I need to question you—" His voice cracked. Questioning the wife of the county's champion investigator was apparently somewhat daunting. Chambers cleared his throat, clicked his pen, and eyed my bloody hand, still wrapped in Tom's handkerchief. "Briefly. If you're up to it."

"May I run some cold water over my hand, while we talk?"

"This won't take long." Chambers' tone was apologetic. "We can't go into the house because it's a crime scene. Just tell me why you're here, when you arrived, and what you saw." He clicked his pen again.

I told him the purpose of my visit and politely added that he could look at the basket of food on the kitchenette counter if he didn't believe me. I told him Burr was asleep in his clothes when I arrived at two o'clock.

"How did he act?"

"Exhausted. As if I'd just awakened him from a very deep sleep. When he went to take a shower, I offered to fix him coffee. He said his percolator was out in his unfinished sun room." I pointed with my unwrapped hand. "When I got there, Gerald Eliot's body was…hanging between the studs. But I didn't see it there right away. If I didn't see Gerald Eliot's body, how could a hiker have seen him?"

Andy Fuller sidled up beside Chambers. "Just answer the questions, Mrs. Schulz. All right?" His expression was arrogant, defensive.

I said, "If Cameron had murdered Gerald Eliot, he would hardly have sent me straight out to where he'd hung up the body, would he? What kind of sense does that make?"

Fuller raised an eyebrow at Chambers, as in *Don't let this pushy woman take over the interview*. Then, without responding to my questions, he turned on his heel and headed back to the patrol car in which Cameron now sat, cuffed and accused of murder.

Chambers held up a soft, plump hand. "Please, Mrs. Schulz. Did Burr mention anything about Eliot when you got here today?" I shook my head. "What do you know about their relationship?"

I exhaled in exasperation. "Gerald Eliot had promised to finish the Burrs' sun room four months ago. He pulled out the wall between the addition and the house, did a subfloor and some framing, and put in three windows. Then he took off for parts unknown." Chambers glanced over at Andy Fuller, whose expression as he stood next to the first cruiser was stone-faced. I hurried along: "At night, it's *cold* up here at eighty-five hundred feet. Even in the summer. Barbara Burr got pneumonia from the chilly air in the house. She's on a ventilator down at Lutheran." Impatience crawled under my skin. "This is common knowledge, Sergeant."

Chambers nodded in a way that told me if it was common knowledge, it wasn't common to him. "Just tell me what else you saw, Mrs. Schultz."

This I did, up to the time of the arrival of law enforcement. Meanwhile, Sheila O'Connor talked on to Tom. Finally he turned his handsome face and nodded at me. I felt a wash of relief followed by the deep urge to leave, to get my hand cleaned and bandaged, to find a way to help Cameron. *Get me out of here*, I pleaded silently to my husband. Unfortunately, not only did my telepathic message not connect, but Andy Fuller chose that moment to sashay up to the van.

He pointedly eyed my wrapped hand. "Did you do anything to try to help Burr? I mean, in his smear campaign against Gerald Eliot, general contractor? Just curious."

Tom lumbered up to Fuller's side. He said, "Leave her alone. She's a witness. She needs a victim advocate."

Andy Fuller whirled to face him. "Oh, really? Why can't you follow my orders, you slob? What's going on here, Schulz?"

Tom's face froze in a bitten, narrow-eyed look that made my heart sink. Fuller shifted his weight, took an angry breath, then leaned in close to Tom.

"Schulz! What did you think I was going to do that I was going to regret? You don't think I can hear you when your radio's on? Are you trying to threaten me?"

"What?" Fuller's fury seemed to baffle Tom.

"How dare you threaten me in front of fellow officers!" stormed Fuller.

"I'm not sure I did," replied Tom evenly. "Goldy, get in the car." My skin iced; I couldn't move. Tom didn't seem to notice. His deep voice rumbled softly. "What are you saying, Fuller?"

"I'm saying you *compromised* this case!" Fuller shrieked.

"*What?*" snarled Tom.

Fuller took one look at Tom's face, then stepped back. I glanced around helplessly: The uniforms were in the first car; Dr. O'Connor was walking back to the sun room, presumably to Eliot's corpse.

"My wife's been hurt," Tom pressed Fuller. "I don't have time for your stupid theatrics."

Andy Fuller took a step in Tom's direction. Tom slammed the van door shut. At that moment, even though he was two feet from Tom, Fuller staggered.

"You're incompetent, Schulz," Fuller crowed once he'd recovered. "How many times have we gone over this?"

"Are you *saying* I can't do my *job*?" Tom replied, undeterred.

Fuller hunched his shoulders, as if he were gathering himself into a cannonball. "I'm saying what I've said lots of times before, that I'm your *boss*. You just don't seem to be able to accept it. Maybe it's time you *did*." Tom glared at him.

"Stop, please stop," I cried. I looked frantically down at the first car. The windows were up. The motor was running. There was no way the other cops would hear me if I called for them to come intervene. "There's no reason to—"

"Shut up!" Fuller barked at me.

I'd heard about their arguments before: Tom had told me how vicious and unreasonable Fuller could be. But I'd never witnessed one of their conflicts. And this one was getting out of control. God forbid that Fuller would lay a finger on Tom. If Fuller were that foolish, my husband would manhandle him so quickly that Fuller would wish he'd bypassed law enforcement altogether.

"Fuller," said Tom, "get into your car. Get the hell away from this crime scene."

"You are intent on ruining this case for me!" Fuller's indignant voice howled. His hands were clenched into tight fists.

"No," I whispered. "Don't—"

"Aren't you?" Fuller cried, lunging toward Tom.

Without thinking, I jumped between them. "No!"

But Tom's warning came too late. I lost my balance. Andy Fuller and I slammed against my van, then hit the ground. Beneath me, Andy Fuller struggled weakly. "Help," he gasped. "I've been assaulted!"

"Goldy, Goldy, oh, Goldy," Tom murmured as he gently lifted me off the assistant district attorney. "What have you done?"

I don't remember much from our trip home. Just leave, Fuller had told us, red-faced and indignant. Watching from their car, the other cops had seen Fuller come at Tom first, had seen me stupidly try to intervene. Still, Tom was very angry. With me.

"Don't you think I can take care of myself,

Goldy? Don't you think I've spent enough time in police work to sidestep some five-foot-tall creep? What on earth were you *thinking*?"

"I wasn't thinking anything," I answered honestly. "Tom, I'm really sorry. I just—"

"Why didn't you get in the van, the way I told you?"

I pressed the handkerchief into my oozing palm and didn't respond. After all, what could I say?

When we arrived at our house, bedraggled, tense, and silent, we found Arch on the phone with his friend Todd Druckman. The two fourteen-year-olds were avidly discussing telephone encryption: whether they needed it, how much it would cost, whether girls would be able to decode their conversations. Still short for his age, Arch was dressed in an oversized burgundy T-shirt and sweatpants. He shook the straight brown hair off his forehead. "It would be worth it if you thought a girl was tapping your phone," he observed. "You *know* how those girls in our class can *be*."

I washed my hand and bandaged it, then asked Arch to hang up. He pushed his smeared tortoiseshell glasses up his freckled nose and sighed. To Todd, he said, "Later."

Ordinarily, our family has heart-to-heart conversations in our kitchen. But in the rosy light of early evening, the plastic-draped hole where the window had once been gave the space the discomfiting feel of an abandoned stage set. The kitchen was no longer the heart of our home, thanks to the late Gerald Eliot. Since we weren't able to retrieve the leftovers from Cameron Burr's guest house—the cops were going through it—Tom and I set the living room coffee table with bowls of cheese, cold chicken, sliced hard rolls, romaine leaves, chutney, and mayonnaise.

"Julian called," Arch announced morosely. "He didn't sound very good. I guess he's not coming." My son threw himself down on the couch and surveyed the spread. "He really wants to talk to you, Mom. Anyway, he said he was going to call Marla."

"Was he in New York?" Tom asked. Arch shook his head and mumbled something about Julian's being on the road.

"I'm sorry, Arch," I said, then asked, "Did André call? Is he doing all right?"

"He left a message," Arch said uncertainly. "He's okay, I guess. Says he's not going to make enough on the shoot to pay the cost of caring for his wife if some guy wrecks all the food. What's the matter with his wife?"

"She has macular degeneration, which is a problem with the eyes. She's virtually blind, and needs a full-time nurse. It's expensive—"

"Who wrecked the food?"

"Just some guy on our job today. Is André's message still on the tape?"

"Sorry. I erased it because Todd and I were doing some experimenting with dialing. You're just supposed to call him back. What's the matter, Mom? You said your hand was just scratched."

"Remember the guy who made the mess in our kitchen?"

Arch smeared mayonnaise on half a roll. "Gerald Eliot? The builder scratched your hand?"

"No, hon. He's dead."

Tom added, "They found his body out at Cameron Burr's place."

"No kidding?" asked Arch, incredulous. He put down his roll. "What happened to him?"

"We don't know yet," I replied, then hesitated. "Anyway, while we were all out there, I...had a somewhat...physical argument with the assistant district attorney. I...sort of lost it when they arrested Cameron," I added.

Arch bombarded us with questions. How did Eliot die? Mr. Burr didn't kill Gerald, did he? I said I couldn't imagine that he would have. Was Mr. Burr okay? Probably, I replied. Did Mrs. Burr know Mr. Burr had been arrested? It was possible Barbara was too sick to be informed of this news, I told him; it might just make her worse. Arch loved the Burrs. He couldn't process what this would mean for them. Instead, he decided to focus on my altercation with the assistant district attorney.

Arch's father, Dr. John Richard Korman—dubbed The Jerk by Marla and me—was currently in jail for assault. Would he now have *two* parents in jail? Arch asked. Jail time for *me* was unlikely, I assured my anxious son, after I'd made us steaming cups of hot chocolate and brought them out to the living room. The other deputies had seen Andy Fuller come at Tom first.

"So who's in trouble?" Arch asked pragmatically. It was hard to tell, Tom and I told him.

The phone rang: Tom held it up so we both could hear.

"Hey!" came a hearty voice. "You should have knocked Fuller out with one of your frying pans!"

"Boyd," Tom announced, and I smiled and nodded. Despite my increasing worries, it was good to hear our old friend, barrel-shaped and straight-shooting Sergeant Bill Boyd. Despite his perfectly serviceable first name, to us and everyone he was always "Boyd," since there were too many sheriff's department deputies with the first name Bill. Boyd had told us he'd gotten tired of getting the wrong calls and worse, the wrong pizza. Now, he was glad to hear we were all right. He promised to stay in touch and hung up.

Ten minutes later, Tom's new captain—a fair-minded, all-business administrator—called. Their conversation was tense and brief. Eliot was being autopsied in the morning; Cameron Burr was being held without bail; his wife was indeed too ill to be notified of the arrest. Moreover, things did not look good vis-à-vis Fuller. We'd know more the next day.

My sleep was predictably fitful. At seven A.M., the phone bleated. Tom, who'd been up and dressed since six, snatched it. He listened and scribbled in his spiral notebook while I hugged a heap of pillows and pretended to be asleep. My hand throbbed. So did my head.

I wondered how Cameron was doing. I wondered how I'd gotten so mixed up in this mess, when all I'd done was try to take food over to a friend.

When Tom hung up, he stood, paced, then slumped down on our mussed bed. His face, ordinarily ruddy, was pale. "Problem?" I asked gently.

"Fuller's demanded a full investigation." He shook his head.

"Of what?"

Tom took a deep breath. "I've been charged with insubordination. And with compromising a homicide investigation."

"I don't believe it."

"Believe it. My buddies protested, of course. Some even threatened to quit."

"Good."

"Don't say that, Miss G. The department has a ton of work to do, even if Fuller is screwing things up. Now listen. You're not in trouble. The deputies all say they saw Fuller swing at me before you got in the way. Still, because this is the bad end of a lot of problems with him, I'm the one being investigated. The process will take four to six weeks."

"Oh, for crying out loud!"

He held me with his gaze. "During that time," he continued, "I'll be suspended without pay."

Chapter 5

Tom hugged me and told me not to worry. I held his handsome face in my hands and kissed him. *Of course* I would worry. And feel guilty. If I hadn't interfered, he wouldn't be in this mess. Tom kissed me, then said he'd fix me an espresso if I'd stop trying to take the blame for the world's wrongs. I followed him to our topsy-turvy kitchen.

"What happens to Cameron?" I asked. "Can you tell me? Or am I considered a witness?"

"I can tell you. It's Cameron Burr who shouldn't get in touch with *you.*" Tom filled the espresso machine with water, pawed through the pile of china on the counter, and finally placed two Norwegian china demitasse cups under the doser. "I'm waiting for a fax from Boyd. He's sending me a map of Blue Spruce showing the Burrs' place in relation to Open Space." He pressed the button and a moment later handed me a small, *crema*-topped drink. "The scenario Fuller is going with is this." He sipped his coffee. "The window frame incident at the Grizzly Saloon occurred just before eleven the night before last. Fuller thinks Cameron Burr followed Gerald Eliot from the Grizzly to his nighttime security guard job at the Homestead Museum. By the way, it was a job Burr got for Eliot. That doesn't look too good, Burr knowing exactly where to go."

The dark, luscious espresso ignited the perimeter of my brain. "Lots of people knew Eliot worked there," I observed. "Marla told me the museum board wasn't happy with Eliot's performance. If *she* knew where he worked, so did the whole *town*."

"Fuller thinks Burr broke into the museum, strangled Eliot, faked a robbery, threw Eliot's body into the back of his pickup, and drove out to the unfinished sun room. There, Fuller claims, Burr stabbed his building contractor with molding, broke a piece of drywall over his head, and hung him up by his Samson-style gold locks. Supposedly, Burr then shot his contractor through the head with a nail gun. For good measure."

I flinched and set down my cup. I thought back to my entry into the sun room, my confusion in trying to find the coffeepot, seeing Gerald's body... "What about that hiker who supposedly saw Gerald? Do you know his name? I don't believe you could see the body unless you were ten feet away from it."

Tom shook his head. "The hiker called from the Open Space parking lot by the trailhead. He didn't give his name. It could be a setup, Goldy. We always have to consider it. Although, with Fuller bucking for higher office, *he* might not consider it."

"Has Sheila O'Connor come up with anything yet?"

"Sheila said Eliot's neck and face were badly bruised when he was strangled. Glass in his scalp is consistent with one of the two breaks in the glass-fronted display cases at the museum. Time of death probably not too long after one A.M. The evidence that Cameron's pickup was used to transport the body is pretty convincing, too." He drank more coffee. "Looks like Eliot's T-shirt snagged on a protruding piece of metal in the truck. A fragment of the T-shirt fabric is still in the back of the pickup. Plus there's grease on Eliot's face and clothing, very similar to the grease in the vehicle." He sighed. "We have no way of knowing if somebody borrowed Cam's truck. He always leaves the keys in it. And it's been so dry, there aren't tire tracks we could analyze. Sheila'll know more after the autopsy, you know how that goes."

I nodded and got up to fix us both more coffee. The fax rang. Tom removed the wall of dishes surrounding the fax machine, pulled out the slick sheet, and perused it. He looked up. "Here's the layout from the fence separating Burr's property and the trail to Smythe Peak." He slapped the smudged map of Blue Spruce next to the cluttered sink; I peered down at it. Most prominent was the Smythe Peak Open Space area, the two thousand acres that surrounded the mountain. All of the land had been sold to the county by the Smythe family. Cameron Burr's property was marked with a rough rectangle. According to thick hand-drawn lines and numbers, the framed sun room was only fifty feet from Cameron's fence.

Tom said, "Cam's lawyer is going to want to know why a killer would strangle a guy, take the time and trouble to rob a museum, and drive the dead or near-dead guy out to his *own house.* Then the killer tortures Eliot or defiles his corpse with building materials, and shoots him with a nail gun? I don't *think* so. You can be really drunk or really angry. To do all that, you couldn't be *both.*" He shook his head.

I slugged back the espresso. "Cameron didn't do it, I'm telling you. Yesterday André told me Leah Smythe—or somebody at the cabin—fired Eliot for sleeping with a model. Maybe they broke up."

"So you think some skinny model killed big, strong Eliot? Then hung him up in Cam's sun room?"

"Not necessarily." I tried to think. "I'm just suggesting other people besides Cameron disliked Gerald Eliot. Take me, for instance, although I didn't really want to see him *dead.* But there might be more to Gerald Eliot than Fuller wants to see. Did you have a look at the Homestead?"

Tom nodded. Before he could elaborate, the phone rang and he answered it. He murmured a couple of questions, took notes in his spiral pad, then hung up. "Interesting update. I'm going to heat muffins. Sound good?"

"Sounds great."

"Okay, early yesterday morning the call

came from Sylvia Bevans about a break-in at the museum. My team covered the call, by the way. I just hadn't told you about it; it seemed so routine. Sylvia was beside herself, babbling about a missing cookbook."

"Cookbook?"

He smiled and spread frozen cinnamon-raisin muffins on a cookie sheet. "Yeah, I thought you'd take some professional interest in the theft. Sylvia Bevans, of course, reamed us out, but good."

"Oh, brother." Now this was a scenario I *could* imagine. The much-feared, seventy-year-old curator of the Homestead Museum would have ushered the cops into the sacred precinct of her cluttered historical society office and puckered her already thin-lipped mouth in fierce and undisguised disapproval. One of her seemingly endless wardrobe of pastel linen dresses—lilac, lime, or pink—would have strained at mother-of-pearl buttons over her ample body as she indignantly demanded the authorities *find the culprit immediately!*

Tom cleared his throat. "Two of the glass-fronted display cases were smashed. Sylvia told us one cookbook was missing. Today, she's screaming about *four* cookbooks being stolen. They were part of an exhibit. She didn't realize they were missing at first, she was in such a state." Tom chuckled. "Only one book was in her initial report, so now Fuller's accusing her of insurance scam. She chewed *him* out, said the Homestead's not insured 'cuz the county's too cheap to pay the premiums."

I thought of the book in the evidence bag found at Cameron Burr's home. "So have they found all four cookbooks?"

"They found one in Cam's trash and a second one underneath drywall in the sun room. Sylvia's up in arms about their historic value, but as far as we can determine, each is only worth a couple hundred dollars." He peered into the oven. "They'll keep looking, don't worry."

Thinking of poor Cameron in the backseat of the police vehicle, I rinsed out our cups and the doser, then ground more espresso beans. I asked, "What's Fuller's big push to nab Burr?"

Tom flipped off the oven light and straightened with a sigh. "He's caught a lot of heat for the plea bargains, and he sees this one as easy. Plus the rumors about him trying for state attorney general have been getting stronger lately. This could be a high-profile case. He'd get a lot of press for being a crime fighter, that kind of thing."

I measured the coffee into the doser, pressed the button, and waited for the espresso to spurt out. "Would they have to find all four cookbooks up at Cameron's house, for him actually to be prosecuted?"

Tom shrugged. "Fuller's got a half-dozen investigators sniffing around the museum and Burr's place. Our guys usually find everything. If they don't, and Burr's defense claims shoddy investigation, Fuller can argue that anything *not* found is excess evidence and unnecessary in prosecuting Burr."

It was my turn to sigh. "So what exactly were these cookbooks?"

He peered at his notes. "The first one we found is *American Cookery* by Amelia Simmons. Famous for its johnnycake recipe, according to Sylvia. This one wasn't the original 1796 edition—apparently the museum's was a nineteenth-century copy—but someone donated it to the historical society, and they put it on display."

Of course the Homestead would put a cookbook on display that contained the seminal recipe for Western Cooking 101. Johnnycake or Johnnie cake, also known as journey cake, had been slapped together and cooked over fires by thousands of folks coming out in covered wagons to Colorado and points west. When I'd served as a docent at the museum, I'd ushered many a class of Furman County fourth graders into the Homestead kitchen to make a cider version of the moist coffee cake.

"The other cookbook they found is a 1903 edition of *The White House Cookbook*. So we need to find a 1910 volume called *The Practical Cook Book* by one Elizabeth Hiller, valued in the range of sixty bucks. The fourth book is something called the *Watkins Cookbook*, from 1936. Worth fifty dollars." He handed me a plate of muffins. "Watkins Cookbook? That's not something Sherlock Holmes's sidekick put together in his spare time, is it?"

"No," I replied, "it's not an English cookbook. And the sidekick was Watson, remember? Thanks for the treat." I bit into the hot, sweet muffin and remembered the humble red spiral-bound volume with its battered cover and spattered pages. "The *Watkins* man came out to Western ranches once a year in his horse and buggy. After the invention of cars, he drove a Model T truck. He brought peppermint, vanilla, liniment, whatever ranch folks needed, including simple recipe-books put out by the Watkins company, based in Minnesota, but with a reach all across the West. Everybody loved to see the Watkins man come," I said with a smile. "And every rural household had a *Watkins Cookbook*."

"Aha! I'm so glad you worked in that museum, Miss G. I never know when I'm going to learn something." He paused. "Anyway, I'm off the Eliot case. I told them my wife's friend was arrested, so if they've got anything, to let me know. How's that?"

"Thank you. For everything. And especially for not staying mad at me."

"You need to stop worrying, Miss G." He pondered the gap above our kitchen sink. Just as he'd done at the cabin, Gerald Eliot had glued plywood over the plaster crevice. He'd certainly never be back to repair the damage. "Think Arch would like to join me for a trip to the hardware store? Better yet, would you like to join me?"

I took another bite of muffin. Was I in the mood to look at galvanized nails after I'd just seen a corpse defiled by them? No. I urged Tom to go and take Arch with him. They could do some male bonding. Tom grinned.

Arch, wearing a faded yellow T-shirt and a pair of too-large red Cornell sweatpants—gifts from Julian—warned that they might be out for a while. He needed to be dropped at the Druckmans' house so he and Todd could finish their conversation on the subject of sending encrypted messages.

"Can you tell me what these messages *are?*" I asked mildly. "Or would that destroy the reason for the encryption?"

Arch opened a new bag of kibble for his bloodhound. "It's no big deal," he replied in a bored tone. "But if you want to come outside while I feed Jake, I'll tell you." I poured Arch a glass of o.j. and followed him through the back door to the deck area designated for his dog. I tried not to glance up at our roof, where the remains of Arch's ham radio—his attempt to communicate long-distance with Julian in the Navajo language—lay like the spokes of an abandoned umbrella. Arch had been fascinated with learning the language because Navajo radiomen had foiled Axis cryptanalysts in World War II. But Julian had only succeeded in teaching Arch *Ya'atey*—hello—when a fierce windstorm had split the radio antenna in two.

Now Arch scooped nuggets into Jake's bowl and began explaining the latest reasons for his interest in encryption. Jake kept his eyes on his food bowl. "School starts in a couple of weeks. Todd and I are wondering which eighth-grade girls will be available to be girl*friends,* and which ones will just make fun of us."

"The girls have high-tech equipment on their phones?"

"Nothing would surprise me, Mom."

From the deck railing, Scout—a cream-and-chocolate stray cat we'd adopted several years ago—kept a watchful eye on Jake and the speed with which he was emptying his bowl. Arch ignored the animals, drank the juice I'd brought him, and checked his appearance in the reflection in the window overlooking our backyard.

The comforting noise of Tom's revving Chrysler floated out of the garage toward us. Jake raised mournful eyes to Arch: *Leaving so soon?* "I'll be back," Arch consoled him. "Look, Mom, double-check the gate, okay? Yesterday, Jake got out somehow. He was barking at elk and got out of control."

"Okay, hon," I promised. Arch hopped down the deck steps. The Chrysler roared away, carrying my family. As if on cue, a sudden cracking noise indicated a dozen elk were shattering branches underfoot as they plodded through our neighbor's yard. Jake, of course, instantly began to howl.

"Stop, Jake. Come on, boy, come in."

But the hound would not budge. Nor would he be quiet. I went inside, closed the door against the canine uproar, and shook my head. In late summer, the huge dun-and-brown elk herds flood through Aspen Meadow, fleeing the first wave of hunters. No respecters of property lines, the elk leap fences, use their powerful necks and big tongues to tear out strawberry plants, strip fruit trees, devour flowers, and gobble bushes. Then they defecate happily and plod on. Our neighbor occasionally bags one with his rifle, hunting season or no.

Only Tom had managed to outsmart the marauders. With great care, he'd lofted nets over our Montmorency cherry trees and tied the nets to the trunks. While awaiting his captain's call the previous night, Tom had patiently salvaged the last of the scarlet fruit. Through the back window, I watched the elk quizzically appraise our trees. *Nothing there, boys, time to move out.*

I crossed to the counter, moved the faxed map showing the location of Eliot's body, and surveyed with a sinking heart the clutter of glasses, plates, and measuring cups. Before Gerald Eliot had revved up his saw, he'd asked me to empty the cabinets on the left side of the window. Then he'd crashed through the window and the right-hand cabinet, and the contents of those shelves had ended up in smithereens.

The next day, Eliot had bounded up my front steps all smiles, sketchy plans for a new kitchen tucked under his arm. He'd claimed he could have my new kitchen done before the first snow. *Ha.* Although it was always difficult for me to believe that people could so heartlessly try to take advantage, I'd been forced to accept Tom's assessment of constructor sabotage. I'd stonily told Eliot to *fix* the window; my *husband* would repair the cabinet. Now my remaining glasses teetered in stacks; the broken cabinet stood on its side in the hallway. How many other people had Eliot tried to cheat this way? And had any other clients wanted to strangle him the way I'd longed to?

I took a steadying breath of the sweet, fresh air pouring through gaps in the dusty plastic. With The Jerk and his violent nature temporarily locked up in jail, I had taken for granted the fact that we could finally relax with our windows open. Or rather, relax with our windows *missing*. I refilled my espresso machine with water, ground a handful of fragrant coffee beans, and rinsed Tom's bowl of homegrown cherries.

As the water gushed over the fruit, my mind snapped back to the traumas of the last two days. What would happen to Cameron now? Had Cameron murdered Gerald Eliot? What could I do? *Interfere and you'll get Cameron, Tom, and yourself into more trouble,* my inner voice warned.

I sharpened a knife, started pitting the cherries, then washed my hands and put in a call to Lutheran Hospital to check on Barbara Burr. I was told she could not be disturbed. Next I phoned the sheriff's department to see if they could tell me anything about Cameron. Burr was being processed, I was told. *Like liverwurst?* I longed to ask.

I energetically mixed the pitted cherries with sugar and cornstarch. I loved the Burrs; both had been extraordinarily kind to Arch when he was eight and I was doing my docent work. Cameron, then president of the county historical society, could talk about Aspen Meadow's history the way some people can croon show tunes. The times I'd had to take Arch with me to the museum, Cameron had kept my son spell-bound with stories of local outlaws, ghosts, Indians, and untold, priceless treasure buried in Aspen Meadow. Arch had been rapt. I hadn't been immune either.

I laid the fruit in a buttered pan and thought back to the photos on the Burrs' guest house walls: Cameron and Barbara with shovels and maps. In the thirties, Cameron had told Arch, Aspen Meadow and Blue Spruce had been aswarm with treasure hunters. A persistent Depression-era rumor held that a stagecoach robber had buried a coffee can chockful of gold pieces in a mine shaft in Aspen Meadow or Blue Spruce. Forget that there was no *mining* in Aspen Meadow or Blue Spruce; Arch had subsequently insisted we follow a trail that—legend had it—led to the gold at the top of Smythe Peak. We'd dug for hours, to no avail, and our only company had been Steller's jays squawking at us for invading their domain.

I beat butter with sugar for the cobbler topping, and recalled Arch's wide-eyed plea that we visit a local ranch where longhorn steer were raised. There, contrary to recorded history but according to Cameron Burr, Jesse James and his gang had buried fifty thousand dollars at the foot of a lodgepole pine. The trick was finding the right tree. Jesse James himself had supposedly pointed a knife downward to the treasure, and embedded the weapon in the pine tree's trunk. If he had, both the knife and the fifty thousand were still there, because Arch hadn't found them.

I measured flour with baking powder,

remembering the time Cameron and Barbara had accompanied us on one of the many treasure hunts Cameron had sparked in my too-imaginative son. The Burrs, Arch, and I had crawled through the crumbling Swiss-built inn west of Aspen Meadow where the *Bund*—Nazis and their sympathizers, posing as bicycling tourists, the story went—had allegedly met during the Second World War. The inn, empty for years and recently renovated as apartments, had given us permission to search the place while the construction crew worked on new plumbing. Alas, to Arch's intense disappointment, we'd uncovered no stash of *deutsche marken* below swastikas carved—by squatters? Or by frustrated treasure seekers?—on closet floors.

Now, at fourteen, Arch didn't drag me out on treasure hunts anymore. Instead, he listened to pounding rock music, worried intensely about his appearance, and yearned for Julian to move back. And though he would never admit it, the only thing Arch truly wanted was *a girlfriend.*

I stirred egg into the cobbler dough and dropped spoonfuls of the thick, golden batter on top of the glistening cherries. No treasure, no girlfriend, and the Burrs in deep trouble. Gerald Eliot dead. And I needed catering business. I slid the cobbler into the oven and contemplated my booking calendar.

This was Tuesday, August nineteenth. Unfortunately, my slimy catering competitor, Craig Litchfield, had so severely cut into my bookings that I had no work until a week from today. And even more unfortunately, that work was unpaid. Tuesday, the twenty-sixth of August, was the date of the rescheduled tasting party at the Homestead. This time, the catering competition for the Merciful Migrations September Soirée would be silent. I would be up against André and Craig Litchfield. The Soirée committee included my frequent catering clients Edna Hardcastle and Weezie Harrington, as well as Marla. How had the committee arrived at the decision that they even *needed* to put the event out for bids? I had no idea.

I loved André. I would enjoy working by his side even if he won the competition. Still, I was sure Craig Litchfield had somehow forced the issue of a contest. What I couldn't imagine—and what was troubling me—was the means he would employ to try to *win* it.

I made another espresso, wished I had one of Julian Teller's indescribably flaky, bittersweet-chocolate filled croissants to go with it, then stared glumly at my calendar. The day after the tasting party was Wednesday, the twenty-seventh of August. That night, I would be doing a birthday dinner party for twenty for Weezie Harrington. Wealthy widows and divorcees always worry that no one will remember their birthdays, so they often give a party for themselves. Weezie was no exception, although she'd had a friend issue the invitations.

I moved my finger across the calendar. My next booking after Weezie's party was Saturday, August thirtieth. That day, Edna Hardcastle's daughter Isabel would finally, *finally* be married, and I would cater the twice-postponed reception. But two booked events and one tasting party would not be enough. With Tom suspended, and no money coming in, I had to find more work.

I put in a call to André's condominium and got the caregiver for André's wife, Pru. Pru's handicap made her extremely shy. I had only met her once, as she disliked going out or having people over. Dealing with Pru's condition, plus the cost of her maintenance, had contributed to André's concerns after his retirement.

"Yes? What is it?" Chef Happy sounded even more brusque than usual.

I told André about discovering Gerald Eliot's body at the Burrs'. I also told him about Tom's suspension. In order to avoid digressing, I left out the details. But André clucked that the Ian's Images people had already had a fit when the police canceled the shoot at the Burrs' house. I told him I was desperate for work. If he could bridge me in to work part-time on the shoot, I promised to take only two dollars over minimum wage.

"Goldy! You worry how the models demean themselves, and then you do it to yourself," my old friend chided. "Yes, come on Friday." He *tsk*ed. "They have agreed to pay me double for that day. Which I am happy to take, since the cost of living in the mountains is so exorbitant."

"Double? For what?"

"The shoot has *many* problems. I have had much overtime. Ian Hood broke his lens. He already destroyed one of his cameras, but does he care? No. The police are at the Burrs' house. So the studio will move up the shooting at their third location, the place Hanna secured for them, the living room at the Homestead Museum. They will do the children's clothes there on Friday—if the police are through *there*. Leah will rent a Santa Claus and the children will sit in his lap. But will the little ones eat what we prepare? Who knows?" He exhaled in disgust. "The models complain the meals are too fattening. Rufus Driggle, the handyman? He likes the blond one, Yvonne. But Yvonne does not like Rufus. Someone put pickles on my crab cakes. But they always want my food. They are pigs."

For Friday, I penciled in *Cater at H. museum* on my calendar. Might give me a chance to snoop a little bit, see if Gerald Eliot had indeed met his untimely end there. "When should I show up?"

"Coffee break, nine o'clock? This kitchen is approved for commercial use, thank the good Lord. Yogurt, fruit, and we will make a sweet."

I hung up and out of habit called Marla. I checked the cobbler—strictly taboo for her, as she'd barely survived a heart attack the previous summer—and listened to her husky-voiced message: *"I'm out being persecuted by the federal government. Leave a message, unless you think they'll trace this call and make your life a living hell, too."*

Ah, yes. Starting this week, Marla was being audited by the IRS for last year's taxes. She had promised to stop by to fill me in on all the odious details.

My business line rang. I sent a quick appeal to the Almighty for a new client.

"Goldy, it's Sheila O'Connor." My heart froze: the coroner. Where were Tom and Arch? "Don't worry," she said, immediately sensing my concern. "I have a job for you, if you're interested. Lunch this Monday."

"*What?*"

Sheila's laugh was earthy and much-practiced. Working with Sheila, Tom had always told me, you developed a sense of humor or you died. Coroner joke. "I'm serious," she went on. "Monday is always the worst day at the morgue. You've got work from the weekend, unidentified bodies piling up, it's a mess."

"Ah," I said, sympathetic. "I see." Not that I really wanted to.

"I've been wanting to treat the staff." Was she trying a bit too hard to sound cheerful? Her words came out in a rush. "So I was wondering if you'd like to cater a lunch for us? Monday? Here at the morgue?"

Tom had always had enormous respect for Sheila O'Connor. Now I did, too, as she wanted to give me work. She must know about Tom's suspension without pay. "Sure," I said, "I'd love to."

"About fifteen dollars a person sound good? We have a soft drink machine, so it could be sandwiches, burritos, whatever you want.

Plus dessert. The six of us usually eat around noon."

"Sounds perfect. Listen, Sheila, what's going on with Andy Fuller?"

"Fuller's a problem," she replied tersely. "He doesn't know how to build a real case. Yesterday was a perfect example."

"But...will he get Cameron Burr convicted?"

She snorted. "Unlikely." She hesitated. Then she added, "I'm sorry about Tom," and hung up.

So was I. I amended my calendar for Monday, August twenty-fifth. *Lunch for Six, Furman County Morgue.* A catered coffee break at the site of a murder and a lunch at the morgue. Things were looking up.

Chapter 6

The doorbell rang. Through the peephole Marla Korman's lovely, wide face grimaced grotesquely at me. I swung open the heavy door, then stared.

For the start of the IRS audit, Marla had apparently decided on a poverty-stricken look. Ordinarily, twinkling barrettes would have held her brown curls in place. Now her hair resembled an ostrich-feather duster. Not a dab of makeup covered her creamy complexion. Instead of the usual rhinestone-studded designer sweatsuit and sprinkling of precious-gem jewelry, she wore a drab gray housedress. The huge dress featured gleaming white buttons, an uneven midcalf hem, and a tear along the shoulder seam. She'd shunned her handmade Italian shoes and stuck her wide feet with their perfectly manicured toenails into hot-pink plastic thongs. Her bright eyes regarded me merrily.

"Marla—" I began.

She gestured for me to stop with empty-of-sapphires fingers. A telltale white line striped her tanned right forearm: no Rolex. I sniffed appraisingly and realized she wasn't wearing any deodorant.

She said, "So you didn't like the prosecutor."

"Don't."

"I'm starving and I want to hear all about it. I'm telling you, Goldy, I *dated* Andy Fuller. *I* didn't even jump on him."

"I appreciate your sharing that, Marla. So, how are the IRS guys?"

"Sons of bitches, they went to a Denver steakhouse. Made a point of telling me about an expensive five-star restaurant on the way, where they could drop me off. I thought the IRS only audited *poor* people." She swept down our hallway, headed for the kitchen. "They never did mention what a good person I was, doing fund-raising in my spare time."

"I don't think they care about charity work," I said as I followed her. "Especially since you didn't join the committees until you got the audit notice."

She snorted self-righteously. "Well, guess what? From the moment I left their office

84

my cellular has been ringing. Seems the whole town knows about your mauling Fuller."

I refused to be drawn in. "Did you drive the Mercedes over here?"

She flopped into a chair. "Yes, but the IRS henchmen didn't see it." She gave me a rueful look. "Word is that Tom's not going to be paid for a while. With Litchfield on the prowl, I tried to hustle up more assignments for you."

"Thanks."

"Don't thank me yet," she said matter-of-factly. "How's your cash situation?"

"Not great."

She stood up and pulled me in for a smelly hug. "The bastards have frozen my accounts. I had my aunt overnight me some cash, and I keep it in a shoe box under my bed. That's how I'll pay Julian's first tuition bills. I'll get a money order, I guess. Goldy, if things get bad, you need to swallow your pride and take some money from me."

Not in this lifetime. But I murmured another thanks and poured her a glass of sparkling water. She flipped on the oven light and *ooh-ooh*ed over the baking cobbler.

I said, "It'll be ready in twenty minutes. But it's not for coronary patients."

She fluffed out the gray housedress and sat back down. "Speaking of coronary patients, how's André doing?"

"Not very well. Lots of thin, temperamental people to cater to," I observed as I scanned the *Ours* section of my walk-in refrigerator for low-fat lunch ingredients.

"Don't say the word *thin* to me," she wailed. "These days, I can't do what I love most. *Eat out. Spend money.* It's a prison sentence." She eyed the demolished window. "Ah, speaking of jail? Heard from John Richard?"

I emerged from the refrigerator balancing a crystal pitcher and two plastic containers. "He calls Arch. Tom or I take him down to visit."

She downed the sparkling water and nodded at the pitcher of iced tea. "I heard the case against Cameron Burr is weak. I want to personally kiss him for ridding the town of Gerald Eliot."

"Marla!"

"Oh, don't. Eliot was a fraud. Did you get a look at the Merciful Migrations cabin kitchen? Eliot was supposed to put in a row of windows. But he fell for a model instead. They didn't just roll in the hay. They frolicked between four-by-fours, screwed in sawdust, porked on plywood—"

"Marla!" I gasped in mock surprise. Then I asked, "Do you know the model's name? Or who caught them—er, frolicking?"

"All I know is that it got Eliot canned."

I shook my head. "How'd he keep getting jobs? How come you didn't tell me he was so bad?"

She sighed noisily. "I didn't know *you* were going to hire him until after he'd made *this* mess." She gestured at my gutted wall. "Plus, other people hate to admit their failures with contractors. When Cameron wanted to hire

Eliot as a night guard at the Homestead, I was in charge of doing the background check, but I was only supposed to find out if he stole stuff, not if he was a good contractor— Cameron already knew his shortcomings in that department. I called his last three jobs. The only thing that disappeared from people's homes was Gerald Eliot himself."

"Nobody told *me.*"

She shrugged. "He was a *terrible* guard at the museum. He swore he'd broken up with that model, but he was pouring tequila for *somebody* into the society's antique shot glasses. Monday morning, we'd come in for a meeting? The place would smell like a bar."

I shook a dollop of nonfat cottage cheese into a crystal cup and surrounded it artfully with sliced strawberries. When I put it in front of her, she smiled her thanks and reached for a spoon.

"Okay, enough chatter," she said after a few bites. I groaned, but she pressed on: "What's going to happen to you? Will you still be able to pick up half of Julian's college expenses?"

My shoulders slumped. I'd forgotten about our responsibility for Julian's expenses. Before we were married, Tom had promised to pay half of our young friend's tuition, room, and board. Marla paid the other half. Also, I realized with a start, I had no idea if John Richard had made any provision to pay for Arch's fall tuition at Elk Park Prep. Before he'd gotten himself into jail, he had been ordered by the court to pay Arch's tuition bills. How could he fulfill his financial obligations if he was behind bars?

"Have you heard from Julian?" I asked Marla. "He called here yesterday but didn't leave a number."

She downed a strawberry and raised her eyebrows. "Talked to him last night."

"You did? Where was he? Is he coming to visit?"

She shrugged noncommittally. "Don't know where he was exactly. He sounded better than he did a few weeks ago, when I told him about the audit and my plans to act poor and virtuous. He even recommended the secondhand store between Mountain Rental and Darlene's Antiques and Collectibles. That's where I found this creation." She smoothed the gray dress and struck a pose. "But it's my turn to ask you questions."

"What about *Julian*? What did he say?"

"Not much, I keep telling you!" She finished her fruit plate and nudged it aside. "So much for the money situation. Does Arch have a girl-friend yet?"

"No. And please don't ask him, he's extremely sensitive."

"Well, then, if we can't discuss cash or young love, is that cobbler done yet?"

"I thought you were going to be virtuous."

"I *am* being virtuous. It's exhausting me." She stood and brought her bowl to the sink, where she ostentatiously rinsed it, to underscore just how virtuous she was endeavoring to be. "Don't worry, I'm not having any of your yummy, artery-clogging cobbler. I need to take you somewhere. So finish your cooking."

"Take me where? To book an event with the IRS? Audit-Time Appetizers? Penalty-Plus-Interest Pizza?"

Her eyes twinkled. She did look much younger without makeup. "Can't tell you. It's a surprise."

Groaning, I slid the puffed, golden cobbler out of the oven and set it aside to cool. Marla, who stubbornly refused to explain further, led me out my front door and motioned down the street. The warm, sweet summer air swished through the aspens and evergreens as we trekked the short block and a half to Main Street, then turned left and climbed the sloped steps to the Grizzly Saloon. There, Marla pointed to one of the old wooden benches lining the porch. She scrutinized the street in both directions. After a moment, she sat down, frowning. Evidently, whatever it was she intended to surprise me with hadn't yet arrived.

The pungent smell of spilled beer and old wood wafted out the saloon doors. Tourists clutching shopping bags came and went from Darlene's and the secondhand store. A runner trotted very slowly down our street, then turned left by the Grizzly. An emerald-green halter top and pants clung to her tall body and set off her gleaming chestnut hair, drawn up in a ponytail. It was Rustine, the model. I was not aware that she lived in Aspen Meadow, much less made slow jogs along Main Street. She glanced up briefly and I smiled. She immediately looked away, as if she didn't recognize me. Maybe this time she didn't need any coffee.

"Why are we here?" I asked Marla after another five minutes. "Are we waiting for somebody?"

"Secret," she said knowingly. "Ah, here we go."

An ancient Toyota with New York license plates sputtered to the curb. A moment passed while the driver and passenger conversed. Then the passenger-side door creaked open. A handsome young man with longish dark hair and a square jaw climbed out of the car, squinted at the bright sunlight, and scanned the front of the saloon. He held his hand up to his forehead to shield his eyes, and frowned. Then he spotted Marla and me and waved.

It was Julian.

He'd let his hair grow out from its bleached Dutch-boy cut. The short, tough, muscled body that I'd usually seen plowing down the lap lanes of our community pool now seemed thinner beneath a faded blue T-shirt and tattered jeans. When he let the hand shielding his dark eyes drop, I could see they were smudged with fatigue.

"Goldy!"

By the time I stood beside the sputtering car, Julian had already unloaded three boxes and a tattered duffel bag from its trunk. Marla trundled up beside me, beaming. The Toyota growled, belched a cloud of exhaust, and chugged away. I hugged Julian tightly. Marla embraced both of us.

"We thought your summer job wasn't over, or that you weren't coming—" I stammered.

Julian pulled away from me. He seemed awkward and disoriented, as if he'd just disembarked from a long flight. His cheeks turned pink. Was he embarrassed? Happy to be home? Impossible to tell.

He said, "Good to see you all, too."

"Marla didn't tell me," I went on, "and I had no idea..."

"Marla." Julian grinned. "Great outfit," he told her.

"Thanks," she purred.

The three of us were suddenly silent. Julian swallowed and shifted from foot to foot. *Something is wrong,* I thought.

Marla chirped, "I'm going to let you two visit. I'll go get my car." She took off before I could protest. Get her car for what?

Julian's voice cracked when he asked, "Is Arch...at your place?"

"He's just doing some errands with Tom," I replied. *What was going on?* His face fell. "What *is* it?" I demanded. He said nothing. "Listen, let's go home, okay? How long can you stay? We were *just* talking about you and—"

He lifted his jaw and I saw a trace of the Julian I'd first known. Rebellion, hostility, and insecurity raged below a forced external calm. "I'm warning you," he said stiffly. "You're going to be very disappointed in me—"

"Never." But I felt increasingly uncertain. So much had been going wrong lately. "What is it?" I asked lamely.

"I quit my summer job at the hotel restaurant. The owner was weird, wanted me to take over the kitchen while she took off. Even the other employees told me I should pack it in. I was wondering if you, if you would be willing..." He cleared his throat. "Could you take me back for a while? Just until I get my act together."

I wondered vaguely about the opening of school, but jumped in with, "Of course! Why would you even *think* we wouldn't—"

He held up his hand. "Wait." His voice crackled with defiance. "Before you say yes, there's something you should know. It's not for a short time. I...didn't just quit my job. I dropped out of Cornell." His eyes were wet. "I was miserable."

I said, "Welcome home, Julian," and hugged him.

This time, he didn't pull away.

Chapter 7

Marla's Mercedes purred to the curb. We loaded Julian's boxes and bag into the trunk and took off.

Jake barked ecstatically when he spotted Julian, even though the dog had only met our former boarder briefly at Christmas. But no matter. When we came through the back gate, the hound jumped up, howled, sniffed Julian's neck and licked his face. Arch was always telling us that bloodhounds belong to the canine equivalent of Mensa. Now Jake seemed to remember that Julian was the great friend and protector of his beloved Arch. In any event, Julian seemed pleased to be so effusively welcomed.

Inside, he eagerly accepted the offer of warm cherry cobbler piled with scoops of vanilla ice cream. Marla and I drank iced coffee and gingerly worked our way toward asking what had gone wrong.

He began by saying he'd *wanted* to go away to college. He'd been eager to try a new place, far away from the West. But he'd quickly become disillusioned, and missed Colorado. His assigned roommate smoked, watched television till midnight, then snored until noon. So Julian couldn't study, breathe, or sleep. Worst of all, he'd become intensely lonely.

"I didn't have anybody to eat with." His spoon traced a circle on his empty plate. "It's something you don't think about, you know? How much of eating is just being with other people. I always thought the important thing was the food, how it tastes. But it isn't."

Contemplating these problems while Jay Leno squawked each night on the roommate's TV, Julian had resigned himself to self-doubt. He'd felt his confidence ebb away. His misery had exacerbated the embarrassment he already felt over Marla and Tom paying so much for him to be in college. With the illogic of the desperate, he'd stopped going to class. He'd begun waiting tables at a coffee shop in Ithaca. Working in a kitchen and being around other food workers had helped his frame of mind. Unfortunately, all those skipped classes and missed assignments had wreaked havoc on his freshman transcript.

At the urging of the coffee shop owner, Julian had taken a high-paying summer job in an upstate New York hotel. But his new boss had required eighteen-hour workdays. Julian had thought about quitting, but he hadn't wanted to return to his hometown of Bluff, Utah. Although he'd learned to make candy and Navajo tacos there, the town possessed few prospects for a food service career. He'd finally phoned a Cornell administrator and talked to various deans. All the university folks had been very understanding; they'd told him to stay in touch. Officially, his departure was classified as a leave of absence. To Julian, it was escape from a black hole.

"So," he said finally. He registered the distress in my face. "Don't take it so hard, Goldy. I'll go back to college eventually. I'll even get better grades. Now, though, I can help with any food job you can think of."

"I don't care about the transcript," I replied. "I'm just sorry you were so unhappy."

Marla interjected, "You know that here in Aspen Meadow, you don't *ever* have to eat alone."

"Yeah, okay, enough about my problems."

94

Julian pointed to the hole over the sink. "Who did that, your ex-husband?"

"Yep," Marla and I said in unison.

I added, "Right before he was arrested. He's still in jail though, so don't worry. And anyway, the hole was actually made a lot worse by a kitchen contractor. And he's *dead,* I'm sorry to say."

Julian exhaled. Then he appraised Marla. "You look so different," he observed. "I mean, besides the dress. Where's all your jewelry?"

"In a strongbox in my garage." Marla giggled. "I've got twenty thousand in hundreds under my bed, too. You want to live at my place? You can be my chef and yard man. Be paid in cash," she stage-whispered, "and have *untaxed* income!"

"Thanks," Julian said with heartfelt appreciation. "But I need to do more work with food." He cleared his throat, then turned back to me. "So, will you have me? Do you still need an assistant?"

"*We* want you. You're part of our family. And of *course* I can use you," I replied. "You're one of the most talented cooks I've ever met."

"Ooh-ooh," said Marla. "High praise from Miss Golden Butter herself."

"How's the *business*?" Julian asked. "I applied to a catering outfit in Ithaca. It was a huge operation. But they said they couldn't justify another guy, even for a few hours a week. They said times are really tough for caterers."

"For heaven's sake," I replied. "It doesn't matter how the business is."

He raked his long hair with his hands. "What do you mean, it doesn't matter?" He narrowed his eyes. "What's going on? Is it good news? Bad news? I'll work for room and board, if that's easier."

His questions dangled while I tried to think of an honest way to inform this proud, easily irritated young man about the recent downward course of events. There wasn't an easy way.

"Better tell him, Goldy," Marla said glumly.

I picked up his plate. Only a few cobbler crumbs remained. "Okay. Tom's been suspended. Charged with insubordination. Scratch his salary. So if you want extra *cash,* you might have to cut Marla's lawn."

"Wait a minute, you skipped the good part!" Marla charged. "Miss Caters-With-Cholesterol attacked the assistant district attorney herself. He *really* ticked her off."

"*What?*" said Julian.

"Oh, it's a long story." I gave Marla a furious *shut up* look. "Plus, business is down," I admitted before Marla could jump in again. "You know, the competitor I told you about. Craig Litchfield. Somehow, he got ahold of my client list—"

"Your client list? With all your prices and menus?" interrupted Julian. "That's stealing, isn't it? How'd he do that?"

The phone jangled. I reached for it without answering Julian.

"This is Craig Litchfield." The imperious tone sawed in my ear. Startled, I glanced at

Julian, afraid he could tell who was on the line. But Julian was angrily clanking silverware into the dishwasher. Litchfield continued, "I'm coming over. I have something to talk to you about."

"I'm not really prepared to—"

"You're never prepared," he quipped back. "I'll be there in five minutes." The line went dead.

I sighed and hung up. "Well, gang, Litchfield's coming over."

"Ooh, fireworks, fireworks," trilled Marla.

Julian banged the dishwasher door shut. He regarded me warily. As a new but unpaid hireling, he did not want to appear nosy. His voice was sharp. "I'll just do some food prep." With that, he started unpacking gleaming red tomatoes from one of his crates.

"You brought vegetables?" I asked.

"Bought them at a farmer's stand in eastern Colorado." He placed a bunch of leeks next to the tomatoes. "I didn't know whether you'd take me back or not. But if you did, I wanted to fix dinner for everybody. There's plenty for you, too, Marla."

Marla checked her wrist, then frowned: no watch. She glanced at my clock. "The IRS hit men said they'd be back at two, so I can only stay a bit longer. Thanks for the invitation, though. If my confrontation with the bureaucratic bottom-feeders ends before next week, which they warned me it wouldn't, I'll take you up on it." She reached out to squeeze his hand. "It's good to see you, Julian," she said warmly. Julian grinned and worked zealously on the vegetables. I poured Marla more iced coffee.

Once the tomatoes and leeks were stacked in glistening heaps, Julian filled the sink with shiny scallions, nugget-sized new potatoes, slender green beans, stalks of asparagus, and fragrant bunches of basil, dill, and rosemary with soil still clinging to the roots.

"So tell me how this Litchfield guy got your files." His voice had an edge. Water gushed into the sink as he began to scrub the rest of the vegetables.

"I honestly don't know," I replied.

"After all that security stuff you went through with The Jerk, you're saying you have no idea how he broke in?" he demanded. "What else has he done?"

Marla took a sip of iced coffee and advised, "Remember, Goldy, twenty-year-olds think the world can be fixed."

I took a deep breath. "Litchfield tried to steal one of my suppliers *and* one of André Hibbard's. Remember my old teacher?" Julian nodded. "He's moved to a retirement community in Blue Spruce. I'll be competing against both André and Litchfield next week, for the Soirée booking. Anyway, Litchfield offered higher prices to our suppliers, and guaranteed orders, if he could be the suppliers' sole client in Aspen Meadow."

Julian muttered, "Some *people*."

"All of Goldy's energy has gone into fighting this guy," Marla interjected. "And that's why she's so on *edge* and why she clobbered the assistant district attorney. At least that's my theory—"

Before she could elaborate, however, a howl erupted from outdoors. Jake. The dog brayed again.

"Maybe Arch is home," I said hopefully. We all listened, puzzled. But this barking was not the usual glad-to-see-you woofing. I headed for the front door. Had I locked the gate? Arch would scold me if I'd forgotten it.

"Sounds as if he's in the street," Marla called. Cursing under my breath, I stepped onto the front porch in time to see Jake tackle Craig Litchfield.

"Jake!" I cried. "Stop! Get down!"

With his massive paws planted on Craig Litchfield's chest, Jake turned and gave me mournful eyes. Mud splotched Litchfield's coal-black shirt. His face was spattered with mud, too, and what wasn't was purple with rage. In the moment I called to Jake, Litchfield smacked the hound hard across the jaw. Squealing, Jake rolled across the lawn.

"Oh, Lord." I ran down the porch steps and across the grass toward our poor dog.

"Stop, stop!" I shoved Litchfield away and dropped to my knees beside Jake. Marla and Julian appeared on the porch and started yelling at Litchfield to back off. "There, there, boy," I murmured. I cradled his head in my lap. Jake whimpered and licked my hand. A thin stripe of blood oozed out of his nose. He shivered with fear. "What do you want?" I demanded of Litchfield. "Why did you *do* that?" I could hear the shrillness in my voice.

With studied nonchalance, Litchfield tugged a pack of cigarettes from the breast pocket of his dirty shirt. With his matching black pants and slicked hair, he looked like a toreador. He shook out a cigarette and flashed a silver lighter out of a pants pocket. He lit the cig, inhaled deeply, and regarded my house like a reluctant buyer. Jake showed his teeth and growled, the last vestige of his police training.

Litchfield blew out a stream of smoke. "That animal is bad news," he announced contemptuously. He lifted his chin, picked at a strand of tobacco on his lower lip, then spit it onto my lawn. "You know, there's a leash law in Furman County."

I stroked Jake's silky ears. "The dog was on our property, so he was perfectly legal." When Jake wriggled in my arms, I pushed his rump down and spoke to him under my breath. He'd always had trouble holding a command to stay. I needed Jake to sit close by me until this visitation from the enemy was over. I didn't trust myself not to do more damage to Litchfield than I had to Andy Fuller. "What do you want?" I repeated coldly. "Tell me and then go. Better yet, go. Write me a letter."

"Yeah, write a letter, you creep!" Marla was glaring.

Litchfield blew smoke at her while appraising the gray housedress and pink thongs. "Who're you? A caterer's helper? Or the maid?" He took another drag on the cigarette. "You can go back to your dusting now."

Marla Korman, the richest woman in Aspen Meadow, head of the committee for the Merciful Migrations September Soirée, laughed in delight. "Hey, baby!" she called back in an uncanny imitation of Litchfield's condescending tone. "How 'bout I start by cleaning your clock?"

Litchfield muttered, "Bitch." He tilted his head and raised a dark eyebrow at Julian, who had stalked down to the sidewalk. He stood beside me, his lean body tensed and ready to strike. Amused, Litchfield grinned. "And who might *you* be? *Another* caterer's helper?"

"I am Julian Teller." Julian bit each word. "I'm telling you so that when I kick your ass, you'll know it's me."

Litchfield chuckled. "Aha! First a threat from the domestic help, then one from the great *Julian Teller*! The *brilliant* young vegetarian chef who used to work for Mrs. Schulz. The power behind the throne, you might say." Jake let out a low growl. Litchfield blew out smoke and contemplated Julian. "I heard you were off in college somewhere. Want to come work for a real caterer? At twice your current salary?"

Julian's voice knifed the soft summer air. "You are so *dead*. You don't even *realize* it."

"What do you *want*, Litchfield?" I demanded for the third time. I gripped Jake's collar.

Litchfield screwed his handsome baby face into a sourpuss. "Well, now," he said. He held his cigarette at his side and bent forward.

"I heard about your *troubles*. I've come to offer you *cash*. For your business. Your suppliers, booking schedule. Recipes, not that those are worth anything. Two-year no-compete agreement." He studied the glowing tip of his cigarette. "Fifty thousand dollars." He smiled. "Take it or leave it."

I was nonplussed. It was like the devil offering cake to a starving person. Still restraining Jake by the collar, I wiped the blood off the dog's nose with my free hand and tried to steady my breath.

"Go away," I said quietly to Litchfield. "And don't ever, ever come back. For any reason."

Craig Litchfield flicked his cigarette butt into Tom's roses. An arc of smoke hung briefly in the air as he thrust his hands into his pockets, rocked back on his heels, and considered us.

"Okay, Goldy Bear Schulz," he said at last. "We go up against each other again a week from today. You change your mind before that, call me."

Chapter 8

Julian and I coaxed Jake up onto the porch. Marla went inside for a clean, wet washcloth. I dabbed Jake's wound; the poor dog squirmed and refused to keep still. Promising to call later in the week, Marla reluctantly left for her match with the IRS. Shortly thereafter, Tom and Arch returned. Arch's joy at Julian's arrival turned to distress when he saw Jake. Tom insisted on taking Jake to the vet; Arch refused to stay home and went with them. Returning to the kitchen, I mentally swore revenge on Craig Litchfield's black heart.

"How does he know about me?" Julian demanded as I rinsed the pork chops I'd bought for the evening meal. I had no idea what to serve meat-shunning Julian. As if reading my mind, he began scrubbing large baking potatoes. No doubt he would conjure up a vegetarian dish more inspiring than anything in my repertoire. "I mean," he went on, "how does he know my background? About college? How does he know what kind of cooking I do?"

"I have no idea," I admitted as I covered the chops and put them into the walk-in refrigerator. "But I'm wondering if he has a rich aunt. He runs huge ads and charges less than the cost of ingredients. He must be losing money on events. Then he offers you twice an unknown salary to work for him. How does he do it?"

"He's a creep," Julian said fiercely as he fitted my food processor with the grating blade. "Don't worry—we'll beat him. We're just going to have to cook better than he does, that's all."

I smiled at him. "That's what André said."

"I just wish I knew how he gets his information."

"Julian, so do I. The man's making me paranoid."

Julian shook his head, then savagely pushed

a hunk of fresh Parmesan cheese into the growling food processor. "You've got an open window right over your sink. Your computer's right on the counter. You have a password for your programs?"

I thought of Arch and his fascination with encryption. "No."

"Install one," Julian said grimly.

◆

Tom and Arch returned with Jake, whose wound had been cleaned and smeared with antiseptic. Tom repeated the vet's warning that we were to watch the hound over the next few days for signs of fever or swelling, indications that an infection might be setting in.

Arch watched Julian's skillful moves as he organized a meal on the scratched Formica counter. "I am *so* happy you're here," he said awkwardly. At fourteen, Arch did not initiate physical affection.

Julian set aside the grated Parmesan and grabbed Arch in a bear hug. "Hey, man, great to see you, too. Still doing magic? What's your latest project?"

"Well...Todd and I are working on some high-tech stuff. I have a whole display of it in my—our—room," Arch replied shyly. "First I have to show you the cat's new spot. Want to see both?"

"You bet."

I followed them upstairs. Tom, mumbling vaguely about woodwork, retired to the basement. While I unfurled clean sheets, Arch proudly showed Julian how Scout the cat had made a hidden home under Julian's old bed. Scout had fled inside during the Litchfield encounter. Now he eased from his spot to rub against Julian's stubbly cheek. Julian howled with laughter. Arch's wide grin made me smile.

Back in the kitchen, I pored over my computer manual and eventually chose and entered a password. Rock music reverberated from the boys' room overhead. At four o'clock, Julian came down to help with the evening meal. I shaped, knotted, and covered rolls from a recipe André had laboriously copied out and given me. Julian put the potatoes in to bake, finished trimming the other vegetables, and set the table. While the rolls rose, I seared the chops and swirled in Dijon mustard with melted currant jelly for a sauce. Julian scooped out the baked potatoes, whipped the steaming mass with cream, Parmesan, salt, and white pepper, refilled the skins, and placed the delicious-looking concoctions back into the oven to puff to a golden brown. While he was cleaning up, I told him about the previous day's modeling shoot, working with André, finding Gerald Eliot's body, and the arrest of Arch's and my old friend, Cameron Burr. Cameron was now sitting in jail while his wife labored to breathe. Julian frowned. Perhaps thinking of Cameron, he dubbed his dish Jailbreak Potatoes.

Just after six o'clock, the three meat-eaters dug into the tender chops, while all of us dove

Jailbreak Potatoes

4 large baking potatoes
2 tablespoons (¼ stick) unsalted butter
½ cup whipping cream
½ teaspoon salt
¼ teaspoon or more white pepper
½ cup freshly grated Parmesan cheese

Preheat the oven to 400°F.

Scrub and prick each potato 3 or 4 times with a fork. Bake the potatoes for 1 hour, or until flaky. Remove from the oven and cool slightly.

In the large bowl of an electric mixer, place the butter, cream, salt, pepper, and cheese. Using a sharp knife, cut at a 45-degree angle to remove an oval of skin and potato from the flat top side of each potato. Using a spoon, scoop most of the potato out of the interior into the bowl with the other ingredients. Leave a thin layer of potato inside the skin. Scrape the potato from the back of the removed ovals of potato skin into the bowl.

Using the whip attachment, whip the potato mixture until smooth. Taste and correct the seasoning.

Dividing the whipped potato mixture evenly, spoon it back into the skins. Place the stuffed potatoes on a buttered, rimmed baking sheet and bake an additional 15 minutes, or until the filling is thoroughly heated.

Makes 4 servings.

into the rich, tangy potatoes and magnificent array of fresh asparagus, leek, tomatoes, and corn braised in white wine and broth. We smeared butter on the feather-light, golden-brown rolls, ate, and talked about Arch's upcoming school year and how long it would be before Tom could be cleared.

We avoided mention of Cameron Burr. We also skirted the subject of Julian dropping out of college. As his self-appointed aunt-cum-godmother, this move of his *did* bother me. No matter how gifted a person was at cooking or anything else, a well-rounded education would help him navigate through life. But this was not the time for parental advice. Julian was a very intelligent, very good kid. I trusted him. If he didn't make a move to go back to school within six months, we'd have a heart-to-heart. For the moment, even under the clouds of Cameron's arrest and Tom's suspension, we could concentrate on enjoying a long-delayed family reunion.

When the dishes were done, Julian ordered Tom, Arch, and me to sit on the back deck while he put together a dessert tray. The sun slipped slowly behind enormous, salmon-colored clouds that hovered over the mountains' silhouette. With a flourish, Julian produced a tray of his trademark fudge, a dark, impossibly luscious concoction dotted with sun-dried cherries. I closed my eyes, bit into the velvety chocolate, and allowed happiness to infuse my senses. The smooth, silky combination of bittersweet and milk chocolate combined with tart, chewy cherries and crunchy, toasted hazelnuts made my spine tingle. My kitchen was a mess, my bookings were down, a friend of ours had been arrested, my husband was suspended. But there was *tomorrow*, I reminded myself. If Scarlett O'Hara could look to better times, why couldn't I? Plus, Scarlett hadn't had her spirits bolstered by Julian Teller's company—not to mention his fudge.

♦

On Wednesday and Thursday we waited for Tom's fellow officers to update us on the Eliot case. No information—not even the results of the autopsy—was forthcoming. Since Eliot's murder was a capital case, Cameron Burr was formally denied bail. One call from the police captain's secretary yielded the information that Tom's suspension was being written up for formal review. The *Mountain Journal* speculated endlessly about the homicide. The headline *Local Cop Suspended Pending Probe* made me flinch.

For my part, I spent the two days drinking coffee, agonizing with Julian over the Soirée, testing menus, and making phone calls. At the Furman County Jail, Cameron either didn't get my messages or ignored them. Lutheran Hospital still insisted Barbara couldn't talk. I also tried—in vain—to hatch more jobs.

When Julian was off at the grocery store on one of our experimentation days—I felt slightly guilty to have such a willing helper—I decided to follow his suggestion and try an autumn-type dish for the Soirée. While I was peeling a Granny Smith apple, Kathleen Druckman—Todd's mother—called to ask about the prospect of Arch and Todd joining a cotillion. While I was chopping the apple, Arch came into the kitchen; I ran the idea by him and he said to for-*get* it. Defeated, I wondered what the mother of a fourteen-year-old was supposed to do. Then again, I remembered as I melted butter and mixed the chopped apples with moist, crumbly brown sugar, I'd sworn off involvement in Arch's social life.

I sifted flour with cinnamon, nutmeg, and allspice—and recalled the beginning of the previous February, when, for the second year in a row, Arch had been approached by a female classmate and asked if he wanted to be her boyfriend. Since it was not the same girl as the preceding year, I'd kept my mouth shut as Arch had *again* ecstatically said, Sure! He'd love to be her boyfriend! Last year, he'd begged Julian to make a heart-shaped chocolate cake with the girl's name and his written in frosting, which he'd given to the girl. This year, he'd enthusiastically spent his money earned from chores on a Valentine's Day basket for the new love. On February fourteenth, he'd floated off to school, bearing his load of chocolates and stuffed animals, and made his offering. By February twentieth—both years—he'd been told that he was boring and the relationship was over.

I stirred the dry ingredients and an egg into the mixture, then slid the whole thing in the oven. When the fragrant scent of autumn spices rolled through the kitchen thirty minutes later, I took the pan out and set it aside to cool. Then I reluctantly called Kathleen Druckman back and said, no cotillion. Thanks anyway. I didn't know whether Arch was unusual in receiving the cruelty of prepubescent females, or whether all the boys suffered from the same gullibility. Whatever had been the reason for the Valentine's Day fiascoes, Arch needed to build up his armor in the gender wars.

♦

Each day, Tom disappeared to the hardware store. He always returned home with bulging paper bags and a secretive, satisfied look. I didn't know what he was up to as he banged away in the basement, and I didn't dare ask. As I felt the reverberations through the kitchen floor, I decided the hammering must be Tom's therapy, like the pro football player I'd seen on TV. With great glee, the athlete had said the NFL was the only place you could beat the daylights out of somebody and not go to jail. And he didn't use the word *daylights*.

Arch followed Julian around like a shadow. As for Julian, he still heaped four teaspoons of sugar into his morning espresso and bounced culinary ideas around until he came up with something he wanted to try. And he cooked. We had ground shrimp poached with herbs and encased in brioche, the savory cheesecake

I'd made for André, crisp-fried crab cakes paired with tangy coleslaw, and grilled fish tacos on homemade tortillas with papaya salsa. Meals were heaven, and a welcome break from the worry over unreturned calls to Cameron Burr, the lack of information about Barbara, and our general lack of employment.

Each evening, Tom and Julian and Arch and I would sit out on our deck and indulge in desserts that ranged from peach pie to bread pudding. We would eat, that is, until Julian's worry about whether he was being helpful enough burst forth in a slew of questions: Had we developed enough recipes for the Soirée tasting party? Would he be allowed to help me at future catered events? I invariably replied in the affirmative. I'd always told my Sunday School class to love unconditionally. The only problem arose when you were dealing with somebody who felt he had to *earn* your love. No matter how many times we showed Julian that we loved and accepted him, he was always looking around wildly and pleading, *Let me do more.*

◆

At seven-thirty Friday morning, while Tom and Arch were still asleep, Julian and I were just beginning to look over our offerings for André's coffee break when the call came.

"This is Rufus Driggle," the husky voice identified himself. "I'm over here at the

Homestead." He paused. Then he said, "I think you better come over and help old Mr. André."

My skin rippled with gooseflesh. "What's wrong?"

Rufus exhaled. The receiver clunked and I could just make out some angry whispers.

"Hello?" I demanded.

"This is Ian Hood. André says he's fine. He gave us your number. But the old guy grabbed his chest when he was putting out the coffee cups." Ian sighed with impatience. "I think he's got a bit of pain down his left arm, he's sweating, and every time I come out to the kitchen, he's sitting down like he's exhausted."

"Did you call nine-one-one?" I demanded.

"They're on their way."

"So are we."

I gripped the dashboard as Julian rocked his Range Rover, inherited from former employers, to the Homestead. *Stay calm,* I ordered myself. *André might need you. We could get there before the ambulance.* I had taken a course in cardiopulmonary resuscitation after Marla had her heart attack. When I'd unexpectedly come on the dead body of my ex-husband's girlfriend earlier in the summer, though, the emergency operator had asked if I knew CPR, and I'd mumbled a negative. Crises will do that: make you forget what you know.

We drew up to the Homestead service entrance. A two-story log octagon with timbered additions and a peaked roof, the former ranch owner's residence-turned-museum always reminded me of one of Arch's Lincoln

Log constructions. As I vaulted out of the Rover, two paramedics trudged out the back door. I confronted one of them: a tall, chunky bald man with a ruddy complexion and a large nose.

"How is he? What happened?"

"He's fine," the man reassured me. "Mr. Hibbard had a little indigestion. He checks out completely."

"What do you mean *he checks out*?" I echoed, dumbfounded. "Did he take some of his nitroglycerin? How come you're not taking him down to the hospital?"

"He didn't take the nitro because his doctor's told him he's sensitive to it. Mr. Hibbard was very angry with us, and insisted he's been told not to take a pill unless he's *sure* he's having an attack, which he *wasn't*. And we're not transporting him anywhere because he's not sick and not in danger," the paramedic said firmly. "Somebody pushed the panic button, that's all."

"Are you *sure* he's all right?"

"He's fine. If he has more symptoms, he knows to put a tablet under his tongue. The nitroglycerin opens up the—"

"I *know* what nitroglycerin does." Reminders of my enforced passage through Med Wives 101 never helped my mood.

"He seems to think he's in excellent shape," the paramedic added with a chuckle. "Are *you* okay?"

I assured him that I was, thanked him for checking André out, and trotted to the glass-paneled back door. Julian followed close behind.

Fussing loudly, André sat perched on a wooden stool by the Homestead kitchen's massive oak table. He was buttoning up his crisp white chef's jacket. Ian Hood and Rufus Driggle hovered nearby.

"—and I don't understand why the two of *you* can't go and take care of Saint Nicholas and the children," André fumed as he elbowed Rufus away from him. "Just wait for us to serve you! I am fine! Stop being such busybodies!"

I nodded to Rufus Driggle, whose neon-orange sweatsuit hung in wide folds from his lanky frame. The carpenter sidled over to Julian and me.

"Goldy, we're so glad you're here," he whispered, as if we were old friends. I blinked: Despite the crisis atmosphere, I couldn't help noticing how the orange suit clashed painfully with *please-call-me-Rufus*'s orange hair and pale skin. "We were kind of worried about old André here—"

Ian Hood was giving André a thunderous, impatient look. "Listen, old man," he reprimanded André, "I saw you grab your chest." I cringed. "Maybe this work is too demanding for you. Maybe you should go home and rest. We can order in some doughnuts."

André folded his arms across his copious stomach and glared. Rufus reached for a glass from an old wooden cabinet and ran water into it. He offered the drink to André. André ignored him.

"Did you hear me, André?" Ian demanded loudly. "*Can* you hear me?"

"I may be *old,* but I am *not deaf*!" André shouted at Ian. When André swiveled away from Ian, he knocked the glass of water out of Rufus's hand. Miraculously, the glass clattered to the tile floor without breaking. André directed his fury at the carpenter. "You *imbecile*! Why did you put that there?" he bellowed, then glared at the two of them. "Didn't you hear the medical people say I was fine?" He caught sight of me. "Now look what you have done! Made my student worry!" He batted Rufus Driggle away with a fleshy palm. "Go spray rocks! Move furniture!"

Ian ran his strong fingers through his thick gray hair, rolled his brown eyes, and tapped his foot. His sensitive features pinched as he worked his mouth slowly from side to side. He was more attractive than I remembered from the first day of the shoot; perhaps then I'd been overwhelmed by the models' good looks. He seemed on the verge of saying something, but then changed his mind and merely shrugged.

I said, "I'm here now, André." I tried to make my voice comforting rather than condescending, which would have made him more upset than he already was.

"Yeah," Julian piped up unexpectedly as he appeared at my side. "I'm Julian Teller, *her* student, Mr. Hibbard. I hope it's okay that I came. Goldy was so worried about you. She's always talking about her teacher," he made his voice appropriately awestruck, " 'a *real* master,' she says, *'that's* André Hibbard.' " With great seriousness, Julian perused the oak island: a rack of cooling muffins sat neatly next to containers of flour, unsalted butter, brown sugar, and eggs. "Are you doing a coffee break cake? It looks super. Goldy was working on one this week. Is it okay if I stay and help?"

André nodded at him and beamed at me. He threw a haughty, I-told-you-so look at Ian and Rufus. Ian wordlessly slammed out of the room, clearly irritated beyond control. I breathed relief.

"I need this scrim adjusted!" he shouted from the Homestead interior. André *hrumph*ed and raised a silver eyebrow. Rufus hustled out the door.

"The coffee break is at ten," said André without moving from the stool. He sighed. "Thank you for offering to help. The Santa is allergic to strawberries and needs a separate bowl of fruit. There are three shots this morning, for three children's outfits." I shook my head: so much work. Why hadn't he asked me to come at eight? "Before you scold me, Goldy," André went on, "let me tell you, I was *not* having a heart attack. When they asked if I had pain down my arm, I told them to go away. And when I told them to leave me alone, I was gasping. So they told the medics that I was short of breath! Nonsense." He inhaled deeply, as if to prove his point.

"So how are you now?" I asked.

"Fine! The *only* reason I placed my hand on my chest was because I was listening to the curator's *terrible* tale...she is quite upset with your husband,"—he wagged a finger at me—"about that robbery by the security guard. I was being sympathetic, not having an attack."

"Aha," I said. *Upset with my husband? About that robbery by the security guard? You mean, the security guard who was murdered five days ago?* I said, "Why is she upset with my husband?"

André wafted a hand. "She had to go down to the sheriff's department. I invited her to our coffee break. She will be back later, do not fear, and you can ask her all about it."

André assigned Julian to trim the fruit bowl components while I prepared the baked snack. Lucky for me, there were apples in with the fruit André had brought, and he'd thought to bring extra aprons, which we donned. Perched on his bar stool, sipping a fresh espresso, offering a wide range of commentary and directions, André appeared not only healthy, but entirely in his element.

"So how are you doing with the fashion models?" I asked him as I tried to recall how I'd put together the apple cake earlier in the week. "Have they been eating the food you've prepared?"

"*Phh-t.* I do not understand why people with no talent earn twelve hundred dollars a day to model clothes, while I struggle to pay my bills."

"But they struggle too, don't you think?" I ventured.

"Listen, and I will tell you." *Oh, boy, here we go,* I thought. André's lectures, I was convinced, energized him. And his strongly held, vehemently expressed opinions proved to him that he was *not* old, after all. He rapped on the island with his espresso cup and waited until Julian and I had put down our knives and given him our full attention.

"You cannot become a *model* the way you become a *chef,*" he began, "through work and talent. A woman needs only a skinny body and a pretty face. And what destruction this wreaks! What I used to see at my restaurant was hundreds of teenage girls who would not eat. Why would they not eat? Because they wanted to be like the models in the magazines. But they could never *become* models because they did not have pretty faces." He sipped his espresso thoughtfully. "Do you know what I have observed this week?"

"Pretty faces?" I said. "May I finish chopping the apples while we listen? So we can offer the snack to those who *will* eat?"

He nodded. "The male models are strong. They work out and have big muscles." To demonstrate, he flexed the arm not holding his espresso cup. "The women may do *some* exercise, but when they come in to model, they are half dead, always begging me for caffeine." He held up the cup. "How can I converse with these women, when I give them coffee?"

Uh-oh, I thought as I set about mixing melted butter with eggs, brown sugar, and chopped apples. To André, *converse* usually meant *you listen; I'll talk.*

André went on: "And so I ask you. What is the message of this Christmas catalog?" He raised his voice. " *'Look like this and you will be happy.'* But this is not true. You can only be insecure. You can only be hungry." He sighed and finished his coffee.

"They won't be hungry with you around," Julian supplied.

"Yes, young man." André slid off the stool and began to lay out the platters.

"Goldy told me that before you were a chef, you were in the Resistance in the Second World War." Julian's voice was filled with awe. "Can you tell me about it?"

Mercy! Now André would love Julian forever. I dropped an egg into the batter. André launched into his tale of the secret network he'd helped build to keep Jews from being deported from Clermont-Ferrand during the Vichy régime. I did not disbelieve my teacher when he talked about this work he claimed to have done fifty-some years before. But if you did the math, André was only eleven while he was helping to build the network he referred to. Still, I would not dare interrupt him.

"They had to avoid contact with police," André said matter-of-factly. "They had to have places to hide, and our network would send messages when the deportation trains were arriving." His tone turned boastful. "The Nazis would come expecting to get two hundred

Jews for a work camp. They would leave with a handful, very angry."

Listening attentively, Julian trimmed fresh pineapple, papaya, banana, kiwi, and grapes for the fruit bowl. While I stirred together the thick cake batter and prayed that I'd remembered all the ingredients from my experimentation earlier in the week, André cast appraising glances at Julian's prep job. Mindful of the stories of French chefs lashing the fingers of kitchen helpers who did not slice, dice, and julienne properly, I felt a bit nervous. But Julian, precision-slicing the fruit, appeared to take no notice of André's scrutiny.

Within twenty minutes, a delicious aroma completely filled the room. We made coffee, arranged the muffins in pyramids, and filled the bowls. I iced the apple cake with a creamy citrus frosting, and dubbed the creation Blondes' Blondies—in honor of the models. The treats weren't truly blondies, but then again, some of the models weren't truly blondes.

"Are you really feeling all right?" I asked André as we prepared to serve the food.

"Goldy!" he admonished me. "When will you learn to believe me? My doctor says I am fine, much improved now that I have begun to work again. What am I always telling you?"

"Let the mood fit the food," I replied promptly.

"All right, then," my mentor fumed as he readjusted his tray. "Stop thinking all the time about death."

Blondes' Blondies

2 cups peeled and diced Granny Smith apples
1 cup firmly packed dark brown sugar
½ cup (1 stick) unsalted butter
1 egg
1½ cups cake flour (high altitude: add 1
   tablespoon)
1 teaspoon baking soda
½ teaspoon salt
1 teaspoon ground cinnamon
½ teaspoon ground nutmeg
½ teaspoon allspice
½ cup chopped pecans or walnuts
½ cup raisins
Creamy Citrus Frosting (recipe follows)

Preheat the oven to 325°F. Butter a 9 x 13-inch metal (not glass) pan.

In a large mixing bowl, mix the chopped apples with the brown sugar. Set it aside while you prepare the other ingredients. In a small pan, melt the butter and set it aside to cool. In a small mixing bowl, beat the egg slightly. Sift together the flour, baking soda, salt, cinnamon, nutmeg, and allspice.

Whisk the melted and cooled butter into the egg; stir this mixture into the apple mixture. Stir the flour mixture into the apple mixture, mixing just until incorporated. Stir in the nuts and raisins. (The batter will be thick.) Spread the batter in the prepared pan.

Bake for 18 to 22 minutes, or until the blondies test done with a toothpick. Cool in the pan, then frost with Creamy Citrus Frosting. Slice and serve.

Makes 32 servings.

Creamy Citrus Frosting

2 tablespoons (¼ stick) unsalted butter, softened
2 tablespoons orange juice
1 to 1½ cups confectioners' sugar, sifted

Beat the butter with the orange juice until the butter is very soft (they will not mix completely). Add the sugar until the desired consistency is reached. Spread on the cooled blondies.

Chapter 9

Just before ten, we carried the frosted blondies, the platter of André's sour cream muffins, the tureen of yogurt, and a silver bowl piled with fresh kiwi, pineapple, cantaloupe, and a variety of berries to the mahogany table in the Homestead dining room. The dining room was a high-ceilinged space that had been added to the original 1866 ranch house by later occupants. Bright sunlight filtered through the row of wavy-glassed windows and shone on polished dark wood paneling. Along the opposite wall, light glinted off glass-fronted hutches displaying Old West artifacts. Unfortunately, the shelves of two battered cabinets lacked their glass and had gaps where the missing cookbooks had been displayed. Yellow police ribbons cordoned off the space.

This room, I thought with a shudder, was where Gerald Eliot had been attacked and probably killed.

"Won't it bother the Ian's Images folk to be eating in here?" I asked André in a low whisper. "It seems sort of, well, macabre."

"I asked Hanna myself," he replied with a sniff. "She said the contract with the models says she has to provide the coffee break food in a suitable area and this is what suits her. She also said the models today probably do not know about Gerald Eliot's death, and they most certainly will not care."

"Nice folks," commented Julian with a wry smile. "Shall we do the coffee, Chef André?"

On the far side of the dining room, Julian and André carefully poured steaming coffee into the gleaming silver urn. I inched up to the cordoned area and looked at the cabinets that I had shown to so many Homestead visitors during my docent days. The shelves of the undamaged display cases were chockful of holsters, knives, and cowboy hats, as well as photographs of early cabins, camp stoves, and other utensils brought across in covered wagons. The cookbooks had occupied the top shelves of the two vandalized cabinets.

I leaned in close to the first cabinet and read the forlorn, skewed label showing the former placement of *American Cookery*. Hanna had put the exhibit together with great care, coupling the cookbooks with old letters that mentioned them or their use. A letter next to the empty spot for *American Cookery* was from a founding member of the German-American Foundation of Colorado, who rhapsodized about his great-grandmother using the book when she first came to Colorado. Dear Great-gran had struggled more with the language than she had with the recipes.

I moved several inches along the police ribbon and winced: The second cabinet had been dented in several places. I could imagine the police report: *signs of a struggle.* On the shelf was the label for *The Practical Cook Book* and a letter from Charlie Smythe, one of the earliest landowners in Aspen Meadow and grandfather to Leah Smythe and Weezie Smythe Harrington, my clients. Old, hapless Charlie had died in Leavenworth Prison. It was from Leavenworth that he had written to his wife, Winnie, and remorsefully recalled her "cookery book" and the bread she used to make in their cabin.

I smiled: Visitors had always relished hearing the tale of a thief who had robbed for the fun of it, although Smythe's life had not ended nearly as romantically as it sounded. The label summed up Charlie Smythe's beginnings as a signalman who'd come west after the Civil War, bought land, become bored with ranching and timbering in Aspen Meadow, and taken up thieving for amusement. He'd apparently robbed successfully until he'd reached his late sixties. Unfortunately, in his last outing, Charlie's gun had discharged unexpectedly—at least he'd so maintained in court—and he'd killed a bank teller before the robbery had even gotten off the ground. He'd died of flu in prison in 1918, at the age of seventy.

I perused the shelves. It had been a long time since I'd worked as a docent, but it didn't appear that any other familiar items were missing. If Sylvia Bevans was upset, then Andy Fuller's investigators must be communicating badly with her. But my husband was *not* the one to be blamed for the museum's woes. If Sylvia hadn't heard *that* bit of news, I intended to enlighten her before we left the premises.

I inched to the end of the wall to get a glimpse into the high-ceilinged area that had served as the residence's living room and now contained more Old West artifacts donated to the museum. On a buffalo-hide-covered wing chair next to the massive stone fireplace, a brightly lit, scarlet-suited, genuinely plump and white-bearded Santa sat staring glumly at the camera crew. Behind the camera, Ian Hood shifted his weight, readjusted the legs of the tripod, and appeared to be checking and rechecking what he was seeing through the lens. Nearby, Rufus, Leah, Hanna, and several other people, including children, fidgeted, whispered, and cast nervous glances in the direction of the tiny office housing the Furman County Historical Society. The strident voice of Sylvia Bevans pierced the air. She sounded very upset with one of her volunteers.

"I have been gone all morning," Sylvia complained, "and these fashion people are *still here?*"

"I have to have *quiet!*" Ian Hood screamed as he stomped away from his tripod. "Qui-*et!*" he shrieked meaningfully in the direction of Sylvia's voice. Julian and André, who had been whispering about the placement of cups and glasses, glanced up, startled. I shrugged.

Sylvia Bevans, her wide face flushed and her silky-haired bun askew, bustled out of the historical society office. When confronted with the hostile faces of the Ian's Images crew, she *hrumph*ed, turned on her heel, and banged back into her office. The door slammed.

The photo folks refocused their attention on the Yuletide scene by the stone hearth.

"All right, try again," Ian said wearily.

A large woman standing on the sidelines scooped up a toddler and placed her next to the fireplace. Santa beckoned to the girl, a pajama-clad, curly-haired brunette with rosy cheeks and an unsmiling bud of a mouth. "Come closer, honey," Santa implored. The girl would not budge.

"Go see Santa, sweetheart!" the large woman pleaded. She was thirtyish, with the same brunette hair and pink cheeks as the child model. "Rosie, I know it's summertime, but go tell Santa what you want!"

"I need a smile," Ian warned from behind the camera. "Is that too much to ask?"

"Look at Mama, baby doll!" called Rosie's mother. "Smile, honey!" Rosie glanced at her mother; the camera clicked on Rosie's grim, unsmiling young countenance.

"Look at what I have!" called Leah Smythe, as she waved a Barney doll high in the air. Little Rosie gave the doll a poker-faced stare and made no response.

"Hey!" cried Hanna, "Look at this, Rosie!" Hanna, beautifully dressed, as usual, blew a perfect strand of iridescent soap bubbles across the room. A startled Rosie opened her eyes wide as Santa laughed. Again Ian Hood's camera clicked and flashed, clicked and flashed.

129

"How's André feeling?" murmured Rufus Driggle at my elbow.

"Fine," I whispered back. "He just gets a little overwrought sometimes."

Rufus shrugged. "Sorry if I worried you. Between him and that lady curator, we've got our hands full, I can tell you." He stroked his scraggly red beard and gave me an unhappy look. "Anyway, we've got a guy bringing Ian's lens to the cabin today, and another guy fixing the picture window. We'll be able to get back in front of our own Christmas tree tomorrow." He tilted his head to indicate the ribboned-off cabinets. "Looks like we aren't the only ones who need help in the glass-replacement department."

Yeah, they need a contractor, I thought, but said nothing. If Rufus did not know how the glass had been broken, I wasn't about to enlighten him.

He whispered, "So what do you think of our set?"

I dutifully appraised the fireplace scene. The errant scrim had been set up over Santa's head to reflect the light. Flats framed both sides of the tableau. A blond boy of about six had replaced Rosie. Perky and obedient, he wore a pair of reindeer-print pajamas as he sat uncomplainingly in Santa's lap and offered wide, toothy smiles to Ian. Leah and Hanna frowned at the scene while Ian clicked furiously.

"Looks super," I told Rufus.

"We'll put flames in the fireplace on the

computer, make the two fireplaces look as if they belong together."

"Look as if what belong together?"

Rufus smiled, showing straight, yellow teeth. "The two fireplaces, of course." He raised his voice to a lilt. "Both from the country home of the same wealthy, but not *too* ostentatious family, with their cute kids and their gorgeous clothes. Having their fantastic Christmas."

"Ah." I decided to plunge in. "Rufus, did you know Gerald Eliot?"

He shifted his eyes to the cold fireplace. "Yeah, we used to work together, I'm sorry to say."

"When?"

"Oh, long time ago. Five years, maybe. We hadn't been together six months when he went off on his own and I came to work for Ian."

"And why are you sorry to say?"

He shifted his weight, suddenly uncomfortable. "You know he's dead? The police came to question me." I nodded. "Well, I felt bad for Gerald. He always sounded so good talking about his skill at carpentry and all that, and how much money we could make together. Then he'd complain about people not paying him, and about supplies not coming in, and pretty soon I realized he was only working three or four hours a day at the most, and the reason supplies hadn't come in was because he was too lazy to go pick them up."

"Why in the world did Leah hire him?"

Rufus frowned. "Oh, hell, I went to Phoenix

to see about a job. Leah knew he worked here at the Homestead and happened to mention that she wanted some windows put in, although I think it was her brother Bobby who had the idea. Anyway, Gerald did his usual snow job and they hired him. Of course, it just turned into a big mess. Which I could have warned them about if they'd ever listen to me." He sighed.

"Do you know why the police questioned you, if you hadn't worked with him in so many years?"

Sylvia Bevans barreled out of her office before Rufus could reply. Short, cylindrical, and bristling with energy, she wore a calf-length pale-green dress, beige silk stockings that had seen better days, and beige shoes, ditto. We moved out of her way as she marched past us into the kitchen. Within a few seconds she was whining, and I heard the clinking of a cup and saucer.

Rufus sighed again. "He owed me money. I'd complained about it in town a few times. I still think Leah and Ian should have waited for me to come back from Phoenix to do the work, but it's almost as if they hired Gerald out of spite."

"Spite?" I asked as Ian clicked away at Santa, now working with a young Asian-American girl.

Dismay clouded Rufus's face, as if he'd already told me more about his private life than he'd intended. "Ian's been losing jobs to New York and Miami for the last decade. With sunny Phoenix so close, a big percentage of the department stores are moving their fashion shoots down there. At least, that's what they tell us. Ian's never been the easiest fellow to get along with. He hates change. Hates the fact that the elk are being driven out of Aspen Meadow by all the newcomers, new apartments, new houses, you name it. He's been dropping hints about concentrating on the nature photography, and saving the elk so he can have more nature to photograph. So I went to Phoenix to look for a new job. I like Ian but hey, a fellow's got to look after himself, doesn't he?"

Leah eyed the two of us narrowly. Was she listening? Hard to tell. André accompanied Sylvia Bevans out of the museum kitchen. She grasped a plate that she piled with goodies from the table.

Rufus went on: "So in comes this macho guy, Gerald Eliot. First he screws up Leah's job, then he says he has to do some consulting on wiring around the windows. Charges Merciful Migrations six hundred bucks delay time. They say they'll pay him and they don't. Maybe Leah finally paid him out of her pocket. But nothing happened because by that time he was getting it on with Rustine. He had to do *something* with his delay time, right? So Leah fired him, but I'm sure Hanna put her up to it, since she was always telling us what a crummy guard Gerald was at the museum, even though she didn't work here anymore. You know, she still thinks of the place as hers."

"What about Leah Smythe? How did she feel about Gerald?"

Rufus whispered, "Well, how would you feel? She had broken plaster and a century of dirt all over her cabin. Maybe she was personally out six hundred for the demolition and six hundred for the delay. Ian had to deal with a model who was pissed off because her boyfriend lost his job. But do we have a single window in the kitchen?"

Leah shot Rufus a dirty look. He closed his mouth.

I whispered, "Wow. Would you like some coffee, something to eat?" I motioned to the spread. "Or do we have to wait for Prince Ian to call the break?"

"Prince? *Please.* Emperor, at the very least. Czar, maybe. And no, thanks, I'll wait."

"Break!" called Ian Hood from the far room. Had he heard us? I hoped not.

The crowd all made a beeline for the coffee and snacks. I checked that Santa had his separate fruit bowl and scampered to the kitchen door. André and Julian were listening attentively to Sylvia, who was drinking a cup of coffee and gesturing with a roll.

"And of course," she went on, "the murder investigation has been hampered by that incompetent at the sheriff's department, Tom Schulz—"

"Ah, excuse me," I interrupted as I stepped boldly into the kitchen. "Sylvia? What are you talking about?"

She turned slightly pink. I folded my arms

and waited for a response. André thrust a tray of blondies into Julian's hands and muttered an order to check the buffet. Julian, glad to be relieved of listening duty, obeyed. André, of course, was desperate to hear the story about Gerald Eliot's murder from someone *in the know.* He clucked sympathetically to Sylvia, refilled her coffee cup, and motioned for me to sit in the chair vacated by Julian. This I did, wondering why André could manage to be courtly toward the curator of the Homestead, who was *not* a client, but couldn't be bothered to be civil to the folks who *were* his clients.

"My husband is off the Gerald Eliot case," I said to Sylvia once I had my own coffee cup in hand. I didn't sound defensive, did I? Well, perhaps a tad.

"Off the Gerald Eliot case?" she huffed. "I thought he was just avoiding me. But his co-workers are accusing me of *theft.* Now they say I must have misplaced the last cookbooks, since I didn't put them into the original report as missing, and the police are too incompetent to find them."

"Did the police ask you about Cameron Burr?" I made room on the counter as Julian returned to the kitchen with an armload of dirty dishes, slid them into the sink, and started running hot water. "Do you know how Cameron's doing?"

Sylvia needed no prompting. She shuddered and clinked her milky cup of coffee into the saucer. "Yes, of course they asked me about Cameron, and no, I don't know how he's doing. But the most important thing," she announced, "was that the police know about Gerald. That he was a terrible guard. One time I came in early and found him here with a woman, for goodness sake! The police asked me what her name was! What? Did they think I came in and asked, 'Whore? What is your Christian name?' " She sipped her coffee, lofted a pinky, and took a tiny bite of blondie. "I should have fired Gerald Eliot right then, but I didn't have anybody else to hire, and Cameron Burr said Eliot needed the money." She sighed gustily, delighted to have an audience for her tale of woe. "Would you like to see exactly where Gerald and his killer had their fight?" she asked with a trace of...what? Naughtiness?... in her voice. I nodded, and André eagerly replied that he would, too. Sylvia downed the last of her coffee and bustled out to the dining room, scooping up another blondie as she departed. Julian ignored us and kept washing dishes. I walked behind André and tried to look inconspicuous.

Except for Hanna, the Ian's Images people were laughing, eating, and talking happily. Hanna was staring at the police ribbons and shaking her head.

"Perhaps we shouldn't have eaten in here," Hanna said morosely.

Sylvia cleared her throat. "Perhaps you shouldn't have come, Hanna, dear. You should just go back to your little department store job."

Hanna shot us an enraged glare, then stalked across the room to have a whispered conference with Leah.

"The police say Gerald and Cameron struggled right next to the cabinets. The glass broke, then Cameron strangled him," Sylvia said in a low, confidential tone to André. She pointed. "Here is where our historic cookbooks were displayed."

André drew his mouth into a pucker. "Very sad." He peered in at the shelves. "What are these letters, then?"

"We put all artifacts that were related to the cookbooks in the exhibit. Cameron and Barbara Burr donated the *Watkins Cookbook* and *The White House Cookbook*. *The Practical Cook Book* was donated by Leah Smythe and Weezie Smythe Harrington." She lifted an eyebrow in Leah's direction. "*American Cookery* was donated by the German-American Foundation of Colorado. As you can see, Eliot's murderer didn't see fit to steal our *letters*, only our *books*."

Suddenly, André gasped. He tried to inhale and reluctantly clutched his chest.

"Oh, dammit! What is it?" I cried as André wheezed. He staggered and I grabbed him. "Julian! Help me!"

"I am fine, I am fine!" André said over Sylvia Bevans's squawking that someone needed to call an ambulance *again*. He recovered his composure and checked the alignment of buttons on his chef's jacket. "I was just surprised, that's all."

"By what?" I demanded.

His eyes had regained their mischievous look; he giggled.

"Goldy?" Julian's worried voice was at my shoulder. "Want me to call nine-one-one on the cell?"

"Goldy! Stop fussing!" André said gaily as he trundled toward the kitchen with Sylvia walking importantly beside him, steadying him by the elbow. "If you want to help, pick up dirty dishes." As if to demonstrate he was just fine, he began an a cappella rendition of "Hark! The Herald Angels Sing."

"I can't believe you worked for that guy for a whole year," Julian muttered in my ear. "I mean, you never know where he's coming from. He nearly keels over, then he's fine. Now he's humming Christmas carols in August, for crying out loud. I want to finish the dishes and leave."

I wanted to leave, too. *Just clean up and then you can clear out,* my inner voice commanded. I picked up dirty cups from an end table, then started toward the buffet. With the sudden disconcerting feeling that I was being watched, I stopped.

The models, their minions, the hair and makeup people, all had ambled back to the living room. But Ian Hood, Leah Smythe, Hanna Klapper, and Rufus Driggle stood at the entryway to the dining room. Hanna glared at the area where André had had his second miniattack, then shifted her reproachful eyes to me. Rufus moved from foot to foot, as if he, like me, wanted to clear out. Leah and Ian conferred, then shook their heads, as if I'd said something incredibly stupid. Confused, I felt suddenly embarrassed to be clutching a nest of empty cups.

"Goldy!" Hanna exclaimed. The authoritarian tone of the former director of docents still had the power to freeze my spine. "What just happened?"

"André just wanted to see the crime scene," I commented lightly as I rebalanced the cups. "He's *fine*! Don't worry."

Not one of them said a word.

Chapter 10

Finally Leah blinked, as if she were coming out of a reverie. She raked her streaked, shaggy hair with her fingers. "Well, fine. We're done for today. Please tell Sylvia I'll see her on Tuesday. And you and André too, I guess."

I nodded. Hanna closed her eyes rather than look at the violated cabinets, somehow managing to convey her conviction that neither the burglary nor the murder would ever have happened if she'd still been in charge at the museum. Ian gruffly ordered Rufus to start packing up the lights and the set. I hustled my tray to the kitchen and asked André how he was feeling. He again assured me he was fine. As if to prove it, he delicately placed plates into the tublike porcelain sink that

Julian had filled with soapy water. Sylvia, once so desirous of our company and our coffee, now did her best to shoo us off.

"How much longer will this cleaning take? I need to bring the fourth graders out here!" she fussed. As is common when someone bothers the catering crew in the kitchen, her presence actually slowed down our cleaning process. But none of us dared point that out, and she finally trundled off.

"Can we help with Monday's food?" I asked André as Julian dried the last of André's pans and I packed them up. "We have another assignment, but we could meet you early...please?" I'd never forgive myself if the stress of Monday's food preparation proved to be too much for him.

"No," he insisted stubbornly. "You make me so *nervous*, Goldy! You do not need to watch me all the time. For Monday, I will do a very simple coffee break and lunch."

"Promise to call and tell me how things went," I urged, as Mountain Taxi pulled up for him. Among his many reluctances to compromise with the times, André had never learned to drive. Julian and I loaded up the cab's trunk. André clambered in and swore he'd stay in touch.

When we reached home, Arch solemnly assured us that Jake was on the mend. The two of them had even gone for a very short walk. To my surprise, Tom had finally taken a break from his mysterious woodworking project to fire up the grill. I was very curious to know what he was up to in the basement, but I had no intention of asking if all the banging was yielding anything beyond ventilation to his frustrations. For my own part, I'd once decided in a fit of pique to construct a gingerbread version of McNichols Arena; halfway through, the walls had collapsed. Therapy projects, I'd concluded, are usually best left undiscussed.

I set the table for lunch and noticed our checkbook jammed up beside a stack of glasses on the kitchen counter. Maybe my husband had taken a close look at our finances and *that* was leading him to pound nails into two-by-fours. Without looking at the check register, I knew that even with the pay from André, only two thousand dollars and change separated us from the morass known as *negative cash flow*. And two thousand wasn't much when sixteen hundred of it represented payments for my two upcoming jobs, and would have to cover the costs of food and labor for those events. Moreover, two thousand was *half* the estimate a hardware store employee I'd called had given when he'd come by to reckon what repairing Gerald Eliot's damage would cost. And then there were the costs of Arch's tuition if The Jerk didn't pay; footing the bill for the free tasting party; keeping the larder stocked for the family. Add to this only a few hundred that might come in as an extra gratuity from Weezie's party and the Hardcastle reception, and financial disaster loomed depressingly large.

When I poured tall glasses of ice water, my stomach rumbled. *Never worry about money when you're hungry*, I'd learned during my lean post-Jerk days. Luckily, deliciously scented grill smoke was curling into the kitchen. I peeked through the back door. Tom had thawed the last of our jumbo shrimp and skewered them with fresh vegetables and fruit. The man was incorrigible.

Ten minutes later, the four of us were digging into tender grilled shrimp, hot, juicy pineapple, and dark, crunchy onion. I murmured thanks to Tom; he squeezed my hand. While we ate, Julian and I filled him in on what had happened at the Homestead: the report and the denial of André's illness, Sylvia's distress, Rufus's tales of Gerald Eliot's mess at the cabin. I peppered Tom with questions: Had Eliot been seeing a woman? Specifically, had he been seeing Rustine the model? Had they found other Eliot clients who might have been willing to kill him? Tom said his buddies at the department were questioning Cameron Burr, Leah Smythe, a country-club couple in the middle of a North Atlantic cruise, and the Montessori School people, where the directress had changed since Eliot had redone a bathroom there. The investigators hadn't been able to find other clients of Eliot's who still lived in Aspen Meadow. All *those* folks, according to neighbors, had had their houses finished by other remodelers, and moved away. Tom asked if I'd obtained a last name for Rustine. I replied in the negative.

"They're looking into Eliot's social life," Tom told us. "He prided himself on being a bachelor. Was frequently seen getting hammered at the Grizzly Saloon. I'll call Boyd, see if any more evidence has turned up at Burr's place. Maybe they've found the last two cookbooks, but they just haven't told Sylvia Bevans. Maybe they won't tell me either."

"Look at it this way," I reasoned, "what if we found out Cameron *didn't* kill Eliot? Which he didn't, of course. It could help to clear you, since you didn't want to arrest him for the murder in the first place."

Arch and Julian exchanged a look. Tom said, "Who's *we*, woman? I'm suspended and you've got your hands full trying to hold your business together."

I helped myself to the last succulent shrimp. "It's just not fair that Fuller gets to do a shoddy job, then blames you."

"You're reaching, Goldy. Besides, it's Fuller's show now. If I go around asking lots of background questions, and it gets back to him, he'll claim interference. It'll work against the investigation into *me*."

"I bet that creep Litchfield who's harassing Goldy had something to do with it," Julian said defiantly. "Where was he the night Eliot was strangled? What if he knew about Eliot redoing Goldy's kitchen and wanted to get rid of him, so Goldy's kitchen stays a mess? Then, as a bonus, Goldy's business falls flat because she hasn't got a kitchen, Tom gets into trouble, and she has to sell out?"

"Now you're *really* reaching," Tom murmured.

"André did say someone had put pickles in his crab cakes," I added, "and I found a hair in the food he served on Monday—a very unlikely mistake for him to make. Food sabotage is a long way from murder, though."

"Don't go off on some investigative campaign, you two," Tom warned Julian and me.

"We'll never even mention your name," I vowed.

"That is *not* reassuring," Tom observed.

◆

Saturday I woke up disoriented, with a vague sense of dread. I stared at the clock. Seven o'clock. Downstairs, Tom was already sawing away on his mysterious project.

The phone rang. One of Tom's co-workers returning his calls about the evidence? No: I suddenly remembered where I was going at ten this morning. To the jail. With Arch. To visit The Jerk. Maybe this was The Jerk calling now, from the cell block pay phone.

"Goldilocks' Catering—" I began, but whoever it was hung up. I didn't have caller ID. But at least I'd put a password on my computer.

I stretched my way through my yoga routine and pulled on a skirt and blouse. Arch met me downstairs, already dressed for his jail visit in dark jeans and an oxford-cloth shirt. On the kitchen table, a large platter of golden homemade biscuits had been stacked on a china platter next to a bowl of what looked like strawberry jam. Next to these delicacies was a note from Julian.

Gone to swim laps. New Southern biscuit recipe. Taste the strawberry conserve. Call the lifeguard at the rec if you need me today. J.

Arch bit into a conserve-slathered biscuit. Mouth full, he mumbled, "All I know is, Julian sure works hard for a guy who's dropped out of college."

"Yes, he does. He's just...trying to prove himself, I think." I sliced a biscuit and spooned on some conserve. The biscuit was light and flaky, the conserve tangy and filled with warm chunks of fresh strawberry. Heavenly. I fired up the espresso machine and told myself maybe this wouldn't be too bad a day after all.

"All right!" Tom announced himself heartily as he banged up from the basement. His arms were laden with wooden panels, rolls of paper, and two large paper bags. "Time for you to see what your new kitchen is going to look like." While Arch and I gave him puzzled looks, he paused and bowed. "Mrs. Schulz, this suspended cop is pleased to announce a metamorphosis. Meet your new contractor: Tom Schulz, kitchen builder extraordinaire."

"*What?*" I exclaimed.

"First," Tom continued, undaunted by my bafflement, "cabinets. Voilà!" He placed a two-foot-by-one-foot cabinet door in front of the cans and glasses cluttering the counter. "You always told me you wanted solid cherry, Miss G. So here you go."

"What are you *talking* about?" I demanded.

Tom sighed. "Just tell me if you like it." I eyed the dark, smooth, cleanly detailed door. It was gorgeous.

"*I* like it," Arch volunteered.

"Well, good." Tom slapped sawdust off his hands. "While your mom's deciding, take a look at this flooring." He pulled several slats of wood from his mountain of supplies and pushed them together. "White oak. Select. It'll lighten up the dark of the cherry." His green eyes regarded me, begging for approval. "You like it?" he asked.

"Sure," I said. A voice in the back of my brain screamed: *This is madness. How in the world are we going to pay for this?*

"And now," said Tom, with a Houdini flourish, "marble countertops." He brought out a pale, gray-veined rectangle of stone. "Buddy of mine works for a granite fabricator," he explained. "We were in the army together and I got the Saigon Special." He placed the stone with its glints of silver next to the cherry cabinet door.

"Tom—" I began.

He straightened and put his arm around me. "Don't say no. You've been wanting a new kitchen for a long time. You deserve one. Let me give it to you."

"No."

"And I took out a loan on my cabin." He continued as if I hadn't spoken. "Line of equity, actually. If I start the kitchen today, I should be done by the time they let me go back to work."

"Tom, I have three bookings in the next week. I have to have a place to cook. What you're talking about is too expensive and too much hassle. Please. Don't do it."

He kissed my cheek and gave me a wide grin. "Don't worry, Miss G. I thought of your cooking needs already. I'm going to drape everything with plastic, set you up in the dining room, no sweat."

I sank into a kitchen chair. "Please, Tom, what you're talking about is a remodeling, not a repair. I would have to close. If the county health inspector came by, which he could at any time night or day, I'd be *dead.*"

"Don't worry, I've already taken out a building permit! If the county health inspector can't be bothered to stop by, that's his problem!" Tom said with mock huffiness. "Besides, I've ordered everything. You wouldn't *believe* how fast some people will move for a cop. The only thing you need to pick out is a window treatment for your bay window and back windows."

"Tom! What *back* windows? For that matter, what *bay* window? Eliot was supposed to put one in. I paid for it but never got it."

"Tha-a-t's why you're married to somebody in law enforcement!" Tom said jovially. "Boyd has all Eliot's paperwork. I may not know about his love life, but I know Eliot ordered your window from The Window Warehouse in north Denver. They've got your bay window sitting on their dock. Unpaid for, of course, but we didn't really think Eliot was going to be *that* considerate, did we?"

I tried one more time. "Please don't do this—"

Tom winked at me. I hadn't seen him so happy since before his suspension four days ago. "You'll love it, Miss G. Promise."

◆

Not long after, Arch and I made our way to the jail. There, another shock awaited us: John Richard Korman had been in a fight. He walked into his side of the three-foot-by-three-foot concrete cubicle and seemed reluctant to face us through the pane of glass. Once I saw him, I knew why. His left eye was purple. There was an ugly cut on his forehead and a slash over his right cheek. His blond hair, always expensively cared for, had been ruthlessly shorn by the prison barber. The orange jumpsuit emphasized the fact that he had lost most of his tan, even though he'd only been incarcerated two weeks. John Richard Korman had always been a handsome guy, but it was clear jail did not agree with him.

"Gosh, Dad, what happened to you?" Arch spoke into the telephone, trying hard not to sound worried and stunned.

"Guy wanted to know why his head hurt all the time." John Richard's voice spiraled loudly out of the phone. He gave me a sour look. "I told him an empty brain echoes. He punched me."

Arch murmured that that was too bad, then launched into his recitation of all the things

148

that had happened to him since the last jail visit. I had asked him not to tell John Richard about Tom's suspension. So, Arch's news covered the fray resulting from Jake leaping on Craig Litchfield. Predictably, John Richard interrupted him.

"Your bloodhound attacked somebody?" John Richard's voice crackled. "You could get us sued!"

"But, Dad—"

"I can't afford to be sued," he announced. "Put your mother on."

"Oh, that reminds me," I said as I took the phone. "How does Arch's tuition get paid? It's due now."

"Ask Leland." His tone was curt, dismissive.

"Leland? Leland who? What happened to your accountant?"

"Hugh Leland's my all-purpose guy now. Lawyer, accountant, the works. He's in the phone book. Need money? Have a heart-to-heart with Leland." He smirked.

Needless to say, John Richard had not jumped right in with an offer to authorize payment for Arch's tuition, which a judge had ordered him to pay in full. In the interest of keeping the peace on what was only our third jail visit, I nodded. But I made a mental note to call my own attorney, if the money was not forthcoming. I tried not to think of what my attorney might charge to pull the tuition out of The Jerk. That's the price for alienation in our day: You have to compensate other people to fight for you.

Arch asked for the phone and I gladly handed it over. "Julian's back," he told his father, who could not possibly have cared less. But Arch talked on, undaunted, about summer vacation, playing with Todd, things he and Jake had done. Finally I relieved him of the phone; we were at twenty-eight minutes, thank God.

"See you next week," I began.

"How's Marla holding up?" John Richard demanded, his face again flattened with a smirk.

I was noncommittal. The Jerk could use information in twisted and cruel ways, I had learned. "Fine. Why do you ask?"

He only laughed and hung up the phone.

Before leaving, I asked if I could see Cameron Burr. The desk sergeant told me Burr had just started a visit with his lawyer, and was unavailable. I scribbled a note to be delivered to Cameron, with our phone number and begging him to call. But I knew he wouldn't. Suspended or no, Tom represented the forces that had put Cameron behind bars; Cameron's lawyer would tell him not to contact us.

When we started back up the mountain, the air was warm, the sky increasingly hazy. I rolled down the window. John Richard's manner at the end of our visit still rankled.

"Does your dad know that Marla is being audited?" I asked my son.

Arch looked out the window. "I guess."

I had heard the entire content of John

Richard's last two visits with Arch; no mention had been made of Marla's troubles with the IRS. As John Richard's new factotum, Hugh Leland might be aware of what was going on. But how then would Arch know that his father was aware of the audit?

"What do you mean, you guess? Dad told you he knew Marla was going through this IRS thing?"

He hesitated. "Well, don't tell Marla I told you, okay?"

I sighed. "He didn't do anything illegal, did he?"

"Oh, no. But when Dad was having financial problems last spring, the HMO's not paying him his money and stuff, he had this idea of how to make money. I don't think he knows that *I* know. I was supposed to be watching TV in his condo, but there was nothing on. When I turned it off, I overheard Dad telling one of his friends about the IRS paying a big reward to whoever turns in a tax cheater. Dad told his friend that Marla was the richest person he knew, and he was going to squeal on her to the IRS. I just thought it was a joke." He shook his head. "I feel bad telling you, because he's my dad and all. But I love Marla. I know it's been awfully hard on her. Sometimes I just think Dad gets sort of like, carried away."

I didn't say what I was thinking. It would have exposed Arch to very bad language.

◆

The next morning, Julian, Tom, Arch, and I went to the early service at St. Luke's Episcopal Church. I called Marla to see if she wanted us to come pick her up; she said she was having severe IRS-produced indigestion and couldn't move from her bed. Given the circumstances, I decided against telling her about The Jerk's hand in her current troubles. Julian had made some hazelnut-caramel rolls—Marla's favorite—that he was eager to offer for tasting at the coffee hour. I didn't tell her about them, either.

As the congregation began to read the Forty-sixth Psalm—*God is my refuge and strength, a very present help in trouble*—I realized that I craved *very present help* in a *very big way*. A friend of ours was in jail; Tom had been suspended; my business was in danger. Compounding these problems were the facts that our living-space was in an uproar and we were teetering on the brink of insolvency.

The Lord of hosts is with us; the God of Jacob is our stronghold. I prayed for Cameron and Barbara Burr. Without warning, I felt the weight of my ongoing resentment of our dead kitchen contractor. When people hurt you, it's hard to let them go, no matter how they end up. But as my Sunday School class often reminded me, God will always take somebody in, even when they're dead. *Right, Mrs. Schulz?*

I conjured up the bloated face of Gerald Eliot hanging between the sun room studs, and silently let him go.

♦

"I'm sorry to put you through all this," I told Tom that night as I pulled two loaves of homemade sandwich bread out of the oven. At my request, and in view of my continuing inability to talk to Cameron, Tom had spent an hour trying to find out about the evidence collected at Burr's home. No one was available to chat about missing cookbooks, so Tom had vowed to go ask Boyd some questions the next day, suspension or no.

Instead of banging about in the wreckage we called our kitchen, Tom had thoughtfully spent the afternoon working on his plans in the basement so we could prepare for the morgue lunch the next day. With Julian's help, I'd stewed a chicken, seared a London broil—both would go into the following days' salads—made vichyssoise and a huge salad of barely steamed vegetables that would chill overnight and be lightly dressed with a raspberry vinaigrette the next morning. Tom received a test bowl of the delectable, chive-scented vichyssoise and pronounced it superb.

Before going to bed, I tried to check in with André. Pru's care-giver said André had done a great deal of cooking this evening and was already asleep. She promised to ask him to call.

◆

Monday morning dawned bright and cool. I chopped tarragon, celery, and pecans to combine with the moist, flavorful chicken pieces, then sliced the beef into thin wedges and mixed it with a spicy vinaigrette. At seven, Julian joined me and mixed flour with yeast and buttermilk to make hot rolls to go with the salads. Arch took off for another walk with Jake. Tom announced he was going for his breakfast with Boyd, where he hoped to hear about the latest Andy Fuller shenanigans. Julian and I were happily engaged in our work until just past ten o'clock, when the phone rang. I scooped it up and gave my business greeting.

"This is Dr. Sheila O'Connor, the coroner. Goldy—" Her voice cracked.

"I'm coming, I'm coming," I replied calmly. At the last minute, clients often fear the caterer will forget to show up. "Don't panic. I'm just putting it all together."

She cleared her throat. "We have a body with only a tentative identification."

I made wrapping motions to Julian and pointed to the salads on the counter. "So do you want me later—"

"This...man had no driver's license, performed no military service," Sheila said. After wrapping the salads, Julian pointed to the cardboard boxes; I nodded. "We don't have

154

any fingerprints. There aren't any dental records." I exhaled and watched Julian fold in the cardboard flaps. Sheila continued, "And his next of kin can't do the ID we need. On the body, I mean. This man's wife— widow—is blind."

The floor under my feet shifted. I stumbled toward a chair and sat down. I whispered, "What?"

"Goldy, we need you here at the morgue. To identify the body," Sheila repeated. "We believe the dead man's your teacher, André Hibbard."

Chapter 11

"Pru." I was clutching the phone so hard my fingers hurt. "His wife. Where is she?"

"She felt she had to come down here, and she's on her way. Her nurse is bringing her." Sheila's voice had become businesslike. "Goldy, I'm terribly sorry to have to ask you to help us. Nobody here seemed to know who else to call."

"You're not sure it's André."

"We're pretty sure." No hesitation. "The arriving crew found him in the Merciful Migrations cabin kitchen this morning. Looks as if he had a massive coronary."

"A heart attack," I said dully.

"We won't know until the autopsy is done. But we can't do what we need to do until a family member or someone who knew him *well* identifies the body." She paused. "Please forgive me. Usually we use fingerprints or dental records or a relative, but none of those are available. His wife said to call you, that you lived nearby and used to work for him."

"I'm sure there's been a mistake. When I get there, I can clear it up."

Sheila hesitated. "Is Tom there?"

"No. Just this...a young man who works for us."

Sheila said, "Please come, Goldy. I can explain what we know once you get here."

♦

"Jeez, Goldy, what's wrong?" Julian wanted to know. "You look terrible. Has something happened to Arch? Has the booking been canceled?"

"No, I...no."

His dark eyes searched my face. "Look, Goldy, if the booking fell through, I can take this food to Aspen Meadow Christian Outreach. We'll find some more jobs. Come on." He ran water into a glass and set it on the table in front of me. "Come on. Drink this. I'm going to call Tom."

"He's...having breakfast. With Boyd."

"No, no, actually he isn't. That's just where he wants you to think he is." Julian hesitated. "Look, don't get mad at him, okay? He's having a polygraph today. About the conflict he's having with that assistant district attorney who thinks he knows everything."

156

I stared at the water glass. A *polygraph*. Tom didn't think he could tell me.

"André...my teacher. He's dead, Julian. He had a heart attack. They need me to come down to the morgue." I gripped my old oak table. This was just a mistake. A stupid error.

Julian snagged the cellular phone from its charger, stuffed it into his pocket, and assumed a calm, pastoral tone. "I'll pack the Rover and then honk from the driveway."

When he beeped not long afterward, I numbly walked outside. This is just a stupid error, I kept telling myself. It's not André. There's been an awful mistake.

Less than an hour later, I took a deep breath and prayed for strength as Dr. O'Connor led frail, bent Pru Hibbard, her nurse, and me down the hall to the morgue's work area. Pru wore a faded pink cashmere sweater and matching skirt, along with a strand of pearls that matched her hair. Her caregiver, a waxy-skinned, thin-lipped older woman with broad shoulders and short, dark hair, nodded at me.

"I'm Wanda Cooney." Her voice was clear but low. "We can talk more later."

The four of us walked through the door toward where I was to do the ID. Dr. O'Connor drew back a curtain on metal rings.

I swallowed. There hadn't been a mistake.

André's body was covered to the shoulders with a sheet. His cheeks were no longer pink, but gray. The small portion of his white shirt that showed was cruddy with dust. His silvery hair was matted.

"Yes." My voice sounded like someone else's. "It is André Hibbard." I turned to Pru. "Are you all right?"

Pru's watery blue eyes wandered around the makeshift cubicle. Her lower lip trembled. She said, "I want to go." Without waiting for me to respond, Wanda slowly guided Pru away.

I turned back to look at André's immobile face, then at Sheila. "Can't you tell me anything more about what happened?"

"We needed the ID first." She moved away from the gurney. "You should go back to the other room."

"Not yet. Please, tell me *something*, Sheila. What was he doing when he had the attack? Was he alone?"

"Rufus Driggle called us," Sheila murmured. "André had phoned to see if he could come early to do some prep work. Driggle opened the gate for the taxi at seven. Driggle didn't stay because he had to go into Denver for film. When he came back at nine, he found André on the kitchen floor. When he couldn't rouse him, he phoned the sheriff's department."

I touched the sheet. "How did André get so dirty? His clothes? His apron?"

"From falling on a *floor*, Goldy." She cocked her head. "Mrs. Hibbard confirms he had a history of heart problems, that that's why he quit the restaurant. He was on Lanoxin, to amplify his heartbeat. We'll get his medical file, see if his condition has been worsening lately."

André. I swallowed. "This past Friday he

had some symptoms while he was at the Homestead, where he was catering. The paramedics came out and gave him a clean bill of health. André swore to me that he was fine." I shook my head; I should have insisted on catering with him today instead of taking the morgue lunch booking. "He was sixty-five. Vigorous, but—" I stopped, transfixed by something I hadn't seen earlier. I pointed toward André's hand. "What's this?"

Sheila leaned in closer. "A burn?"

"No. No way."

Sheila peered at the curved, inch-long mark on the back of André's left hand. "Yeah, it's a burn. Recent." Her eyes pleaded with me. "Time to *go,* Goldy."

I stared at the mark on André's hand. "But," I protested, "there's nothing out at that cabin that he could have burned himself on. I mean, not that looked like that."

Sheila sighed.

I stared at André's right hand, motionless on the gurney. "What's this?"

Sheila O'Connor reached into her pocket, retrieved a pair of surgical gloves, and snapped them on. She picked up the hand I was pointing to. On the side of the other hand, there was another, smaller dark spot.

"Another burn, looks like. He was a *cook,* Goldy. You have to *trust* us. We haven't started to do our work here yet.... He could have burned himself just before or while he was having the attack. People lose control during a coronary."

I was having trouble breathing. "Sheila—"

"The department is already doing a sweep of the cabin."

"Can you give me the autopsy results?"

She snorted. "You must be joking."

"He was my teacher, Sheila."

"Let's go." Her voice was increasingly chilly, and I wondered if she was afraid I was going to get hysterical on her.

"I need to go help Pru," I replied. "André would want me to be with her. But I'm not going anywhere until you promise to call me."

She *tsk*ed. "Have Tom give me a ring in a couple of days." She took my arm. "Right now, you and I are going to the lunchroom."

We came through the opaque glass door to the brightly wallpapered lunchroom. A sudden noisy wash of people engaged in conversation made me reel back. Sheila murmured something about going to her office and left my side.

My mind seemed to splinter; I observed that Julian had done a superb job serving lunch. The salad platters were littered with shreds of lettuce and crushed cherry tomatoes; the roll baskets were forlornly empty. The morgue staff was digging into their dessert. Julian was chatting with two older women. When he saw me, he left them and walked quietly to my side.

"Well?" When I nodded that yes, it was André, he said, "I'm sorry. Are you okay?"

"I don't know. You did a nice job here. But...I need to help Pru now."

"I called Tom at the department. He offered

to pick me up with all the equipment. I thought…you might want my car. But now I'm worried about you driving."

"I just need some coffee, please, Julian. And maybe a glass of water. I have to help Pru," I repeated, as if giving that help would structure my next few hours and make things clear. How could André—so full of life and mischief—be gone?

Julian brought me water and coffee and handed me his keys. I mumbled a thanks. "Goldy. Are you sure you can drive?"

I sipped the dark coffee; it tasted like ashes. "Yes, I think so. Where did the rest of them— Pru, Sheila—where did they go?"

He rummaged in one of the boxes, pulled out my purse, and handed it to me. "They're talking in the office. The Rover's on the far east side of the parking lot, remember? I'll meet you back at home."

I waved at the detritus on the lunchroom table. "But—"

"Go."

In the office waiting area, Sheila O'Connor talked quietly with Wanda Cooney. Another morgue staff person was shuffling papers and asking Pru questions. Pru, seated next to the desk, mumbled answers. The gist of their conversation had to do with Pru not being able to see and therefore not being able to sign the necessary papers. The papers were being sent on to an attorney. Wanda acknowledged my arrival with a nod, then walked over to attend Pru.

Sheila O'Connor told us: "We'll release the body for burial in three or four days. There's a committee at St. Stephen's Roman Catholic Church in Aspen Meadow that helps with a memorial service or funeral arrangements when the spouse or family can't."

Pru's voice rose, tremulous. "Goldy? Are you there? You were his favorite."

I went over to Pru's side and leaned down to embrace her. "Let's go back to your place. You should be home."

Sheila motioned me over for a last message. "Tom called. He wanted to know if you'd prefer to wait for him." When I bit the inside of my lip and didn't reply, Sheila added, "I promised I'd call him back, if you want to leave right away."

"Tell him I'll meet him at home in a couple of hours. Tell him I'll be fine—not to worry."

I headed west in Julian's black Range Rover behind Wanda Cooney's dull green Suburban. Overhead, the sun shone briefly between mushrooming gray clouds. One of our summer thunderstorms was brewing. The half of my brain still operating logically recalled that the drive to the Blue Spruce condo would take forty-five minutes. Time to focus on Pru, whom I barely knew, despite my long friendship with André.

But I could not. I ground the gears and felt my mind shift from rationality to despair. André dead. It wasn't possible.

Raindrops spattered across the windshield.

The wipers scraped noisily over the glass as the van crested the interstate; the Continental Divide, thickly shrouded in mist, came into view. *A heart attack.* *Two burns.*

Tongues of lightning flicked above the near mountains as we turned into Aspen Meadow. At the turnoff to Blue Spruce, I glanced down Main Street. Stupid, unexpected worries about the tasting party the following day loomed. How would I gather supplies? When would I manage to finish the cooking? How could the packing and serving get pulled together? Julian will do it, I told myself. Thank God for Julian.

Water splatted on the glass and I turned on my lights. Beside the road, Cottonwood Creek gushed and foamed. A memory of André trying dinner menus appeared from nowhere. He would always offer the cooking staff dishes laden with possibilities: cranberry-glazed pork with sweet potato pudding; seared steak Hong Kong with creamy risotto; poached Dover sole nestled in steamed artichokes and hollandaise. He would concentrate intently as he drizzled blackberry sauce over a spill of crêpes, then have me taste as he meticulously wrote out times for prepping and cooking. He would cap his pen and say, "Now, Goldy. All is well?"

No. All is not well.

I needed information. I needed to know what had happened to him. How it could have happened to him. I picked up my cellular phone and punched in the number for information. When the operator answered I asked for the number for Mountain Taxi. Yes, I replied to the operator's query; I would like her to connect me.

The taxicab dispatcher's voice crackled. I identified myself as a cook who worked with André Hibbard, and could I speak with the driver who brought Mr. Hibbard to work this morning? The dispatcher put me on hold. It was unlikely that the police would have questioned the driver already, I figured. If for some reason the sheriff's department didn't want me to talk to the driver, then I would have to come up with another strategy.

The line filled with static and then cleared. "Yeah, this is Mike. I took the chef this morning. I've been driving him out to that job site. Who're you again?"

"It's Goldy Schulz, the caterer. I used to work with André."

"Yeah, well, I've been taking him to work lately. The old guy couldn't drive. I gotta call here, whaddaya need to know?"

I asked about his schedule this morning. Mike had picked André up at six-thirty, an hour earlier than usual. When I asked why so early, Mike replied, "I don't know. I ast the chef, What you cooking out there this time of the morning? You already got two big boxes of food. Ain't you done yet? And he got all huffy, the way he does, you know, and said, Yeah, he was done with the cooking, but that he still had work to do. That was it. Told me he'd call when he was done, the way he usually does, only he didn't. Did you take him back?"

"No." I wasn't going to tell Mike that André was dead; he'd find out soon enough. I forced myself to concentrate on my driving. The Rover hurtled along a winding paved road bordered by a steeply cut cliff. I glanced at the creek and meadow on the right and said, "Was anyone else there? Anyone at all?"

"Nope. The gate was open, and that was what I was worried about, but André had called ahead about that. No cars. I helped him carry the boxes across the creek the way I usually do, then I left."

"And what was in the boxes?"

"His food and his beaters and whatnot. Why? Somethin' wrong?"

"What food? Did he tell you?"

"He told me, but now I can't remember. Wait...individual custards, he told me. People love 'em, he said."

"No fruit to slice, no coffee cake to make?"

"Nope. He'd made muffins to go with the custards. He even gave me one, had orange peel in it. It was good."

I took a deep breath. "Did you notice his hands? Had he been burned? Did he complain that he'd been burned?"

"I didn't notice anything wrong with his hands, and he didn't mention them. What is this about?"

I told Mike it was nothing, thanked him, and signed off. When I'd replaced the cell I gripped the wheel. André had made custards and muffins ahead of time, gone to work early to do unknown extra work, burned himself before or during a coronary attack, and died. Made perfect sense. I wrenched the wheel to the right and turned into the Blue Spruce Retirement Village.

Wanda had Pru settled in her small blue-and-white sitting room. I offered to make tea. The condo was a tribute to Pru's love of teapots. Every available table, shelf, and cupboard in the sitting room and kitchen was crowded with teapots: fat and gold-rimmed, slender and blue, pink and detailed, new and antique. I'd been in their home only once before, when Pru and André had first moved in and I'd brought over a loaf of oatmeal bread. I veered away from *that* memory as I found cups, bags of Pru and André's favorite English Breakfast tea, spoons, lemon slices, sugar, cream, and arranged them on a tray with a plain ivory pot.

"Pru, I want to help," I said, once I'd served her tea and we were settled in the sitting room on plump blue-and-white slipcovered chairs. Wanda Cooney had excused herself to make phone calls. I told Pru about the church and funeral arrangements. She nodded, sipped from her cup, and smoothed the folds in her pink cashmere skirt. The wall above the couch where she sat was crowded with mounted photos of André: offering a full-size fudge football to a Denver sportscaster, frosting his renowned Stanley Cupcakes for our triumphant

Avalanche. I'd later begged for the recipe; of course, he'd given it to me.

"Thank you for the tea," Pru murmured, her unseeing eyes fixed on her hands, clasped around her fragile teacup.

I took a deep breath; the doorbell bonged. Wanda's voice murmured into the phone in the next room. When the bell rang again, I rose to answer it.

Through the peephole I was surprised to see Leah Smythe's half-brother, Bobby Whitaker. The handsome male model was quickly combing his long, dark curls in anticipation of the door being opened. Unfortunately, Bobby, now dressed in a shiny suit, did not appear much more confident than when he'd been ordered to take off his shirt a week ago.

I opened the door. "Bobby? Why are you here?"

"Ah, are you a relative of the deceased?" he said nervously. He was clutching an expensive raincoat. He did not remember me from the auditions. I told him who I was and why I was there.

"Are you here to see Pru?" I asked, confused. As before, I wondered, what *is* the deal with this guy?

"Yes, well, I'm with High Creek Realty." He scooped a business card out of his inner pocket and handed it to me. "We...try to meet the needs of mountain residents. You don't know if...Mrs. Hibbard's going into a nursing home, do you?"

"I thought you were concentrating on modeling."

"I do both, actually. Modeling and real estate. I'm here to see if Prudence Hibbard wants to sell the condo."

Anger fizzed through my frayed nerves. "We just got home from the *morgue,* you idiot."

"Yeah, but I've got a client ready to buy this condo—"

I thrust his card back at him. "Go away."

"You don't know if she needs the money," Bobby objected. He held up his hands in a defensive posture. "Hey, listen to me for a sec. How do you know Mrs. Hibbard doesn't need the cash that's tied up in the equity of this place?" The wide shoulders inside the shiny, fashionable suit lifted in a gesture of helplessness.

"Scram," I said tersely. "Don't *ever* come back. And if any more vultures like you show up, I'll boil them for stew to serve at the next High Creek Realty lunch."

He backed away. I gripped the door hard. Much as I wanted to slam the heavy wood into its casing, I restrained myself. *Pru mustn't be further upset. Think about Pru,* I told myself as my heart hammered. *And calm down,* I added as I leaned against the closed door. *Pull it together for André's sake.* After a few moments, loud knocks banged against my head. The doorbell bonged, followed by more rapping. I wrenched the door open. If it was another real estate agent, I would kill him with my bare hands....

168

It was not a real estate agent.

It was a caterer.

Chapter 12

Craig Litchfield's hair was neatly coiffed, his handsome face carefully blank. He was dressed in a collarless dark brown shirt and matching pants, the mahogany equivalent of the coal-black outfit muddied by Jake the previous week. Was this a uniform you could get in different colors? I wondered. Did he order it from a catalog?

"What are *you* doing here?" he demanded. He cocked his head and grinned when I didn't answer. "What, that big dog of yours got your tongue?"

"I'm here to help Pru Hibbard," I said in a low voice.

"Oh?" he replied, mock-polite. "May *I* help her, too?"

"I doubt it."

He glanced down the row of town houses. "Okay, Goldy. I've had enough. Let me in. I'm here for the same reason you are."

Had I missed something? "What *reason*? Please. You need to leave. You couldn't be here for the same reason I am. He was my teacher. And an old friend."

He bristled. "Let me talk to her."

"No."

"I'll take you to court."

"For what?"

He reconsidered, then softened the muscles of his handsome face and passed a hand over his helmet of manicured hair. Of course, these conciliatory gestures put me even more on my guard. "I want to offer forty thousand for André's client list, menus, schedules, prices, and recipes. Cash." He tilted his head, oozing sympathy. "You know you can't match that. You need to let me see the widow. She might need the money right away, to pay for the funeral, whatever."

From the sitting room, Pru's thin voice called my name. I told Litchfield, "I don't know how you found out André had passed away. But I'm going to close this door now. Don't knock. Don't come back. If you want, call Pru's caregiver and set up an appointment with their attorney."

His face darkened with fury. He put out his foot. But I was too quick for him and slammed the door.

I returned to the sitting room. The telephone had rung and Pru was speaking into it. Wanda Cooney tugged my arm. I followed her into the kitchen. André's gleaming copper pans hung clustered from a thick wrought-iron ring suspended from the ceiling. It was a beautiful, spotless kitchen, lined with pans and teapots that André would never sauté with or make English Breakfast in again. Tears pricked my eyes.

"Pru will be all right," Wanda told me. "I've called several of her friends. They all want to talk to her or come over."

My shoulders relaxed with relief. "Thanks."

"Who was at the door? We're expecting Monsignor Fields, but he said he couldn't be here for about an hour."

"Nobody, really. Just...a couple of creeps wanting to buy the house, André's business, even his recipes. I sent them packing."

Wanda was incredulous. "How could they have known—?"

"Oh, somebody at the morgue probably gets paid to tip people off. Anyway, they're gone, so don't worry. If anybody comes to the door that you don't know, call the Furman County Sheriff's Department." Wanda, speechless, nodded. I glanced into the sitting room. Pru held the phone to her ear, weeping softly. I took a deep breath and asked, "Should I stay?"

"We'll be fine," Wanda replied.

"Do you need food? Shopping done? Please tell me."

"No." Her voice was doubtful. "Not that I can think of."

I went into the sitting room and knelt at Pru's feet. She told the person on the phone to please hold for a moment, then reached out to touch my hair.

"It's Goldy," I said.

"Dear Goldy. Thank you for being with us. He loved you so much." Tears streamed down Pru's pale face. "He always bragged about you."

"I'll stay in touch," I assured her. "Call me if you need help with the church, or anything else. Anything at all."

171

Pru nodded and went back to her phone call. I checked through her lace curtains to make sure the road in front of her condominium was empty. There was no sign of unwelcome visitors. "I'll call tomorrow," I told Wanda Cooney, then left.

I piloted the Rover from the paved maze that wound through Blue Spruce Retirement Village onto the wide dirt road that ran past the complex. The dirt road leading to dense housing was not an uncommon sight in Colorado. A developer would buy acreage in a remote spot along a wide, unpaved road. At such remote locations, the county usually wouldn't pave roads through residential areas, so the builder took on that task himself, naming his byways "Huntington Green" and "Foxhound Ridge," as if his subdivision were an outpost of an English manor instead of dense housing in the middle of nowhere. Once the residents realized they were forty minutes from the nearest grocery store, and four times that long in a blizzard, they'd already bought in.

Rain drummed on the Rover roof. I passed a lumbering road grader and tried to ignore the emptiness gnawing my insides. André was now part of that group we ambiguously referred to as *the departed*. As my signal blinked to make the turn to Aspen Meadow, I cracked my window. Next to the state highway, the wind shuffled through a stand of aspens. A new blue-on-white metal sign swayed in front of the trees: FOR SALE—COMMERCIAL-ZONED LAND—EIGHT MILES AHEAD! 200 acres! Great, I thought as

I negotiated the turn. The Blue Spruce folks might get a snazzy grocery store yet.

A hunger headache loomed and I realized belatedly that it was almost four o'clock. I'd had a minimal breakfast and no lunch. When I'd left the morgue, Julian had been cleaning up salad detritus. Hardly appetizing, but the memory made my stomach growl. Funny how dealing with death does not remove the exigencies of life.

Cook, I decided. *Go home and fix something that André would have made for you.*

The mist of rain had lifted by the time I nosed the Rover into our driveway. Tom was making a show of feeding his roses; absurdly, I wondered if he'd found Craig Litchfield's cigarette butt. By the look he gave me, I knew he'd been worried. I felt a pang of guilt: I'd turned off the cellular after calling Mountain Taxi.

"I swear, Goldy." Tom dumped the last of a solution on a pink-blossomed rugosa. "You were gone so long, I couldn't—" His shoulders slumped. "I'm sorry. Please. Come here." I walked toward him and he held me in a very long hug. He smelled of laundry fresh from the dryer. "Are you all right?" I nodded into his shoulder. "How is Pru?"

"Not too bad," I murmured, holding him tight. "Where are Arch and Julian?"

"Arch is at the Druckmans'. Julian's cooking for your shindig tomorrow. I was so worried about you I couldn't stay inside. Come on in," he urged. "I've got something to show you." He took my hand. Of course I assumed that Tom had been cooking, too. With no job to go to, he'd probably prepared a fudge meringue or tower of shrimp. But when we came into the kitchen, Julian merely glanced up and nodded. Then he went back to cutting a pan of polenta into diamond shapes. I scanned the room. It looked odd. Except for the polenta, there was no food. Come to think of it, there wasn't even a back door.

"Oh my God, Tom," I said, astonished. I glanced from the plastic-covered area over the sink on the side wall to large plastic sheets covering a huge, *new* gash in the back wall. *Act grateful,* some inner voice warned, but it was once again drowned out. "What have you done?" I murmured to Tom as I gaped at the hole in the wall. "Do you know what's going to happen to me if the health inspector sees that? I'll be closed down. I thought you weren't going to...I mean, how could you...Tom!"

He dropped my hand. "I've been working all day on this. At least take a look. I'm going to take out the wall, too."

I pointed to the area beside the place where, up until this morning, there had been a door. "That wall?"

"That's where your new windows are going to go." There was a tick of impatience in his reply.

A buzz filled my brain. "I thought we were just *talking* about this—"

"Look, Goldy, I am *sorry*—" Tom began. "But this is what you wanted—"

"I *never* said—"

"Uh, guys?" interrupted Julian as he rinsed his hands in the sink. "Goldy has, or we have, a big tasting party tomorrow? And we need to work on it. Or *I* need to work on it." He dried his hands and then crossed his arms, uncertain. "Look, Goldy, I know I said this before, but you were a great pupil for André. He must have been very proud to be *your* teacher."

"Thanks."

Julian squinted at us and shifted from foot to foot. "I don't mean to intrude with details, but do you just want *me* to do this party? I know it's only for three people, at least, that's what you told me. I can't check because I can't get into your computer anymore, unless you tell me the password—"

Tom held up his hands. "Julian, can you give us a few minutes?"

"Sure." With his brow furrowed, he levered the polenta diamonds onto a waiting platter, tucked plastic wrap around the edges, and placed it in the walk-in refrigerator. He stripped off his apron. "Want me to go get Arch, pick up some food for dinner?"

"That would be great," Tom replied warmly, as he pulled two twenties out of his pocket and handed them to Julian. *My out-of-work husband, the money man,* I thought bitterly. Julian picked up his wallet, keys, and a plastic container that looked as if it contained cookies. He pointed at the plastic-draped hole in my wall.

"May I go through that way, or will I screw

something up?" he asked. Tom made a go-ahead gesture. With a rustle of plastic and quick-step across the deck, Julian was gone.

Tom sighed. "Let's start over," he said. A moment later, he carefully placed two crystal glasses of sherry on the table. "Please sit down."

"Thanks." I looked at the amber liquid without touching it. "I haven't had any food, so this will probably go straight to my head."

Tom opened the door to our walk-in refrigerator. In the door's black reflection, my face looked drawn and angry. Tom brought out some cheese, then pulled a box of crackers from one of our few remaining cupboards. A moment later, he slid an offering of butter crackers and fat wedges of Brie to the center of the table.

"Eat something. Then we can talk about André. That is, if you want to."

I stared at the crackers and cheese. "I had to identify the body."

"I heard. I'm sorry, Goldy. Honestly, I am." He leaned over and squeezed my hand. "And I'm sorry I sprang the kitchen stuff on you before you were ready. It's just that I have to get started."

"It's okay." I bit carefully into a crisp cracker topped with the creamy cheese. The sherry was like fire in my chest. *Fire*...I said, "Tom, there's something that's been bothering me all day. André had burn marks on his hands."

"Burn marks? What kind of burn marks?"

"He wouldn't have *done* that to himself," I

rushed on. "Plus, he went out to the cabin an hour early to do extra food prep, and that's not like him, especially when the kitchen there is so small...and for him to die right after Gerald Eliot, and Cameron's arrest...I mean, it's all pretty weird...."

Tom's eyes searched mine, which had again filled without warning. "Start over," he told me solemnly. He scooted his chair over so he could rub my back.

The comfort of his warm, accepting presence made talk possible. I told him about the call from Sheila O'Connor, about going to the morgue, having the conversation with the cabdriver, who said André had gone to the cabin early. I told him about visiting Blue Spruce, dealing with the intrusions from Bobby Whitaker the Realtor and Craig Litchfield the caterer. I told him about poor Pru. Thinking about what André's death had done to Pru's world, a sob closed my throat.

Tom nodded. "So Sheila's thinking heart attack?"

I exhaled. "Can they find out exactly *when* he had the heart attack?" I asked. "And how he burned himself?" My voice sounded suddenly shrill.

"I'm sure the department will check it out," Tom said quietly. Outside, the rain started up again. Mist rolled into our yard and pressed against the dining room windows. Raindrops pattered on the plastic sheeting Tom had put up. "You know the drill," he went on. "They secure the scene, sweep it to determine what happened. There'll be an autopsy, toxicology, to see what actually caused his death, whether it was a heart attack or what." I closed my eyes. "If Sheila said I could call her about it, I will."

I said, "You can ask around, can't you? Please?" It was part statement, part plea.

"Of course." His voice was a murmur, like the rain. "I just need to go easy. And so do you, Miss G. You know, if this had happened to someone I didn't know, I'd say you need a victim advocate. You're not the victim, but you were close to André, and it was an unexpected death."

"You can be my advocate."

He smiled at me. "Can't. I'm your new kitchen contractor."

"Don't joke."

"I'm not."

Julian and Arch banged in before he could reply, laden with three bags of carry-out Italian food: ziti with marinara, fettucine alfredo, pizza bianca. I looked at my watch: incredibly, almost half an hour had gone by. The few crackers with cheese had filled me up. But I ached to be with people.

Arch gave me a brief hug and whispered that I was a good mom, his standard assurance in rough times that things would turn out fine. His cheek was like sandpaper. Although he had no beard yet and his voice only occasionally cracked, he had begun to shave with great hopefulness on his fourteenth birthday. The razor had been a gift from Tom; I would never have thought of it.

"André was old, wasn't he?" My son's voice was anxious, even though he had only met André a few times during my stint at the restaurant. Still, he wanted to put a spin on sudden death. "I mean, he had retired and everything, right?"

"Yes, hon."

Julian dressed a green salad with balsamic vinaigrette, heated some breadsticks I'd made the previous week, and set out all the food. When we said grace, I offered a silent prayer for Pru. Despite the problems besetting our family, at least I had companionship and comfort. Except for her nurse, Pru now had no one, and my heart ached for her.

As Julian expertly twined fettucine onto a fork, he again brought up the following day's tasting party. "Thought we could do that fantastic grilled fish, with grilled polenta and a fruit salsa. What do you think, Goldy? I called your meat and seafood supplier, and she had fresh escolar. I had her deliver five pounds of it while you were out at André's place. She said she'd put it on your bill. I hope that's okay." He paused, eager but embarrassed. "I mean, does this sound good to you? We do sort of need to discuss stuff."

I struggled to remember the menu we'd finally decided on for the postponed tasting party. Oh, yes: I had been planning to roast a pork tenderloin and serve it with Cumberland sauce. Pork is plentiful and inexpensive in the fall, and people enjoy its heartiness when the weather turns colder. But the escolar would be good for dieters, or at least for people who think eating fish entitles them to dessert. "I don't know about grilling fish at the Homestead," I told Julian uncertainly. "But it might work. Maybe with an exotic slaw to complement the salsa and polenta."

Tom smiled and I knew what he was thinking: At least we weren't talking about death or remodeling.

"You can grill at the museum," Julian said authoritatively. "I know because I went over in the van once your supplier brought the escolar. I had a chat with the curator lady, Sylvia. Took her some truffles left from lunch."

"The Soirée committee might see that as cheating," I pointed out gently.

"No, it isn't," Julian protested. "Besides, Sylvia's not even one of the people who decides." He looked at me innocently. "Is she?"

"No, but she'll probably be there and influence the decision-makers, who are Marla, Weezie Harrington, and Edna Hardcastle."

"Oh, brother," said Julian.

"Do we have to talk about this?" Arch piped up. "Can't we have some of the truffles, too?"

"Absolutely," Julian replied. He retrieved a foil-covered platter, and uncovered his special dark truffles dipped in white chocolate.

"You are too good," I said to Julian as I bit into the exquisitely smooth, densely creamy *ganache.*

"Sylvia Bevans loved them. Had a couple

while she told me her problems." He measured out coffee for espresso. He pulled the shots, then dumped them over glasses half-filled with ice and whole milk. "Oh, by the way, she said they found one of the missing cookbooks."

"What?" I demanded. "When? Which one?"

"A piece of evidence was returned?" Tom asked sharply. "The department found it at the site, or Sylvia had it all along?"

"That *Watkins Cookbook* she kept complaining had been swiped, remember?" He handed the iced coffees to Tom and me, fixed one for himself and dosed it with sugar, then sank into a chair. "The cops told her they found it in the back of Mr. Burr's truck. But they finished their search of the house and guest house, and never found the last one. They told her it's probably gone for good, tossed out in the road or something."

"Thrown out of the truck?" I asked, incredulous.

"Gosh, Goldy, I'm sorry. Mrs. Bevans doesn't believe someone could have tossed her beloved copy of *The Practical Cook Book* out on the road, but if the killer was that stupid, she said to ask *Tom* if he could search for it. She wants everything back the way it was. The woman was a wreck. Remember all that complaining she was doing to André? Since the cops think the museum theft was just an attempt to cover up the murder, they're sticking with their the-last-cookbook-got-chucked-away theory. Sylvia doesn't care about their theory. She says she has to have *The*

181

Practical Cook Book, because some old handwriting of Charlie Smith is scrawled across one of the recipes. Who's Charlie Smith?"

"Smythe. Grandfather of Leah Smythe and Weezie Smythe Harrington," I supplied. "He built the Merciful Migrations cabin." *Where André died.*

"Oh," said Julian. "According to Sylvia, Charlie Smythe's handwriting could make the cookbook real valuable, like a collector's item, at least in Aspen Meadow. And here's something else: Sylvia said André called her up this past weekend, after we catered together at the Homestead? He said he was interested in some recipes."

"Some recipes?" I echoed.

"Yep. André asked if Sylvia had photocopies of their historic cookbooks in the museum files, and if so, could he have his own photocopy of *The Practical Cook Book.*"

"You're kidding. A copy of the entire cookbook?"

"Nope, I'm not kidding, and yep, the whole cookbook. Sylvia told him sure, she'd make a copy for him. But he never showed up to get it." He gave me a wide-eyed look. "I'm really sorry I brought this up. You probably don't want to be reminded of your teacher right now."

"Why would André want a photocopy of *The Practical Cook Book*?" I asked, but of course none of them had a clue. Nor did I, since I knew that André never gave two turkey drumsticks about American cooking. Plus he prided himself on being a chef of great stature. I could not *imagine* why he would want photocopied recipes for dishes he would have scoffed at: white bread, brown sauce, yellow cake. "This doesn't make sense," I said to Tom.

"It's strange," he agreed. "Four cookbooks are stolen. Eliot is killed. All but one cookbook are retrieved. A chef who asks for a photocopy of the last missing cookbook—which is almost a hundred years old—turns up dead before he can get it."

Tom dialed the sheriff's department. I used my business line to try to track down Sylvia Bevans.

Chapter 13

While we were on the phone, Julian insisted on doing the dishes. I tapped the counter impatiently. *Sylvia now claims* The Practical Cook Book *is a collector's item...and André wanted a photocopy of it....* Could André really have cared about early twentieth-century American cookery? An answering machine picked up at the Homestead Museum. I hung up and dialed Sylvia's home. The phone rang and rang. The curator, apparently, did not embrace telecommunications technology.

Charlie Smythe's handwriting across one of the recipes makes it valuable...so what? To the best of my knowledge, André had never *been* in the Homestead before Friday. He'd never seen the cookbook, or any recipes therein, had he?

Who would know about this? Someone in the Furman County Historical Society? Marla. But I got her machine, too. Was the IRS holding her hostage? I stared glumly at the hole in our back wall as I listened to my friend's bright voice on tape. Of course, there was Cameron Burr...I wondered if his lawyer had told him yet about the incriminating evidence retrieved from his pickup. There was no way Cameron would have staged the museum burglary and then left the old cookbook in his truck. So where was the fourth cookbook? And who on earth had reason to steal it? I left a message on Marla's machine asking her to call, and hung up.

Arch announced he and Julian were taking Jake on an evening walk. Did I want to go? The rain had vanished, leaving the air cool and moist. I declined, anxious to hear what Tom was learning from the department. Realistically, what could they tell him? So they found another of the stolen cookbooks? So what? I fidgeted with my iced coffee glass.

"Okay, there's not much but here it is," Tom said after twenty minutes of conversation with his departmental cohorts. "Fuller's guys did find the *Watkins Cookbook*. No sign of the other cookbook, although they have the photocopies of all four from the Homestead files, and this is the first they've heard about the cookbook possibly being a collector's item. As far as they know, it's worth less than a hundred bucks. But here's something more interesting: The department got the tip about

Eliot's body being at Burr's house just a little more than three hours after my team answered Sylvia's call about the robbery at the Homestead. So in Fuller's mind, the whole thing looked like a homicide-masquerading-as-burglary pretty quickly. See what I'm saying?"

"Yes, I think so...that once he decided it was a homicide, you couldn't think of it as anything else?"

Tom nodded and poured us two cognacs. Well, why not? We'd already splurged on the last of the shrimp, carry-out food, and a loan for a new kitchen. We might as well finish off the Courvoisier. Tom placed a crystal liqueur glass in front of me and continued: "Andy Fuller ordered Burr arrested without taking the time to hear his story, and without a lot of evidence. Burr didn't have any alibi for that night beyond being drunk. He had brawled with Eliot earlier in the evening, and Eliot's body was found on Burr's property. Q.E.D., according to Fuller, who claimed Burr knew when Eliot would be working at the museum, killed him there, then faked the burglary as an inebriated afterthought."

I sipped the cognac: It was sweet, smoky, and soothing. "Didn't they ever investigate it as a *robbery*? Especially with what Sylvia is saying now about the last cookbook being a potentially valuable collector's item?"

"They don't put much stock in Sylvia, Miss G." Tom shook his head. "Fuller had his homicide-not-burglary theory. The department had already recovered the first two cookbooks, and those weren't very valuable. I mean, we're not talking the Gutenberg Bible or anything, right? Plus, Sylvia's original report didn't even mention all the stolen cookbooks, so they're reluctant to change their theory now."

"I hope this is Sylvia's last term as curator."

"Patience, Miss G. Her position pays less than fifteen thousand a year. She's dedicated, but she's not superwoman. Most of the collection was donated from old-timers in Furman County. The missing cookbook was donated by Leah Smythe, and apparently she's been completely disinterested in whether it's found or not."

"So are you telling me a stolen collector's item doesn't hold *any* weight with the department? It couldn't be a motive for murder?" I offered Tom another truffle and he bit into it thoughtfully.

"I told Boyd to run a burglary-gone-bad theory by Fuller. But you know the golden boy won't want his original theory being questioned by a cop on suspension." Tom went on: "The department is sending somebody up to the museum to talk to Sylvia tomorrow about her call from André regarding that cookbook. Maybe Boyd can get us some inside information."

"I want to know why he wanted that book," I insisted. "We're talking about a French chef who couldn't have given a flipped pancake for historic American cooking."

"It may have been his...nosiness, Goldy. Wanting to see what had been stolen."

"But this is like the burns on his hands," I objected. "It doesn't fit. It isn't the way he *was*." I hesitated. "Look, Tom, I *need* to know what happened to André. If I went up to the cabin, I could poke around a little—"

"You're not serious," my husband interrupted gently. Then, knowing me far too well, he added, "Don't even *think* about doing that."

I sipped the last of my cognac and didn't reply. The boys returned and took Jake up to their room, unaware of Scout stealthily scampering after them up the stairs. Typically, the cat refused to be left out of anything.

A pearly twilight suffused the sky. Swamped with exhaustion, I decided to go to bed. But first I called Lutheran Hospital: How was Barbara Burr? I asked. Stable. And unable to talk, I was told, for the umpteenth time. I hung up and phoned to check on Pru Hibbard. Wanda Cooney said Pru had taken a sedative and was asleep. So much for asking about André's reasons for wanting a photocopy of a historic cookbook. Wanda added softly that the memorial service for André would be held at St. Stephen's Roman Catholic Church this Thursday at four o'clock.

♦

The scent of baking bread woke me just before seven the next morning. I checked the thermometer outside our window: sixty degrees. Despite a stiff breeze lashing the trees, Tom slumbered on. I stood at the window and watched shiny puffs of cumulus race across a delft-blue sky. Pools of shadow swiftly followed the clouds' path on the far mountains. The sound of barking dogs mingled with the hesitant chug of a school bus on a practice round.

I tried to ignore that stunned, painful hope that threatens to drown your common sense the day after a tragedy. Had this really happened? Had I seen André's body at the morgue the previous day? Was he really gone? Yes.

I stretched and breathed through my yoga routine, trying hard to empty my mind and let energy flow in. This was the day of the Soirée tasting competition. I couldn't have been less in the mood.

While dressing, I wondered if there was anything I could do for Pru today. I'd call her later from the Homestead, where I also wanted to find out about André's request for photocopied recipes. Sylvia and I needed to have a little heart-to-heart...Wait a minute. Heart-to-heart. *Need money? Have a heart-to-heart with Leland.* With a sinking feeling, I realized I'd completely forgotten to call John Richard's lawyer-accountant, Hugh Leland, about Arch's tuition payment at Elk Park Prep. Several rounds of phone tag were coming up on that score, I knew.

I brushed my teeth, combed my hair, put on a minimum of makeup, and attempted to focus on the tasting party. *You can worry about your work or you can do your work,* André used to lecture. *A chef doesn't have time for both.*

The kitchen was chilly because of the missing

188

walls. But this apparently put no damper on Julian, who was up already, zipping energetically from the cluttered counter to the cluttered table and back to the counter. Smiling brightly, his hair neatly combed, his young face scrubbed and enthusiastic, he wore a rumply-soft white shirt, dark pants, and a spotless white apron. He gestured for me to sit. With a mischievous look, he set a plate with a single cupcake in front of me. It had an uneven top and a small scoop of frosting for garnish. The eager, approval-seeking expression on his perspiration-filmed face surely mirrored my own, when I'd first offered poppy seed muffins to André.

"What's wrong?" Julian demanded in a rush. "They're right from the oven. Miniature bread puddings with hard sauce."

I cut a mouthful of the crusty, moist cake and spooned up a judicious amount of the hard sauce frosting along with it. The crunchy, caramelized pudding mingled with the smooth, creamy rum sauce. "Delicious," I pronounced. And it was.

"I even came up with a name," Julian went on. "Because they're for Merciful Migrations' fund-raising? Big Bucks Bread Puddings." His eyes glowed with pleasure.

"Great." I glanced around to check Julian's preparations, resolved to get going cooking. But how on earth could I do that? This was no longer a kitchen; this was a ruin littered with bowls, pans, and foodstuffs. Only half of the upper cabinets remained. The back wall was now utterly gone. Tom had widened the gap

over the sink. The place looked like a solar-
ium in ruins. "Lord," I murmured. "If the
health inspector shows up, I'll be deader than
week-old aspic."

"No, you'll just punt," Julian replied cheerfully. "You want to start on the rest of the appetizers or do you want me to?"

"I'll do it. I just need some caffeine first."

"The next batch of puddings will be out in
twenty minutes." He removed the plastic bag
of escolar fillets from the walk-in. "I'll fix
you some French-press coffee while you look
up exactly how many folks we're serving
today. I still can't get into your computer. You
need to give me your password." He set water
on to boil and ground coffee beans. "By the
way, you were right about more than three people coming to the tasting. Sylvia Bevans told
me she'd be there, plus a couple of extra
women from Merciful Migrations might show
up. Hanna and Leah. How come Leah Smythe
and Weezie Smythe Harrington are so involved
in everything in this town?"

"Oh, Julian, they're old-timers. Their grandfather, Charlie Smythe, was one of Aspen
Meadow's original settlers, and he left his
son Vic land-rich. Vic passed the land to his
family, and that's why the daughters are so
involved in mountain land preservation."

"Well," he said defiantly, "I don't really care
who comes, as long as they vote for *our* food."
Clearly, he did not want to talk about Weezie
Smythe Harrington, the widow of his biological father, Brian Harrington. Julian was

no relation, blood or otherwise, to Weezie Harrington, and he avoided my eyes as he poured boiling water over coffee grounds in the press, then set the timer for four minutes.

I said, "I don't need to check the computer. We'll probably have six total, up from the original three." Julian nodded. "Oh, and we'll be doing Weezie's birthday party tomorrow night. You can skip it if you want."

"No, I'll do it. So it's Marla, Weezie, and who else again?"

"Edna Hardcastle. We're doing her daughter's wedding reception on Saturday. If we can snag the Soirée assignment, by the time of André's funeral on Thursday," I concluded, "we'll be back in business." Although how we would prepare the food, I thought, looking around at my mutilated kitchen, the Lord only knew...

"He'll be there today, won't he?" Julian asked darkly as he poured me a richly aromatic cup of coffee.

I was startled, thinking he'd read my thoughts. "Who?"

"Litchfield."

"Oh. Yes. And before you ask, I don't know what his menu will be."

We set to work in earnest. The dinner was advertised as a five-hundred-dollar-a-plate champagne dinner for thirty. The relatively intimate number of diners was all the historical society could fit into the Homestead dining room. County law forbidding liquor on government property had been waived for

Big Bucks Bread Puddings with Hard Sauce

5 tablespoons unsalted butter, softened
½ cup Demerara sugar (sometimes sold as raw
    sugar or Hawaiian washed sugar) *or*
    granulated sugar
2 eggs
1 cup milk
½ cup whipping cream
¼ teaspoon ground nutmeg
1 teaspoon vanilla extract
8 slices white bread, torn up (9½ ounces)
⅓ cup raisins
Hard Sauce (recipe follows)
12 fresh mint sprigs (optional)

Butter a 12-cup nonstick muffin tin. Preheat the oven to 325°F.

Cream the butter until fluffy. Add the sugar and beat until well combined. Beat in the eggs, then beat in the milk and cream. Stir in the nutmeg and vanilla. Thoroughly stir in the bread pieces. The mixture will look like mush. Stir in the raisins.

Using a ⅓-cup measure, ladle out a full scoop of batter into each muffin cup. Bake 15 minutes. Remove from the oven and, using a nonstick coated spoon, quickly stir each cup of half-risen batter to break up the crust on the sides. Return to the oven for an additional 15 to 20 minutes, or until the puddings are set and browned.

Quickly unmold the puddings on a wire rack and set upright like cupcakes to cool slightly. (The puddings can be served hot, warm, or at room temperature.) Top each pudding with a scoop of Hard Sauce. Using a toothpick, insert the stem of a mint sprig into the top of each scoop of Hard Sauce.

Makes 12 servings

Hard Sauce

5 tablespoons unsalted butter, softened
¼ whipping cream (more, if necessary)
2 cups confectioners' sugar, sifted
¼ teaspoon rum extract

Beat together the butter and whipping cream until thoroughly combined. Add the confectioners' sugar slowly and beat until thoroughly blended. Stir in the rum extract. If the mixture is too stiff, add a little more cream. To serve with bread puddings, chill the mixture until it is easily scooped out. Using a small ice-cream scoop, measure out even scoops of the chilled sauce onto a plate covered with wax paper. Cover with plastic wrap and refrigerate the scoops until ready to serve.

Any leftover Hard Sauce can be thinned with cream and used to frost cookies or cake.

the one evening. Thankfully, the champagne and other wines would be supplied gratis by a member of the historical society. Expensive buffets could quickly turn into pig troughs, so I was glad the historical society wanted a seated dinner and large—but controlled—portions. Even better, the society was paying the winning caterer seventy dollars a plate. With any luck, if I won the tasting today, I could buy supplies, amply remunerate Julian, and still clear forty bucks per person to make the first payment on Arch's tuition. Just in case The Jerk or his lawyer-accountant forgot.

I savored the coffee and studied the menu Julian and I had decided on. We had enough for eight tasters, following André's cardinal rule to bring enough for your planned group plus two. For appetizers we were serving Julia Child's stuffed mushrooms, artichoke hearts roasted with a mayonnaise-Parmesan mixture, and hot herbed shrimp wrapped in crisp bacon strips. These would all go beautifully with champagne. The main course consisted of a choice of the grilled escolar, polenta, and salsa, or pork tenderloin with Cumberland sauce, and Yukon gold potatoes mashed with cream and roasted garlic. Both meat offerings would be served with baked garden tomatoes stuffed with asparagus and buttered bread crumbs, Caesar salad, and rolls. This would be followed by the white chocolate-dipped truffles and/or Julian's Big Bucks Bread Puddings, served with Vienna Roast coffee. Sounded like a winner to me.

Julian had made the salsa along with the polenta and stuffed a dozen mushrooms the evening before. I snipped bacon strips into quarters and slid them into the hot oven. For the tomatoes, I lightly steamed the asparagus and started buttering bread crumbs. Once I'd stuffed eight tomatoes, I whipped together an eggless Caesar dressing and washed and dried all the greens. By the time Tom came down an hour later, Julian and I had finished the preparation and were packed and ready to boogie.

"Please don't do any more tearing apart," I begged Tom, who wore old work clothes. "And please, please clean up what you've done."

Tom hugged me. "Just go win your party."

◆

Main Street was thick with the last wave of summer tourists. Shoppers rushed into boutiques selling candles embedded with aspen leaves, wooden lamps carved into the shapes of giant squirrels, and wind chimes purportedly fashioned of genuine Colorado silver. A queue of men waited for the first beer of the day outside the Grizzly Saloon. Julian sat beside me, his face intent with worry. I hooked a left onto Homestead Drive and gunned the engine.

"It's going to be okay," I assured him, feigning confidence. "No matter how it comes out. Especially after all that's happened...please,

Julian. Listen. I couldn't have gotten this far without you. I'm *very* appreciative of your help."

"Thank me when you get the booking."

Sylvia Bevans trundled out the museum's service door just as we began to unpack the van. She wore a lace-trimmed powder-blue linen suit and squat powder-blue heels. "We were very upset to hear about André," she announced, her voice quavering. Her pale, rheumy eyes regarded me as I heaved up a box. "I know you must be devastated."

"He was my teacher, Sylvia."

"Yes. Well, life does go on, doesn't it?" Her dismissive wave said: Back to work, no time to grieve. Well, we would see about that.

"You mentioned to Julian that André wanted a photocopy of a cookbook."

"Yes, Goldy, but he never came to get it." She exhaled impatiently. "You don't suppose the little episode André had here in the museum contributed to his demise, do you?"

"Sylvia, I don't know." I handed Julian a box. "Sometimes severe heart attacks are preceded by mild ones."

She sniffed. Then, insincerely, she added, "I am sorry we couldn't cancel the tasting because of André's death. It would have been more respectful. But the next time these busy women could all meet together was after the Soirée had taken place. Now please pay attention, Goldy, I must tell you about the events of the morning. Edna Hardcastle and Weezie Harrington have arrived. Marla Korman has

197

not. Also, your competitor is here." She indicated the brand-new cream-colored Upscale Appetite van by the kitchen door. She pursed her mouth and reconsidered. "And you can tell that husband of yours that the sheriff's department refuses to discuss *The Practical Cook Book*." She marched away as Julian returned.

He opened his eyes wide. "She didn't seem happy."

I hoisted the platter of bread puddings. "She never does."

Once we'd hauled our cache into the Homestead kitchen, Julian busied himself with the grill while I set about unpacking the foodstuffs, or trying to. Unfortunately, Upscale Appetite bags, boxes, and platters occupied ninety percent of the available counterspace. Craig Litchfield—dressed today in star-patterned pants and a dapper tan chef's jacket—swaggered in from the dining room. He refused to acknowledge my presence.

"Excuse me," I said stiffly. He did not respond. "Please," I tried again, "could you move some of your stuff? We need a bit of space."

"*We?* I thought this was supposed to be a solo operation for both of us. How many helpers did you bring?"

"Just one. And no one told me we had to work alone."

He scowled disapprovingly, but said nothing, as if he couldn't be bothered to scold me for a gross infraction of rules every *real* caterer already knew. Then he pulled a sheet of diagonally sliced egg rolls out of the oven and slithered through the door to the dining room. They looked good. I glanced down at my watch: just after ten o'clock. We weren't supposed to begin serving until eleven-thirty. What was he doing? And where was the committee?

As if in answer, the lilting voices of Weezie Harrington and Edna Hardcastle floated out to the kitchen.

"Oh, yum! Craig, you doll!" cried Weezie. "You're going to put this recipe in the newspaper? Fantastic!"

Doggone it. I wedged my greens into the crowded refrigerator. Why was Marla not here at the Homestead with her committee? And what was I supposed to do: appear empty-handed in the dining room ninety minutes before serving time? I glared at a framed article on the dingy kitchen wall. It was a July 1915 issue of the *New York Times* proclaiming that gunmen had held up a Yellowstone stagecoach. I sighed and forced myself to put on a cheery visage as I walked into the dining room.

Edna Hardcastle, her tight curls as gray as the inside of an aluminum pot, wore a red-checked pantsuit and red-and-white spectator pumps. She held a glass of fizzy champagne aloft. For some reason, my entry made her glance guiltily at the tray of flutes on the sideboard.

"Oh, Goldy, here you are, finally," cooed Weezie Harrington, brandishing an egg roll. In her early forties, with a trim body and dyed blond hair zinging out in improbable waves, Weezie wore a trio of thin gold necklaces, a tailored lemon-yellow blouse, navy shorts, and navy flats with perky bows. "*So* glad to see you." She giggled. "And to see *this.*" When she snagged a champagne flute from the tray proffered by Craig Litchfield, the enormous diamond ring on her left hand threw off a huge beam of light. What was going on with the booze? Not only was the champagne illegal—this was government property, after all, and our dispensation to serve wine was only good the night of the Soirée itself—but drinking was strictly banned under the terms of our tasting party. Craig Litchfield whisked past and set his tray down. I looked to Sylvia Bevans for direction, but she was showing Edna Hardcastle the damage to the display cases wrought by Gerald Eliot's killer.

"Hello, everybody!" called Leah Smythe as she breezed in. Unlike the preppily dressed committee members, Leah wore black pedal pushers, a black shell, and large, modernistic silver jewelry. She fluffed her streaked coal-and-gold hair with one hand and dropped her oversized leather sac on the floor. Tall, blond Yvonne, the model I'd last seen a week ago at the first P & G fashion shoot, hovered behind her.

"Check out Yvonne's shirt, ladies!" Leah exclaimed as she stepped to one side and pointed theatrically. One thing I had begun to wonder about models: Didn't they have last names? I'd met Rustine, Bobby, Peter, and Yvonne, and the only last name I'd heard was Whitaker, for Bobby. Yvonne mutely cocked a narrow hip and lofted an arm to better show her forest green sweatshirt. Leah declared, "We're going to sell them at the door. Catchy, no?" The shirt was emblazoned with the white silhouette of a buck elk's horned head and the phrase *Lawrence Elk Loves The Bubbly!*

Craig Litchfield jumped in with: "Oh, my God, that's the best-looking sweatshirt I've ever *seen.*"

Weezie touched her sister's arm. "You are *too* creative, Leah," she gushed. "People will snap them up."

Edna frowned. "How much will they cost? Will the Welk people sue us? Or demand a cut?"

"Sue us?" said Leah. She winked at her sister. "For what?"

Sylvia Bevans turned to Craig Litchfield and me. "I believe we're ready to start," she said frostily. Litchfield grinned, lifted his chin, and shook his shoulders, like a runner eager to start the race.

"Wait a minute." I pressed my sweaty palms on my apron. "Marla Korman is this committee's chairperson. The tasting isn't supposed to start for another hour. She would want us to wait for her. Not only that," I added boldly, "but no wines were to be served."

Weezie waved this off. "Goldy, look. We all know Marla's your friend, but hey, the poor dear's in an audit. Lord knows when those IRS people will let her go. And we've just started drinking a *tad* of champagne, to *celebrate.*" She giggled again, then held up the hand with the diamond ring.

"Celebrate what?" I asked, but she ignored me.

"Marla will be along," Edna Hardcastle said sweetly, adjusting the belt on her red suit. She looked slightly apologetic. "We know it's early. We'll make allowances for that."

"But we *have* to wait for Marla," I said stubbornly.

Sylvia Bevans moved so close to me I could smell her lavender talcum powder. "I don't *know* when Marla is coming, Goldy. I only *know* this party has already been postponed once because of *you,* and the other chef who was supposed to come is *dead.* We've got a group of fourth graders coming at one o'clock and you need to be out by then. We must stop talking and get cracking. Is that clear?"

"Yes, Sylvia," I said in my most placating tone. "Absolutely." I glanced at Craig Litchfield's confident smirk, then wished I had not.

I sailed back to the kitchen and out the service entrance.

"Julian, forget the grill," I said tersely. "They're starting now. We'll have to broil the fish and not serve the polenta."

Julian swallowed a curse and tossed water on the smoky coals to put out the fire. Like me, he'd learned that in food and client situations, argument is fruitless.

Unfortunately, the tasting did not go well. The mushrooms were barely warm, not hot, as the Homestead oven labored to heat my pans as well as Litchfield's. Broiled, the escolar was quite good, but absent the succulent grilled flavor, it merely tasted like high-quality fish. I'd had to turn the oven up to the highest temperature to kill any bacteria in the pork, and the result was dry, rather than juicy and tender.

And yet, although my meats were not as tasty as I would have liked, I was certain they beat Craig Litchfield's braised salmon, stir-fried scallops with green peppers, eggplant and rice pilaf, and avocado salad. Many people do not eat salmon or scallops, and even Arch got indigestion from bell peppers. Surely the committee had to be mindful of food allergies?

By the time Marla finally showed up, we were halfway through the main course.

"Marla, you scamp!" squawked Weezie. "Are you starved, darling? Or does being audited make you lose your appetite?"

Marla complained that they had started the tasting early. Unfortunately, she was still sporting her gray housedress, and lacked the authority of power clothing. She did not dare look at me, nor I at her. Although the tasting was supposed to be silent, Edna and Weezie kept telling Craig Litchfield how cute he was.

At twelve-thirty, Julian took out the tray of bread puddings. To my chagrin, I realized I'd forgotten the truffles. Litchfield offered a low-fat lime dessert. While the women all were duty-bound to try both desserts, all except Marla gobbled the lime and only took small bites of the luxurious pudding. And

Marla, of course, should not have been eating *that*. But I could tell she was remorseful—for not coming earlier, for wearing her Minnie Pearl outfit, and for sending elk burgers to the head of Merciful Migrations.

"It's over," Julian informed me glumly when he brought the barely touched pudding tray out to the kitchen. "They don't even want coffee."

Craig Litchfield, triumphant and glowing, lofted his empty bowl of lime glop and swiftly packed up his serving platters. Before Julian and I had begun to gather our dishes, Litchfield was gone, claiming over his shoulder that he had a "huge" job at the country club and much as he longed to, couldn't stay to chat. Yakking gaily, Edna, Leah Smythe, and Yvonne departed by the front door. The tasting had been a disaster.

"Sit down, Goldy," Julian commanded. "Let me finish taking the boxes out. You look like hell."

"Thanks, but I'll work," I replied as I rinsed off the pork roasting pan. I tried to console myself with the thought that even if we'd lost this booking, we still had Weezie's party and Edna's reception.

Marla hustled breathlessly into the kitchen. "God, I'm sorry!" she exclaimed. She hugged me, and I was reminded once again that her current austerity program did not include deodorant. "We make the decision by conference call later in the week. You know I'll call you. I'm sure you'll get it."

"It's okay," I said stoically.

"You know about Weezie?" she asked tentatively. "You know who's picking her up?"

"She's celebrating something," I replied dully. "And no, I don't know who's picking her up."

"Better come look out the dining room window."

Marla and I went back to the dining room and peered through the wavy glass. A dark Furman County government car had pulled in front of the museum. Weezie ran out to it as a short man with strawberry-blond hair emerged from the car. The two embraced. The man was Assistant District Attorney Andy Fuller.

"Don't tell me," I said to Marla, my eyes fixed on the embracing duo.

"The day Gerald Eliot's body was found? Fuller and Weezie got engaged."

Chapter 14

I walked quickly to the kitchen and scrubbed viciously at the scarred countertops. Why hadn't Weezie told me about her engagement? Perhaps she thought I knew. Maybe she didn't like me anymore; maybe I was just being paranoid. After all, I *was* catering her birthday party the next day. Still, you'd think she would have mentioned her upcoming nuptials, if only to refer to catering the wedding reception....

"I'm sorry," Marla murmured.

"Me, too," said Julian.

"I doubt Andy Fuller has any say over who caters the Soirée," I said unconvincingly. I looked at Marla's sad, round face and Julian's square-jawed, stoic expression. "Will you two quit?" I demanded. I grabbed the platter of puddings. "I'm going to tell the museum people we're leaving." I rushed out of the kitchen, desperate to be away from them and their pity.

The dining room was empty except for a couple of dirty champagne glasses. I passed the living-room fireplace where Santa and the child models had posed so unhappily, and arrived at the doorway to the historical society office.

"Hi," I said brightly to a volunteer worker with buckteeth and loopy brunette curls. Four plump mixed-breed dogs lay coiled on the floor. The canines scrabbled to their feet at the sound of my voice and wagged happy tails. A plastic gate barred the entrance of the office. Probably this was to keep the dogs from wandering through the museum. "Uh," I said, and offered the volunteer the leftover puddings, "I'm Goldy, one of the caterers from the party. These are for you."

The woman spoke lovingly to her dogs. Denied immediate access to dessert, all four grunted and flopped around her desk. "Thanks, nice to meet you." She bit into a pudding and looked ruefully down at her pets. "Mm-*mm*. Sorry about my sweethearts here. Sylvia puts up with them so I'll come in and do her paperwork."

"My helper and I just wanted to let you know we're leaving."

"Okay! I'm Annie," she said brightly. "The back door is self-locking. Sylvia is out talking to a group of fourth graders in the parking lot, or I know she'd be in here thanking you." She munched the pudding. "Did I ever need a break! This is super! Here, sweeties, taste this yummy treat." The four canines scrambled to their feet. At least someone was eager to sample my cooking, I thought bitterly, then scolded myself for being a bad loser.

"Well, good." If she needed a break, maybe she wanted to have a chat. "So...what kind of work do you do here?"

"Oh," Annie replied in a friendly tone, "writing letters asking for money. Sometimes asking for a historical item." She shared another cupcake-sized pudding with her dogs as she talked. Sylvia would have a stroke when she saw the mess the food was making on the floor. "Or answering a question about one."

"Really! I catered here last Friday—"

"With the chef who had the heart attack! Were you close?" Her breath whistled between her gaping teeth.

"We knew each other," I replied noncommittally. "Actually, I'm friends with the Burrs, too. I just...can't accept that Cameron strangled Gerald Eliot here, just because Gerald was behind on a remodeling. It's not the kind of thing you think of the president of a historical society doing."

"Oh, I know, no way." The shiny bark-colored curls flapped as she shook her head. "Old Cameron has a temper, that is true. I've seen him lose it at historical society meetings enough. And I guess he and Gerald could have broken the exhibit cases when they were fighting. But why would Cameron ruin display cases that he'd donated to the museum?"

"To make it look as if he didn't do it?"

She shrugged skeptically. We both hesitated. I leaned back on a closet, trying to appear relaxed. In truth I was tense about being once again in the gray area between interest and nosiness. There was an item I wanted, and I didn't know how convincing a lie I could develop on short notice to get it. "Since you mention André, the chef who died, I was wondering about something he mentioned...a photocopy of *The Practical Cook Book*? The reason I'm asking is that...I'm doing a party tomorrow for a member of the historical society. So I need to troll for authentic historic recipes. Any chance you'd let me borrow the photocopied version of *The Practical Cook Book*? To get ideas?"

"Well..." Annie cocked her head and gave me a doubtful look. "I'm really not supposed to let a whole facsimile go out, although Sylvia was going to make an exception for André. We could wait to ask her. But I don't know how long that would take. If you told me a recipe or two you liked, maybe I could help you—"

Ah, bureaucrats. "No, that's okay," I interjected

as I backed away from the half-gate. The four overweight dogs watched me greedily, perhaps hoping I'd accidentally drop a bread pudding. "I'll just go to the library," I tossed over my shoulder to Annie. Of course, I had no intention of doing any such thing.

"Isn't this pudding to die for, sweeties?" I heard Annie call cheerfully as I departed.

♦

When Tom heard us drive in, he put his special crumb-covered crab cakes into the oven. As soon as we had our boxes unpacked and ourselves cleaned up, we were digging into hot, crispy, divinely spicy little cakes. I said a prayer of thanks that I had such a wonderful husband...and that fish, owing to a doctor's warning that he wasn't getting close to enough protein, was now occasionally included in Julian's diet. We raved over the crab cakes and had seconds. I stretched the truth and said the tasting party hadn't been too bad. Just as I was actually beginning to forget the wretched day I'd had, however, the lights flickered, went out, then flickered on again. Tom announced he had to check the fuses. He'd been working on the kitchen's electrical outlets during the day, he told us cheerfully.

I rinsed our dishes and told Julian he *had* to take a break. What I didn't say was that if he wanted to cure the loneliness he'd felt so keenly in college, he needed to go out and make friends. Hopefully friends of the female variety. Thanks to my experience with Arch, however, I'd learned long ago not to give advice to young people. The lights flickered and went out. Great. I wondered how we'd manage to prep Weezie's party in the morning without electricity.

The lights came back on. Then they went out again. "It's okay!" Tom called from the basement. "I've turned the power off!"

"No problem!" I called back cheerily, then groaned.

"Where's Arch?" Julian asked. He glanced anxiously around the kitchen space, as if he couldn't bear a moment with nothing to do.

"In town," Tom supplied as he returned with a handful of tools. He frowned at the first set of electrical outlets. "Having hot dogs with a couple of eighth graders in front of the Grizzly Saloon. If you're wanting company, they'd probably enjoy chatting with a college student."

"Tom," I reprimanded when Julian banged out the front door. "That wasn't very sensitive."

He put down his screwdriver and frowned at the outlet. "Sorry. But the kid has to kick back a little. All he does is work, with occasional bursts of so-called relaxation when he swims a hundred laps all by his lonesome. I only said he should walk into town and maybe meet up with Arch. It'll be good for him. Besides, I need to talk to you."

"We do need to talk," I agreed. I pulled unsalted butter and eggs out of the dark refrigerator. "But I lied about the electricity being no problem. If you're done with those outlets, I need you to turn the power back on so I can make Weezie's birthday cake."

To avoid another disagreement, he trundled off silently to do as bidden. The lights blinked back on as I readied my recipe for orange poppy seed cake, Weezie's favorite.

On his return, Tom pulled out a metal tape measure and extended it across the floor with a clinging *thwack*.

"Speaking of lying," I said casually, "how did the polygraph go?"

"Ah, so you ferreted that out. Well, don't know yet about the results. But I did speak to Sheila about the autopsy. Looks like André somehow burned himself, had some chest pain, then took an overdose of his nitroglycerin, maybe because he was confused. Apparently, he was extremely sensitive to the nitro. I know you know how nitroglycerin works, opens the blood vessels to the heart. He took too much and his blood pressure crashed. The cops interviewed the photo people. Everyone at Ian's Images feels bad. They claim to have loved André."

"Right." But of course none of this was right. On Friday, the paramedics had mentioned that André's sensitivity to his medication had made him reluctant to take any, even at the first sign of symptoms. On the other hand, maybe these symptoms had been much worse, and he had indeed become confused.... "What caused the burn marks?" I asked.

Tom snapped the measure; it slithered back into its chrome housing. "The guys who secured the scene couldn't find a pan or burner that exactly matched the curve of the burns on André's hands. They found his empty bottle of medication. But there's no indication of foul play, and it's not a suspicious death. So they're not going to pursue it." He cracked the tape across the floor the other way. "End of story."

I sifted flour and shook my head. "Come on, Tom. On Friday André's his usual temperamental self. The following Monday he uncharacteristically burns himself with no-one-knows-what, then takes an overdose of a medication to which he knows he's extremely sensitive? And Sheila says that's the end of the story?" I set the beater to whip the egg whites. Delicately scented strands of orange zest curled onto my cutting board as I reminded myself that Tom was not the enemy.

He finished his measuring and scribbled numbers into his trusty spiral notebook. "Sheila's not done, of course, but she's *probably* going to rule the death an accident. They've put one investigator on it and he agrees." He pocketed his measure and notebook and enclosed me in a bear hug. "I thought you should know. I'm not saying it's right."

"Well, it isn't."

As he traipsed back down into the depths of the basement, I scraped the light, seed-specked batter into a buttered pan and set it in the oven. The kitchen clock indicated it was exactly four o'clock. After a moment's hesitation, I reached for the phone and punched in the number of the morgue. I counted it a blessing that I was only put on hold four times while waiting to get through to Sheila O'Connor.

"Listen," I began breathlessly after identifying myself. "André was *extremely* careful about his pills. And I think it's really *odd* that he would have burned himself—"

"Goldy, please. You always think that something's suspicious—"

"No, please," I interrupted, although I knew Sheila's scenario of burn, symptoms, overdose, hypotension, death, was not impossible. I took a deep breath. "I was at a tasting party today, a contest between caterers for a big booking. André was supposed to be there, but he wasn't, of course. He probably would have won. The other caterer, Craig Litchfield, is a real scumbag."

"Goldy, I'm not the one—"

I took another steadying breath, inhaling the tart-sweet orange scent, and ordered myself to be patient. "But you *are* the one, Sheila. If you rule André's death an accident, no one at the department will do anything. Tom's not allowed to poke around. He certainly doesn't want *me* to go out to the cabin to nose around the kitchen—"

"You'd *better* not," she cautioned.

"So when was the last time anyone out at the cabin saw André alive?"

"Friday. André called Rufus Driggle on

Sunday night and asked to be let in early to do some prep work. Rufus opened the gate for him at about seven, and then left to get film. The cabdriver confirms the gate was open when they arrived. When Rufus came back at nine, André was already dead."

"And Pru didn't tell you he'd burned himself over the weekend?"

"Nope. I asked her specifically."

"Is anybody at Ian's Images admitting they were out at the cabin early Monday?"

"No."

"All right then, listen to this," I went on urgently. "Within an *hour* of Pru leaving the morgue, Craig Litchfield practically broke down her door, trying to buy André's client list and recipe book. The guy is bad news, Sheila. I wouldn't put anything past him. Where was Litchfield early Monday morning when André died? Has anybody asked?"

"Goldy, look. I like you and trust you. So I'm going to tell you that Craig Litchfield called Andy Fuller yesterday and complained that *you* should be investigated. I only know because Andy ran it by me. I told him it was nonsense, just sour grapes from one of your competitors. But Litchfield said *you* can't deal with competition. He told Andy about some incident with a cake plate?" I groaned. "Litchfield claims you were at the Hibbard house yourself trying to get the clients and the recipes, and that you knew André's schedule, so you had the means, motive, and opportunity to kill him."

214

Stunned, I was speechless for a moment. "Sheila, you *know* I went to be with Pru. And André's always given me all the recipes I've ever asked for. Fuller can't, the department can't—"

"Of course not, and that's exactly what I told him. But you see how it looks. So if you'd rather not be investigated as the leading suspect in a homicide case, you'd better let me close the books on André Hibbard's death as an accidental overdose of nitroglycerin. An *accidental* death, Goldy," she said meaningfully. "Now, please, I have a ton of work. I have to go." She hung up.

I cursed silently and stared at the kitchen timer as it ticked down to the cake being done. *Think,* I told myself. *First Gerald Eliot, then André. You don't just have two unexplained deaths like this, with so many connections and yet no connections....*

The cake was almost done; the oven would still be hot; I decided to make us an early dinner. Anyway, I thought better when I cooked. How about a rich Mexican torte layered with chiles, Fontina cheese, and tortillas—a creamy entrée even a vegetarian could love? I grated cheese and chopped chiles, and as I did, I reconstructed what I knew.

Gerald Eliot had been doing his usual on-again, off-again remodeling work at the Merciful Migrations cabin. And for Cameron Burr. And for me. Supposedly, he'd been having an affair with the one-name model, Rustine. And he had been working as a security

215

guard at the museum, where he'd been killed, and from where his body had been moved. There had been a burglary at the museum. Or had there? Annie-the-volunteer-secretary had insisted Cameron Burr wouldn't have made it look as if a burglary had occurred, when his real motive was murder.

I beat eggs with half-and-half. I didn't know what the motive was, didn't even know which crime had come first, the murder or the burglary. Nor did I know how the strange death of André—who'd incomprehensibly asked for a copy of the one cookbook that had been stolen and was still missing—was related to either. But I owed it to André to answer all these questions. If only I could snoop around at that damn cabin! But I couldn't, at least not yet. Right now, the only thing that might help would be to have a look at some evidence, or facsimiles of evidence. I slid the cake out, turned the temperature down slightly, put the torte in, and set the timer for forty minutes. Then I ran upstairs to get the white gloves I'd bought to wear to Arch's confirmation.

It shouldn't take me that long to break into the museum, I reflected as I hustled out to the van with the gloves tucked in my pocket. After all, they no longer had a security guard. *And* because that very afternoon, after the tasting, I'd duct-taped over the Homestead kitchen door's so-called self-locking mechanism.

The museum closed at five, so the parking lot was predictably empty. Still, I exhaled in relief. I pushed open the door I'd rigged and strode purposefully into the kitchen, trying not to think of what Tom would say if he knew what I was doing. My story, just in case I was caught, was that I'd left a baking pan in the kitchen. Which I had, just before I'd taped the door.

Tom had told me that the forcible entry on the night of Gerald Eliot's death had been through the front door, which opened onto a reception area adjoining the octagonal living area, at the opposite end of the museum. Wouldn't the president of the historical society have had keys to that door? Maybe, maybe not, since the museum was government property. On the other hand, the president of the historical society would certainly have figured out how to break through the kitchen, wouldn't he? I didn't know. Nor did I know whether the intruder had been deliberately lying in wait for Gerald Eliot to make his rounds, as Andy Fuller contended. Was it possible Gerald surprised someone in the middle of a burglary?

I trotted into the dining room. This was where the struggle and strangling had taken place. I looked carefully past the police ribbons. Tiny shards of glass were still visible in the doorframes of the two violated display cases.

My watch indicated I'd been away from the house for fifteen minutes. In my mind's eye, the rich, creamy custard in our oven began to puff. The cookbooks...Where was the photocopy Sylvia had made for André from the files? No telling. And why would he want it, anyway? Wasn't what was valuable the cookbook *itself*?

Well. I knew enough from working as a docent here that it was possible to find what I wanted. And what I wanted was what André had requested, although I didn't have a clue why he'd requested it. I walked quickly to the historical society office, which smelled distinctly of dog, and scrutinized the four file cabinets.

Correspondence between the historical society and donors, government officials, and teachers was filed by years. Each drawer of the cabinets nearest the wall contained three years of correspondence. No help there. I headed to the other file cabinets, and was immediately rewarded for my efforts by tabs for *Acquisition Files: Permanent Collection*.

Unfortunately, each of the files within the drawers was labeled only by series of numbers. I pulled out one and read that 90.12.3 was a Hopi basket plaque acquired in 1990; 90.14.6 was apparently a Colt revolver donated in 1990. I pulled all the drawers open: all filed by number. I had no idea when *The Practical Cook Book* had been given to the museum. And there was no way I would be able to go through all these files, even if I stayed all night.

My eyes locked on Annie's computer. As a

docent, I'd never used it. But if a cross-reference for the files existed, the museum staff would surely enter it into the computer, wouldn't they? On the other hand, Sylvia didn't strike me as the data-processing type; maybe she left it all to Annie. I pressed buttons to boot the computer up, held my breath, then clicked on Permanent Collection. No password! That would teach them. I entered a word-search for *cookbook*.

The permanent collection contained twenty-three historic cookbooks. Ten of them, plus the letters from the German-American Society and from Charlie Smythe while he was incarcerated in Leavenworth, had been in the cookbook exhibit. I clicked on *The Practical Cook Book* by Elizabeth Hiller, and read rapidly through the accession sheet's description: *Brown cloth-bound volume with dark brown lettering; the owner's name and the year—Winnie Smythe, 1914—inscribed on the title page. Note from husband on second page.* The measurements and *overall good condition* of the book and its *heavily yellowed pages* were scrupulously noted, including *letters of the alphabet written randomly in brown ink on pages 32, 33, 112, 113.*

The book had been donated in 1975 along with letters and other items from the old Smythe cabin, now headquarters for Merciful Migrations. At the bottom of the accession sheet was the name of the donor: Leah Smythe.

The computer file itself was made up of two pages: the accession sheet and a list of items found in what the museum called the *object file.*

In the object file, I read, I'd find a photo of the book, photocopy of the pages, and a photocopy of a letter written from Charles Smythe to his wife from Leavenworth in 1916, mentioning the cookbook. Had I found pay dirt? Or was I on a wild-goose chase for a book dumped by Gerald Eliot's killer somewhere the police hadn't found yet? Why had André requested this cookbook? And why, two days later, had he ended up dead? Was there a connection?

The cookbook's accession number was *PC—1975.011.001a.* I grabbed a ballpoint, scribbled the number on a piece of paper, and shut down the computer.

I flipped through the accessions for 1975 and came upon the thick file for 75.011.001a. I checked my watch: the torte needed to be out of the oven in ten minutes. I yanked the cookbook file out of the cabinet, slammed the drawer shut, and raced to the museum exit. Before leaving, I glanced at my decoy baking pan on the kitchen table. Should I take it? Perspiration dampened my face. What about the duct tape on the door's self-locking mechanism? I riffled the photocopies in my hand. The hundred sixty pages of the small cookbook had been copied as double pages; the whole file looked as if it contained less than a hundred pages. I closed the unlocked door, trotted out to my van, and revved up the engine. I would shoot to the library and photocopy the file, bring it back, and pull the tape off the back door at the same time. Before going to the library, though, I needed to zip home, to take my torte out of the oven before it burned to a crisp.

Cooking puts such unfortunate constraints on criminal behavior.

Chapter 15

Jake howled a greeting as my van crunched into our driveway. I tucked the stolen file under my arm and prayed that Tom hadn't noticed my absence. I also hoped he wouldn't be there to ask what I was toting.

The heavenly smell of hot Mexican food greeted my entry through the plastic sheeting covering the hole that used to be our back door. The golden-brown cheese torte steamed on a rack on a cluttered countertop. Julian, who'd undoubtedly taken out the dish, was now gallantly offering a ceramic platter of crudités to none other than Rustine. I was so surprised at the sight of the model, I almost dropped the purloined folder.

She sat serenely at our kitchen table, her chestnut ponytail loosened to soft waves that fell just to the straps of her black sport bra. She appraised a hillock of glistening grated daikon on the platter Julian offered her. When she crossed her legs, her skintight black leggings made a silky, rustling sound. I gripped the file and tried to look delighted that Julian was making

221

friends. The former lover of Gerald Eliot, no less, although she probably wasn't in the mood to chat about *that.*

"Hey, there..." I faltered. "Welcome, Rustine. Julian? Thanks for saving the torte." When he nodded, I asked, "Any idea where Arch is?"

"He's with my sister Lettie on your front porch," Rustine supplied smoothly, before Julian had a chance to answer. "Lettie and your son and I all go to Elk Park Prep, as it turns out."

"How nice," I murmured inanely.

"It was okay, wasn't it?" mumbled Julian. His brown eyes crinkled in puzzlement. "Bringing people home?"

"Of course." I was aware that Rustine was staring at me. Did I look as if I'd just committed a burglary? I wondered if any of the identifying numbers on the file tucked under my arm were visible. "So," I asked her, too brightly, "you all just ran into each other?"

"Yep." Rustine lifted a tiny handful of Julian's meticulously grated carrots and inspected it.

"Are you looking forward to school starting?" I asked politely.

"Not really." She popped the carrot shreds into her mouth and munched thoughtfully. "Our dad is supposed to get back from Alaska right after Labor Day, so the only thing Lettie and I are looking forward to is seeing him. We've been so busy with the shoot we haven't been able to think about much else."

"*We've* been so busy with the shoot?" I prompted.

Rustine shrugged. "Lettie models, too."

Julian plunged in with: "Rustine thinks Goldilocks' Catering might be able to book the rest of the Christmas catalog shoot. She said Litchfield's already been out to the cabin, nosing around to pick up the assignment. Why don't you sit down, Goldy, have some coffee with us?"

I headed across my wrecked kitchen, stepping over a hammer, two saws, and a nail gun abandoned on the floor. *Cater the rest of the shoot where my teacher just died? No thanks.* Julian sprang up beside the espresso machine. I said, "I'd love some coffee. I'll be back in a sec."

"We should call Ian or Leah just as soon as possible, Rustine says," Julian persisted. "Want me to get a bid together? For the photo shoot?"

I stopped in the kitchen doorway, still clutching the file. Wait a minute. *Litchfield* had been out there. I gave Rustine a sharp look. "When exactly did Craig Litchfield go out to the Merciful Migrations cabin?"

She bent back her slender wrist in nonchalance. "Late afternoon, yesterday." I calculated: Litchfield had gone from André's condo, where he'd confronted me, directly to the cabin? Rustine went on, "Leah told me this other caterer named Litchfield offered to fix hors d'oeuvre to serve at the end of that day's shooting."

"And did he?"

She flicked a wisp of carrot off her fingertip with her tongue, then nodded. "Ian had had to send Rufus in for sub sandwiches, and they weren't very good, so Leah told Litchfield he could heat up whatever he wanted. They were just egg rolls and spinach turnovers, but everybody liked them." She chewed the strand of carrot. "Leah thinks Litchfield's really cute. She offered to give him an audition for the cruise section. But it would be great if you guys did the food. Your stuff was better."

Julian raised his eyebrows. "So, Goldy, should I put a contract together for coffee breaks and lunches for Prince and Grogan? They should be shooting through Labor Day." He twinkled as he mouthed: *More work.*

"We already have catering jobs for this week," I replied matter-of-factly. "There'll be a huge amount to do that will take up most of our time." I fidgeted and gripped the file. Upstairs, I could hear Tom's low tones: He was probably on the phone. I hated to feel on the spot, but here I was. Plus, had Rustine and Julian really *just run into each other* in town? Why the sudden urge to have us cater at the site where my teacher had died? Did I *really* want this chance to be out there, as I'd thought half an hour ago?

"Whatever feels right to you. But as I said, your stuff was better," Rustine commented sweetly, and turned her smile back to Julian.

"I'll think about it," I muttered before

heading down the hall. I pulled open the drawer of Tom's antique buffet and dumped the Homestead file inside, then stepped out the front door.

On our porch swing, my son was sitting next to an impossibly lovely blond girl dressed in a navy blue shirt and shorts. Freckles splashed over her tanned cheeks as she chatted brightly, blinked thickly lashed eyes, and twirled a French braid dotted with tiny navy blue bows. Arch sat beside her, entranced. I teetered, wondering briefly about the availability of shock medication. Arch glanced up when he felt my presence. Crimson flooded his cheeks.

"Oops—Sorry." I cleared my throat. Lettie turned enormous questioning eyes to me. Good Lord, she was pretty. "I'm Arch's mom. Would you two like some lemonade?"

Arch's expression turned instantly thunderous. Miss Sparkle-Plenty scuffed at the porch floor with the toe of her sandal and gave the swing a forceful nudge. "Sure. Can you make lemonade with artificial sweetener?"

"Absolutely." Would a snack be appropriate so close to dinner? Should I invite Lettie and Rustine to stay for dinner? When did the library close? I tried to think. Arch caught my hesitation.

"You can go now, Mom."

Ten minutes later, a cowardly mother to the core, I sent Julian to the porch with a pitcher of lemonade and a platter of chilled poached shrimp with cocktail sauce. I averted my eyes while mixing more lemon juice with generic aspartame, and invited Rustine and her sister to dinner. Rustine replied that they could stay, if the two of them could only have shrimp and salad. She was scheduled to model on Friday. She and her sister needed to watch their figures, she reminded me. *And what do you think Arch and Julian are doing,* I couldn't help thinking, but asked instead, "How long has your dad been in Alaska?"

"Since mid-July," she said. "He's looking for a job in Juneau. I've been taking care of Lettie. Our mom lives in Florida with her new family."

"And...will you both withdraw from Elk Park Prep if your dad finds work in Alaska?"

"Well, I guess. I'm taking a year off from school anyway, and Lettie won't start eighth grade until after the P and G shoot's finished."

"Why?"

"Because," Rustine replied in a *you-moron* tone, "we each clear a thousand to fifteen hundred dollars every day we work. We make as much as our dad, and he's an engineer." She slipped out of the kitchen, presumably to join the other young people on the porch. That girl did have a way of making me feel aged.

I gratefully swigged the iced latté—made with fattening whipping cream—and brought water, seasonings, and the lemon skins to a boil so I could poach more shrimp. With a plentiful salad, the Mexican torte, and a frozen rice pilaf quickly defrosted in the microwave, we'd be okay. I needed to talk to Tom and start prepping Weezie Harrington's party. But most of all, I knew I absolutely had to copy the Smythe cookbook file and get it back to the museum before it opened in the morning.

"Look," I said when Julian returned to the kitchen, "I can't think about going out to work at the cabin right now. If you want to put together a proposal for them, I'll look at it tonight. But right this sec I really need to do an errand in town." I took out the frozen pilaf and pointed to the salad ingredients. "Can you defrost the pilaf and make a salad for the rest of the dinner? I'll be back in less than an hour."

"Sure," he said enthusiastically as Rustine glided back into the room. I snagged the file, sprinted out the front door, and waved a hasty good-bye to the occupants of our front porch, who ignored me. In a cloud of dust, I reversed the van down the driveway. I doubt they noticed.

At the Aspen Meadow Public Library, I laid out crisp dollar bills on the copier farthest from prying eyes, and flipped through the file. *The Practical Cook Book,* written by Elizabeth Hiller—whose stern cameo was featured opposite the title page—had been published in Chicago in 1910. Only two or three recipes were printed on each of the small pages. Although I'd determined to work as quickly as possible, I was puzzled by a note written after the page with Winnie Smythe's name and the date 1914. In a different hand that featured severely slanted letters and fine long curlicues was the inscription: *My Dear Wife, when you make my Favorite Dessert, remember to make the Rolls the way I taught You.* It was signed, *Your Loving Husband.*

So, Charlie Smythe gave cooking advice in addition to being a rancher and unsuccessful bank robber, eh? Busy fellow. I slapped the file sheets madly into the machine, and frowned at two pages with random rows of letters in the outside margins. Page 33 contained the recipes for German Coffee Cake and Parker House Rolls. In the margin was a row of slanted ink letters that spelled nothing: **U, A, A, Z, N, B, K, R, D, L, M, I, E, W, P, Q, R, V, Z, X, T, S, A, U, H, G, F, D, E, Y, T, R, E, P, A, S, L, W, I, C, E, X.** Page 113 contained two more grids, with rows of different letters in the margin next to the recipes for Bread Pudding and Steamed Apple Pudding. This was the handwriting that made this cookbook a valuable collector's item? What were these letters? Directions on how to make the rolls the way Charlie had taught Winnie? Now *that's* what I called secret recipes.

The last item in the stolen file was a copy of the letter written to Winnie from Charles when he was in Leavenworth. I'd seen the original in the shattered case at the Homestead:

My Dear Wife,
You must know how very much I love you, and how I would tear out my Heart to see you again. To get to my cell, I pass a wall

*in which I have tried to carve your name.
I remember our cabin Kitchen with its
smell of Bread and Pudding, how you
would use Cookery to show your love for
me. I have only read one book. Sky here is
seldom seen. I long for our bed, children,
Family tales, rifle, horses, cabin, and
beautiful land where I believed to find
Riches. One day, my Love.
Your Loving Husband*

Hmm. More references to bread and pudding; and it was the pages with those recipes that contained the random letters. But this eighty-year-old puzzle would have to wait until I could go over it, preferably with Tom. He wouldn't be happy about how I'd obtained a copy of the file, but he'd live.

I finished the photocopying, reassembled the original file as well as my packet of copies, and hustled out of the library. It didn't take long to sneak back into the Homestead, replace the original file, and tear the tape off the back door so that this time, it really did self-lock. It wasn't until I was pulling back into our driveway that I realized I'd left my stupid baking pan on the table of the museum kitchen.

Arch was standing in the driveway when I returned. He looked embarrassed and frantic, and I had the feeling he'd been lying in wait for me. He hopped out of the way so I could pull into the garage, where I hastily tucked my photocopied file under the van's front seat. At the moment, Tom was the *only* person with whom I wanted to share the contents of the pilfered book.

"Hon, what's the matter?" I demanded when I hopped out.

"Lettie and I want to have dinner at the Chinese place."

"Tonight?"

"Please, Mom, may I borrow twenty dollars? I don't have time for you to take me to the bank to get into my own account, and I don't want to ask Tom because he's suspended with no pay. Lettie and I will walk down to the Dragon's Breath and walk back. So you don't need to take us." He kicked at a pebble in the driveway and sent it hurtling down into the street. *"Please."*

I pulled two ten-dollar bills out of my pocket. "Forget borrowing, just take it."

"Thanks, Mom."

"Remember not to have peppers, they make you sick."

Arch just shook his head and ran off.

In the kitchen, Tom wedged a crowbar behind a drawer to pry it loose. With a sickening shriek, the drawer and cabinet below it tore from their moorings and crashed to the floor. Ignoring the sound, Julian packed up food on our one remaining counter. Our kitchen table had been pushed against the wall. Standing beside it, Rustine watched the destructive drama with undisguised interest.

"Why are you doing this *now*?" I cried.

Tom, who had been peering at the rubble with a satisfied expression, appeared surprised. "I have to get rid of the old stuff today so I can go pick up your new cabinets." He raised a bushy eyebrow. "I would have asked you about it, but nobody knew where you were."

"Where am I supposed to work?" I wailed. "How are we supposed to *eat*?"

Tom and Julian exchanged a look. *Women,* it clearly said. Julian picked up two grocery bags loaded with foodstuffs. "Tom said to pack up the shrimp and torte for a dinner picnic. It'll just be the four of us here. Did Arch tell you he and Lettie were going out for Chinese? And Tom has some secret picturesque spot for us, right?"

"You bet," my husband said cheerfully. He put down his crowbar. "Let me just go get showered. Miss G., why don't you come upstairs and talk to me?"

As I sat in the steamy bathroom listening to the shower patter, I realized this was the wrong time to bring up stolen paperwork, especially to a cop. Even if that cop was on suspension. I tried to focus instead on Tom's patient explanation that he'd be done with the kitchen in a mere month or so.

"I need you to decide if you want a lazy Susan as the under-counter cabinet in the corner six feet to the right of the sink. And I need to know if you want a double or single sink, and if you want stainless or some color."

"I'd love a lazy Susan cupboard, thanks. And

I'd prefer a double sink, stainless, please. And don't forget three separate sinks are required by the county for food service."

"My dear Miss G. Trust me, okay?"

I could see his body through the steamed-up glass of the shower stall, and immediately thought of better things to do than discuss kitchen amenities. Tom turned the water off, wrapped a towel around his middle, and shot me a quizzical look. "Okay, so I can ask you questions about what you want, and you won't be upset with me?"

I smiled. Of course, it wasn't *what I wanted* that was bothering me, it was the mess, the cost, the fear that when he finished, I'd have something rich and strange, like oysters with sour cream and truffles, that made me sick to my stomach just to contemplate.

Tom paused in his toweling-off and regarded me questioningly. "Why is this red-haired young woman here, exactly? Rustine. The one who was getting it on with Gerald Eliot, right?"

I shrugged. "Right. She's a model for the Prince and Grogan shoot. *I* think *she* thinks Julian is sexy. Of course, the only man I think is sexy is standing half-dressed in front of me, while the bed is beckoning."

Tom chuckled. "How about when we don't have people waiting for us to have dinner with them?" He finished drying off, pulled on the clean yellow shirt and khaki pants he'd brought into the bathroom, and gave me another quizzical expression. "This model. Did she and Julian hook up before now? Or did she just show up here?"

I remembered when I'd unexpectedly seen Rustine in her green outfit, jogging down our street just before Julian arrived. "I don't think they hooked up before now. Why?"

"What do you know about her and her sister?"

"Well, let's see. Because of Rustine's relationship with Gerald Eliot, Merciful Migrations fired Gerald. Rustine and her sister Lettie go to Elk Park Prep and model, too. I think Julian ran into them in town when you sent him off to find Arch, and they all came back together. Why the big interest?"

He rubbed the towel over his hair. "Not sure. I just don't trust her. Could you ask her some questions about the fashion photo people?"

"Like what?"

"Be the good cop, Miss G. Ask some friendly questions while we drive, see if she's on the up-and-up. I'd like to know what the real story is."

"Do you think she's lying about something? And I should ask her questions when we drive *where*?"

"Look, Goldy." He dropped his comb on the countertop, took my hand, and led me down the stairs. "What is it they're always telling the yoga people? Just go with the flow."

"Okay, but could we at least take Julian's car? Please? It's cleaner." *In every sense,* I added silently.

♦

"So where are we headed?" Julian asked once we were all in his Range Rover and he was driving us toward Main Street, ten minutes later.

"To the Smythe Peak Open Space area," Tom replied. "I'll direct you."

A cluster of blush-rose clouds rimmed the horizon as the summertime sun slowly sank. I bit the inside of my cheek as we passed the ornately carved entry to the Dragon's Breath Chinese restaurant. Back at home, I had left a note for Arch under the front doormat, our agreed-upon spot for messages. *Gone out for a picnic dinner, just in case you get home first. Home by eight. Please stay on the porch with your friend.* I doubted Lettie's dad would approve of a fourteen-year-old boy inviting his daughter up to his bedroom to see his ham radio equipment.

Rustine, who sat next to Julian, turned around to smile at Tom and me. She was so pretty, so perfectly made up, so disarmingly clothed in what I usually considered underwear, that it was challenging to come up with casual chatter, much less a friendly interrogation.

She said matter-of-factly, "You must be *freaked out* about Chef André. That day you worked with him and gave me the coffee? I didn't know he was your *teacher*. Julian told me. And to think he died in that same *kitchen*...spooky."

I frowned. Was she offering sympathy? How was I supposed to respond to *freaked out*? We whizzed past the library and headed out of town. "Did you...get to know André at all during the shoot?"

She shrugged her bare shoulders. "He seemed...a little weird, you know. But *real* lovable."

I glanced at Julian, who was frowning at the road. Given the nature of Rustine's alleged relationship with the late Gerald Eliot, I wondered how she defined *lovable*. "Oh," I commented knowingly, "André had his ways. But when you say *weird,* do you mean *eccentric*? How was he...during the shoot?"

"Well," she said, "like if anybody put salt on food before tasting it, he had a fit. One time Ian blasted Rufus to go get him some soy sauce from the kitchen. *That* didn't go over very well with André, who yelled that Rufus was an imbecile." She giggled. "Rufus really isn't very smart, but he hates it when people draw attention to it." Her tone turned mock-serious. "And you can't *imagine* how upset André got when some *catsup* got poured into a raspberry sauce he'd made for a cake, or some *pickle* ended up on his seafood stuff. Plus," she added resignedly, "some people just have bad manners. You know, they stick their fingers instead of vegetables into bowls of dip. So Chef André would get after us in the hygiene department. Anyway, with all that butter and anger, it's no *wonder* he had a heart attack."

My heart ached. She could be right. So why was I so convinced there was something amiss about André's sudden death? I glanced at Tom. His face was expressionless. His cop face, Arch liked to call it. "Ah, Rustine?" I asked innocently. "Have you had much experience with other caterers on modeling jobs?"

"Ha!" she chortled. "Usually it's cold cuts and iceberg lettuce followed by brownies." She shuddered. "André was the best we'd ever had. Ian's always made plenty of money to *spend* on catering. But he hasn't exactly been generous about spreading it around. Or in treating his helpers or the models very well."

"That's too bad," I murmured sympathetically, myself a veteran of a cheapskate ex-husband. "What do you suppose changed his mind this time?"

"Oh, having André was probably Leah's idea. She tries to smooth out old chintzy Ian's rough spots."

"Turn at the next right," Tom ordered Julian as we approached the flashing yellow light by the You-Snag-Em, We-Bag-Em Trout Farm.

"So..." I didn't want to jump right into asking about Ian and Leah; that would surely seem nosy. "Have you known Ian long?"

"Two years. Ian noticed me when he was shooting an ad at the athletic club. He recommended that I audition as a model, and mentioned a couple of agencies in Denver. I hooked up with one."

236

"Do you enjoy it?"

"The money is super. But the work's hard, and it's off-the-charts stressful."

"Because of not being able to eat?"

Rustine turned around so abruptly I was startled. "For us, our bodies, our faces, the bookings we get, the money we make...it's our whole lives. We get a zit, it's a disaster. We gain a pound, we're on the phone to Kevorkian, you know?"

"I guess I don't," I murmured.

"Plus the jealousy, if we don't get chosen for a shoot?" She rolled her eyes. "Eats us alive. And then you see what's coming: One day, it's just *over*. A model goes in for a cattle call, sure of a booking with a client they've worked for for years. The client says, 'We can't use you anymore.' Believe me, you don't want to be around when that news breaks. I've seen it happen, and it's not pretty."

"Is that what was going on the day I was there? With Leah's half-brother Bobby?"

"Oh," she said with forced vagueness, "who knows? Bobby has an in because of Leah." She made a noise to indicate her disgust. "It really stinks. You think the world's fair, and then you see old potbellied, red-eyed Bobby get a job, and you know it isn't."

Tom gave me an exasperated look. Guess he didn't approve of my interrogation methods. I went on: "Do you...have much time for...you know, hobbies, extracurricular activities, schoolwork, whatever, between shoots?"

Rustine didn't reply. I glanced at Julian, who

scowled into the rearview mirror. Guess he didn't approve of my interrogation methods, either.

"Take the next driveway on the right," Tom instructed.

We chugged along. Rustine's hands tightened on the dashboard. The next driveway on the right led to the house of Mr. and Mrs. Cameron Burr.

At the end of the rutted drive, I expected to see the bright yellow police ribbons that usually marked a crime scene, but there were none. A stocky uniformed policeman sitting in front of the guest house got to his feet and lumbered to the car. Julian powered down the window.

"Schulz?" The cop's voice was surprisingly high and querulous. His dark eyes swept the interior of the car. He lifted his chin in acknowledgment of Tom. "Yeah, you were right," he observed laconically before walking heavily back to his perch on the deck.

"Right about what? What's going on?" Rustine asked as her eyes followed the policeman. "I thought we were going on a picnic. Isn't that what you said?" she demanded of Julian. Julian shrugged and glanced at Tom.

"We can still have dinner outdoors," Tom said amicably. "You can drive over to the Open Space picnic area now, big J."

Julian torqued the wheel. The Rover rocked down the Burrs' driveway.

"Okay, let's see," said Tom when we were out on the two-lane road once again. "A week ago, about here," he pointed out the window, "the officer we just met saw a red-haired woman scavenging along this road. It was in the late afternoon of the day after Gerald Eliot's body was found at the house we just left. I called the cop back there to see if he'd take a look at you, see if he could identify you as the one searching through the grass."

Rustine exhaled. Her beautiful eyes remained locked on the road.

"I can't arrest you, Rustine." Tom's voice was gentle. "Can't even take you in for questioning. But there are a couple of things that have my curiosity up. One report tells us you were going out with this fellow Eliot before someone murdered him. Then you were seen near here, right after Goldy found Eliot's body. You were obviously looking for something. Now you're hanging around us, with your we-just-ran-into-Julian line. You want to satisfy my curiosity?"

Chapter 16

"I don't have to talk to you, you know," she said defensively, still refusing to look at him.

"You're right, you don't. And I'm not accusing you of anything." Tom maintained his calm, soothing tone. "I'm not allowed to do that. Nor can I keep you here against your will. I'm suspended, remember?"

She whirled in her seat and gave him an icy look. "I did not kill Gerald."

"Good for you," Tom countered with a smile. "We're just wondering what's going on, that's all. Eliot was murdered. He was a terrible contractor and an even worse security guard. He had done work for a lot of people who didn't like him, including unfinished work for Ian's Images, out at the Merciful Migrations cabin. Then right after his death, my wife's teacher died suddenly, just when *he* was working for Ian's Images. Is there a connection?"

"I don't know," Rustine said uncertainly.

Tom went on: "But you must *not* have found what you were looking for when you were out here searching around. If you had, you wouldn't be hanging around us, saying you just happened to bump into Julian." He paused, then said, "Is it because you think André might have told us something? Something that somehow got him into trouble, too?"

She immediately muttered, "Oh, crap."

Julian's face in the mirror registered distaste mixed with disappointment. Some picnic.

Rustine seemed to be turning something over in her mind. After a moment, she gave me a girls-only grin. "Actually, my little sister really *does* think your son is cute, Goldy. And smart, too."

"If your cute little sister breaks my son's heart," I retorted calmly, "I will lop off her cute little blond braid."

Rustine wrinkled her nose and scowled at me. "Man! What *is* it with you?"

"Sorry," I mumbled. I felt a sudden wave

240

of sympathy for Rustine. After all, what *had* she been doing out here? Playing detective in the wake of losing a loved one? Wasn't that precisely what I was doing?

Julian pulled up to the picnic tables at the trailhead for Smythe Peak. Tom opened the back door of the Rover and announced that we could continue talking while we ate. We set out the platter of shrimp, the torte, a basket of rolls, and two salads Julian had made. The first was comprised of avocado chunks, romaine lettuce, and sugared walnuts tossed with a champagne vinaigrette; the second was a delectable mélange of fresh grapes and pineapple chunks robed in a buttermilk dressing. I put a pitcher of iced tea next to the rolls and recalled my first day at the cabin, when Rustine had come into the kitchen seeking coffee. What had she said? *You're the caterer who figures things out.*

"Start with your relationship with Gerald Eliot." Tom proceeded to pull the tail off a shrimp, dunk it in our homemade cocktail sauce, and stick it in his mouth. He chewed and winked at me, as if to say, *Good food. Good interrogation.* I was happy to discover that Julian's green salad was out of this world.

Rustine ran her fingers through her luxuriant red hair and shook it over her shoulders. She waited until she had our attention, then announced, "Gerry had found something that was going to make us rich." Julian moved his gaze to the rosy-feathered clouds fringing the mountains. Less assuredly, Rustine added, "Or so he said."

"What was it he found? And when did he find it?" asked Tom. "Was it at the cabin or at the museum?"

"I think I should begin at the beginning," she said, almost apologetically. "Gerry and I started going out in June. I was up there doing the shoot for Prince and Grogan's July R.O.P.—that's *run of press*—their ads for July, to be in the *Post* and *News*. Gerry was tearing out the wall in the cabin kitchen to put in windows. He never finished, of course."

I groaned.

Rustine's tone became defensive. "Look, I know all about Gerry taking your money. But...he'd been fired by Ian's Images in the middle of July. They never even paid him for his work, even though he'd given Leah his bills. *Rufus* said that *Hanna* wanted Gerry out because Gerry was involved with me. But I never believed that."

Tom studied another plump pink shrimp. "Why did Eliot—Gerry—scam my wife and keep a crummy security job, if he'd found something to make him rich? And are you going to tell us what it was? Or do you even know?"

Rustine's perfectly powdered brow furrowed. "I...don't know what it was exactly...whether it was a *thing,* or some *dirt* on somebody...or what." She faltered. I had the distinct impression that she was lying. "Gerry was in a real financial bind, though," she went on. "His last credit card had been canceled. He'd had to put down *cash* for some of

242

the windows he'd ordered for projects." I thought of Cameron and Barbara, with their pink and blue sheets of glass winking in the sunlight, of the cabin kitchen and my own cooking space, both with glued plywood over the sink. Rustine assumed a sad tone. "Yes, Gerry took the Burrs' money, and Goldy's, too. But it was just to stay afloat until he could get to the next project."

Rather than dwell on how dumb and trusting I'd been, I helped myself to more avocado salad.

"So he didn't tell you what he'd found, or found out?" Tom pressed.

The edges of Rustine's lipsticked mouth turned down. "He said he'd found a weapon."

"A weapon?" I interjected. I immediately thought of the strange marks on André's hands. Could they have been caused by a weapon? "What sort?"

"I don't know. I was hoping *you* guys might tell *me*. Like, that you'd come across…something?" She looked at us expectantly. "Or maybe," she continued, "that André had told you some secret he'd found out? Say, about Charlie Smythe, who used to live in the cabin? Maybe something to do with cooking in that kitchen, that Gerry and André might *both* have found out," she added desperately.

Julian cut himself some more torte. "That makes a lot of sense, Rustine. Something to do with cooking in that kitchen that would have contributed to two guys' deaths."

Rustine closed her eyes and shrugged.

"Well, André cooked, didn't he? And Gerry had been doing work in the cabin kitchen, too, right?"

My mind went back to *The Practical Cook Book*, but I said nothing.

"Here's what we've got," Tom said. "A contractor hated by his clients gets fired from a job where he's having an affair with an employee."

"I wasn't an employee—" Rustine interrupted indignantly.

Tom cocked an eyebrow. "Item two." Rustine pressed her lips together. "Eliot claimed to this Ian's Images *employee* that he'd found something, or maybe found *out* something that he claimed would make them rich. It might be a weapon or it might be information, right?" Rustine nodded once, quickly, then licked her lips. "At Eliot's second job," Tom went on, "security guard at the Homestead Museum, where he arrived the evening of Sunday, August seventeenth, he was strangled to death in what appeared to be a faked burglary attempt. Law enforcement officials believe the perp was one of Eliot's disgruntled clients. Of whom there are at least three still living in or near Aspen Meadow." He pointedly avoided looking at me. "The perp— and at this point we still think we're looking at one person, one crime—stole some things from the museum. Is that what you were looking for?"

"What?" Rustine asked innocently.

"Something stolen from the museum?"

"What was that?"

Tom tried again. "C'mon, Rustine, help us out. Were you looking for something?"

Rustine replied, "What are you missing?"

The blankness of Tom's cop face made me smile. I'd read enough about law enforcement cat-and-mouse to know that the *last* thing he'd identify for Rustine was what the sheriff's department was still missing. And if Rustine knew about the fourth cookbook, then she knew a lot more about Gerald Eliot's murder than she was letting on.

Tom cleared his throat, then said, "André Hibbard also worked at the cabin, in the kitchen, in fact, and he died under what may be questionable circumstances. And yet, the coroner is about to rule Chef André's death accidental."

Rustine added eagerly, "But who knows what really happened? André worked at the Homestead Museum one day of the shoot, don't forget that. And that guy who's under arrest for Gerald's murder? Burr? He's like, the president of the historical society, which has its headquarters at the Homestead. So...I figure somebody with connections to *both* Merciful Migrations and the Homestead *must* have murdered Gerald and André."

"The Pope was in Denver last year," Julian commented solemnly as he served himself fruit salad. "It doesn't mean Goldy catered to the cardinals." Rustine shot him a furious look, but Julian was right. When it came to conclusions, this girl definitely won the long jump.

"Okay, people," Tom soothed, "I'm going to call a buddy of mine at the department and see what we can find out about Ian's Images, Merciful Migrations, *and* the Homestead Museum. Financial problems, people problems. Maybe there's a public record that would give us an insight into whatever it was Gerald Eliot stumbled on that was going to make him rich."

"Look," I said to Rustine, "maybe there's more that's gone on at that cabin than you're aware. You're the one who could find out if someone, say, didn't get a modeling job. That person could have argued with Ian or Leah, and maybe André overheard the fight. Or someone might tell *you* that Eliot knew about some other conflict, or saw or found out something he shouldn't have. What if Ian Hood fired Eliot because Eliot was trying to blackmail him? Then if André stumbled on the same incriminating piece of information, it might have made things dangerous for him."

"I can't find that stuff out." Rustine's whine was full of complaint. "I'm telling you, these people *scare* me."

But you want *us* to figure it out, I thought. Have *us* work on it, and find out what happened to your boyfriend, and maybe in the process, find whatever it is that's going to make *you* rich. The conversation ended. Julian encouraged everyone to finish up. Rustine nibbled three shrimp without sauce. She forked a pile of romaine onto her plate, sorted away the avocado, blotted off the vinaigrette with paper napkins, and downed the damp leaves. It was painful to watch.

Locusts whirred from their hidden perches in the tall grass. A breeze smelling of pine whispered down the mountains while the sun slid into the purple outline of craggy peaks. Again I found my mind wandering back to that *something stolen from the museum*, Winnie Smythe's 1910 copy of *The Practical Cook Book*, the facsimile of which was tucked under the driver's seat of my van.

♦

When the Rover ground over the gravel by our curb, Julian curtly ordered Rustine to fetch her sister. Without looking at me, he announced that when he returned from dropping the two girls off, he would unpack the picnic leftovers.

A knot of sadness twisted in my chest. But I knew better than to worry about Julian's love life. Or lack thereof.

Seated side by side on the porch swing, Arch and Lettie were speculating on the meanings of their fortune cookie prophecies. Lettie offered us her full sunlit smile. Arch narrowed his eyes at our intrusion.

"Time to groove," Rustine informed her sister.

Lettie grabbed her backpack and asked for Arch's e-mail address, which he wrote on the back of her fortune. On the way to the Rover, he walked slightly behind her, like an attendant to a princess. Unbidden, he climbed into the backseat beside her. I repressed a sigh.

About to step inside the car, Rustine turned. "Goldy, when will I see you again? Will you call me?"

I reflected on the mountain of work still to be done for Weezie Harrington's party and the Hardcastle wedding reception. And yet, like Rustine but for very different reasons, I wanted to know what had really happened at the cabin.

"We'll see," I promised. "Hurry back!" I added belatedly, with a hopeful vagueness intended for Lettie.

"We will!" Julian assured me pointedly from behind the wheel. I don't think he'd even looked at Rustine since her confession at the picnic table. "Unless Rustine has someone else she wants to run into!"

♦

I checked our messages: nothing from the Merciful Migrations people about the Soirée. So maybe I still had a prayer of winning the competition from Craig Litchfield. Fat chance, the way that charming sleaze operated.... I called Marla and left a message on her machine, saying I hoped she was surviving the audit. Next I called Pru, as I'd meant to earlier, and again got her nurse. "She goes to bed around seven these days," Wanda told me flatly. "But she seems to be doing all right."

I assured her I would see them at the

memorial service Thursday. Then I hustled out to my van and pulled out the hidden photocopy.

"I have something I want to show you," I murmured to Tom.

Tom was proudly surveying the wreckage of the kitchen. He'd stripped the cabinets off the walls so that all that remained were the wooden studs. Looking at the way the studs marked off coal-black paper torn here and there to reveal bright pink insulation, I tried not to think of how much my kitchen now resembled an eighteenth-century prison. I sighed.

"Miss G. Here's where your lazy Susan will go." He motioned to the shadowy corner far to the right of the gutted sink area. "Oh, by the way, do you want a soffit above your cabinets, or do you want the cabinets to go all the way to the ceiling?"

"Tom, *I* don't know."

He whipped out his measuring tape and snapped it along the wall. "All the way up, I'd say. Have more storage space." He frowned at the dark wall. "Do you want under-cabinet lighting? If so, we'll need to cover it with molding. We don't want the molding to come down so low you can't use your food processor."

"Agh!" I cried. "Who's *we*, cop? I just need to get my workspace back!"

"Now, take it easy. I've set up space for you and Julian in here." He led me out to the dining room, where he'd stacked the furniture against the wall by the hutch. In the center of the room, four sawhorses supported two four-by-eight pressboard work surfaces. Large cardboard boxes had been carefully labeled to show their contents. I read one list: *Large mixer, bowls, beaters. Food processor.*

"Great. Thanks." This was not the time to squabble with Tom about my working conditions. I had to show him the cookbook facsimile and see what he thought. "Now *please,* may I show you something, Tom? In the living room?"

He nodded, nabbed a few of Julian's truffles from a covered dish, and followed me to the couch. "While you were outside, I put in a call to Boyd. He's going to get back to me tomorrow on our questions about unusual goings-on at Merciful Migrations and the Homestead. Meanwhile, I need to set up a third temporary counter for you and Julian."

"I promise, this will just take a minute." I handed him the thick sheaf. "It's a photocopy of the missing cookbook," I explained. "Check out the inscription. Also pages thirty-three and one-thirteen."

He put the pile of paper down on the coffee table and tapped it with his forefinger. "How'd you get this?"

"The museum keeps photocopies of all the volumes they possess, Tom. I was a docent there, remember. I know how they operate."

"And this is the museum copy?"

"Will you stop being such a fussbudget? No, of course not. I made my own copy."

"With their permission, of course."

"They don't own the frigging copyright, Tom."

"Aha!" he said triumphantly as he picked up the sheaf of papers. "So you didn't steal it, you only borrowed it for a little bit. Who else knows the museum keeps photocopies of their volumes?"

"Well, anybody who's worked there, I guess. Plus, André asked, remember, so he knew."

Tom nodded thoughtfully as he went through the pile one page at a time. He took several minutes to peruse the two pages with their bewildering list of random letters. Then he shook his head. "Presumably, this is the handwriting that is supposed to make this book valuable, right? So Fuller's guys must have already taken a look at it, and think there's nothing to pursue."

"And we all know how competent Fuller is," I observed tartly.

He offered me a truffle and I took one. "So what do *you* think?" he said mildly.

I frowned and savored the dense, dark, velvety sphere of chocolate. But it didn't help me come up with a theory. "I want to know why Gerald Eliot was killed. If the motive was really *murder*, and you wanted to make it look like *robbery*, why not take something really valuable from the museum? If the motive was *robbery*, and the object was the cookbook, the killer could have just taken the file, forget about stealing the actual volume. Forget about killing a contractor-guard."

Tom licked chocolate from his fingertip.

"Unless the robber didn't know the photocopies existed."

"Sheesh."

"Tell you what: I agree with you about one thing, Miss G.—I'm convinced that Cameron Burr didn't kill Gerald Eliot. There are just too many loose ends. Eliot was on to, or up to, something. Rustine, despite her lack of forthrightness, has convinced me of that. And whatever Eliot was up to got him killed. And got the museum messed up in the process."

"I just keep thinking about reverse psychology," I said. "General Farquhar used to tell me that a good burglar will always try to make it look as if he *hasn't* broken in, so that it takes longer to discover the crime and longer to find him. But this burglar-killer didn't do that." I hesitated. "Your anonymous hiker who phoned in the tip about Gerald Eliot? Exactly when did he call?"

"Monday afternoon, the eighteenth. We left immediately for Burr's house."

"Okay. Say the true motive is burglary, *not* homicide. You want to make it *look* like *homicide*, though. You need to distract people from the real crime. So you steal stuff you *don't* want and dump it in the trash of the guy you're trying to frame. And the guy you're trying to *frame*—Cameron Burr—is someone you know hated Gerald Eliot. Now, Eliot was guarding the thing you're stealing. The thing you're *really* stealing, not the things you're stealing as *decoys.*"

Tom frowned at my logic and drummed his

fingers on his knees. "If you wanted the original of this cookbook, why not just steal it, and plant some other stolen stuff at the house of the person you're trying to frame? Why kill the guard and try to frame that other person for *murder*? And why, when this was all over, did *André*, now dead, ask for a photocopy of this exact cookbook? It's like the damn thing's the kiss of death."

I shook my head, baffled, as Arch and Julian came through the back door and called for us. I said, "I don't understand it."

With a heavy sigh, Tom got to his feet. "Beats me, too, Miss G. But in the meantime, I've got a counter to set up."

Over my protests, Julian volunteered to work in the dining room to get a few things started for the Harrington party. I reminded him that he was not a servant, he was a member of our family. But he was in the mood for cooking, he insisted, and if he was a member of the family, he should do what he was in the mood for. I was too tired to argue. Instead, I put in a call to Sylvia Bevans. She answered on the third ring, sounding annoyed.

"I'm sorry, Sylvia," I said after identifying myself. "Is it too late to be calling? I just had some historical questions about...Charlie Smythe. Would tomorrow be better? It's very important," I added in the same apologetic tone.

"I do not discuss historical society business at night," she told me crisply. "However, I will call you at precisely seven o'clock tomorrow morning. Is that too early for *you*? I have an early meeting with our board of directors."

253

I told her seven was fine, then hung up and told Julian I'd meet him in the kitchen at six A.M.

"I have something to tell you," Arch announced in the living room, when it was just the two of us. "Lettie and I are going out."

"You just *went* out. To the Chinese place."

"Jeez, Mom." Arch was impatient. "You don't *get* it, do you?"

My son had run up the stairs before I realized he'd told me he finally had a girlfriend.

Chapter 17

I dreamt of a sinister figure spinning strands of caramelized sugar in the cabin kitchen. Then André appeared in his white apron, and the dark figure strangled him with smoking strings of sugar. I tossed uncomfortably and finally rose at dawn, when the slanted light of late summer streamed into our bedroom. Outside, all was hushed. Most songbirds had already fled Aspen Meadow for points south. Their absence and the attendant silence seemed a bitter reminder that cold, short days, blizzard-closed roads, and the increasingly uncertain future of the catering business, all lay ahead.

Work well today, I ordered myself. *Concentrate on food and life, not death.* I finished my yoga routine, pulled on a sweatsuit, and reflected that I certainly had plenty of prep to concentrate on. The dip; André's coq au vin;

rice pilaf; two salads. At least the cake was made.

In the dining room, Julian was already grating Cheddar for the layered Mexican dip. He'd processed a fresh bowl of guacamole and was stirring sour cream to make it ultrasmooth. He smiled a greeting, then washed his hands in the small bathroom between the dining room and the kitchen. Then he filled a container of water for the espresso machine.

"Sorry I was in such a bad mood last night," he offered. "After what I went through with Claire..." He ran steaming water into demitasse cups to heat them, unwilling to pursue the subject of his tragically lost girlfriend from the summer before. "Anyway, I feel so dumb. I really thought that model was interested in me."

"How do you know she wasn't?" I eyed the dip recipe and the jewel-colored heaps of tomatoes, olives, and scallions that Julian had laid out. I pulled out a knife and cutting board.

But the phone rang before he could answer. It wasn't seven yet; could this be Sylvia already? More importantly, where *was* the phone?

"I'm going to start on the coq au vin." Julian hightailed it to the kitchen.

The phone rang again. I finally located the portable extension: Tom had placed it on the end of the sawhorse and someone had laid a towel over it. I nabbed it.

"Goldy, it's Weezie Harrington." Her voice came out in a rush before I could even launch into my customary greeting. "I just wanted to save you some trouble. I mean, I figured you'd be up cooking for my party, and I wanted you to stop—"

On his own portable sawhorse, Julian began beating chicken breasts between sheets of plastic wrap. I pressed the phone to my ear and started slicing the first ripe tomato into juicy, sweet cubes. Pre-party anxiety, I thought with a *frisson* of unease. Happens all the time. "We've already started, Weezie. Don't worry, it's going to be a great dinner. By the way, happy birthday."

"I told you, *stop*," she rasped. "Goldy, I've hired another caterer."

My knife clattered to the cutting board. *Be calm. She's a client. The client is always right.*

"Weezie," I said, attempting to assume a voice of reason and patience, "you *can't* hire another caterer. You've already paid in full. I...I've got all the food here." *The client,* I thought, *is always—*

"I know I have to pay for the food. But, well..." She cleared her throat, as if she were reading from a prepared text and had lost her place. Behind me, Julian thumped relentlessly on the chicken. "I want a refund on the labor and gratuity cost. I have the contract in front of me." Her voice was turning shrill. "Two hundred for the labor and ninety for the gratuity. Please send it today. If I don't receive the refund in four working days, I'll have to contact my lawyer." She hung up.

I gently put down the phone. *Is your lawyer your fiancé, honey-bunch?* Julian had piled up the flattened chicken pieces and was grating black pepper onto a plate loaded with flour. He saw my face and froze. "What?"

"Weezie Harrington's party is canceled." I stared in dismay at the tomatoes. "Or rather, *we're* canceled. The party's still on."

"What? Why?"

"She didn't say why," I murmured. I thought of Arch's tuition that was still unpaid, of Tom's paychecks that were not forthcoming.

"Sit down, Goldy, for crying out loud. You look like you're going to keel over."

I stared around the makeshift workspace. Our dining chairs were stacked, weblike, against the far wall. Sawdust lay in heaps on the floor. Tentacles of wiring stuck out from walls with half their plaster missing. Bent nails littered the corners like so many dead bugs. The phone rang again.

"I'll get it." Julian dived for the portable. "Goldilocks' Catering. You're calling this early, you'd better have a *great* booking for us." He paused. "Oh. No, Goldy can't come to the phone at the moment. This is her assistant."

"Julian, stop!" I cried. "I'm waiting for a call from Sylvia Bevans! Please, it's important!"

He covered the phone with one hand. "It's not Sylvia. Just drink your coffee and let me handle this, okay?"

I reached for my espresso, which was now lukewarm. Too bad it wasn't Marla calling.

I absolutely hated the IRS consuming her every minute. If hot gossip was burning through town on Weezie Harrington's motives for canceling us, Marla would be the first to hear. "*I* can help you," Julian insisted. As the person on the other end spoke, Julian struggled to keep his face composed. "Why?" he asked belligerently. "Oh, yeah, *who*?" After a moment, he said, "We'll just have to see about *that*," and banged the phone down.

I finished the espresso. "Weezie again? What did she want, for me to drive over with her check? If she doesn't get her two hundred and ninety dollars back in the next hour, Andy Fuller will prosecute me and demand it in equal installments of brownies? Or better yet—"

But the pain in Julian's dark eyes brought me up short. Whatever he had just learned from this caller, it was more serious than Weezie's treachery. "That was Edna Hardcastle," he said. "She's canceling us for the wedding reception Saturday. She's hiring another caterer. And get this, she wants a refund on her labor and service charge."

I pictured the bags of wedding reception hors d'oeuvre crowding our freezer. I thought of the checks from Edna and Weezie that had formed the solitary cushion in our checking account. Sometimes people hit you to be cruel. Other times, they just act viciously behind your back. "Did she tell you why she's canceling? Or who her new caterer is?"

"Craig Litchfield. His prices are much lower, she said."

Tom, freshly showered and dressed, came into the room. "Give me an apron and a knife. I want to help. Plus, I figure something must be going on, the phone's ringing so early. Is everything all right?"

I told him what had happened. He was perplexed. "They *both* fired you?"

"Not only did they both fire me—they both want refunds. Two hundred labor for Weezie, plus ninety in service charge. Five hundred labor for Edna, plus two hundred ten for gratuity, since it's figured on the total cost of food and labor." I glanced at Julian, who was slapping the flattened chicken in the flour, then setting the pieces aside, as if nothing had happened.

"So you get to keep the food? What have you got here,"—Tom stared at my printout—"appetizers, chicken, rice, sugar-snap-pea-and-strawberry salad, greens and vinaigrette, cake that you've already made. What are you going to do with the food you have? I'm available to eat it."

But I had already reached for the phone book. It was just before seven o'clock. I looked up Merciful Migrations, punched in the buttons, got a recorded menu that gave me options and another number. I took a deep breath and called that number. A groggy Leah Smythe answered.

"Hello? This is Merciful Migrations. We can't help if you're trying to get rid of elk on your property."

Now *there* was a greeting. "It's Goldy Schulz,

Tom's Layered Mexican Dip

2 avocados, peeled and seeded
2 tablespoons lemon juice
2 tablespoons medium or hot picante sauce
2 tablespoons grated onion
2½ cups regular or fat-free sour cream
16 ounces fat-free spicy black bean dip
2 tomatoes, chopped (about 3 cups)
6 scallions, chopped, including tops
1½ cups sliced pitted black olives
8 ounces regular or low-fat Cheddar cheese, grated
Tortilla chips

Beat the avocados with the lemon juice, picante sauce, grated onion, and ½ cup of the sour cream until the mixture is smooth to make a guacamole. Set aside.

Using 2 large platters or 2 9 x 13-inch pans, place half of the bean dip into the bottom of each pan. Carefully smooth half of the guacamole on top of each bean layer (about 1 cup on each layer). Place 1 cup of the sour cream on top of each guacamole layer.

Layer half of the tomatoes, half of the scallions, half of the olives, and half of the grated cheese into each pan.

Chill the platters and serve them with tortilla chips.

Makes 24 servings

André's Coq au Vin

3 tablespoons butter
1 carrot, diced
1 medium onion, chopped
2 garlic cloves, crushed through a press
3 tablespoons chopped fresh parsley
1 cup dry red wine
½ cup beef bouillon
1 tablespoon tomato paste or catsup
1 tablespoon cornstarch
4 skinless, boneless chicken breasts
     (approximately 1½ pounds)
1 tablespoon flour
½ teaspoon salt
¼ teaspoon freshly ground black pepper
1 tablespoon olive oil

In a large skillet, melt the butter and slowly cook the chopped carrot, onion, garlic, and parsley until the onion is soft and translucent, approximately 10 to 20 minutes. Add the wine, bouillon, and tomato paste or catsup. Simmer, covered, over low heat for 20 minutes. Stir 2 tablespoons water into the cornstarch until smooth. Mix into the wine mixture and stir

until the sauce is thick and clear. Set aside, covered, over very low heat, while you prepare the chicken.

Pound the chicken breasts between sheets of plastic wrap until they are approximately ½ inch thick. Mix together the flour, salt, and pepper, and dredge the chicken breasts in this mixture.

Heat the oil in a large, heavy skillet. Over medium-high heat, sauté the chicken breasts for 2 minutes per side, or until almost cooked through. Place the chicken breasts in the wine mixture, cover, and cook over medium-low heat another 6 to 10 minutes, until the chicken is just cooked through. Serve immediately.

Makes 4 servings

the caterer." Leah groaned, and I took a deep breath. Was I ready to step into André's job? Probably not. But I was going to give it a go, anyway. For André and for myself. "Listen, Leah, I have a lot of wonderful food here, and I was wondering if you were still looking for meals for the shoot."

"Goldy," interjected Tom. "Forget it."

I ignored him. On the other end of the receiver, masculine-sounding mumbling stopped Leah from responding immediately. She covered the mouthpiece, then came back. "This is just like the other guy," she said drowsily. "He'd do free catering for me if I'd vote for him for the Soirée. I told him I didn't have a say in it. The votes belong to Marla, Weezie, and Edna. I don't have a *vote*, Goldy."

My skin went cold. "I would never try to bribe you, Leah. Nothing I do is free, but my services *are* reasonably priced. You need a caterer and I'm already familiar with the site and setup. The food will be ready when you need it. How many more days of shooting do you have?"

"It's Wednesday," she said with a yawn. "Two, if nothing goes wrong. Today and tomorrow. Stretch into Friday if there's a screwup." She sighed, as if what she really wanted was to go back to sleep. "All right, you can have the booking. But you'll need to abide by André's original contract."

"I may not be able to provide the exact food he was offering to you. Only the price."

She yawned again. "Just a minute." More

muffled conversation. "If you can be there by ten to do a breakfast-type coffee break and then lunch for fifteen people, that would be great."

"No problem."

"I'll call Rufus and have him open the gate for you. What time should he be there?"

"Eight-thirty. And, is that Ian Hood with you there, by any chance? I'd like to talk to him later today about the voting for the Soirée."

Leah covered the phone, then returned to say Ian could chat with me after the lingerie shots today. Super, I thought, hanging up. If they wanted a coffee break during the lingerie shoot, I had just the recipe for the occasion.

"We're on," I informed Julian and Tom. "Coffee break and lunch. There's fresh fruit in the walk-in we can slice. We'll pick up yogurt on the way, and I'll make cakes on the griddle when we get there. In Scotland they call a griddle a 'girdle,' but it's really just pancakes. Girdle cakes for a lingerie shoot. Pretty cute, eh?"

"I don't like this," Tom commented as he pulled out strawberries to slice. "I don't want the two of you going up to that cabin unaccompanied."

The phone rang again and we all looked at it.

"It might be Sylvia," I said. The way this morning was going, she would be calling to say Litchfield had won the tasting.

"I'll let you know if it is," Tom offered as

he hugged the strawberry bowl to his chest and snagged the phone from the sawhorse. After a moment of silence, he put down the bowl and pulled out his ubiquitous spiral notebook.

"Go ahead," he ordered. He wrote furiously. "Thanks. You free today?" A pause. "Think you could go out to Gerald Eliot's former workplace? A cabin in Blue Spruce. Goldy's catering up there and it'd make me feel better if you'd stay with her." I shook my head furiously; Julian groaned. Tom raised an eyebrow at me and grinned. "Sure. Come by our place about seven forty-five. Oh, wait. Could you pick up a couple of gallons of fat-free vanilla yogurt on the way?"

"I'm going to the cabin, too," Arch announced from the doorway. "Lettie might be there. I want to talk to her about my radio equipment."

"You are *not* going," I said firmly. Why was everyone in this house up before seven on a summer morning? How were Julian and I going to get the prep done with all these interruptions? "They're doing a lingerie shoot today, and Lettie's too young to wear lingerie. And if she isn't and she is in the shoot, it would not be appropriate for you to be there."

"Call her up and invite her over for lunch," Tom interjected wisely, while Arch was still trying to puzzle out what I'd just said. "I'll be working on the kitchen. You can have sandwiches on the deck. Eleven-thirty."

"I sent her an e-mail about my ham radio

equipment, and she can't *wait* to see it," Arch said earnestly. "Get this—her dad taught her how to put an antibugging device on her phone."

"Wow," the three of us said simultaneously. Arch vanished up the stairs to shower and agonize over his clothing for the day.

Thick, sweet slices of strawberry fell before Tom's expert knife. "That was Boyd," he announced. "He told me I passed the lie detector test." When we exclaimed our congratulations he held up the knife to stop us. "That only means I wasn't *consciously* compromising an investigation. But I did get the background we were looking for." He deftly cored the pineapple. "First off, Boyd interviewed that cabdriver you talked to, Goldy. The one who drove André out to the cabin Monday morning. Nothing unusual about the chef, just a lot of grousing about how he was serving more gourmet dishes for skinny people who wouldn't understand or appreciate his food. No complaining of tightness in the chest, pain down his arm, anything."

I could just imagine it. "Did he talk about the food being done for that day? Or why he was coming early?"

"Yup." Tom frowned, gripped the juicy pineapple, and began carving the sides. "According to the cabbie, André insisted the food was already done. But the chef had some 'other work' to do that meant he needed to get to the cabin early. He just didn't say what kind of work. As to Merciful Migrations and the historical society? The society's in pretty good shape. They've got a few big donors who keep 'em going. Ian Hood's group is another story, though. He supports most of their work with the fashion photography, but he's been losing bookings because he's so hard to get along with, and so many photography studios are opening in Phoenix. Leah Smythe? She's land-rich only. Plus she works for the studio and for the charity for very little remuneration. Donations and the money from the Soirée make up the rest of the budget. According to Boyd, if Ian stopped supporting the organization, the elk would be on their own."

"Hmm." Would it be so bad if the elk were left to fight developers on their own? *Probably*, my inner voice replied.

"I asked Boyd to find out just how land-rich Leah was. He said he'd have to check—"

The phone rang again. "Fourth time's the charm," I announced, and politely gave my greeting into the receiver.

"This is Sylvia Bevans, returning your call."

"Oh, *thank* you," I gushed. Should I get her opinion on Craig Litchfield's mode of stealing clients? No: what I really needed to know had to do with a murder, not any kind of theft. "Listen, Sylvia, I called for some historical background, if you don't mind. I'm doing catering out at the Merciful Migrations cabin today. I've become so fascinated with Charlie Smythe," I raved as Tom rolled his eyes, "I was wondering if you could tell me a bit about him. Do you have time for that?"

"Well. I suppose. Of course, I'm always glad when Aspen Meadow people want to know their roots. It certainly is more important than adding extra lanes to the highway, which seems to be the main area of interest anymore. What do you want to know about Charlie?"

"Everything," I said as I hit buttons on my espresso machine to fuel myself with more caffeine.

"I presume you know that Charlie Smythe was the grandfather to Leah Smythe and Weezie Smythe Harrington, yes?" When I *mm-hmm*ed, she went on: "Charlie Smythe settled at the cabin after the War Between the States, which is what *he* called it, as a member of the losing side. Like a lot of restless army men, Charlie came west, but only after he'd scammed ten thousand dollars off his aunt in Kentucky. Ten thousand was big money in 1865, my dear."

Julian was peeling kiwi. Tom dumped the sun-yellow pineapple chunks into the big blue bowl we were using. He picked up a cantaloupe and began slicing off the ribbed skin. I reached for the bananas. "He stole ten thousand from his aunt? The creep."

"Yes, I'm sorry to say, and the story is that the poor woman died of grief. And Charlie was no one-time scam artist. He became addicted to thievery. It kept life interesting, I suppose." She sighed deeply, as if she were discussing a piece of lovely china that had been carelessly broken.

"Back up, Sylvia, okay?" I sipped the foam

from the espresso. "What about this aunt? She had ten thousand dollars in *cash*?"

"Oh, no," Sylvia said sternly, as if I'd flunked a history class. "She'd buried a strongbox of gold coins before the war, but after Appomattox she was afraid the victorious Yankees would find them. Charlie promised to deposit the coins in a bank, and that was the last anyone in *Kentucky* saw of him! Next thing you know, it's 1866 and Charlie and his wife, Winnie—grandmother to the two Smythe girls—are buying land in Colorado with a whole lot of gold coins. They purchased a thousand acres in Aspen Meadow and twenty-seven hundred in Blue Spruce. Wait a moment while I pour myself some tea, would you?"

"Sure." I was the last one to deny folks caffeine.

"Where was I?" she asked a moment later. "Oh, yes, Charlie's land. The Aspen Meadow acreage was to be an investment. The Blue Spruce land was where Charlie was going to have his ranch and his timber business, according to his boasts. He cut down trees, built the cabin, and got bored. So he abandoned Winnie and their small son Vic, the story goes. Charlie turned to crime, alas. He stole horses in the early years, then robbed stagecoaches in the later ones. He ended up trying to rob a bank. That's how he was caught, in the end. He was in his sixties, if you can imagine. And then he died," she concluded sadly, "at the age of seventy, in Leavenworth, during the flu epidemic of 1918."

Puzzled, I stopped slicing. Something wasn't

right. "In the letter to his wife, he waxes euphoric about the rural life they shared."

"You don't need to tell *me* the contents of that letter, Goldy. Perhaps he honestly repented, and missed his family. Prison does that sometimes. Now I must go."

Prison brings repentance? I wondered as I replaced the receiver. I thought of The Jerk, and shook my head.

"So what's the deal?" Julian asked impatiently, eyeing the clock. We had a little over an hour before we needed to be at the cabin. As I was giving the two of them a summary of what Sylvia had just told me, the doorbell rang.

It was Sergeant Boyd, a half hour early, no less.

"Escort service," he said cheerily when I opened the door. His black crew cut stood up in short, clean spikes. He was wearing a white shirt and dark pants. A white apron hugged his huge belly.

"Nice getup, Sergeant."

"We aim to please, ma'am."

With assurances from Tom that he would put in the first batch of kitchen windows in our absence, we packed up the foodstuffs for coffee break and lunch—formerly Weezie's birthday dinner—and took off. I had written refund checks for Weezie and Edna; when I dropped them into a mailbox on Main Street,

I murmured a prayer for that elusive psychological phenomenon, *perspective.*

A breeze stirred the trees as Boyd, Julian, and I headed out to Blue Spruce in my van. The air was balmy, the sky porcelain blue. On the far mountains, a breath of early autumn gold stained the swaths of aspen trees. *Time to start over,* I told myself.

I asked Boyd if he could tell me anything else about the department's interview with the cabdriver who'd brought André to the shoot Monday morning. Boyd replied that he'd told Tom all there was to tell. He himself had never officially been on this case. If he had, he wouldn't be able to come out to help today. Undercover, more or less, he concluded solemnly, so that no one recognized him. Well, great, I thought as I frowned and tried to process what Sylvia had told me.

Charlie Smythe built the cabin and got bored...became a thief, died in Leavenworth.... But what could any of this have to do with Gerald Eliot, really? How could it affect what Rustine had told us, that *weapon,* that unknown *something Gerald had found that was going to make him rich?* What had happened to the land and the cabin after Charlie Smythe died, before Leah and Weezie inherited it? And what did any of this have to do with André burning himself, overdosing on his medication, and dying of hypotension? As we pulled up to the dirt road to the cabin, I realized I had no more clue to what was going on than I'd had when I'd broken into the Homestead yesterday. So much for amateur sleuths. But I was not going to give up. I was going to be in the cabin where André died, and I was going to poke around and ask some questions. Even if I had to be obnoxious or bribe people with cake. Preferably the latter.

At the gate, Rufus Driggle greeted us with a wave. He was wearing worn cowboy boots, torn jeans, and a misbuttoned red-checkered shirt. A jaunty scarlet bandanna was tied around his neck. It didn't match his scruffy red beard. He peered into the van.

"I see you have a new helper."

"Boyd the Baker," the fat sergeant replied matter-of-factly. Julian suppressed laughter. "At your service."

"Rufus?" I asked sweetly when he'd closed the gate and squeezed into the van, "when we finish up the coffee break, could we chat for a few minutes? I'm looking for people to taste some poppy seed cake I made for another assignment."

His cheeks flooded with color. "Uh, sure. I love poppy seed cake."

We parked in the lot, lifted the first of our boxes, and headed past the elephant-shaped boulder, across the rushing creek, and up the stone steps to the cabin. As he heaved up one of the boxes, Rufus informed us that only two models would be working that day. Neither had arrived yet. The independent contractors—a stylist and hair and makeup peo-ple—were already in place. This was good news. If we were lucky, Rufus went on, the day's shoot should end soon after lunch. I smiled, thanked him, and told him not to forget about being a taste-tester.

While Boyd and Julian unloaded supplies, I made a large pot of coffee, set out sugar and cream, and eyed the uneven, dusty wooden floor. This, presumably, was where André had clutched his failing heart one last time, and fallen. There was no blood or other sign of what had happened. I opened all the old wooden drawers and cabinets: they scraped, stuck, and yielded nothing more than rusted spatulas, broken knives, mismatched measuring cups, and a few dented pans. Next I eyed the stove: it ran off a propane tank, as was common in the mountains. The burners all faithfully produced circles of knobby blue flames. What had burned André? I didn't have a clue. Finally, I examined the sink and the wall above it. I ran my fingers over the rough edges of glue and plywood, Gerald Eliot's legacy of yet another unfinished job. Something looked different about the plywood from the time we'd catered here before....

The sudden commanding voice of Hanna Klapper made me jump. "Looking for something?"

I turned. Carrying a black briefcase, Hanna was a vision in black: T-shirt, jeans, bandanna, and black tooled cowboy boots. *The Pony Express meets Polo, at a funeral parlor.* Only Hanna wasn't in mourning; she was being chic. With her free hand, she hitched precision-cut dark hair behind one ear. I said,

"No, just looking at the mess. Gerald Eliot worked for me, too."

"Well, then. You must be *very* familiar with his inability to get a job done!" Her voice was as severely clipped as her hair. I sighed: No matter what Hanna said to me, even when she was trying to be jovial, I felt an edge of criticism. It wasn't my *fault* I'd hired Gerald, was it? Hanna went on: "I need to talk to you about the schedule for the day."

"Sure. How about some coffee? I brought you a cup and saucer." Hanna accepted a china cup of coffee—with a matching saucer I had brought specially for her, since I remembered from my docent days that she would decline any hot drink brought to her in a mug—and ladled in sugar, then poured in cream. "Hanna? Before we get into the schedule, there's something I just have to ask you, I mean if you don't mind. It's sort of in the social life department."

Her facial expression became coy. "Well, Goldy, what kind of problem are you having? I am probably not the one who can help."

"Well, really, it's about Gerald Eliot," I said hastily, as I got out the buttermilk and flour mixtures for the girdle cakes. "Did Leah really fire him for having an affair with one of the models? You see, my assistant, Julian Teller, is interested in one of the young women, and I didn't want Julian to get into trouble..." I let my voice trail off.

Hanna sighed. "Yes, that is why he was fired. He was a lustful, secretive man. Of

275

course, he did not confide in me." She put down her coffee and swung her briefcase up to the counter. I was surprised to see strong, rippling muscles in her arms, quite a different appearance from her modest blouse-of-a-pioneer-woman look during her time at the Homestead. "I *tried* to be his friend, which is what I told the police. But I think I made him nervous. You know, there are some people you can joke with, some you cannot."

"Ah," I said, trying to imagine *anyone* who could joke with Hanna. "How far did he get before he was fired? And what was he doing with this wall, anyway?" I pointed to the plywood.

She motioned to her cup, which meant I was supposed to pour more coffee into it, which I did. She sipped some of her drink, then clinked the cup down in the saucer. "Just outside where that window was situated, there used to be a small stand of pine trees that obscured the view of the mountains. In the late seventies, the pine beetles destroyed them. So Leah had the trees taken out. Then Bobby Whitaker had the bright idea to put in large windows here, so a person in the kitchen could see the mountains. Leah hired Gerald to tear out the wall and put in windows. But he was fired once he'd torn down the wall."

I fingered the edges of the wood, where dried glue protruded roughly from the edge next to the old plastered wall. "Why was the old wall plastered instead of being made of logs?"

She sighed impatiently. "Don't you remember the exhibit we had on log cabins at the museum?" I shook my head. She said, "It's all that *butter* clogging up your mind, Goldy!" I smiled brightly as she continued: "These old cabins are just made of trees, laid on their sides, stacked, and plastered. Inside the cabin, for some living areas such as the kitchen, the early builders would cover the logs with home-made two-by-fours. Then they put up diagonal lath strips, and covered the strips with three coats of plaster. Eliot pulled it all out. He made a terrible mess." She touched her temple as if the thought of Gerald Eliot had brought on a sudden headache.

"A terrible mess," I repeated, staring at the plywood. Finally I saw what I seemed not to have noticed the week before. Or had something changed since then? Along the corner nearest the stove, the wood was compressed and broken, as if Gerald had glued the plywood over the opening, then decided to pry it open to do something else. Near the corner, he'd hammered in a finishing nail.

"What happened here?" I asked. "It's like he glued the plywood in place, then decided to move it."

Hanna peered at the place I was indicating. "I don't know what stage of construction Gerald was in when he was fired," she said, "and I told the police that." She waved her cup dismissively. "Gerald became secretive after he found what Leah's grandfather hid in the wall."

"What?"

"Oh, yes," said Hanna calmly. "One day I was out here with Ian and Leah, planning this shoot. Gerald found the gun that Charlie Smythe had hidden in the wall before he put up the lath strips and coated them with plaster."

"Gerald pulled out a hidden gun?" I asked, nonplussed.

Hanna's fingers waggled at the wall. "In there. Can you imagine? How was he going to get a weapon out quickly, if he actually needed it to protect his family?" Something flickered in Hanna's dark eyes. "It took Gerald a week of destruction just to find that antique rifle. Although I was impressed, of course, that that old criminal Charlie Smythe had taken such care to wrap his rifle so well in oilcloth. It was ready to go out and shoot somebody with! I mean, if that's what you wanted to do."

Chapter 18

"Did you all tell the police Gerald found a rifle?" I asked breathlessly.

"Of course we did." She tilted her head. "Leah has it hung out in the living room. Haven't you seen it? Of course, *I* wanted it for the museum. You must try to talk her into donating it, Goldy. No one will ever see it, way out here in Blue Spruce."

The Winchester. Yes, of course I had noticed the rifle on the wall.

Hanna narrowed her eyes. "Leah kept asking, Why would an outlaw hide his rifle in a wall?"

But of course *I* did know. Or I thought I did. Tom had concealed his extra Colt .45 and his own Winchester '94 behind a false wall he'd built in our garage. Then, if someone broke in, his valuable firearms wouldn't be stolen. Or be in the hands of someone who could use them for crime. But it didn't take a week to get to those weapons; Tom's rifle could be accessed by removing a rectangle of drywall in mere minutes.

To Hanna I said, "That was it? The rifle was the only thing Eliot found in the wall?"

"I think so." She shrugged, a tiny gesture of impatience that I interpreted as *we need to get on with our business*. "Now, we need to talk about the schedule for the shoot," she reminded me. When I nodded, she pushed her cup and saucer away, pulled out a black loose-leaf notebook from the dark briefcase, and hooked black half-glasses over her nose. This woman's fashion palette was so limited, she might as well have worked for a mortician.

The somber notebook held about twenty plastic-encased pages. Hanna flipped through the sheets, each of which contained a photocopied sketch of that page's layout in this publication, the first of three Christmas catalogs that P & G would be mailing to its customers. Hand-drawn outlines of bed and table linens, jewelry, shoes, belts, and handbags, splashed across the accessories section. Ian had finished up the still-life shots the first week, before André came on board, Hanna told me. The proofs for these pictures were paper-clipped onto the sketches.

Then came the fashion sketches, with printed notes about what shot should fill each section. *Santa in chair with boy in reindeer pajamas. Yellow bikini & blue maillot for cruise section.* Snugged within each plastic envelope were three or four flash-lit Polaroid shots of the items to be modeled. Suspended from coat hangers, the cruise outfits, nightwear, chinos, sweaters, blouses, coats, and dresses looked painfully unglamorous. Hanna flipped through to show three pages of women's clothes, two of men's. Each page represented a day of shooting. There were only two pages left. Barring any more equipment failures, the P & G Christmas shoot should finally finish by the next day, Thursday, or, worst-case scenario, Friday. André had been making between six and eight hundred dollars a day, depending on how many people showed up for each meal. I closed my eyes. I would have preferred that André be alive, of course. But I'd known him long and well enough to be sure he would have been glad that I was the one taking over his booking. I also knew he would have rejoiced that this new income would be enough for me to recoup the money lost to the Harrington and Hardcastle refunds.

To my surprise, I'd recognized the outfits from the two pages with Santa and the children. Even I had to admit these pedestrian outfits had looked pretty good when worn by adorable kids. Especially when those kids were being visited by Santa himself! The trick, of course, lay in seeing that the clothes were still the same bland outfits. Most folks, of course, were fooled. And that was why models were paid so much. It was also, I reflected sadly, why bad caterers—who only care about presentation and not the quality or taste of their food—were able to stay in business. If I ever resorted to that kind of cheating, I hoped to be stripped of my spoons.

Hanna pointed to the lingerie page. She explained that a black push-up bra with matching panties, a white lace bra and half-slip, and a pastel green granny-style nightgown were to be the outfits of the day. Zowie! I was *so* glad I hadn't brought Arch. I told Hanna we were going to offer girdle cakes at the coffee break.

"That's pancakes to you and me," I translated.

"Fine, then. But at least now you are aware there will only be today and tomorrow or Friday for catering. Depending on how things go. So, that's it. I'll take more coffee, if you don't mind."

I poured her a refill and commented, "You seem to manage the uncertainty of when you'll be shooting pretty well."

Her eyes glimmered with seriousness. Her thin lips set in a slight scowl. "I need to work. So I have learned to deal with people's idiosyncrasies. Or at least, I make a very good show of working around people's weaknesses," she said proudly.

Oh, *right,* I thought, remembering her caustic words to Bobby Whitaker during the cattle call. I said, "Do you miss working with the folks at the museum?"

"No, actually." Without warning her voice turned bitter. "I am *sorry* for all the years I gave to the Homestead, with no thanks from the historical society, and certainly no *monetary* appreciation. I know you're keenly aware of how divorce can leave you financially stranded, Goldy. I certainly did *not* expect my husband to leave, forcing me to live from paycheck to paycheck in my midfifties. I did *not* expect to have to buy a used station wagon from a person selling it by the side of the road. I did *not* expect to be living in a tiny apartment at the Swiss Inn, that my parents used to own! And of course, I did not expect to pay a lawyer more for an hour of his time than I spend on a month's groceries." She gave me a mirthless, knowing smile. "And I guess in my heart, I hoped the historical society would give me a little monetary gift when I left. Of all people, *I* am aware of the funds they can spare. But the society did not see fit to do so."

"It's tough," I murmured sympathetically. When you suffer through a postdivorce reduction in circumstances, it's a miracle if your attitude *doesn't* turn to vinegar.

"I was lucky to find this job," Hanna went on, her voice defiant. Her tone was threaded with the old authority. The implied message was: *And I'll be damned if anyone's going to take* this job *away from me.*

"Hanna, I am happy for you." Impulsively,

I hugged her, but when she remained as stiff as a board, I realized an embrace was a bad idea. I stepped back. "Did you enjoy working with André? He helped me become a caterer back when I, too, was lucky to find a job. Did you like him?"

She twisted her mouth to one side as if trying to decide how to say something negative. "Oh, Goldy. André was an old man with a lot of stories to tell. He told them whether people were interested or not. I would tease him because he talked too much. When he would tie up one of the photo people with his chatter, then you had *two* people who were not working." She picked up her briefcase, as if I had lured her into the same idleness. "My only concern has to be that the shoot run efficiently." She marched out of the kitchen before I could ask just which photo people André had tied up with his chatter.

As soon as she left, I asked Boyd about the rifle. He said Fuller's people had looked at the Winchester, and found that it was clean of fingerprints and had not been fired. I told him what Rustine had said about Gerald's claim that he'd found a weapon that would make them rich. Boyd said a gun only made you rich if you used it to rob a bank. *Great.*

By nine-thirty, Boyd and Julian had set out a crystal bowl mounded with homemade granola and another containing a glistening array of sliced strawberries and kiwi. Crystal pitchers contained cream and skim milk. Carafes of coffee, decaf, and hot water were poised above lit cans of Sterno. I nestled assorted juices and waters into a table-size ice bath. Julian and Boyd had scuttled back to the kitchen, claiming they needed to assemble lunch. I suppressed a chuckle. Apparently, both men were embarrassed to appear openly interested in Rustine's lingerie shoot.

They would have been disappointed, I reflected, after I watched Rustine go through her paces. The mother of all granny gowns concealed everything. Since I'd just seen the Polaroid of the gown hanging forlornly on its coat hanger, I knew it was quite ordinary, despite Rustine's coy looks, dipped shoulder, and hands on hips. Behind his camera, Ian prompted Rustine with *That's it, baby. Keep it coming. That's it. Don't lose it now.* Rustine simpered and kept moving through her poses. I wondered if the lace-trimmed gown could survive the restless insomnia a worrying cop's wife endured every night, while waiting for her husband to come home with his bulletproof vest intact.

Back in the kitchen, I put these thoughts out of my mind and returned to that old soul-restorer: working with food. I hummed as I mixed the cottage cheese, buttermilk, and egg mixture with the sifted dry ingredients to make the girdle cakes. On the griddle, they would rise, develop a crunchy exterior and featherlight interior, and bring joy to the heart, no matter what you were wearing.

"I'm not staying out there to serve," Julian announced fiercely, his cheeks pink. "That blond girl, Yvonne, is mean as a skunk. When

I asked her what she was doing today, she told me to trot on back to the kitchen and mind my own business. At least Rustine *pretends* to like me."

I murmured sympathetically and skimmed oil onto my electric griddle. I was studiously avoiding conversation with Rustine. I did not want anyone at the shoot even to suspect that she wanted me to act as her informal P.I. I hustled the griddle out to the central room, set it on a table, and plugged it into one of the numerous crooked wall outlets. Yvonne sauntered across the set in black bra and panties while Ian fixed his lens and swore. I frowned and remembered Rustine's words from the first day: *The blonde's…wearing flesh-colored falsies.* Was Yvonne dishonestly stuffed now? And how far had I come from pondering questions of eschatology while catering to the Diocesan Board of Theological Examiners?

Ignoring these mental digressions, I retrieved the batter and waited for the signal from Ian and company to start heating the skillet. With any luck, the bra shoot would only take twenty minutes. But the voices on the far side of the room rose suddenly, as did the level of activity. There was general scurrying and knocking into chairs. My heart sank as I gave the batter a gentle stir and wondered if we were in for another ruined meal.

"I told you so, didn't I?" muttered Rustine at my elbow.

I jumped and barely avoided spilling the batter. "For heaven's sake, Rustine! You told me what?" No *wonder* André had a heart attack, I thought uncharitably, as I righted the bowl.

Rustine, now clad in a tightly cinched sky-blue terry-cloth robe, gestured toward the far side of the room. Yvonne, in the lacy bra and panties, sat slumped on a chair beside one of the flats that formed the artificially lit three-sided stage that had been constructed for the day's shoot. What—mountains were too suggestive a backdrop for department store lingerie? In any event, Yvonne blended in with the flats, which were painted a very light, neutral beige. Hanna, Ian, Rufus, and Leah were huddled in a hasty conference. Behind them, the day-contractors—female stylist, younger male hairdresser, older male makeup artist—shook their heads in bemusement.

"She doesn't have any cleavage!" Rustine whispered. "She may be blond, but it's not enough. She can't fill that bra." Rustine lifted her chin and shook her red hair in triumph. Up close, I could again see that her face was flawlessly, if heavily, made up. "They're going to *have* to use me. That's great, because we need the extra money."

"Why will you make extra?" I asked innocently.

She stared at me as if I had just offered to don the black bra and underwear myself. "Because more *skin* shows in a lingerie shot. They *have* to pay extra, and especially for yours truly, who will now be used for both shots."

"Ah." I cocked my head toward the set. "How close would you say we are to the coffee break?"

She frowned, then assessed the conference.

"Dammit!" Ian was yelling at Rufus. "Why can't you check out the equipment before we start?" Ian stomped toward his tripod, then tripped. Flailing wildly, he crashed to the floor. "How many times," he shouted angrily at Rufus, "have I told you to get rid of Eliot's damn air compressor? Are you brain-dead? Were you deprived of oxygen at birth, Driggle? Get that damn thing out of here!"

Rufus, head bent in embarrassment, picked up the heavy compressor and struggled across the great room. He passed me without a glance, pushed the compressor against the wall outside the kitchen, then hustled back to Ian's side to see about the problematic equipment. Ian's cursing got more colorful. Still slumped in her chair, Yvonne was scowling at her gleaming fingertips.

Rustine continued as if nothing had happened: "The coffee break will be earlier than if they'd done the shot. They'll break in about five minutes." Time to cook, I thought. I turned on the skillet. "Getting me ready will take at least half an hour." Rustine sniffed the batter, then whispered, "Have you been able to figure anything out about Gerald?"

I considered her question as I dipped a measuring cup into the bowl, then poured

Lingerie-Shoot Girdle Cakes

1 egg
1½ cups or more buttermilk
½ cup cottage cheese
1½ cups all-purpose flour
2 teaspoons baking powder
½ teaspoon baking soda
1 cup blueberries, plus more for serving
Butter and maple syrup for serving

Oil a large skillet or griddle (the Scots call it a "girdle," hence the name) and preheat it over medium heat.

In a large bowl, beat the egg lightly. Stir in the buttermilk and cottage cheese.

Sift together the flour, baking powder, and baking soda. Sift again into the egg mixture. Stir in the dry mixture very lightly, mixing only enough to combine. If the mixture is too dry, stir in a small amount of additional buttermilk. Gently stir in the blueberries.

Scoop the batter into pancakes into the hot, well-oiled pan. After the cakes have set on one side, lightly loosen them with a metal spatula to make sure they do not stick. When the edges of the cakes appear dry, flip the cakes carefully to cook until cooked through and golden brown on both sides. This can take from 2 to 5 minutes per side.

Serve immediately with butter and maple syrup or more fresh blueberries.

Makes 8 to 12 cakes

the contents out on the steaming griddle. The pale golden batter sputtered invitingly. This was not the time to get into a discussion of the Winchester, I decided. "Is there anything you haven't told me?" I asked.

She blushed. "Like what? The names of other remodeling clients who were mad at Gerald?"

"*Anything* else. About that weapon, say."

"Break!" called Ian. He turned to catch my eye. I grabbed my spatula and hastily loosened the undersides of the sizzling cake.

"Rustine!" cried Leah. "Dressing room!"

Rustine couldn't conceal her grin as she scampered down the hall. Yvonne rose and stalked out behind her. As she went by, I noticed a fat roll of toilet paper tucked under the bra's back strap. The toilet paper roll pulled the bra tight across Yvonne's breasts, but apparently, not tightly, or alluringly, enough. The black panties, smooth as cream over her abdomen, had been pinned in a multitude of folds on her buttocks. *For crying out loud!* I reflected as she passed me. *No wonder* lingerie never fits me right!

For the next twenty minutes I was occupied flipping and serving girdle cakes, which I heaped onto the famished workers' plates next to their bowls of granola and fruit. Yvonne and Rustine did not choose to indulge in the coffee break goodies, despite the low-fat offerings. Leah reappeared from the cabin bedroom used for hair, makeup, and dressing only long enough to snag herself a bowl of granola and duck into the second bedroom, the space devoted to storage. She re-emerged with a rack of jewelry and whisked back to Rustine. For their part, the hair and makeup fellows devoured their girdle cakes, then answered Leah's call to tend to Rustine. I had only peeked in on the hair-and-makeup-and-dressing room once. The endless mirrored reflections of hot curlers, hair spray, honey-beige foundation, and racks of clothing had made me dizzy.

"This is really good," commented Bobby Whitaker at my elbow. Wearing a bright yellow shirt, black pants, and black-and-gold striped tie, he looked like a handsome, if somewhat plump, bumblebee.

"I didn't expect to see you here."

"Yeah, I'm always turning up! Didn'ja expect me?" he crowed.

"Oh, really? How did you happen to turn up at the Hibbard house right after André died?" I ventured calmly.

He blushed and straightened. "High Creek Realty has an agreement with the morgue. Look, I'm sorry we had that little argument after your teacher died," he added ruefully. His curly dark hair fell forward provocatively. "I'm under a lot of pressure to get a sale, Miss Caterer Lady. One thing I need to do is check out all the dead people. I'm supposed to see if their survivors want to sell, and if the house has a designer kitchen. Sometimes my showing up doesn't go very well."

"Forget it." I heaped a spill of girdle cakes

on his plate. "Did you see André at all when he was here?"

He shook his head and dug into the cakes with gusto. "This is my first day out here since the cattle call. I brought some papers for Leah. But she says they've had some scheduling glitches, so she's going to use me tomorrow or the next day, after all."

I raised my eyebrows. "Congratulations. So, do you prefer modeling or real estate?"

"Oh, modeling, no question. Lotta money. But I'm getting out of it now. I've got some other things going on." His eyes flickered toward Rustine, who was striding confidently toward the set. Now *she* wore the black bra pulled tight across ample breasts by the toilet paper roll. The black panties had been nipped and tucked into place. She stretched her neck and assumed a provocative stance between the lighted flats. As Ian cued her, she began to move, smile, cock her hip, and otherwise seduce the flashing camera. Drawn by the action, Bobby moved away.

I picked up the coffee break detritus—there wasn't much—and hauled it out to the kitchen. Boyd relieved me of the tray of dirty dishes and filled a sink with hot, soapy water. I felt thankful for his diligence in maintaining the charade, especially when it extended to cleanup.

Julian had finished plating an extra appetizer: *crostini*, small rounds of toasted baguette generously smeared with goat cheese and topped with a fat, spicy walnut that would provide crunch. The three of us quickly divvied up the task of heating up the Harrington birthday dinner to serve outside. We devoted the first deck table to the plates and appetizers: the layered Mexican dip, chips, and *crostini*. The adjoining table squeaked under its load of coq au vin, rice, and sugar-snap-pea-and-strawberry salad. For dessert, I sliced the orange poppy seed cake while Julian and Boyd carried out the beverage bottles, silverware, and glasses.

I finished my work, hefted my tray, then stared across the rushing creek to the sand-bank. I tried not to think of André directing the cabdriver to carry his boxes across the bridge for the last time. Tomorrow afternoon was the memorial service. An ache swelled in my throat and I hurried back inside with three pieces of the cake wrapped in plastic for Rufus.

He was waiting by the door to the kitchen.

"Ready for tasting?" I asked merrily.

"Am I ever. Gotta get this thing back there. Ian's splitting a gut 'cuz he keeps tripping over this thing"—he bent over and started scooting the compressor along the hallway, grunting mightily—"and of course"—he scooted and grunted, scooted and grunted—"it'll be *my* job to put a notice in the paper and sell it."

I followed him into the empty storage room and watched as he savagely kicked the compressor toward a corner cluttered with grotesque skeletons of photographic equipment. When he turned to face me, I offered him the cake. His large, somewhat dirty hands delicately pulled apart the plastic wrap, then broke off a huge chunk, which he popped into his mouth with glee.

"Tastes pretty good to me!" he said after the third chew. "Who didn't like it?"

I sat in an ancient rocking chair that was missing an arm. "Nobody, really. Listen, Rufus, do you know much about Leah and this cabin?"

He snorted. "Well, I should. I've had to listen to Leah talk about this place these last five years. Why?"

I shrugged. "Just interested, I guess. I used to work at the museum as a docent, but I really never knew much about the Smythes apart from Weezie and Leah having land." *This cabin,* I thought. *This cabin links the deaths of Gerald and André.* "What do you know about this place?"

Rufus took another thoughtful bite of cake. "Nobody ever asks me anything. You know, I'm just the stupid equipment guy."

"*I'm* asking you."

"Well, you know Charlie Smythe died in that big flu epidemic at the end of World War One?" I nodded. "Charlie wasn't in the war, though, he was in prison. His wife, Winnie, died in the same epidemic. As to this cabin, well, Charlie and Winnie Smythe left it to their son, name of Victor." He took a bite of cake and looked at the ceiling. "Let's see, now. Vic Smythe married a woman named Carrie, and she was the mother of Leah and Weezie. When Vic died of emphysema about twenty-five years ago, it turned out he'd left Weezie a parcel of land that was a thousand acres. Now it's called Flicker Ridge. Fancy pants."

I nodded. This I did know, but I didn't want to interrupt Rufus. Weezie Smythe Harrington, a few years after receiving her land inheritance, had given her gently sloping acreage to her much-beloved, unfaithful, and ultimately fatally unlucky husband, real estate developer Brian Harrington. When Brian died, Weezie had inherited back what was left of Flicker Ridge and promptly donated it to the ecological group, *Protect Our Mountains*. Ecological concerns ran in the family, apparently, even if long-lived, happy marriages didn't.

I asked, "What about Vic's wife Carrie? What exactly did he leave to her and his other daughter, Leah? Do you know about them?"

Rufus stood up and wrapped the thick cord around the compressor. "Yeah, yeah. Vic Smythe left two thousand of the Blue Spruce acres to his wife, Carrie. The remaining seven hundred acres and the cabin went to Leah. After Vic died, Carrie remarried and sold her land to Furman County Open Space. That's why they named Blue Spruce's biggest mountain 'Smythe Peak.' Anyway, Carrie and her new husband, Mike Whitaker, had Bobby, Leah and Weezie's half-brother. Helping with Merciful Migrations and taking care of Bobby are Leah's two big concerns. She's always worrying about him. 'What is the matter with

Bobby?' she's asking all the time. *Weezie* doesn't care if her too-tubby-to-model, fail-ure-as-a-Realtor half-brother Bobby lives or dies." Rufus chuckled. "But when *Leah* passes to the Great Migration Area in the Sky, Bobby gets three hundred acres; Merciful Migrations gets the cabin and four hundred acres surrounding it. Only none of that inheriting of land may actually ever take place." He fin-ished wrapping the cord and frowned know-ingly. "Leah's negotiating to sell the whole seven hundred acres, including the cabin, to the paint pellet people. Know 'em? Guys who wear camo gear and spend the day hunting for their friends so they can shoot pellets of red paint at 'em?"

"Good Lord," I said.

"She wants to split the proceeds of the sale with Bobby. It was Bobby who thought they'd get more for the cabin if they put a row of windows in the kitchen, so's the cabin could appear to be modern. Ian will have to move, and he's not too happy about that. So they fight about the sale. All the time. And I get to listen."

"Uh-huh." I hesitated. "Did you get along with Gerald Eliot? I mean, was he nice to you even though you hadn't worked together for five years?"

He shrugged. "He was okay. But you know I wasn't tight with him anymore. When I got back from Phoenix, he and Leah and Ian were always yakking. I thought they were talking about the windows, except I could never find any plans, you know? I figured

296

maybe Bobby had 'em." He paused and stroked his uneven beard. "Y'know, I think even old Hanna got jealous or suspicious of their yakkety-yak. So she got this private sort of joke going with Gerald. I don't think he thought it was too funny, after the first few times."

"Joke? Hanna?" I suddenly recalled her saying that she had *tried* to joke with Gerald.

"Yeah, something about cooking the way they used to in the Old West, you know?" From the great room, Ian hollered for Rufus. He gave me a pained look. "I gotta go."

"Please, wait. What about cooking in the Old West? Please tell me, it's *really* important."

He sighed. "I don't know how it got started. Gerald asked Hanna about her work at the museum, and if she knew how to make rolls using an old-fashioned cookbook."

"What cookbook?" I asked breathlessly. *Make the rolls the way I taught you,* in Charlie Smythe's handwriting, loomed in my mind's eye.

"I dunno," Rufus replied. "Hanna asked why did Gerald want to know, was he going to start doing some baking? Bring us rolls along with his glue gun in the morning? And then Gerald told her just to forget about it. But Hanna kept after him, kept saying, 'Where're our rolls, Gerald?' and he'd say, 'Just shut up, Hanna!' until finally Ian yelled at the two of them to quit it. And then Gerald started up with Rustine, and Leah axed him." Loud footsteps shook the walls. "Look, I really gotta go."

"If Gerald and Ian and Leah were such great friends, why would Leah fire Gerald for having an affair with one of the models?"

He opened the door. "Look, Goldy, I'm looking for another job right now. If I knew why these people around here act the way they do, I wouldn't be fixing to leave, would I? Now, you gonna let me go, or you gonna wait till Ian comes stomping in here, having a fit?"

Confused, I hurried out after him. Tapping her foot at the kitchen door, Leah asked if lunch was ready. She resembled a hothouse poppy in her orange T-shirt, green pants, and orange-and-green sandals. Her streaked pixie looked wild and uncombed. She clutched a thick manila file from which bits of paper poked out.

"Nice outfit," I observed.

"The Mimaya has failed again," she announced petulantly. I decided that the Mimaya must be a camera, not a piece of lingerie. "Rufus will take it down to Denver for repair, but we're done shooting for today. In all likelihood, there won't be shooting tomorrow, either. So, can you serve lunch now?"

"It's ready." I kept my voice cheery.

"You still want to talk to Ian?"

"Sure. If that's okay."

"He doesn't have much time."

With failed equipment about to be hustled to Denver by a kind man everyone treated like a drone, and work canceled for the next day, what was pressing in on Ian's time? I couldn't imagine, but I smiled anyway. "This won't take long."

"Here are André's bills and menus, since you said you needed them to plan the food." She thrust the overstuffed file at me.

"He gave it to you like this?"

She sniffed. "I don't remember." She turned on her sandaled heel and departed.

I waited for everyone to go through the food line. Hanna methodically consumed a small plate of chicken and strawberry salad. Rustine, Yvonne, Rufus, Ian, Leah, the *per diem* contractors...Since Leah had told me fifteen people, and we'd brought enough for twenty, that should be plenty of food, right?

Wrong. At first I thought something was wrong with Rustine's and Yvonne's food, the two models kept going back to the platters so many times. Tried this, and didn't like it? Tried that, and still weren't pleased? But no: they were binging. After four trips to the buffet, Yvonne could have beat any bear foraging for hibernation.

I sidled over to where Ian sat alone nursing a cup of coffee and smoking a cigar, his back to the mountains. Every now and then he turned his shoulder to send a stream of smoke over the creek.

"Hi there," I said happily, instead of asking: *If you really care about the environment, what's that thing in your mouth?* "Can we talk?"

He glanced behind me to see if anyone was watching. Suddenly paranoid, I looked around myself. Leah, Rustine, Yvonne, Bobby, and the day-contractors were still on the deck, but no one appeared interested in us. Ian inhaled, bobbed his chin, and exhaled out of the side of his mouth. "Heard you need something from me." He dabbed at his gray moustache. "Is there a problem?"

"Ah, no." I sat down. Was Ian acting defensive, or was it my imagination? "Well, actually, yes. It's about who's doing the catering for the Soirée."

"Oh, for crying out loud," he snorted. "What do I look like, *Court TV*? You catered it last year."

"Just give me five minutes," I promised. "Maybe less. If you *knew* monkey business was going on, monkey business that might get into the paper, say, wouldn't you want to prevent it?"

He took his cigar out of his mouth to sip his coffee. "I've got competitors in Phoenix and Miami and New York who are breathing down my neck. I've got real estate development all through the mountain area threatening wildlife migration that I've tried to protect for over a decade." He squinted at me. "And you're dangling *bad press* in front of me? Am I going to be sorry I let you come here today? Your food isn't that good, if you want to know the truth. The chicken has too much red pepper and the rice tastes like dirt."

I stared at his barely touched plate. "I'm sorry you didn't enjoy the meal," I said softly, while thinking, *If you'd lay off the stinky cigars, your taste buds would work.* "I'm not going to the newspaper. But catering is my livelihood, even if today's meal isn't to your liking. Listen, Craig Litchfield is doing *free* parties for two of the three women judging the tasting party, in exchange for their vote."

"And you're sure of this."

"He offered to do a free party for Leah, until she told him she wasn't voting." I steeled myself. "Weezie Harrington and Edna Hardcastle both canceled me out of catering their parties after *Litchfield* said he could do them at no charge, I firmly believe."

"But it's not as if *you* weren't trying to bribe them. It's just that the damn price was different. Right?"

I took a deep breath. What did Leah see in this person? What had it been like for André to work for him? "I wasn't—"

Ian stubbed out his cigar and again glanced along the deck. "Listen, I'd do anything to try to save the elk in this state."

"I realize that—"

He stood up. "Don't drag me into your stupid squabble over who caters the damn fundraiser. The other guy won the booking. Live with it." He grinned. "Suck it up, caterer." And with that he strode off the deck.

Wow, was that *fun,* I thought sourly.

Julian and Boyd had cleared the plates and were working inside. I picked up the mostly empty platters. A mass of red pepper flakes speckling the coq au vin sauce gave me pause. A closer inspection showed the flakes were not *in* the sauce, but on top of the last chicken breast; they had been dumped on. For heaven's sake, Ian had been right. The only condiments

301

we'd placed on the tables had been salt and pepper. The strawberry-sugar-snap-pea salad appeared okay. My examination of the rice revealed more foreign flakes, this time very thin and orange and brown. Only it wasn't dirt. My experience with Arch's aquariums told me this was fish food. What the heck?

I didn't have time to find out what was going on. There was a loud crash inside the cabin, accompanied by an unearthly scream of pain. I dropped the platter and ran to the window as more howling erupted. I squinted through the wavy glass. One of the flats had broken loose from its clamp. It had crashed to the floor, with Leah underneath. For one ghastly moment, I saw Leah's blood-covered face. *No,* I thought, *no. Please God,* I prayed, *no.*

By the time I got inside, Boyd was commanding Julian to help him lift the heavy flat. When Boyd saw me, he shook his head.

Chapter 19

"What happened?" I demanded of Rustine, who didn't reply.

"Help us!" Julian yelled at Rufus. Bobby Whitaker stood to one side, seemingly paralyzed. Rufus and Ian ran to the far side of the flat and lifted at Boyd's command.

"Don't touch anything!" Boyd commanded.

Leah's body was inert. She was breathing, but her entire right side appeared unnaturally folded. Her arm stuck out at a cruel angle; her leg wouldn't move. She cried and moaned. Ian knelt down beside her and began to murmur words of comfort. Boyd snapped open his mobile to call an ambulance.

I looked at the flat. Secured by an A-clamp to a pole that extended between the floor and ceiling, I couldn't understand how it could suddenly come loose. Just at that moment? To hurt someone? It seemed very odd. Or very convenient?

Boyd ordered me to bring clean, damp cloth napkins to wipe the blood off Leah's face. Meanwhile, he gently checked her for shock and broken bones. When the E.M.S. arrived twenty minutes later, the paramedics shooed everyone away from her, then took great care getting her on a stretcher and across the creek to their vehicle. As suddenly as the crisis had developed, it was over. I asked one paramedic how she looked, and his tight-lipped answer was something along the lines of *We can't say.*

Boyd quietly told me he was going to examine the flat and the clamps to see if there was any evidence this was anything besides an accident. Rufus had already informed Boyd that flats occasionally came loose, but that this was the first time in a while one had actually fallen on somebody. Feeling disoriented, I walked back out to the deck and picked up the platter I had dropped. In the kitchen, I showed Julian the pepper-flake and fish-food additions and asked if he'd seen anything suspicious going on out at the tables.

Julian's face was dismayed. "No, nothing. Sabotage. Unbelievable."

I told him that I had suspected the same thing had happened with André. Maybe he had caught the saboteur?

"Maybe," Julian mused. "Or maybe it's just somebody's idea of a practical joke."

When Boyd came out to the kitchen, he said he could see nothing that would indicate someone had jerry-rigged the clamps or the flat. He even wondered if Leah had been trying to move it, as the flat had fallen on her front rather than her back. As usual, he said, no one had seen anything.

I sighed. Julian showed Boyd the platters of tainted food. He shook his head. "Cover them up and I'll take them down to the department. I'll see if the guys in the lab have any free time to analyze 'em."

When we left, Hanna seemed subdued and far from her usual bossy self. So much for dealing with idiosyncrasies, I reflected. She said she would see us Friday morning unless the equipment could not be fixed. Leah's job of casting for the auditions was largely past, and she could manage all the details. Coffee break, lunch, all right? she asked. With any luck, that would be their last day. I nodded and tucked André's bills and menus under my arm. Two more days to figure out what was really going on at this place.

On the drive home, Julian fell asleep. Quietly, I asked Boyd if he'd be willing to talk about the people at the cabin or its history. He nodded.

Remembering the bitterness in Hanna's tone when she'd visited me in the kitchen, I told him I was wondering about Hanna Klapper. Her parents had owned the Swiss Inn, now apartments. She was in dire financial straits because of her divorce. But what I didn't know, I said, was if there was any history between Hanna and Gerald Eliot.

Boyd kept his eyes on the road and his voice low. "The department looked into Hanna because she knows the museum so well, and that's where Gerald was killed. But since she's familiar with the collection, they asked why a knowledgeable thief would take cookbooks, and leave those antique Hopi dolls—"

"Kachinas," I supplied automatically.

"Right," Boyd continued. "Those things are valued in the thousands. A person without a whole lot of money wouldn't take a book worth sixty bucks, would she?"

"The missing cookbook has strange markings in it from Charlie Smythe."

"So? She knew that place inside and out. She wouldn't need to kill somebody to get pages that she knew could be photocopied from the museum files, right?"

"Gerald Eliot asked Hanna about Old West-style cooking. Making rolls. She even teased him about it. And Charlie Smythe had written to his wife in the stolen cookbook about making rolls."

Boyd glanced at me. "So?" His response to everything, it seemed. "I don't know anything about making rolls. You asked about Charlie Smythe and the Merciful Migrations cabin. I've heard the rumors about a Denver outfit wanting to put one of those paint-pellet courses out there. Don't know if they're true yet or not. And of course, everyone's heard about old Charlie Smythe." Boyd chuckled. "Guy's a legend. He was the greediest old bastard in the West. You wouldn't catch me trying to rob a bank when I was in my late sixties."

"But he *was* caught," I interjected.

Boyd tilted his head in acknowledgment. "Yeah, finally. Basic rule of law enforcement: A criminal keeps breaking the law until he's in jail."

"Keeps breaking the law. Do you know of any *other* crimes Charlie Smythe committed?"

"Nope. But that doesn't mean anything. Sometimes they won't give you a hint as to what they've done until they're behind bars. Then they'll use their stories to keep you hopping. Sometimes."

We passed a meadow where a small herd of grazing elk was barely distinguishable from the boulders dotting the prairie grass.

"The Swiss Inn," I said slowly, thinking of André's early history. "What do you know about *its* background?"

Boyd said, "That place is an *ongoing* problem because skinheads are always trying to meet there. B'nai B'rith called us a while back, wanted to know about the swastikas on the floor of the old section, and the rumors from the war.

We've never come up with anything except totally unsubstantiated rumors about the Heinzes, Hanna's parents. Financially and in every other way, Hanna is absolutely as clean as a whistle. She belongs to no organizations beyond the historical society, and has been loyal and generous to them, at least until she had to quit and get a higher-paying job. Before the Swiss Inn was turned into apartments, whenever neo-Nazis tried to meet there, Hanna would call us." He rocked the van from the dirt road onto the highway toward Aspen Meadow.

Julian groaned as he awoke. I assured him we were almost home, although in truth, I was only paying half attention. An idea was forming in my mind. Did Charlie Smythe, a greedy con man who robbed for the fun of it, still have a tale to tell?

At home, the yawning garage door revealed that the entire interior was filled with boxes: the kitchen cabinets had arrived. *Just shows how eagerly retailers will part with discontinued merchandise,* I thought. Boyd greeted Tom, filled him in briefly on what had happened at the cabin, and then took off with the tainted dishes. Tom handed me a note from Arch saying he and Lettie were listening to music at Todd's house. Not to worry, he'd scrawled: Mrs. Druckman was making them sub sandwiches for lunch. Lettie would eat a sub sandwich? I doubted that. Matter of fact, what had she had at the Chinese place? Steamed squid?

Tom, after asking us how we were, went back to sawing. His old friend Sergeant Zack

Armstrong had come up for the morning to help him. Where the back wall had been, there were now three dusty windows decorated with the manufacturer's stickers. The sudden vista on our backyard opened up by the wall of glass was disconcerting. I knew I'd get used to it, even love it, so I told myself not to make any negative comments.

Zack and Tom had moved on to nailing down the strips of oak that were to be our new floor. Unfinished and dusty, it was hard to tell how they would look. Tom had brought in one of the cherry cabinets; it lay tilted against a hole-pocked wall. Julian and I gushed over how stunning the dark, carved box was. Tom, sweaty and intent, thanked us and then asked us to let him get back to work.

Julian and I brought our crates of dirty dishes through the front door, wiped them with wet paper towels to remove dirt and food particles, and washed them in the downstairs bathtub. *If only the health inspector could see us now....* I shuddered. It was nearly four o'clock by the time we finished. Julian offered to pick up Arch, take Lettie home, then get pizza and calzones for dinner. I handed him money from my wallet. It would appear that remodeling a kitchen, in addition to being expensive, was fattening.

While Tom and Zack banged and hammered on the first floor, I took a long shower, wrapped myself in a thick terry-cloth robe, and settled down in our bedroom. First I called Lutheran Hospital, where the E.M.S. said they were taking Leah. No one at the hospital could give me any information yet, unfortunately. Next, I pulled out the packet Leah had given me. The disheveled pages of André's menus and bills to Ian's Images were meticulously numbered and dated but out of order. I put them in order and opened my calendar. I needed to reconstruct what André had told me about his meal-service plans, and how those had been disrupted by Ian's breaking the window with the temper tantrum that had also cost him a camera and a whole lot of glass.

The first day I had worked with André had been Monday, the eighteenth of August. I smoothed out the menu for that day and felt a twinge when I read *Models' Mushroom Soup* and *Goldy's Vegetarian Dish*—the Florentine cheesecakes. I traced the letters with my fingers, admiring André's faithfully kept resolution to write as well as speak English. *Burnt Sugar Cake.* He'd given me careful instructions on not burning myself. I steered away from that particular irony while noting that beside the lunch menu for Tuesday, a different hand had written: *André: Could you please serve lunch inside for the next 3 days? We'll be working on the deck and need the space. L.* Leah. That day, he had proceeded with *Vichyssoise, Chilled Stuffed Artichokes, Marinated Beef Salad, Brioche, Fresh Fruit Skewers,* and *Grand Marnier Buttercream Cookies.*

On Wednesday the twentieth, he'd done a coffee break that consisted of *Scallion Frittata,*

Fresh-fruit Pineapple Boats, and *Scones with Lemon Curd.* Wednesday's lunch had featured *Cream of Corn Soup, Lump Crab Salad, Green Beans Vinaigrette, Dill Rolls,* and *Chocolate Cake.* On Thursday he'd treated the assembly to *Spiral-cut Ham, Fruit Plate,* and *Pecan Rolls* for the coffee break, while lunch had been an offering of *Western-style Barbecue Ribs, Coleslaw, Potato Salad, Corn on the Cob,* and *Brownies.* American cooking? Incredible.

Friday we had catered together at the Homestead Museum, heard Sylvia's sad tale of her violated museum, seen the children model. And he'd had his miniattack.

He'd died before serving the Monday coffee break. He'd written the prep plans, though: *Crème Brûlée Cups for 20—start Saturday.* To that he'd added *Peach Compote—make Sunday.* Heavy on the cholesterol and sugar, but that was the French way.

His bills had been uncomplicated: figuring ten to twenty people per day, service, tax, and gratuity included: ten dollars a pop for the coffee break, eighteen for the lunch. He'd averaged a daily gross of about seven hundred dollars. On Friday afternoon, he had written down the check number of the payment Leah had made to him for the first week's work. I did not know whether he had ever deposited the check. I sighed and closed the notebook. Downstairs, the loud *pow* of Tom's nail gun split the air.

I would be seeing Pru Hibbard the following afternoon, at the memorial service. It would not be tactful to pose any questions about André's week with the fashion folks. The last thing a bereaved widow needed was to imagine there was anything unusual about her husband's death. Which, of course, there was.

Slowly, I read back over the menus. I visualized André working on Sunday, peeling peaches for the compote he would serve on Monday morning for Ian's Images. First, he would have placed the thickly sliced peaches in a baking dish, then reamed out a lemon for its juice, mixed the juice with some red wine, sugar, a cinnamon stick, and some cloves and a bit of salt. This he would have heated and poured over the glistening peaches before placing them in the oven. Then, for the other dish...Wait a minute.

I closed my eyes and remembered André bustling about to prepare *crème brûlée.* He'd insisted on teaching me his old-fashioned way, although I'd ended up developing my own method. André would stir and heat eggs with cream to a rich custard, then chill the dish overnight, which is why he would have started it on Saturday. Then on Sunday he would have covered it with a thin layer of light brown sugar, and...Hold on.

To caramelize the sugar, he did not use a hand-held propane torch, as I did. No: André used his own salamander, an old-fashioned iron tool heated over a fire and then run over the top of the *crème,* to make it *brûlée.* Like his butter-baller, his balloon whisks, and battered

311

wooden spoons, André's salamander came from the time before modern kitchen equipment was common. It was a curved, fancy implement that I'd seen many times in his red metal toolbox.

In my mind's eye I saw André's dead body, his burned hands. *Crème brûlée* crusted by the heat of a salamander. Strangely shaped burns carved into the skin followed by death...or something like that. In any event, because of the shape of the burns, I knew the salamander *must* have caused the scars. How had it happened? When could the burning have happened? Not Sunday when he'd originally made the custards, or he would have put salve on them, wouldn't he? Or bandages? He'd told the cabdriver he'd finished making the food...but he had to be at the cabin early for prep. Why? Could there have been some reason why he'd felt he had to make *more* custards Monday morning? What would that reason be? Could someone have startled him while he was cooking, as Rustine had startled me today, so that he burned himself, had chest pains, and took an overdose of nitroglycerin? If someone had surprised him, why wouldn't that person have called for help when André collapsed, as Boyd had called for help today?

It still didn't make sense. But at least I knew one thing. André had been burned by his own salamander.

I checked my watch: just before five. I put in a quick call to the morgue, and was astonished to be put straight through to Sheila O'Connor.

312

"Sheila, it's Goldy…look, I just didn't know who else to call—"

"No problem."

"Remember those marks on André's hands?" When she *mm-hmm*ed, I took a deep breath. "I know what caused them." I told her about the menus, the *crème brûlée,* and the salamander.

"So, what are you telling me?" she asked patiently. "That he was burned while he was cooking? I never thought anything else."

What *was* I telling her, exactly? "Of course he was burned while he was cooking, but it just doesn't add up. Why would he tell the cabdriver he was all done, and then proceed to make more food? If one of the photo people came to the cabin and told André extra people were showing up, and then André burned himself and collapsed, why didn't the photo person call for help?"

Sheila took a deep breath. "Goldy, you loved your teacher. I know you did. I know you hate to think of him as old and vulnerable. But he *was.* Our guys found his empty bottle of nitroglycerin, by the way. His doctor says the bottle should have been full."

"He took a whole bottle? When he was sensitive to it? Why would he do that? How much was in his system?"

"About two hundred milligrams. It's a lethal dose. Goldy—"

"Did he have any…internal bruising that would have shown someone forcing pills down his throat?"

"You're always telling me about Med Wives one-oh-one, Goldy. Remember? Nitroglycerin dissolves in the mouth."

"Do you have *any* evidence that might indicate this wasn't an accidental overdose? Please, Sheila, he was my teacher."

"Have Tom call me tomorrow." Then she clicked off.

♦

Sometimes problems, like a well-simmered stock, *must* be put on the back burner. I couldn't obsess about André's death any more that day. Nor could I contemplate how long it would be until my kitchen was back in service. Nor did I even want to *think* about being replaced as the caterer for Weezie Harrington's birthday party, or of my replacement, Craig Litchfield, wowing the country club divorcée set.

Instead, I forced myself to shove all that aside, and relaxed into our lovely dinner on the deck. If the pizza was a bit cool, the calzones a tad mushy, no one mentioned it. Arch raptly contemplated the sun slipping behind burnished copper clouds. The only thing he told us about his day was that he and Julian had been invited to Rustine and Lettie's house the next afternoon for lunch. Tom, exhausted from his carpentry labors, fell asleep on a deck chair before Julian could proffer take-out tiramisù. I gently woke him and tugged him up to bed. Julian, bless his heart, offered to clean up. He said he was actually starting to like washing dishes in the tub.

◆

The next morning, Tom was once again up early and hammering away as I pulled myself out of bed and stretched through my yoga. Julian and Arch were sleeping in. We had no catering jobs, although Julian had vowed to experiment with something to take to Rustine's. Maybe he didn't dislike her quite as much as he pretended.

When I came into the kitchen, Tom appeared to be about a third of the way through nailing in the lower cabinets. Unfortunately, huge piles of boxes obscured my ability to admire all of his work.

"What do you think?" he asked happily. He wore a sweatshirt and jeans, a carpenter's apron, and two days' worth of beard.

I smiled. "I love it." No matter what I thought, I had learned over the last few days to say his work was *fantastic*.

"You'll have to get your coffee in town, I'm afraid," he told me. "I had to shut off the water, just for the morning. And Marla called. She's almost done with the IRS and wants to meet you at St. Stephen's at three-thirty, before the service."

Relief swept over me. My friend was finally going to be released from audit agony! "That's super." I located the phone and called Lutheran

Hospital. Leah Smythe, I was finally told by a nurse I knew, had two broken ribs and lacerations on her face, arms, and legs. The doctor was in seeing her, but the nurse would relay the message that I'd called. And could she find out about Barbara Burr, I asked. I was put on hold, then told sadly that Barbara's condition hadn't changed. Next I called Pru Hibbard; the line was busy. I put nightmares of bottom-feeding Realtors out of my head, and hoped the engaged line meant other people were making sympathy calls to André's widow.

Tom eyed me skeptically. "You seem awfully perky for a caterer with no kitchen, no water, and a tenuous business. You must want something *wicked* bad."

"Actually, I need you to call the morgue."

"Oh. Is that all?"

"Tom, listen. Just ask Sheila if there's any possible evidence to show that André's nitroglycerin overdose wasn't an accident."

Tom put down his nail gun and came over to give me a hug. "Miss G., I know you loved him. But you're going to have to let it go."

"If I'd been there helping him, he wouldn't have died."

"For crying out loud, Goldy, you know how many lives I could have saved if I just would have been someplace at the right time?"

"Please, Tom, I'll let it go just as soon as I know how and why he died." I reached for my van keys.

"Now where are you going?"

"Into town for coffee," I replied innocently.

"You've got that purposeful look about you that's not just desperation for caffeine."

Ah, how well the man knew me. "No bail was set for Cameron Burr, right? Because it's a murder case."

"Correct."

"So the next event in Cameron's life is his preliminary hearing?"

"Ye-es."

"I need to go visit him at the jail. To talk to him about another outlaw."

One of the marvelous additions to Aspen Meadow in the last year was one of those drive-through espresso places where you order, answer a trivia question, get a card punched, and lay out in cash the cost of an entire fast-food breakfast for a triple-shot latté. Still, a treat was a treat, I thought as I sipped the luscious, caffeine-rich drink and zoomed down to the Furman County Jail.

Visiting hours during the week were from nine to eleven in the morning and one to three in the afternoon. I arrived just after nine and still had half of my expensive coffee to savor. So I put the cup on the dash, got out pen and paper, and started to scribble the questions I needed to pose to Cameron Burr, president of the historical society, the one person in Aspen Meadow who might know enough to figure out the puzzle of Charlie Smythe. Unwritten, but first on the list, was:

Would Cameron, who had not answered any of my phone calls, see me?

Hunched over my paper, my heart quickened unexpectedly when someone passed by the back of my van. I did not move, only looked up at the rearview mirror and followed the movement. The dark-haired man was smoking, walking fast. Usually visitors to the jail at this hour were attorneys. Occasionally, out-of-work family members would straggle in. The man glanced over his shoulder to determine if I was watching him. Catching my eye in the mirror, he flicked his cigarette onto the grass and sprinted to the Upscale Appetite van. A moment later, he revved his vehicle and took off in a nimbus of grit and dust.

Well, now, there was a question I wouldn't have thought to write down.

Who at the sheriff's department—or in the jail—had just received an early-morning visit from Craig Litchfield?

Chapter 20

The desk officer, a fresh-faced fellow named Sergeant Riordan, was not someone I knew. I handed my driver's license over the counter and announced my desire to visit Cameron Burr. Riordan nodded and cheerfully tapped an unseen keyboard.

"Do you know my husband?" I ventured. "Investigator Tom Schulz?"

"Schulz. Sure. By reputation, mostly." Riordan handed my license back. "Why?"

"Well." How to sound friendly instead of nosy? There wasn't a way. "The last guy who was here? Craig Litchfield? I...*we* were wondering...Could you just tell me who he was visiting?"

The cheerful expression drained out of Riordan's face. "No. No, I can't tell you that, Mrs. Schulz." He picked up a phone, punched buttons, and murmured. When he hung up, his warm hazel eyes had gone from friendly to flat. "You have thirty minutes with Cameron Burr, Mrs. Schulz."

♦

Cameron Burr's ill-fitting orange prison suit didn't flatter him. He looked older, thinner, and paler than he had just ten days ago at his home. He flattened his long gray hair against his scalp in a vain attempt to make it appear less mussed. The look in his bloodshot eyes was defeated, angry. With his right hand he picked up the phone.

"Cameron, I'm sorry," I blurted out. "I had no idea—"

He rubbed his stubbly cheeks. "How's Barbara, have you seen her?"

"I've called Lutheran several times. She's still on a ventilator." He nodded as if he knew this already. I said, "How are *you*?"

He sighed. "Terrible." The bloodshot eyes

turned wary. "Are you going to screw up my case by being here?"

"I hope not." I gripped the grimy phone. Overhead, a whirring air conditioner labored unsuccessfully to keep the metallic air cool. "I'm trying to help you. You're right, I probably shouldn't be here, since I found Eliot's body and I'm technically a witness. But I'm not here to talk about what I saw up at your house, which is what your attorney would prohibit us from discussing."

"Then why are you here?"

"Please, Cameron, first...can you tell me if you were the one who just had a visit from Craig Litchfield?"

He cast a rueful glance at the painted cinderblocks lining his side of the booth. "No, he wasn't here to visit me."

"Do you know who he *was* here to visit?"

His voice turned rough. "Is that why you came up to see me, Goldy? To ask about some other caterer?"

"No, no," I said as gently as possible. "Don't be angry. I was just curious. Actually, I have a few history questions, and you're the one person I think could answer them."

"*History* questions?"

"Yes. About Charlie Smythe. But listen, Cameron, if you want me to leave, I will."

His free hand splayed against the scratched glass between us. Curiosity momentarily sparked his face, followed fast by fury. "First, I have to tell you something, Goldy. That ridiculous assistant district attorney, Fuller, is a disgrace. The man should be disbarred. I didn't kill Gerald Eliot."

"I know."

He hesitated. "Why do you want to know about Charlie Smythe?"

"I'm just...trying to figure out what Gerald Eliot was up to." I took a deep breath. "Pulling out a wall in the Merciful Migrations cabin kitchen was one of Gerald Eliot's last jobs. Have you spent much time up there?"

He shrugged, again wary. "A fair amount."

"The Merciful Migrations people fired Eliot in July. He was killed in August, right after a number of items, including a cookbook once used in that same kitchen, were stolen from the Homestead Museum. Then last Sunday, my catering teacher, a French chef named André Hibbard, died unexpectedly after working in that same cabin kitchen."

"I read it in the paper. You have my sympathy."

I nodded my gratitude. Then I said, "André had asked for a photocopy of the stolen cookbook before he died." Cameron looked confused, so I plunged on. "Hanna Klapper told me that back in July, Gerald Eliot found a rifle that had been hidden inside the kitchen cabin wall. I think the rifle belonged to Charlie Smythe."

Cameron Burr frowned. "A rifle? Do you know it belonged to Charlie Smythe? How do you know it wasn't hidden after he died?"

How *did* I know the rifle belonged to Charlie Smythe? I didn't. I'd just assumed it, after *the weapon* and *Charlie Smythe* were put together in the same thought by Rustine. She had told Tom, Julian, and me about the weapon, then wondered if *André had told you some secret he'd found out? Say, about Charlie Smythe, who used to live in the cabin?* How had she happened to put the weapon and Charlie Smythe together? Good question. "Look, I don't know *when* it was hidden. But Gerald Eliot told his girlfriend that he'd found, and I quote, 'something that was going to make us rich.' "

"Like what?" Cameron's voice was like gravel. "And why didn't Leah Smythe notify our society that an item of historical significance had been found at her cabin?"

"Maybe she did." I bit down on my impatience. "But...say Gerald Eliot discovered something out at the cabin—something besides the rifle—that got him killed at the museum."

"And this is related to the missing cookbook you just mentioned? The one André wanted a copy of?" His forehead furrowed.

"I *don't know.* I'm just trying to figure out how and why my teacher died, working in the same place that Eliot did. This summer, Eliot worked for the museum, for Merciful Migrations, and for you and me."

Cameron Burr rubbed his chin. "He didn't actually finish his work for you, though, did he?"

"Of course not. He took my money, made a mess, and disappeared. Next thing I knew, he'd been killed at the museum in the course of a fake robbery that might not have been fake.

Why might it not have been a *faked* robbery? Because the cookbook of Winnie Smythe's that was in the museum still hasn't been recovered. Now two people are dead, and the only thing linking them is that they both worked at the Smythe cabin. What am I missing?"

His long, snorting laughter came across the phone like a truck braking on a curve. "You're missing Charlie Smythe."

I glanced at my watch. Twenty minutes left. "I know Charlie was a thief, and ended up in Leavenworth in 1916 for killing a teller while he was trying to rob a bank. He died in prison two years later. What else is there?"

"All right, Goldy. First, you should know where I heard what I'm going to tell you. Vic Smythe, Charlie's son, was a friend of mine. Vic was an old-timer with the fire department when I was a recruit."

"How long ago did he tell you these stories?"

"Thirty years." He went on: "Charlie Smythe was a Confederate signalman during the Civil War. Came out here like a lot of folks after the conflict, restless, wanting a fresh start. Only difference was that he had money. Obtained fraudulently, as it turned out, but still his. He was only seventeen or eighteen, but smart as a whip, and ambitious. He bought land, got married, built that cabin, tried to start ranching and timbering the way mountain folk did. But he couldn't settle down. He was always leaving Winnie out there in Blue Spruce to fend for herself."

"Leaving for where?"

Cameron shrugged. "According to Vic, Charlie would go wherever there were horses, money, or anything valuable to be stolen. He'd be gone for weeks at a time in the summer, which was the only time you could dependably get around on horseback, if you were avoiding the roads. Word was he was up by Jackson Hole for a while, then down in New Mexico. He'd come back with a lot of cash that he would spend on boozing through the winter. Charlie Smythe never missed his family, according to Vic."

Never missed his family? That sounded familiar; Sylvia and I had discussed just that fact. She thought Charlie had repented in prison, of course. "Do you understand that letter they have on display at the Homestead? The one that mentions his wife's cookbook? In that, Smythe sounds as if he loved family life."

"I know, I've seen that letter. Only one he ever wrote her that the family kept. Know what? Vic didn't even believe his father had really written it, it was so full of malarkey. Soon as Vic was old enough, he had all of his parents' possessions packed up and put away. Leah and Weezie, Vic's daughters? They gave the whole lot to the Homestead Museum without even going through the boxes."

"Could... Charlie...have hidden anything else in the wall, besides a rifle? Did Vic ever say his father boasted about something hidden? There are some strange markings in the cookbook—"

"I know, I know, I've seen them. Barbara tried to figure them out, too, but she didn't have any luck."

"So nobody *ever* figured out what those random rows of letters mean?" I asked disconsolately. "If anything?"

"Nope. Winnie had a stroke right after Charlie went to prison. She was incapacitated and never even used the cookbook after he was sent away. So if she ever *did* know what the letters meant, she couldn't tell anybody. Plus, before Charlie was finally caught, he was secretive as all hell, according to Vic. Charlie would lie about anything. Vic even thought his father would *read* about crimes, then boast that he was the one who'd committed them. When the James gang went up to Minnesota, Charlie claimed to have been with them. When Butch and Sundance ended up in Bolivia, old Charlie swore he was there, but he escaped."

"Marvelous. Great reliable source." I smiled at Cameron. Even if this story wouldn't help figure anything out, it was good to see him relishing a tale, instead of being angry with me.

Cameron held up a finger, as if he sensed that he wasn't giving me helpful data. "Wait, though. There is one thing that's interesting.... Every now and then, old Charlie'd get remorseful, the way a drunk always does when he sobers up. One morning, Charlie sobbed to Vic that he was sorry he'd been such a rotten father. He'd been a small-time thief, he said, but he'd pulled off one last big heist and never been caught."

325

I swallowed the words *fish story,* and only murmured, "One last heist..."

"On this particular dawn he was feeling *very* penitent. Old Charlie told his son that he'd never been caught for gettin' back into his Army of the Confederacy uniform and robbing the last stagecoach that ran in Yellowstone Park."

"Oh, please."

Cameron shook his head slowly. "That may actually be the one true boast Charlie Smythe ever made. Although no one knows for certain, of course."

I sighed. "Right. He made it from Yellowstone back to Blue Spruce on horseback. Alone. Carrying his loot, no doubt. For crying out loud, it takes twenty hours to drive—we're talking a car, here—from Blue Spruce to Yellowstone. What time of year was it?"

"You want to hear the story or not?"

"Go ahead."

"Morning of July nineteen, 1915, it was raining hard when the last commercial stagecoach started its run from West Yellowstone on its way to East Yellowstone."

I grinned. Of course Cameron would know the date, even the weather, for this historic event.

He went on: "Folks weren't allowed to carry firearms into the park, so the amazing thing is that *more* of the stagecoaches weren't robbed. One thief, Ed Trafton, had already been caught for robbing the stagecoach the year before. But old Trafton was sitting in jail when this particular robbery took place."

I sneaked a peek at my watch and nodded. Ten minutes to go.

"The story gets confused some, whether it was one person or two who did the robbing of that last stagecoach. But one thing's for sure: Whether it was one or two robbers, he or they wore soldiers' uniforms. One account says a man seated above the carriage box recognized the robber. Saw him the next day at a dance and called him by name. Called him 'Charlie.' "

"Uh-huh."

"And guess who was on that last stagecoach? New York financier Bernard Baruch. The robber got *him* for fifty dollars."

"Right. How much did this last stagecoach robbery net, *in toto*?"

"Five hundred dollars, they say."

I took a deep breath. "And that's it?"

"Not quite. The way the story goes, a sixteen-year-old named Eugenia Braintree was on that stagecoach. She was running away from her parents. The Braintrees, very wealthy banking people from Pittsburgh, were feuding with their daughter. Eugenia wanted to work for women's suffrage. Her parents thought this was a *very* bad idea. She was headstrong and took off, but not before she'd stolen a ruby necklace, a diamond brooch, and sapphire earrings from her mother. The jewelry was supposed to finance Eugenia's escape to San Francisco, but it ended up in the robber's sack with Bernard Baruch's cash." He chuckled. "Whoever took that five hundred dollars hit the jackpot with Eugenia's jewelry. It was worth a fortune. Plus, whoever it was got away and was never caught. Supposedly, the guy named Charlie disappeared from Yellowstone the next day."

"You seem to know the story pretty well."

The glee that had suffused Cameron's face as he told the old legend abruptly left. His voice filled with sadness. "Yeah, I do. But only because Vic had researched it after his father died. The Braintree part he only got from one source, in Pittsburgh. The Braintree parents never reported the robbery, according to this source, for fear that a story of their daughter stealing all that jewelry would somehow cause a run on their big bank in Pittsburgh. Vic didn't care. All he wanted was the story. He went to great lengths to obtain the front page from the *New York Times* that ran the article about the robbery, and he framed it. Leah even gave *that* to the museum. Anyway, in all our hours at the fire station, old Vic told that story well, and often, to the recruits." Cameron sighed deeply. "It was like Vic didn't have a father, really. But he had this story."

"Sounds as if Vic Smythe was like a father to the recruits."

"He was."

My thirty minutes were over. "I'd better be going—"

"Listen," Cameron said hesitantly, "I'm glad you came. You've been so nice since Barbara got sick, bringing food, checking on me. I'm sorry I didn't call you back, but my lawyer..." He exhaled softly, too defeated to finish his thought.

"It's fine, Cam. If I can figure out this mess, maybe it will help you."

"You have no idea how much your visit has cheered me up. I didn't think it would, but it has."

I tapped the glass. "You're a good man. And a good friend."

Cameron Burr looked over his shoulder to see if he was being watched. He lowered his voice and covered the phone with his hand as he said, "Your ex-husband is in here."

"So you've met The Jerk. Poor you."

"You can't tell anybody I told you this, 'cause he's a guy who gets in fights and I can't risk that. Plus, he didn't actually tell me this. It's what I heard from somebody else, who heard it through the gossip mill, which operates at a pretty hefty clip in here. It relates to what you asked me about when you first came in."

A familiar queasiness threatened. I tried to sound normal. "Why? What's going on?"

Cameron Burr's gritty whisper spiraled through the phone. "He's trying to get revenge on you and Marla, his other ex-wife."

"Revenge?"

"Before he got caught for beating up his girlfriend, he was having money troubles. Marla was giving him a hard time, you know how she can be. So he turned her into the IRS. Since he got in here, he's started bankrolling Craig Litchfield to undercut you. Your ex used your son to get your client list, assignments, schedules, menus, and prices off your computer, to give to your competitor."

The air conditioner fan whirred overhead. I said, "Thanks, Cameron," and stood up.

His bloodshot eyes watered. "I hope I can see you again soon."

"You will," I promised.

◆

A cool breeze whistled through my half-open windows as I reflected on stagecoach robberies, a rifle in the wall, escape from prosecution, unsolved crimes, and the manipulation of my son, my dear sweet son, to do one of his father's vicious errands. If I had the rifle from the wall, Charlie Smythe's escape route between Yellowstone and Blue Spruce, and John Richard Korman standing in front of me, would I shoot The Jerk and be done with it? Goodness, but it would be tempting. The nerve of that man, to try to wreak revenge on his two ex-wives. Leopards don't change their spots. Especially those big cats who use power to hurt people.

At a red light, I again called Lutheran Hospital to check on Leah Smythe. A new nurse told me Leah couldn't talk. But the patient was doing fine. Punching in Marla's home number on the cell, I swerved out of my lane. I swung back to safety and listened as her phone rang over to her tape.

"It's me," I said to the machine. "Yes, I can meet you at the St. Stephen's parking lot at three-thirty. I'd say more, but I'm afraid the IRS is bugging your phone." I punched off and called home.

"This is Goldilocks' Catering," a male voice answered happily, "but Goldy's out with the bears right now. Can I help you?"

"Tom, please. How likely is it that potential clients would book me after that greeting?"

"Aha, Miss Happy-go-lucky. You must have had a super time at the jail."

"How's my kitchen coming?"

"Great. I know you want to see it, but Arch needs his swimsuit. Julian took him over to Lettie's, but the suit's in your van, left there after some lock-in at the rec center two weeks ago, he says. Anyway, you'll have to wait to see your kitchen until you get the suit to Arch."

Patience. "Tell me how to get to Rustine and Lettie's place."

"Sure. Don't you want to know what I found out from Sheila?"

"Hold on." I pulled onto the shoulder under the bridge that overlooked the Continental Divide. Forty miles west of the gloom overhead, the peaks shimmered under a cloak of new snow—another chilly harbinger of the winter to come. I pulled my notepad from my purse. "Go ahead with the directions."

"The girls live in Aspen Hills, at the western end of Troutman Trail. That's the third hairpin turn after Brook Drive turns into a dirt road. You taking notes? Pass a *For Sale* sign, pass a gray house with red trim. Their house is the first place on the right after the last set of mailboxes on Troutman. Brown house, green trim. You get to a dead end, you've gone too far."

"Got it." If that wasn't an Aspen Meadow set of directions, I didn't know what was.

"I called Sheila—"

"Go ahead." I put my notebook away.

"Remember what you asked about how André took too much medication?"

"Yes."

"There was a very slight amount of bruising around his mouth, but it is inconclusive. So it is not *impossible* that he was forced to keep the pills in his mouth, although Sheila still doesn't think so."

I checked my rearview mirror and pressed the accelerator to get back on the road. "Thanks, Tom. You're the best."

◆

Rain splatted gently across my dusty windshield by the time I reached the western end of Troutman Trail. When I drove up to the very plain-looking brown house with peeling green trim, Lettie and Arch were jumping on the trampoline in the front yard. Julian was nowhere in sight.

I parked under a lodgepole pine and considered my wet-haired, happily leaping son. He was dressed in a clean but faded polo-style white shirt as well as too-large navy shorts—both hand-me-downs from Julian, both now quite wet. He was bouncing on an unstable, steel-framed trampoline, in the rain, when lightning could strike any moment. And all this with a girl, no less. Should I tell him to stop? Or

332

confront him about sharing my confidential client information with The Jerk? Neither. The first could be finessed, the second would wait until we were alone.

"Arch! I don't know where your suit is! You'll have to find it." I pulled open the van door. "Lettie? Are Julian and your sister inside?"

When Lettie nodded, I knocked on the front door. Julian, his finger marking his place in the new edition of *The Joy of Cooking,* admitted me.

"Catching up on your reading?" I asked.

He blushed. "I brought it with me, along with poached veggies for the girls. Arch ate at home, which is probably a good thing. Have to warn you, this place is a mess. I didn't feel right about cleaning it up, but I don't know if Rustine would want you to come in. They had a housekeeper, but she quit a month ago. Anyway, Rustine's doing some beauty treatment. I hollered to her that you were here."

"No matter what, I want you to keep an eye on Arch," I said quietly.

"That's why I'm sticking around."

Rustine, sporting newly painted toenails and toes separated by wads of cotton, appeared behind Julian. She was wearing a white shorty robe. Underneath a shower cap, her hair was covered with green goo. Her face was plastered with mud.

I said, "Are you going like that to the rec center?"

She *tsk*ed. "It's almost time to rinse this stuff

off. Have you been able to find out who wanted to kill Gerald?"

"May I come in?"

She moved in front of Julian, opened the door, and ushered me into a space so cluttered with furniture and boxes that it was hard to make out where to go. It was a contemporary-design house, with the dining room, living room, and kitchen all open to each other. The dining room table was covered with papers: résumés, letters, files, want ad sections of old newspapers. Every chair in the dusty living room was heaped with boxes of papers.

"Want something to drink?" Rustine eyed the sinkful of dirty dishes, which probably included every glass in the house. "Check the refrig."

Opening the refrigerator door, I was dazzled by gleaming rows of bottled water, flavored with everything from passion fruit to mango. I looked longingly at the kitchen faucet and ended up choosing water flavored with kiwi. In the living room, Rustine perched on the arm of a once-white, now charcoal gray, wing chair filled with a pile of papers. I sat on a stool close enough to the black wall-to-wall carpeting to see it was embedded with hair and dust. Julian hunkered down on the undusted hearth of a moss-rock fireplace. So much for models living in surroundings as gorgeous as the ones in which they're photographed.

"Where did you say your dad was?" I ventured.

"I told you, in Alaska, looking for a job. Then

he's going to Orange County, then he'll be back after Labor Day. If he gets a job, he's going to hire a new housekeeper."

Julian closed the cookbook. "You want me to clean up that kitchen for you?"

"No, thanks," she said dismissively.

"Aw, I'm used to doing dishes." He grinned and made for the kitchen. "That way you can ask Goldy about your former boyfriend and not be embarrassed."

"I'm not embarrassed." She watched Julian filling the sink with hot sudsy water, though, then stood up and beckoned for me to follow. A few minutes later I was perched on the edge of a tub in a large, messy bathroom tiled in avocado and lemon, while Rustine rinsed the mud off her face. As she was patting her cheeks with a dingy towel, she said, "I just need another few minutes for my conditioner, then Julian and I will take the kids swimming. That's okay, isn't it?" I nodded. She went on: "So, what have you been able to find out about Gerald?"

Two things I had learned from Tom: always take charge of an interrogation. Even when you're sitting on a tub. And when you think a criminal might have done something, first pose a question he can truthfully deny, then ask him what you really want to know. If he hesitates, you've got him.

I studied Rustine's reflection in the mirror. "Are you the one who's been sabotaging my food up at the cabin?"

"No! What sabotage?"

I kept my eyes on her. "Foreign matter has appeared in the food. Whoever's putting it there might have sabotaged André, too. I suspect Craig Litchfield's behind it."

"Well, *I'm* not the one doing it. And it sounds disgusting. I'm going to stop eating your food!"

"Rustine, you told Tom and me that Gerald Eliot found a weapon. Then you immediately asked us if we'd found out some secret about Charlie Smythe. But it was a rifle Eliot found, and something *told* you it was Smythe's, right? You were Gerald's girlfriend. I think you know a lot more about what he found."

Rustine reddened; she checked her eyelids for specks of mud before responding. "I didn't say...I don't remember saying—"

"Cut the crap."

"I—" She sighed. "Okay. Gerry found Charlie Smythe's old rifle. You've seen it on the wall of the cabin's great room, haven't you? Leah put it there."

"What else? Tell me. Otherwise I'll call the department. You'll be arrested for withholding evidence in a murder case faster than you can say *anorexia nervosa.*"

She tapped the side of the sink, thought for a moment, then shrugged. "All right. I used to be at the cabin with Gerry, kind of keeping him company, you know, when he was working. It was fun to watch, all that destruction. He'd take off his shirt, Mr. Rippling Muscles, you know—" She giggled, then said, "He pulled everything away from the wall, and used his sledgehammer to rip the plaster off the kitchen wall. When he got to the laths underneath—"

"I don't need a course in construction, thanks."

She pulled the shower cap off and checked her hair. "Right. Tucked between the laths, he found this...package, wrapped in oilcloth. He was really excited, and kind of afraid, too. Like he'd discovered a ghost or something. Inside the oilcloth was this old rifle. But Rufus barged in right after Gerry unwrapped the rifle. So Gerry had to give it to Rufus, who left to give it to Leah and Ian. Gerry felt...gypped."

"So you knew all about the rifle, but you only told us it was a weapon. What exactly were *you* looking for up at *Cameron Burr's* place?"

"I need to rinse my hair—"

"You want me to call the sheriff's department? Then you can rinse it in the jail shower."

She turned red. "I was looking for Winnie Smythe's cookbook, okay?" I waited. "After he'd found the rifle, Gerry came across something else in the wall. It was also a package, and it was wrapped in oilcloth, too. It was...a note from a man to his wife. From Charlie to Winnie."

"Do you have it?"

She ran her fingers through her slick hair. "No."

She was lying. "So help me, Rustine—"

"Oh, all right, I have a photocopy that Gerry made. He thought the letter was going to make us rich, and all it did was get him killed. I figured if you could find out who really killed him, or where the cookbook was, then I could...If I help you, will you split what you find with me?"

"Rustine! Show me the note and tell me why you need the damn cookbook!"

"Just listen for a sec. Gerry was so excited about finding this stuff, he was asking all around about the history of the cabin. Everybody knew he was on to something!"

"Would you please give me that note?"

Her excited eyes met mine. Again I recalled her first appearance in the cabin kitchen. *You're the caterer who figures things out.*

Rustine's medicine cabinet door squeaked when she opened it. She pulled out a folded, zippered plastic bag and handed it to me.

Chapter 21

"Mom!" called Arch from the door. "I found my suit. Can Rustine take us swimming now? We're ready."

"Can you just...hold off for a few minutes, hon? We're talking."

"Let me show you my ham radio," Lettie added. "Does yours still work?"

"No," I heard Arch reply. "How do you keep your antenna on your roof?" Their footsteps pattered down the hallway.

I pulled a folded sheet of paper out of the zippered makeup bag. The handwriting, with its bold pen marks, was identical to the handwriting on the letter from Leavenworth:

My Dear Wife,
You are my Treasure and I am yours. If
there ever comes a time when I am in
Heaven and you want me, you know you
have only to use my Rifle and your Cook-
ery book, and make the Rolls as I showed
you. Thus will you have our Treasure.
Your Loving Husband

"Well, now, that makes a lot of sense," I said after I'd read the note twice. "Use the rifle. Make the rolls according to a certain recipe. Then you'll be rich. Do you stir the batter with the rifle butt? And would that be Parker House or cloverleaf rolls?"

Rustine shrugged. "I just wish I knew who else Gerry showed the note to. Or who has that cookbook. We have to have the cookbook!"

I stood up. No need to mention the photocopies to Rustine. I said, "I need to take this to my husband."

I missed Arch on the way out, which was probably just as well. In the kitchen, Julian was up to his elbows in sudsy water, singing an a cappella riff on "Hark! The Herald Angels Sing." Just like André, I thought with a smile, although Julian probably didn't even realize it. He'd somehow cleared off a spot on the cluttered counter, laid down a dish towel, and heaped up a pile of washed and rinsed pans to drip-dry.

"Please have Arch home by three," I asked him. "The service for André is at four."

He nodded, and I took off for home. To my astonishment, Tom had finished the plumbing and put in the rest of the bottom cabinets. *This is what it must be like to have a contractor who works full-time,* I mused. Without a counter, our kitchen still looked like a dusty warehouse, but at least it was beginning to take on the look of a *culinary* warehouse.

While I looked for lunch fixings, Tom washed his hands, poured a glass of water, and stared at the note I'd given him. "Why in the world didn't Rustine tell us about this? It affects a murder case, for crying out loud."

"She was hoping to cash in, once we found out what was going on." I handed him a wobbly paper plate containing one of two peanut-butter-and-cherry-preserves brioche-toast sandwiches I'd just made fresh in our cramped dining room space. It didn't look very fancy, but when I hungrily bit into mine, the crunch of homemade toast mingling with slightly melted peanut butter and sweet cherry preserves was out of this world. Now all I needed was an iced latté to go with it.

"This is delicious." He wolfed his down and reached for the phone to call the sheriff's department. "You know they're going to come get this," he informed me. "And they're going to want to question Rustine."

I shrugged. It was time to get ready for André's service. I made a slick fax-copy of the note for my own file. It wasn't ideal, but with needing to shower and change, I didn't have time to go to the library and photocopy more copies of stolen historical documents.

♦

In a black Chanel suit and spectator pumps, her freshly coiffed curls tucked behind rhinestone-and-onyx earrings, Marla had morphed back to her old self when I found her in the parking lot of St. Stephen's Roman Catholic Church. The rain had stopped, but my irascible friend lofted her Louis Vuitton umbrella over her head in triumph.

"I'm done, I'm finished!" she sang. Her peaches-and-cream complexion was flushed with joy. She bustled up to my van. "The IRS guys left today, saying I'd hear from them soon. I said, 'How 'bout never?' They weren't amused. But here's the deal: they think I'm going to get a *refund*!"

I hugged her tightly and felt unexpected tears burn. "Oh, Marla. I've missed you so much. And there's something I have to tell you, but you weren't feeling well, and I wanted to wait until your audit was over, because—"

"Calm down, will you? I can't listen to whatever it is until I've had some food. Let's see if the guys from André's old restaurant have any goodies set up yet. Where's Arch?"

"Tom's bringing him. And the food is for afterwards!"

"You want my stomach to growl through the service?" she threatened as she linked her arm through mine and led me up the steps. "Have to tell you, Goldy, one of those IRS agents *was* kind of cute." Her voice turned wistful. "I suppose it's unethical for him to date an accused tax-chiseler.... And if he did ask me out, I'd have to wonder. I mean, now he *knows* I'm rich."

We entered the parish hall, a long, vaulted-ceiling addition to the ultramodern church. The enticing scents of roasted ham, chicken, pork, and beef wafted toward us. My heart tugged as I waved at two of the servers I knew from the old restaurant days with André. After Marla had deftly nabbed a couple of what looked like André's Grand Marnier Buttercream Cookies, I steered her into the stone vestibule. There, lanky, balding Monsignor Fields talked in a hushed tone with Pru Hibbard and Wanda Cooney.

"What I want to tell you is this," I whispered to Marla as she munched on her cookies. "John Richard has been, and is, trying to get revenge on us. He turned you in to the IRS before he went *to* jail, and he's been bankrolling Craig Litchfield *from* jail."

Her beautiful brown eyes widened with shock. She swallowed the last mouthful of cookie. "Revenge on us? For *what*? That son of a bitch!" she hissed. "I'll kill him!"

"Don't start!" I warned as I sent the startled monsignor a conciliatory nod. I tugged Marla into the airy, modern church. Because Saint Stephen had been martyred by stoning, the only decoration on the high, pale blue walls was a mass of irregular stone-shaped windows filled with pale blue stained glass. Light abruptly flooded the windows as the sun emerged from behind a cloud. The wall suddenly resembled a jeweler's cloth strewn with aquamarines. "Look, Marla," I said softly, "I just wanted you to know he's being vengeful. In case anything else unexpected happens. Are you vulnerable in any other way?"

"The *hell* with vulnerable." She slid into a pew and smoothed the Chanel suit. "That creep has so much money to throw around, I'll sue him myself. And don't tell me you can't sue somebody in jail, because *I will find a way.* Oh, I can't *wait.*" She patted my knee. "Now, I have *good* news for *you.* Litchfield's dinner for Weezie was *dreadful.* I know because I sneaked out on the IRS and went—as an invited guest, but of course as a spy, too, once I'd found out she'd canceled you. Anyway, he tried to cheat her— naughty, naughty. Weezie had ordered poached salmon from him. He made *coulibiac,* which everybody knows is a carbo-load made from bits of salmon sandwiched between crêpes and covered with brioche. I heard that Weezie now suspects he had the salmon left over from another job. *And* get this: She wants Andy Fuller to investigate!"

So. Maybe instead of bothering my husband, Andy Fuller would be investigating Craig Litchfield's fraudulent use of salmon? Now *that* was what I called having bigger fish to fry, I thought, as an usher handed us each a service leaflet for the memorial service.

"There's more," Marla whispered conspiratorially as the pews around us began to fill. "Weezie wanted a buffet. Craig insisted on a sit-down affair so he could limit portions. Worse, he inflated every dish with either frozen chopped spinach or—you're going to *die*—bread stuffing. Even the pasta had *bread crumbs* in it." She unsuccessfully suppressed a giggle. The woman on the other side of me looked up and glared. But Marla went on happily, "Edna Hardcastle is in for a *huge* surprise on Saturday. Maybe she'll call and rehire you at the last minute."

"Maybe her daughter will cancel her wedding again."

Marla laughed out loud at the prospect of a wedding that might be postponed a third time; the woman glowered; I shrugged apologetically. Life in Aspen Meadow is never dull.

Tom, Arch, and Julian slid in next to us. Pru had been accompanied by Wanda Cooney to the front. The widow had apparently made the decision not to have her husband's coffin present. Arch gave my shoulder a quick squeeze when the organ began to play.

An altar boy had opened the side door overlooking the mountains. A breeze scented with pine wafted over us. The huge church was about half filled with mourners, which I found gratifying. André had touched a number of people, despite his eccentric ways and long-winded tales of his own history, real or imagined. While the lessons from Isaiah and Paul's second letter to the Corinthians were read, I prayed for my teacher. I gave thanks that he had given me the gift of cooking as a way to care for people. I gave thanks that he'd come into my life just when I'd needed him.

The monsignor gave a brief homily on not fearing death. He took his seat, and the congregation waited. According to the service leaflet, a remembrance was to be offered by Rabbi Sol Horowitz. This was something I'd never heard of in a Roman Catholic church, and I mentally gave them points for open-mindedness. After a few moments, a stooped, white-haired man shook off offers of assistance and climbed to the pulpit.

"The organist has agreed to help me," the rabbi began in a heavy accent. We waited, but no music was forthcoming. The rabbi pursed his lips, looked out over the congregation, then opened a folded sheet.

"This is my remembrance, from the time of the war." Holding the sheet with one hand, he removed a handkerchief from his pocket and dabbed his forehead. "In my brother's town of Clermont-Ferrand, André Hibbard was a fearless Resistance fighter, despite the fact that he was but eleven years old. Although André was a child, he hated the Nazis, and he helped my brother and his wife avoid deportation to the camps." The rabbi faltered, then went on.

"André Hibbard concealed my brother and his wife, an Italian Jew, in a barn. My brother was a violinist. Every day, André brought them cheese and milk." The rabbi cleared his throat. "The Resistance was organized, and they taught codes to all their trainees. But André had no radio, of course. So when the trains to take the Jews away arrived, André Hibbard used music to alert my brother's family. If there was danger, André would whistle 'Für Elise' to my brother." Rabbi Horowitz waited while the rippling notes of Beethoven's tune rolled through the blue-lit church.

When the organ music faded, the congregation was still. Rabbi Horowitz went on: "One night, a man waited to take my brother and his family out, to try to get them to Switzerland, to safety. André's job was to watch for the Nazis and whistle again to my brother's family, to indicate it was safe to move. The tune he chose was from Felix Mendelssohn."

The entire congregation listened intently as the organ pealed forth with "Hark! The Herald Angels Sing." Marla's face brightened. Arch smiled broadly. The rabbi folded his paper and pocketed it with the handkerchief. He grinned and nodded down at us.

"With the help of André Hibbard, my brother and his wife escaped to Zurich. After playing many years with the Boston Symphony, my brother retired. Last year, he died. But he always made a good joke, about how the French boy fooled the Nazis, by using a Christian hymn to save a family of Jews."

The congregation broke into spontaneous applause as Rabbi Horowitz found his seat. Visibly moved, the monsignor led us through the Lord's Prayer, the intercessions, additional prayers, and the final commendation and blessing. One of the cooks from André's old restaurant led Pru down the nave. The congregation followed. As we all filed out, the organist broke into an enthusiastic, multiversed rendition of "Hark! The Herald Angels Sing."

◆

After the service, I dimly registered Monsignor Fields walking toward me across the church's large patio. Marla was eating, but I couldn't. I was sitting on the patio's stone wall—in a state of shock, I think—realizing that the stories André had told, the stories that I'd doubted, that I'd only been half listening to—had been true. The monsignor interrupted my thoughts.

"Pru is extremely tired. She does not want to stay for the reception, but she would like to visit with you at her condominium, if you feel up to driving out there." He seemed almost apologetic.

"I'd love to."

When I told Tom where I was going, he chuckled. "I told the boys this buffet food was it for dinner, so we'll be here for a while."

On the way to Blue Spruce, dark-bellied clouds again gathered and spit raindrops on my van as I followed Wanda and Pru in Wanda's Suburban. *André had indeed been a Resistance fighter,* I thought with newfound admiration. *He was a genuine hero.* I felt like a better person, just from knowing him. I turned on the wipers as the road snaked beside a creek edged with cottonwoods and wild daisies bowed by the rain. A golden eagle soared gracefully downward, then skimmed the tops of the lodgepole pines before disappearing from view. I braked as Wanda slowed to enter the Blue Spruce Retirement Village.

"I'm going to go take a shower, if you don't mind," Wanda confided once she had Pru settled on a chaise longue in her sitting room. We were standing in the small condo kitchen. "There's something about a funeral that just...makes me want to get out of my clothes and start over." She placed André's old tea ball stuffed with leaves into one of the many teapots and checked the water she'd set on to boil. "You'll tend to her if she needs anything? She just wanted to see you again, since you've called so many times."

"No problem," I said softly. "It's unlikely our visit will be disrupted by visitors this time. Has anyone called to bother you in the last week?"

"Two more real estate agents appeared, plus that horrible caterer dropped by again." She shuddered and carefully poured the steaming water over the tea ball. The scent of orange and black pekoe wafted upward. "I told Litchfield if he had the nerve to come here again I'd report him to the police. He hasn't been back."

"Wanda," I said suddenly as I glanced

around the kitchen, "where are André's cooking tools?"

"You mean the ones he kept in his red box?" When I nodded, she answered, "The police brought them back, along with his apron and pans. Pru had me put them in the spare bedroom. Why?"

"No reason." I took the tray. "Thanks for the tea."

Pru was fast asleep by the time I returned to her sitting room. With her head tilted back, her mouth slightly open, she looked as young and innocent as a bride. I put the tray down and sat on an ottoman by the chaise lounge. When I heard the shower water running, I quickly went looking for the spare bedroom.

It was upstairs, a spotless, sparsely decorated room featuring white curtains and chenille bedspreads. My heartbeat sped up as I pulled open the closet door and heard it creak. I held my breath; Wanda's shower continued to run. André's red metal chef's toolbox had been placed on the floor of the closet.

The old metal hinge squeaked when I cracked back the top. Again I froze and waited for some response in the house, but heard only running water. I opened the partitions of the box that I knew so well: butcher and paring knives, balloon whisks, can openers, butterball scoop, vegetable brushes and peelers, garlic press, spatulas of all sizes, old wooden spoons. Only one item was missing: André's salamander.

Although André had never used the bottom

compartment for tools—he liked having his tools out where he could see them—I lifted the top layer just to see if I'd missed something. The spoons clanked and the metal layer scraped the sides of the box as I heaved the compartment free. When it was finally out, I gaped, uncomprehending, into the bottom of the box.

There was what I sought: André's salamander. But next to it was a tool I'd certainly never seen André use in a kitchen: a crowbar.

Chapter 22

What to do? My thoughts raced. I did a double-check of all the tools; nothing else was unusual or out of place. The water stopped. I hastily closed the box, slid it back into place, shut the closet door, and descended the stairs on tiptoe. Pru slumbered on. I poured two cups of ultrastrong room-temperature tea and slugged one down. When Wanda reappeared, I motioned toward Pru and then whispered that I would find my way out.

I sprinted to the van and drove back to our house. Tom and the boys were not yet back from the reception. Hunger knotted my stomach. *Cook,* I told myself. *That will help you figure this out.*

Cook? I surveyed the buckled rectangles of plywood that covered two thirds of the counter area; the rest was just gaping holes revealing cabinet drawers. The new floor, still unfinished, looked like it belonged in a barn. I did not have the foggiest idea where my recipes were, but I knew Arch well enough to predict that no matter how much food they had at the reception, he would want dinner. Not because he was hungry, but because the comfort of order, including meals served at regular times, had been one of the ways he'd restructured his universe after our family life had first fallen apart. So I decided to make Slumber Party Potatoes, his favorite.

Within ten minutes, I had started bacon cooking, scrubbed four potatoes in the main-floor bathroom, shuttled them along with washed broccoli out to the kitchen, and placed them in the oven. I trimmed the broccoli stems and set them in a small amount of boiling water just as the thick slices of bacon began bubbling in my sauté pan. Despite a messed-up kitchen, despite Craig Litchfield's attempts to undermine my business, I still loved to cook.

Craig Litchfield. He'd shown up in the most unlikely places, including at André's house the day he died. I knew he was a smarmy competitor, but was he engaged in something even more sinister than stealing clients? Someone was sabotaging my food up at the cabin. I was fairly certain the same vindictive prank had been played on André. Could the prankster be Craig Litchfield? Could Litchfield have been so insane as to get through the locked gate, or climb the fence of the Merciful Migrations property, to try to harm a competitor? Or could he have hired someone

351

Slumber Party Potatoes

4 large baking potatoes
2 tablespoons (¼ stick) butter
3 tablespoons all-purpose flour
1 tablespoon chicken broth granules
1½ cups milk
1 cup grated Cheddar cheese
1 pound fresh broccoli, trimmed of stems and
  separated into florets, lightly steamed
1 pound thick-sliced bacon, cooked until
  crisp, drained, and chopped

Preheat the oven to 400°F.

Scrub and prick the potatoes in 3 or 4 places with a
fork. Bake them for about 1 hour, or until flaky.

While the potatoes are baking, melt the butter in a
large skillet over low heat. Stir in the flour; cook and
stir just until the flour bubbles, 2 or 3 minutes. Add
the chicken broth granules, stir, and then gently
whisk in the milk. Heat and stir constantly over

medium heat until the sauce thickens, about 10 minutes. Add the cheese and stir until it melts, 2 or 3 minutes.

Split each of the hot potatoes in half and place them on a platter. Place the steamed broccoli florets and chopped bacon into bowls. Pour the cheese sauce into a large gravy boat. Diners serve themselves assembly-line style, ending with the cheese sauce.

Makes 4 to 8 servings

to do it? And could that person have meant merely to scare André and gone too far? I couldn't believe that Craig Litchfield would be willing to take a homicide rap, but then again, as I'd learned so often with The Jerk, some folks won't hesitate to use violence in order to get their way.

I turned the sputtering bacon slices. Fat popped in the pan, and a tiny, stinging droplet spattered my forearm. I frowned and rubbed the spot. That first morning we had worked together at the cabin, André had given me such meticulous instruction in caramelizing—"burning sugar"—for that day's dessert. He was always careful in the kitchen, citing tales of cooks who had sliced fingers or burned their hands or faces. He'd warned me repeatedly about burns. So, on the morning he died, I'd say the chances he had burned *himself* with his own salamander were slim, unless he had had cardiac symptoms *while* he was doing the caramelizing.

I finished flipping the bacon and turned down the heat. So the burns on his hands still bothered me. What else? The fact that he was even preparing more *crème brûlées* that day was a puzzle. André always brought backup food. So why would he have been making still more *crème brûlées* in the kitchen? Had he come to the cabin to prep the fruit, and then been told he needed to make a lot *more* custards? Who could have delivered this message, and when? Had that same person interrupted André as he was making the *crèmes*? Maybe even seen him using the fiery-hot salamander? And why had André, or someone else, hidden or stored the salamander and a *crowbar* in his tool-box? Had the crowbar been used as a weapon, or for something else?

I turned off the heat under the broccoli and tried to envision André that last morning. Maybe he'd been working in the kitchen and heard somebody in the great room. Could he have seen someone tinkering with the flat that so nearly crushed Leah? Maybe he'd seen or heard something, picked up a crow-bar, tiptoed out to the great room, and...And what? And tried to hurt somebody with it? What about the hot salamander? And the nitro-glycerin? Were the slight bruises in his mouth nothing, as the coroner seemed to think? Or had someone forced him to swallow the pills?

I drained the fragrant, sputtering bacon slices and the bright green steamed broccoli florets, and tried to construct a different sce-nario. What if André had brought the crow-bar with him, in order to try to find something? That would surely explain why he'd come early, with all the food made in advance. But what would he have been seeking? André had never seen the letter hidden in the old wall, the letter which had pointed toward using Winnie's stolen cookbook to make rolls. To find treasure. He had never shown the least interest in either American history or weapons, and it seemed highly unlikely he had any regard for Charlie Smythe's old rifle. But he had had *some* glimmer of what was going on when he'd asked for a photocopy of Winnie

Smythe's cookbook. Why? What made the cookbook so important? If André had known something—something Gerald Eliot had known, too—what could it have been?

I cut a stick of butter in half and set it to melt in another pan for the cheese sauce. Had there been a tidbit of gossip André was waiting to share with me—something that had made someone on the set dislike Leah enough to try to kill her? I turned that over in my mind for a moment, and discarded it. Any gossip he had, he would have told me instantly as soon as the paramedics left on Friday, when we worked together. That day, instead, he'd clucked sympathetically to Sylvia's tale of woe about the robbery. He'd talked to Julian about his work with the Resistance during the war, and helped us prepare and serve the coffee break goodies. What else? André had gasped later in the morning. I'd thought he was having another attack. But he hadn't been.

I quickly grated a heap of Cheddar cheese. What had immediately preceded this *appearance* of a seizure at the museum? He'd been staring with a disconcerting intensity at the smashed cupboard which had held the missing cookbooks. What else? He had read Charlie Smythe's letter to Winnie from Leavenworth. So what?

I stirred flour into the butter for a roux, and waited until that mixture bubbled over low heat. *Gently cook the flour,* André had admonished me so many times, *gentleness is one of the secrets of the sauce.* I added seasonings and hot milk to the roux and delicately whisked the sauce.

Outside, Tom's car turned into the drive-way. I stirred the cheese into the thickened sauce and watched it turn golden.

"Oh, Mom, thanks!" cried Arch, dashing into the kitchen. "Slumber Party Potatoes, and we're not even having a slumber party!"

Tom kissed and hugged me and announced that he'd had plenty to eat, and that he had some work to do in the kitchen. Was there any way Arch and Julian and I could eat outside? Arch said he needed to feed Jake and Scout and give them fresh water. Julian quickly offered to help me set up on the deck. When we finally had scraped the outdoor chairs together, covered the picnic table with a bright tablecloth, set out silverware, plates, bowls of crisp bacon, steamed broccoli, hot cheese sauce, and steaming potatoes, Julian abruptly declared that he needed a break and was going to go back to the rec center to swim laps. He left without eating a bite.

I raised my eyebrows at Arch, who had finished his animal care duties. "Any reason for the sudden interest in swimming?"

Arch dabbed cheese sauce on half a potato and licked his fingers. "Rustine's not there, if that's what you're asking, Mom. Rustine said there was too much chlorine in the pool, and it would wreck her hair, so she didn't go in. Neither did Julian. And Lettie saw some friends from school, so she didn't really talk to me very much."

"Arch," I said, "there's something I need to talk to you about."

357

"Oh, brother. Now what?"

"Did you print out my client list and all my schedules, assignments, and prices for your father?"

"No! No way!"

"Did you print it out for anybody?"

"Yeah," he said immediately. "That guy who's trying to do Dad's finances? Hugh Leland? Mr. Leland called when you were on a job. He said he couldn't figure Dad's portion of my tuition at Elk Park Prep while he was in jail until I faxed him a copy of your client list and prices, to verify that *you* couldn't pay the tuition."

"Arch, that is complete baloney. Your dad pays the tuition, as ordered by the court."

"Well, that's not what Mr. Leland said, Mom."

"Please, hon. Please don't give out any information about me, or us, or the business, to anyone." I heard the sharpness in my voice, but couldn't suppress it.

"I'm *sorry*." Arch looked stricken. "I was just doing what I thought I was supposed to do, Mom."

I swallowed my anger. Despite what he had done, it was impossible to blame my son: He'd just been trying to help. And yet, John Richard's ability to manipulate him appalled me. I glanced upward, trying desperately to think of something else to talk about. On the roof, Arch's ham radio antenna still dangled like a forgotten spider web. "How was Lettie's ham radio set? Did it work any better than yours?"

Arch set his plate aside, the food virtually untouched. "Look, Mom, I know you really want me to be happy and all that, but don't ask me a bunch of questions about Lettie, okay? Please?"

"Sure." He was at an age where trying to establish a conversation was as treacherous as navigating a mine field. I was forever veering away from one subject where I was tempted to give advice, to another, where I would have to bite my tongue not to lecture. I looked up again at the forlorn antenna, the remnants of Arch's first obsession with high-tech encryption. Wait a minute.

Arch had always been fascinated by a bit of history told him by Julian, whose adoptive parents in Utah had taught him to speak Navajo. During the Second World War, Navajos serving in the American military had spoken in their own language, over the radio, to other Navajo soldiers, who'd passed on details of troop movements and other matters of military importance to Allied military intelligence. Navajo is one of the most difficult languages in the world. It was a code never broken by the Germans.

What was the one thing everyone said about Charlie Smythe? *He was a signalman for the Confederacy....*

Rabbi Horowitz had told us: *The Resistance...taught codes to all their trainees.*

One of the secrets of the sauce...André had never seen the cookbook or the letter in the wall. But he *had* seen the enigmatic letter from Leavenworth, the later letter Charlie Smythe had written to his wife...not the earlier letter, which had remained hidden in the wall all these years.

"Arch," I said suddenly. "You know your work with telephone encryption? Did you ever learn any codes that are universal? I mean, besides Morse."

He eyed me. "There are codes and ciphers that have been used over and over. But the question isn't whether you can put something *into* a code, Mom. The question is whether the person receiving it can *understand* it." He pushed his glasses up his nose and tilted his chin. "Why?"

"If I showed you a letter that a man wrote from prison, that might be in a fairly common code, do you think you could read it?"

"Is it in English?" he asked dubiously.

I told him that it was and ran inside for my file. When I handed Arch the photocopy of Charlie Smythe's letter to his wife from prison, he pondered it, chewed his tongue, then reread the paper in his hands. He did not know that Winnie Smythe, incapacitated by stroke, probably never had understood the letter. He did not know the history of the Smythe cabin. He did not know about the aborted remodeling work that Gerald Eliot had begun there. So it was with true astonishment that I heard Arch's next set of questions.

"So. Did this woman, Winnie, tear out her kitchen wall? Did she use a"—he peered down at the letter—"cookery book? Is that a cookbook?" I nodded, speechless. "And let's see—this guy's gun? To find some treasure?"

"Show me," I whispered.

"It's a real common code, Mom. It's one a lot of prisoners used over the years, because it usually gets past censors." He pointed to the paper and I read it again.

My Dear Wife,

You must know how very much I love you, and how I would tear out my Heart to see you again. To get to my cell, I pass a wall in which I have tried to carve your name. I remember our cabin Kitchen with its smell of Bread and Pudding, how you would use Cookery to show your love for me. I have only read one book. Sky here is seldom seen. I long for our bed, children, Family tales, rifle, horses, Cabin, and beautiful land where I believed to find Riches. One day, my Love.

Your Loving Husband

Arch said, "You just read the first two words in each line. So it's: *You must tear out wall in cabin kitchen use cookery book skytales rifle find riches.*" He paused. "Did this lady know the code?"

"No. At least, I don't think so." If she had been able to act on the letter, Winnie would surely have found the precious rifle her husband had so carefully hidden in the wall. "What's a skytale?"

"It's another way of encoding a message,

Mom. It's been used for a really long time. Say you have a message. You write it on a long, thin piece of paper. That's called the plaintext, that you wrap around a cylinder of a certain size; *that's* called a skytale. But on your plaintext, you put lots of numbers or letters in between your message, so that nobody can read what you're saying, see? The person who's decoding the message rolls your sheet of letters or numbers around the skytale cylinder. Then the extra numbers or letters aren't seen. Just the one line of letters is seen, and that's your message. Get it? The trick, once you have a strip of paper, is to know which cylinder to roll it around."

I remembered Rustine's copy of the note in the wall: *Make the Rolls as I showed you.* It wasn't *bread* Smythe referred to, but *strips of paper.* I closed my eyes and shook my head.

Arch asked, "Do you have the cookbook?"

"I have a copy. There are letters written on two of the pages. They must form the strip of words, somehow." My heartbeat sounded loud in my ears.

"What about this rifle?"

"It's up at the cabin where I'm catering tomorrow. Where André was working." I did not add *when he died.*

My son's eyes were solemn. "Do you think Chef André knew the code in the letter from prison?"

I remembered André gasping, staggering, looking triumphant and secretive when he read the letter. "Yeah, I do." And he needed money, I added mentally; he'd complained about his wife's bills and the cost of living in Aspen Meadow. The chance of finding a treasure isn't something he would have told me about. Besides, he just didn't know how much money, or how little, might be hidden out at the Smythe cabin. But he'd taken a crowbar with him to the cabin and tried to get behind the kitchen wall. And someone had discovered him, I was convinced.

"What about Leah Smythe?" Arch asked. "Do you think she read it and that's why the flat fell on her?"

I let out a nervous laugh. "I don't know, Arch. Hon, don't worry about it. André was getting on in years and had heart problems. I think a clamp came loose somehow and Leah was just in the wrong place at the wrong time." If I focused on the possibility of danger at a site, Arch would fret about my catering away from home. His fear would not be expressed in begging me to stay home, but only in pained looks and agonized questions: *When will you be back? What if something goes wrong?* In addition to all my other problems, I did not want to worry that Arch was anxious about my safety.

Arch had turned away to look at a butterfly perched on the deck railing. It was a monarch. The butterfly clapped its black-edged, dark orange wings slowly, soundlessly, before lifting from its perch and drifting down to the picnic table.

"It's lost," Arch announced. He pressed

his lips together. "So. Do you want me to look at these two cookbook pages? I could see if I could cut it into plaintext to wrap around a skytale for you, if you want."

"Sure." I scrambled up. "That would be fun. Maybe you and Tom could do it together."

"The two of you seem pretty excited," Tom said when we came into the kitchen. "Why don't you let me do these dishes? You guys go get an ice cream in town."

"Forget the dishes," I told him. "Arch has just figured out an interesting aspect of the Smythe history."

I grabbed the pages of letters from the bread and pudding recipes in *The Practical Cook Book,* and began to make copies with my fax machine. Through the evening, Tom, Arch, and I photocopied, cut, and taped together strips. We made strips of the letters horizontally, vertically, and sideways. My kitchen began to look as if a confetti parade had marched through a bomb site. Finally we had several dozen strips constructed. While Tom pried open the garage wall and pulled out his Winchester '94, I brought a sour cream coffee cake out of the freezer to defrost for the next day's catering.

We took turns wrapping strips one way and the other around the rifle. It took us hours to assemble long and short lines of nonsense. Julian came home and joined us, asking questions, offering suggestions, sharing our excitement.

Finally, close to exhaustion and ready to concede defeat, Arch had the idea to make a strip from all the vertical rows of letters on the Parker House Rolls and the bread pudding pages, and wrap them around the rifle's magazine, the ammunition-storage cylinder under the barrel. This gave him a very long string of letters, the longest yet.

"Hold on," Arch ordered. The slippery fax paper scritched and slid across the gray metal of the gun as Arch nudged it into place. Then, triumphantly, he showed us Charlie's message to his wife.

UNDER THE ELEPHANT ROCK.

Chapter 23

"Well, I am impressed." Tom patted Arch on the back, and he beamed. "And I know that when Sylvia Bevans hears that Leah might loan her museum a stash that's been buried for eighty-some years, even she will be ecstatic."

Arch's face fell. "You mean we don't get to *keep* whatever's there?"

Tom, Julian, and I laughed. I told him if there was anything there, it would belong to the robbery victims' descendants, if any could be found. Arch asked if he could call Lettie to tell her the news. No way, Tom informed him, you can't tell *anybody*. Disappointed, but still savoring the victory of breaking the codes, Arch retired to his room with Julian to play music. Listening to the muffled thud of rock-and-roll, I took a hot bath and thought about the painful events of the past eleven days.

"You know I'm going to have to report what Arch figured out," Tom told me, joining me later in the bedroom. He had taken a shower after my bath, and now rubbed his wet, sandy-colored hair with a towel. The room was luminous with moonlight. Outside, a breeze shuffled the pines. It was late, and I was bone-tired.

"Of course. But at the moment, no one knows except us." I patted the clean sheets, made lustrous in the creamy light. "I have one day of catering left at the cabin."

The bed creaked as Tom got in. He pulled me close. "Uh, Miss G.? You should cancel for tomorrow." He kissed my ear and I shivered. "And if you *must* go, Boyd's coming with you again, no argument. Somebody on that photo shoot could be, probably *is*, a killer."

"Listen. I know something now. And what it is, I think, is the location of some very valuable jewelry, plus about five hundred dollars in cash, heisted from the last stagecoach to run in Yellowstone Park." Tom's embrace muddled my thinking, but I didn't mind. "All hidden away," I pressed on, "by a guy who was a signalman, a thief, and a rotten father."

He kissed my neck. "You're changing the subject."

"Wait. You're making it hard for me to think. What *else* I know is that someone is trying to sabotage my food. I need to figure out who it is, or face a risk whenever I do a booking."

His hands touched the small of my back and I nuzzled against him. "Goldy, stop nosing around in old crimes. Just finish your job."

"I might say the same for you, Mr. Contractor."

He groaned. "Don't joke."

I kissed him. "I'm not."

And then we made love, and for a while, I forgot all my problems, even my wrecked kitchen.

♦

A brief rain shower swept in very early the next morning. When I looked out, the leaves on the neighborhood aspen trees sparkled and drooped with their weight of water. Freshly stretched from yoga, and dressed in my caterer's uniform, I swallowed a few greedy breaths of cold, moist air before shutting the window.

Coffee break and lunch. I had the coffee break food ready to go—defrosted sour cream coffee cake, Cointreau French toast, strawberry and banana kabobs, cottage cheese mixed with mandarin oranges. For lunch, we would be serving an array of cold cuts and brioche. Julian had promised to make a soup and salad. We were also thawing some Blondes' Blondies made earlier in the week, while I turned over ideas on how to catch a saboteur. In that department, I'd had a couple of thoughts during the night.

When I entered the cluttered, unfinished

kitchen, Julian immediately handed me a hot espresso dosed with cream. I took the coffee with my usual gratitude. Through the trio of glittering new windows, I watched Jake and Scout cavort in the bloodhound version of cat-and-mouse. It was as if the move into colder weather brought out more energy in the animals: *Have fun now, before two feet of snow prevent us from romping around.* The delicious smell of baking puff pastry made me turn around.

"What are you making?" I asked Julian.

Snappily dressed in black with a white apron, his hair still damp from his shower, Julian gave me a quick grin, then went back to stirring. "Forget the soup. I'm heating the hors d'oeuvre from the wedding reception we're not doing. And a crab dip." His dark eyebrows knit as he cocked his head and studied my face. "What's wrong? André's memorial service got you down?"

"Yeah, a bit. Plus, the last day of a job, you always feel kind of sad." Especially when you don't know who's dumping garbage in your food, how your teacher met his death, or why one of your clients was almost squashed by a falling flat.

Julian, less obsessed with crime and criminals, turned his attention back to the hot dip. "Just think of the check you're going to get at the end. That's what I always do. Our boxes are packed, by the way. As soon as the first batch of appetizers is done, I'll cool it down and we can go." I slugged down the espresso, picked up the first box, and felt my shoulders and back strain from the weight. What had Julian said? *Think of the check.* Sure. If I was not mistaken, *thinking about the money* had produced a great deal too much illicit activity in the last month.

Sergeant Boyd was waiting for us at the library, steel thermos in hand. He had circles under his eyes. His feet hurt, he said. The sergeant's mood was not as jovial as it had been two days before. Most people think catering is just cooking, but it's not. The stresses of organizing, preparing, serving, dealing with people, and cleaning up either energizes or utterly exhausts you. Julian and I relished it; Boyd, the volunteer, was in culinary hell. When I asked if the crime lab folks had been able to find anything in the platters of food, he only muttered that they had not gotten to them yet.

"Which brings me to my current plan of action," I announced. I told Julian and Boyd that whoever was putting stuff into the food had always done it as soon as my back was turned. So, what if *I* wasn't the server of, say, the cottage cheese? One of them could bring out the platter and put it on the counter by the window. I'd be stationed on the deck, almost out of sight. The server would then go back to the kitchen, our saboteur would make his move, and I'd see the whole thing. "And you'll be there to arrest 'em," I told Boyd triumphantly. "How convenient."

"You gonna have a camera or something, catch this perp in a way that'll make it possible to prosecute?" he asked skeptically.

"Maybe Ian will loan me his Polaroid." I pulled the van through the open gate to the cabin. The damp, gold-tinged aspens clicked in the chilly breeze. Soon this road would be closed to traffic and open only to elk. I gunned the van through. Of course, that wouldn't be true once the paint-pellet people took over the property: They shoot at each other in all kinds of weather, elk be damned. We expertly unloaded our boxes in the parking area. As we headed down the trail to the cabin, the sun emerged from behind the clouds and shone brightly on the rock I'd noticed the very first morning I'd come here to work with André: the one that looked like an elephant. Tom was probably on the phone with the department, proposing a time to bring in a crew to dig. I wondered how *that* was going down with Andy Fuller. I forced myself to take my mind off the treasure by contemplating pitching a catering job to the paint-pellet guys. Pellet *pipérade*? Probably not.

Even though it was not quite seven, the final day's photo session was already in full swing. Out on the cabin deck with the assembled crew, Ian Hood seemed to be in a particularly good mood, calling good-natured orders—*Come on, baby. That's it. That's the way*—to a nightgown-and-slipper-clad Rustine. She was smiling coyly and moving this way and that on a bed made up of robin's-egg blue linens.

Even without Leah, the workers seemed to know exactly what to do as they hovered nearby. A new hairdresser and stylist I didn't recognize moved in and out swiftly between shots, expertly fluffing Rustine's hair with a tiny comb, checking the gold anklet that shimmered just above the heel she'd daintily exposed on the bed's coverlet. I recognized the makeup man from earlier in the week: from time to time he darted forward to dust Rustine's nose. On the occasional gruff order from Ian, Rufus adjusted the scrim. Hanna, black-clad as usual, like a fashionable cat burglar, scowled at everyone and tapped her foot. Behind Ian, Bobby Whitaker crossed his arms over his slight paunch and pretended to look bored. He had mentioned modeling today, but he certainly didn't look any thinner than the last time I'd seen him.

"Damn, that model looked cold out there," Boyd muttered as he opened the kitchen door for us. "Wouldn't catch me out on a deck in my pj's first thing in the morning. 'Cept if an elk was across the creek and I could get a clean shot."

"Shh!" Julian and I warned in unison. Even though the elk-lovers were all outside working the shoot, you couldn't be too careful. And we had work to do. The last thing I'd done after our code-breaking session was to put thick slices of French bread into the refrigerator, to soak overnight in a decadent combination of eggs beaten with cream and Cointreau. Now these sputtered on the hot, oiled griddle. When the fragrant, drenched slices formed a deep golden crust on one side, I flipped them. I checked my watch: The coffee break was scheduled to start in twenty-five minutes. We heated the oven, ran water for coffee and tea, and poured sugar and cream into a china bowl and pitcher. I slid a platter of the French toast into the oven while Julian began unmolding the cottage cheese rings and Sergeant Boyd brought out the coffee cake, fruit skewers, and silver platters.

"Ten minutes," I told them, and zipped out the kitchen door.

Someone had built a fire in the cabin's old fireplace, probably for the afternoon shots. I didn't know if this meant they wouldn't be dropping in the flames by computer, but I'd leave that to them. The great room seemed unusually cheery, good for the break. I nipped out to the deck, where a damp breeze sent a chill down my arms. Rustine eased off the blue sheets and raised her eyebrows questioningly at me. I ignored her.

"Ian." I caught up with him as he was conferring with Rufus about the next shot. "How's Leah? Have you visited her?"

He thoughtfully brushed his salt-and-pepper moustache with his finger. "I went down to the hospital last night. She broke a couple ribs when she fell. She's having some trouble breathing."

Out of the corner of my eye I could see Bobby Whitaker impatiently crossing and recrossing his arms. I said, "I'm glad she's okay."

"Ian?" pressed Bobby. Ian gave me an indulgent, *anything else?* look.

I cleared my throat. "I won't keep you. But could I borrow your Polaroid for a few minutes? Just during the coffee break."

He tilted his head in suspicion. "Why?"

"Oh, well..." Ian couldn't be the one sabotaging my food, could he? From all accounts, he ran a faltering photography studio, but he was the ambitious leader of a successful charity. He'd been unsympathetic to my pleas of unfair competition regarding the Soirée. Was there any way *he* could be in cahoots with Craig Litchfield? I gave Ian a soothing look, but his black eyes yielded nothing. *Basically, I don't trust anyone,* Tom was fond of saying. "I want to take a picture of my food through the window, that's all." I shrugged, as if I were just a kooky caterer looking for an angle. Which, of course, I was.

"Sure. Get it from Rufus." Ian's words trailed over his shoulder like smoke.

Balanced halfway up a stepladder, Rufus was adjusting a scrim for the next shot. He listened to my request, frowned, then gestured to the equipment sacks on the far side of the deck. "In one of Ian's bags. If you can find it, you can use it."

I rummaged through collapsible stands, lenses, rolls of film, and every kind of focus before my hands finally closed around the Polaroid. I nonchalantly picked it up, frowned at it as if it were a missing piece of cooking equipment, and walked purposefully back to the kitchen. Once there, I explained to Julian and Boyd exactly how I wanted to proceed.

They nodded, picked up the first fruited cottage cheese ring and hot water for the French toast chafer, and banged out the kitchen door—right into Yvonne, who shrieked and crumpled to the floor.

"Oh, gosh, we're sorry," Julian mumbled. Luckily, no food had spilled. Boyd, who had not yet learned that no matter who causes the problem, the caterer always apologizes, shot Yvonne an irritated glance.

She ran her fingers through her blond hair and hollered up at him, "What're you looking at, barrel-man?"

I hustled to her side and helped her to her feet. Muttering irritably, she brushed dust off her clothes: white mohair jacket, white pants, white leather boots. "I'm really sorry," I told her. "They should take that door off the kitchen entrance."

She fluffed her hair. "Don't worry about it. Do you like the outfit? Think anyone will notice the dust?"

"I love it," I lied smoothly. "It looks perfect."

While Boyd and Julian put the French toast and condiments on the buffet, I circled the folks on the deck to tell Hanna we were ready. She rocked on her small heels and nodded impassively. When Ian announced that the roll of film was done, Hanna efficiently signaled the break. I snagged the Polaroid from the kitchen and scuttled outside.

Through the window, I could see the line forming for coffee. I strode to the far side of the last window, pretended to be looking out at the creek, and smiled at Rufus as he climbed down the ladder and headed for the food. Then I waited.

Hanna, Ian, the day-contractors, Rustine vamping Bobby: All these folks came through the line. Ian and the stylist had two pieces of French toast. Rustine had only cottage cheese. Rufus must not have eaten breakfast; he piled his plate high. Behind him stood Yvonne, who reached into the pocket of the mohair jacket, pulled out a jar, and held it close to her as she unscrewed the lid. My heart thumped; I raised the camera. Yvonne dumped the jar's contents into the cottage cheese. I pressed the yellow button. The Polaroid flashed and spit out the picture. Yvonne looked up, glared, and hurried away from the line. But I had her.

"Arrest Yvonne." My breathless order to Boyd took him by surprise. "I've got it, it's in the picture, she endangered the food supply at a public function."

Boyd peered at the image slowly clarifying out of the murky film. "Yup." Laconic guy. But efficient. He had handcuffs in the pocket of his apron. When he swung the door open to the kitchen, Yvonne was scampering out the front door. Boyd rushed forward and grabbed her by a white-mohaired wrist. "You have the right to remain silent," he began tersely. Yvonne slithered up and down, her back to the front door, her eyes wide with fear. "If you don't hold still," Boyd warned, "I'm not going to be able to tell you the rest. You have the right to have an attorney present during questioning...."

Time to tell Ian and Hanna what was going on. They were conversing intently, heads together. Rufus and the day-contractors, their mouths agape, watched Boyd cuff Yvonne and talk to her in low tones. Bobby, still appearing impatient, appeared to take no notice.

"There's been a bit of a problem," I began, then proceeded to tell Ian and Hanna what I had captured on film.

"That fat caterer is really a *cop*?" exclaimed Ian, as if I'd just informed him that his elk were all migrating to Mexico. He looked at me incredulously. "That's why he had a mobile? I thought he got Leah's ambulance here so quickly because you guys had to be on the lookout for food poisoning!"

When I shrugged, Hanna grabbed my apron bib. "I *have* to have the mohair outfit and the boots. He can take her to the peni*ten*tiary if he wants, but I need her *clothes*. It's a twenty-thousand-dollar loss if I have to go over a day. Please, Goldy. Please. I'm begging you."

The things we do for clients. I headed back to Boyd and conveyed Hanna's request. Yvonne was crumpled against the door, whimpering. I resisted the urge to slap her face.

Boyd held up the jar. "Salt, she says. But we gotta have it analyzed anyway. She admitted some guy named Litchfield is paying her. She wants to stay and finish modeling for the day. I told her no way, and I've called for transport. Department has a unit in Blue Spruce, they'll be here in about ten minutes." When I conveyed Hanna's plea for the garments, he shook his head. "I can't risk losing her if she changes. She's gotta wear those clothes. Sorry."

Hanna's shoulders slumped when I told her. "Get Rustine into the Go-Gear Ski outfit," she snapped at the stylist. To me, she snarled, "Clean up the food and then go see if you can help Rustine. And lunch will have to be at two. We *must* complete this catalog today." *Hey,* I wanted to shout, *your model sabotaged my food! This is not my fault!*

The harried powwow that followed centered on whether the orange ski outfit would work with Rustine's hair, and whether or not they should move the shot inside. Two uniformed policemen appeared as Julian and I were clearing the buffet; they took the plate with the cottage cheese ring into evidence. I felt a great weight lift off my shoulders as Boyd left with Yvonne and the officers.

I scooped up the last French toast platter and started back toward the kitchen. Julian appeared and asked if I thought the clients would be wanting more coffee. I looked around. Across the cabin, Hanna and the day-workers were squabbling over photographs in the loose-leaf notebook. Rufus and Ian were arguing about the equipment. Bobby caught my eye and waved madly.

"Hey, I get it!" he cried. "That first day you were watching me undress, you weren't interested in my bod! Were you, Goldy? You're like, *undercover*, right? Is that why you were over at that old guy's house right after he died? Snooping around? Trying to find out what happened? Cool!"

To Julian, I muttered that we didn't need more coffee. I gripped the platter and wondered, for at least the tenth time since I'd come on this shoot, *What is the deal with Bobby?* No wonder Leah felt her twenty-four-year-old half-brother wouldn't be able to survive on his own—his immaturity seemed to guarantee long-term failure.

Bobby crowed, "So, Miss Caterer Lady, didja find anything at André's place?"

I stacked cups on the platter and realized I should be making some snappy comment. Or maybe I should have put down my load and held up my hands as in *Who? Me?* But I was embarrassed and suddenly insecure at the silence and the fact that everyone in the front room was staring openly at me. Could they guess how close Bobby had unwittingly come with his stupid questions? Could they imagine I'd ransacked a dead man's condo until I found his salamander and crowbar?

"Would you bring me some coffee?" Rustine simpered as she floated past me toward the dressing room. "With nonfat nondairy?"

"I'd like some, too," Hanna announced imperiously as she marched along behind Rustine. "Black. We'll be in the hair and makeup room."

"Sure," I replied, glad to have a reason to

scoot back to the kitchen. Luckily, Julian had made an extra pot of coffee. "I need to get out of here," I told him. "And I'm glad you're here, because I am sick to death of these people."

"No kidding. It's almost over, right? Three more hours, and we'll be done with this place for good." He slid a tray of miniature quiches— formerly for the Hardcastle reception—into the oven. "And, maybe it'll rain in the next three hours, too." He closed the oven door and waved his hands, as if conjuring up a vision. "Picture all the wedding-reception guests at the Hardcastles' place getting soaking wet as they chomp into soggy cheese puffs. I'll bet you a *thousand* bucks Craig Litchfield's hors d'oeuvre can't touch ours."

I grinned, poured the fragrant coffee into a large silver pitcher, clamped the top down, and put it along with nonfat creamer, artificial sweetener, and cups on a tray. But Hanna barred me from entering the door to the hair and makeup room. Inside, Rustine and the hair fellow were shrieking at one another about how Rustine's French twist should be held in place.

"Not yet with the coffee," Hanna snarled. "Go get us the barrette stand, would you? Do you know what it looks like, and where it is, in the storage room?" When I nodded, she said, "Then go get it so we can deal with this crisis."

Crisis? I hoisted the coffee tray, walked to the storage room, and kicked the door open with my foot. Was there *anything* having to do with a *hairdo* that could truly constitute a *crisis*? Sheesh!

I glanced around the room for barrettes. Along the back wall, by an old pole-mounted strobe and Gerald's broken compressor, a tilted card table was piled with racks of bracelets, necklaces, and earrings. I crossed to it, banged down the coffee tray, and was so intent on pawing through the racks looking for barrettes that I barely heard the storage room door quietly click shut.

"How close were you to old André?" Ian Hood asked as he started across the room. "Did he tell you something about this cabin that you felt you had to tell the police? Is that why you brought them here?"

"I—"

But he was already too close. He grabbed for my shoulder; instinctively, I jerked backward. His dark, dark eyes bored into mine. His fingers clamped my arm. *He knows,* I thought. *He's the one.*

"Who else knows?" he demanded.

I scarcely heard him. He had me pushed against a rack of dresses lining the wall and his fingers had closed around my neck. Black spots formed in front of my eyes.

The burns are deep, instantaneous, André's voice came from some distant part of my brain. *They are like molten lava....*

I kicked at Ian frantically. *Too late,* I thought as I tried to scream. Julian was busy with the food. Boyd was gone. Everyone else was staking a claim to hair, makeup, or ego. *It will be over by the time anyone misses me.* Ian's hands tightened. Visions of Arch, of Tom, flashed and vanished. I stretched my arms behind me, groping for anything. I couldn't get my breath. We struggled and fell away from the dresses; he lost his hold on my neck. My hands clawed futilely at the wall: I couldn't breathe. Where was the cord to the strobe light? Could I blind Ian if I plugged it in? My fingers closed around the cord. Ian lunged for me, hands outstretched. He tripped over something as I groped along the wall for the outlet. A piece of metal skittered across the floor. Ian righted himself and lurched toward me. I pushed in the plug as I wrenched away from him.

Nothing happened. No strobe, no light. *Dammit!* I'd plugged in Gerald's fool compressor, now minus its loose housing that Ian had sent sailing. I charged toward the door. Ian lunged to block my way. I charged the other way and knocked into the card table.

Swiftly, Ian grabbed the strobe pole. An idea seemed to form in his mind. "This has been a most unfortunate shoot," he said. "First André, then Leah, and now you. This very heavy light is going to fall on you, and a terrible accident will befall our *second* caterer."

He advanced toward me. The light stand scraped as he yanked it along. There was nothing between us except the compressor, its engine guts exposed. *Coffee,* I thought wildly. *All I need is coffee....*

I yanked the pot from the tray and heaved the contents at Ian.

He jumped sideways so that the steaming, dark liquid missed him and sloshed onto the compressor and the floor. Ian cursed and lunged at me. *I'm dead,* I thought. *Poor Arch won't have a mother. Tom was right—I should never poke my nose into murder.*

And then it happened. As Ian careened toward me, intent on ending my life, he stepped into the lake of coffee and the exposed, live current of Gerald Eliot's broken air compressor. The surge of voltage caused his body to jerk up and away from me. Before he fell to the floor, he was dead.

Chapter 24

"Leah told us Ian wanted the road to the cabin kept closed," Tom proclaimed matter-of-factly as he drove me to the museum from Lutheran Hospital on Monday, the first of September. "If he had the place to himself all winter, she said, Ian was sure he could figure out the code and find Smythe's stolen treasure."

It was Labor Day, except we weren't working, even though Tom had finally been taken off suspension by his captain. With a search warrant in hand, the investigative team had toiled through the weekend at the Merciful Migrations cabin. Underneath the spare tire in the locked trunk of Ian Hood's Mercedes, they had found *The Practical Cook Book* and the original note Gerald

Eliot had discovered tucked in oilcloth inside the kitchen wall.

"Leah says, early last Monday morning, Ian told her he'd remembered some equipment he needed. Of course, he knew André wanted to get into the place early. He just didn't know why. Ian must've surprised André prying up the wall, and told him much more food was needed. But he knew André had figured out Smythe's code at that point. He just didn't know what or how—only that the secret the wall had held was exposed. When André was involved with extra cooking, Ian burned him with the salamander. Maybe Ian meant to startle him, make it look as if André had an accident." Tom turned on Homestead Drive. "But from the heart-problem incident at the museum, Ian knew André kept the nitroglycerin with him, and that he was acutely sensitive to it. So when the hot salamander had done its damage, he must have overdosed him. André died and Ian nailed the plywood back over the wall."

"But why did Ian feel he had to kill *both* André and Gerald?"

"He was greedy." Tom glanced at me. "He wanted the treasure for himself, wanted to start up someplace else saving the elk. Leah had told him he could have Charlie Smythe's cache if Bobby could keep the proceeds from the sale of the cabin. Ian took her at her word. What Leah didn't bank on was that her boyfriend Ian would try to eliminate anyone else who knew about the code and his secret. He didn't want to share. Couldn't stand competition."

Oh, brother, I thought as guilt and insecurity reared their unattractive heads. *Now who does that remind me of?* Craig Litchfield hadn't played fair, and had been in cahoots with The Jerk. And yet I had to admit I didn't have catering in Aspen Meadow to myself anymore. So, the same insecurity that had plagued me the last month had eaten up Ian Hood, and driven him over the line to murder.

Our cellular rang as we pulled into the Homestead lot: it was Cameron Burr. He had been released and would join us at the cabin for an early dinner, thank you very much, to work with Sylvia and a crew of volunteers. And he had great news: Barbara was finally off the ventilator. The doctors were certain she was well on her road to recovery. Tom and I promised to visit her soon. And, Cameron asked, did we know Leah Smythe had vanished? We knew, we said, and hung up.

While Leah was still in the hospital, she had been questioned by Andy Fuller and two investigators from the sheriff's department. Her face had still been bandaged; her broken ribs had made talking difficult. After they left, so did she. The hospital had called the department when they'd discovered her gone. She wasn't a suspect in any of the crimes that had taken place at the cabin, and yet why had she slipped out? When Tom called Bobby Whitaker to ask if Leah wanted to join us at the cabin, Bobby had replied that his half-sister was too busy. Too busy, to come see historic treasure buried by her grandfather unearthed? Too busy doing *what*? She was at the museum, Bobby confessed, just looking at her grandfather's old stuff.

So we were at the Homestead. We were going to talk to Leah together because I was a friend, not a cop. Besides, I wanted to know for myself what had happened with that falling flat.

But as Tom and I crossed the Homestead dining room, we immediately heard Leah arguing with Sylvia Bevans in the kitchen. Between them, on the island, were the letter from Leavenworth and the framed *Times* article on the 1915 stagecoach robbery. Apparently Leah was demanding that the letter and the article be deacquisitioned so she could have them for mementoes. And Sylvia, fiercely protective of the museum, as usual, was telling her that she absolutely could have neither the newspaper article nor the letter.

"But *why* do you want them?" huffed Sylvia, trembling indignantly inside a lime-colored linen suit. "After all this time? The police told me you want *The Practical Cook Book,* too. Have you gone insane? Why don't you just take a photocopy?"

Leah, bandaged and holding herself at an awkward angle, shot back: "No, Sylvia, I have *not* gone insane. I'm leaving Aspen Meadow. I'm moving to Arizona, okay? The only things I want to keep are the messages my grandfather sent, and the newspaper reporting his last caper."

"You absolutely cannot take museum property—"

"We need to talk to Miss Smythe, Mrs. Bevans," Tom interposed gently as we joined them. "If you would excuse us. And please bear in mind all that Miss Smythe has done for the museum," he added. "Especially this afternoon."

Snapping her mouth shut, Sylvia stomped past Tom, back toward the sacred realms of her office. She did not acknowledge me.

Leah shuffled over to one of the stools and sat gingerly. A bare spot above her ear had been shaved and stitched. Her face was still swollen and covered with bruises, and the streaked pixie haircut looked disheveled and shorn.

"Are you here to arrest me?" she asked Tom defiantly.

"No," Tom replied easily. "Why don't we sit and talk?"

Leah gestured impatiently. "I'm leaving the Smythe land. When I have the property, everyone wants it. They *use* me to try to get it. That's why I'm going away."

"Begin at the beginning," Tom advised. "Goldy hasn't heard your story yet."

Leah raised one eyebrow at me and *hrumph*ed.

"I'm sorry about Ian," I said, and meant it.

"Don't be. Ian and I have...had been together for ten years. What kept us together was preserving wildlife migration routes." Leah touched the bare spot on her scalp. "I guess even a good cause isn't enough when you're not getting along, especially when the person you thought you loved turns into a self-centered, temperamental guy." She shifted her weight on the stool and

386

winced. "They're doing a lot of shooting down in Phoenix now, what with the good weather...anyway, Ian said he didn't have the capital to set up in a new place. But I wanted to leave, and I wanted Ian to move his studio somewhere, anywhere, away from my cabin, so Bobby could sell it. I feel responsible for Bobby, and I'm the *only* one who does. I wanted to let him sell that land to the paint-pellet people, so he could have a way to live, now that the modeling was finished for him." She took an unsteady breath and shook her head. "I don't give a damn about anything buried up there. If they don't find any of the victims' heirs, and the county historical society people want it, they can have it. I have a big family house in Aspen Meadow that I'm about to put on the market—"

"Three people are dead," Tom reminded her.

"Okay, okay. Sorry." She stopped and tried to construct her thoughts. "Bobby said the place would show better if we did a little work on it. We hired Eliot because he was available and said the job could be done in a week, before we got going on the Christmas catalog. The liar."

She fell silent; her fingers stroked her bruised cheek. Tom prompted: "And?"

She moaned. "That moron Eliot found the rifle in the wall, and a note from my grand-father saying you needed Winnie's cookbook *and* the rifle to find his treasure. Ian's Images put out the story that we'd fired Eliot, but that wasn't quite true. Ian and Gerald Eliot were in on it together. Eliot was going to get Ian the

387

cookbook. They were going to find the treasure together. But Ian...oh, God, I didn't
want to believe he could have killed Eliot. I
didn't even ask him about it. I didn't want to
know. And he knew better than to mention it."
She gave me a quizzical look. "How did *you*
find out about what was in the wall?"

I said simply, "Gerald Eliot had Rustine photocopy the note. But André didn't have the
note." Leah's confusion deepened. I told her
about André's knowledge of the very common
code, showed it to her in the Leavenworth letter, then explained that André had requested
a photocopy of the cookbook. "That's why he
went to the cabin so early on Monday morning." Leah's eyes watered; she raked her hair
again.

She said, "So...Ian managed to make it
look as if André had died accidentally?" When
I nodded, she began to cry. She said, "He must
have thought he was in too deep, by then. Anyone who figured out the code would be on to
him, about what he'd done to Eliot to get
the cookbook. It all got so out of control. I knew
it, but I didn't want to face it. I was afraid."
Tears streamed down her face. "I loosened the
clamp on the flat. I wanted to die. That way
Bobby would still get half the property. And
if the flat didn't kill me, at least I would be far
away from Ian. I knew he'd kill me next."
Sobs wracked her slender body.

"Let us take you back to your place," Tom
told her. "You need to rest."

"Aren't they going to start the digging up

388

at the cabin in a couple of hours? Don't you want to be there?"

"It's more important for you to take care of yourself," Tom replied. "Let us help you get home."

She picked up the Leavenworth letter and shook her head. "I can drive. I'm *fine*. You all go on to the cabin. I never want to see the damn place again." With her free hand, she smeared the tears from her eyes and forced a sour laugh. "I must look awful. I need to do something about my makeup, don't you think?"

◆

We followed Leah to her old house overlooking Main Street, then went home. I surveyed my lustrous cherry cabinets, bright new windows, and gleaming Carrara marble countertops. This was a kitchen I could enjoy, I decided, as Tom and I began to pack up for our meal at the cabin. Arch, joining us, announced: "Elk Park Prep called and said after Tom talked to Leland, he paid my tuition." While I offered a quick prayer of thanks, my son looked around and exclaimed, "Man, this place rocks! The marble's cool. I told Lettie she could come over after school tomorrow to see it. That's okay, isn't it?"

"Yes," I said with a smile. "Invite her for dinner, if she can stand the smell of paint. And you're right, Arch, this kitchen positively *rocks*."

Tom beamed wordlessly, surveying the

result of his labors over the past weeks with unconcealed pride. It wasn't quite done, but who cared? The floor still needed to be sanded and finished, the walls painted, the molding put in, and a hundred details attended to, but Tom, unlike the late Gerald Eliot, would take care of everything. My spirits soared.

"One thing I forgot to tell you," Tom said as we were packing up chilled wine and salads. "Litchfield's attorney tried to cop a plea on the charge of criminal mischief, tainting your food. Andy Fuller turned him down until Litchfield told Fuller that John Richard's guy, Leland, was paying him, Litchfield, to sabotage the food. *And* that John Richard was calling the shots during the weekly visits that Litchfield made to the jail. That bit of info motivated Leland to pay Arch's school bill. It looks as if *Litchfield* will get probation, which probably upsets him less than the facts that Edna Hardcastle's daughter put off getting married again, and Merciful Migrations has yanked him from doing this year's Soirée." I blinked. Litchfield had lost two jobs in one day? Things were looking up. Tom went on: "Your ex will be charged as a principal in the criminal mischief situation. Might add to his jail time."

"Might make him think before he tries to wreak vengeance on his ex-wives," I observed. "So. Eventually, I'll still be dealing with Litchfield." I thought about that while mixing fresh basil into tomatoes vinaigrette. Was I secure enough to deal with the competition? You bet. "On an even playing field," I said finally, firmly, "I can compete." To Arch, I said, "Are you ready?"

My son nodded. His face had turned tight with apprehension. This was, after all, a big day for him.

On Sunday night, Rustine and Lettie had called to invite Arch to accompany them the next day, when they met their father's flight from Juneau at Denver International Airport. Their father had given up on finding a job and was skipping the California leg of his trip to come home; he missed his daughters. Julian had generously offered to help the sisters clean their house Monday morning. I shuddered, remembering the chaos and dust we'd encountered on our visit. For his part, Arch had spent the morning getting clean himself and deciding on his wardrobe.

Julian returned; half an hour later, Rustine finally pulled up in front of our house. By that time, Arch was so nervous you'd have thought *he* was flying in from Alaska. I didn't hug him good-bye. I didn't tell him to be polite to Lettie's father. I told him to have fun.

Julian had proposed that Marla, Hanna Klapper, and Sergeant Boyd join us at the cabin dig. *To celebrate,* Julian added, we should have a feast for all the workers: crab cakes, pasta, salads, Parker House Rolls from *The Practical Cook Book,* and André's famous Grand Marnier Buttercream Cookies, which I had given a new name. They were a delicious treat my teacher had left for me to serve my clients: Keepsake Cookies. Plus, I had made

a flourless chocolate cake that was really a collapsed soufflé...when you *want* a soufflé to fall,
it can be delicious—like life, once you've put
it back together.

But Julian's words haunted me as I packed
the food. Celebrate *what*? I'd wondered. I
hadn't had the heart to ask what Julian's
plans for the future were, but I sensed the feast
was a kind of good-bye. He'd declined to
accompany us to church on Sunday. I concluded it was because he was on the phone,
making his plans to get a ride back to Cornell
so he could plead his way in for the fall semester.

"Time to go," Tom said. "I swore to Sylvia
that we'd be there by one o'clock. They aren't
allowed to bring anything out of the ground
until we get there."

Boyd and Tom carefully packed a chilled
white chocolate cream sauce I'd made for
the cake into the cooler; I covered the rest of
the food with foil.

By the time we arrived at the Merciful
Migrations cabin, the crew of diggers made
up of members of the Anthropology Department of the University of Colorado and volunteers from the Furman County Historical
Society, including Cameron Burr, were hard
at work at the base of the elephant rock. We
set up our feast on the deck of the cabin. The
diggers had vowed to have no treat until they
found what they were seeking.

"Good school, the University of Colorado,"
Julian said idly as I handed Marla a very small

advance taste of the tomatoes vinaigrette. "I just finished a transfer application. For the spring semester, of course."

I gasped. Marla giggled. Boyd brought his mouth into an *o*. Tom shook his head and said softly, "I knew it." Even Hanna Klapper smiled.

"Something else," Julian went on mildly, his eyes sparkling. "I called Leah Smythe on the cellular, on my way home from Rustine's house. Woke her up, I think."

"You called Leah?" Hanna demanded. "Why?"

"Well," Julian said as he tilted his handsome face knowingly at Tom and me, "you know, Leah and I are related, sort of. I'm her nephew once removed, since Brian Harrington, her brother-in-law, was my biological father. I mean, Weezie has made it very clear she doesn't want to be involved with me. But I thought Leah might want to know she had more family than just Bobby. That she could, you know, call on me—"

"You never said *I* could call on you," Marla *hrumph*ed good-naturedly. "And I'm your biological *aunt*."

"I didn't need to," Julian rejoined. "You *knew* you could call on me day and night, and you did, when I went through rush and was visiting all the fraternities, and you called every night to make sure I'd gotten back to my dorm safely."

"Marla, you never mentioned this," I accused. "Calling like a mother hen when he was going through *rush*!"

393

Labor Day Flourless Chocolate Cake with Berries, Melba Sauce, and White Chocolate Cream

7 ounces (1¾ sticks) unsalted butter
7 ounces best-quality bittersweet (semi-sweet) chocolate (recommended brands: Lindt Bittersweet, Bernard C. Semi-Sweet, Godiva Dark)
1 tablespoon espresso or strong coffee
5 large eggs, separated
2 tablespoons best-quality unsweetened cocoa (recommended brand: Hershey's Premium European Style)
7 tablespoons granulated sugar
1 tablespoon vanilla extract
1 small package fresh blueberries (approximately 6 ounces)
1 small package fresh raspberries (approximately 6 ounces)
Melba Sauce (recipe follows)
White Chocolate Cream (recipe follows)

Place the oven rack in the middle to lower (not the lowest) part of the oven. Preheat the oven to 350°F. Butter the bottom and sides of a 10-inch springform pan. Make sure you have the bottom of another 10-inch springform pan on hand.

Place the butter, chocolate, and coffee in the top of a double boiler and melt over boiling water. Transfer to a bowl and allow to cool slightly, then stir in the egg yolks and whisk until smooth. Sift the cocoa and sugar together, then sift this mixture directly into the chocolate mixture and stir until smooth. Stir in the vanilla and set aside. Beat the egg whites to soft peaks. Fold half the egg whites into the chocolate mixture, then pour the chocolate mixture on top of the remaining egg whites and fold in. Pour the batter into the prepared pan and set it on the lower rack of the oven. Bake for 25 minutes, or until the cake is puffed and the center no longer appears moist.

Remove the cake from the oven and immediately press another springform pan bottom onto the cake to deflate it. Allow the cake to cool on a rack.

When the cake is cool, remove the springform ring and place the cake on a serving platter. Decorate the top with concentric rings of blueberries and raspberries. When serving, ladle large dollops of Melba Sauce and White Chocolate Cream on top of each slice.

Makes 8 to 12 servings

Melba Sauce

½ cup currant jelly
2 (6-ounce) packages fresh raspberries, sieved
   (approximately 1 cup after sieving)
2 teaspoons cornstarch
7 tablespoons sugar

Heat the jelly and sieved raspberries in the top of a double boiler (placed directly on the burner) over medium heat until bubbly, about 4 or 5 minutes.

Remove from the direct heat and place on top of the bottom of the double boiler that is filled with boiling water. Mix the cornstarch with the sugar and stir into the jelly mixture. Cook and stir until thickened and clear. Remove from the heat, cool, and chill at least an hour before serving.

White Chocolate Cream

6 ounces best-quality white chocolate,
    coarsely chopped
1¾ cups whipping cream

Over low heat, melt the chocolate with ¾ cup of the cream, stirring constantly. When the mixture is melted and smooth, remove from the heat. Pour into a bowl and, stirring occasionally, allow the mixture to come to room temperature. Whip the remaining cup of cream and, whisking constantly to ensure smoothness, stir into the chocolate mixture. Chill before serving.

Keepsake Cookies

Cookie
⅔ cup blanched, slivered almonds
2 cups (4 sticks; 1 pound) unsalted butter,
    at room temperature
1 cup confectioners' sugar, sifted
2 teaspoons very finely minced orange zest
¼ cup Grand Marnier liqueur
3⅓ cups all-purpose flour
½ teaspoon salt
Granulated sugar, for preparing the cookies

Filling
½ cup (1 stick; ¼ pound) unsalted butter, at
    room temperature
3 cups confectioners' sugar, sifted
3 tablespoons whipping cream
1 tablespoon Grand Marnier liqueur

Grind almonds in a blender until they resemble large bread crumbs; set aside. In the large bowl of an electric mixer, cream butter until it is very smooth and creamy. Slowly add the confectioners' sugar and beat until the mixture is very smooth. Beat in the zest and liqueur. In a small bowl, combine the flour,

salt, and ground almonds. Stir the flour mixture into the butter mixture until very well combined. Chill the mixture for at least 3 hours, or overnight.

Preheat the oven to 375°F. Butter two cookie sheets. Measure out the cookie dough into ½-tablespoon increments. Roll each spoonful of dough into a ball and place them, two inches apart, on the cookie sheets. Butter the bottom of a glass, then dip the glass bottom in sugar. Flatten each cookie with the buttered and sugared glass bottom to a diameter of 2¼ inches. (Do not make the cookies too thin.) Dip the glass into the sugar before flattening each cookie. Bake approximately 7 to 10 minutes, or until the cookies are just cooked through but *not at all browned*. After removing the cookies from the oven, allow them to cool 1 minute on the cookie sheets. Then transfer them to racks to cool completely.

For the filling, in the large bowl of an electric mixer, beat the butter until smooth. Add the sugar, cream, and liqueur, and beat until very smooth and creamy. Spread about a teaspoon of filling on the flat underside of half the cookies; make a sandwich with the flat underside of the other half of the cookies. Store tightly covered.

Makes 64 sandwich cookies

"I thought we agreed you weren't going to *tell*, Julian," Marla said.

"Well, just don't give me this stuff about how you never call," Julian zinged back. "Plus, Arch and I have decided it's an effect Goldy has had on you. Arch told me, 'You'll never be able to do anything again, without Marla checking to see if you're still alive, or telling you that whatever you're doing is dangerous or will make you sick.' "

"Uh, excuse me," I interjected, smiling. "If people want to eat, they need to be *nice* to the caterer."

Julian patted my shoulder. "Let me finish about Leah, okay? I think at first she was relieved I wasn't her biological nephew. She figured I wanted money, or land, or her cabin, just like Bobby and Ian. I told her I just wanted her to know that she has another relation besides Weezie and Bobby. So then she got like, all teary, and said she was just so vulnerable since Ian had died. And did I want to move in with her in the big family house in Aspen Meadow until she sold it, that she would enjoy having family around her, besides Bobby. And I could help her with her move to Phoenix, she said. There was lots and lots for me to do, to help her."

A familiar fear gripped me. *Don't leave us,* I thought, *not again.* Not daring to look at Julian's happy face, I picked up the serving spoons and moved them around. *You can't hold on to people,* I warned myself. *You can't keep them, any more than Charlie Smythe could protect his wretched treasure.*

A whoop arose from the elephant rock.

"They found it!" Hanna cried. She had brought bird-watching binoculars, which she now swung into place. "Goodness, it's just an old coffee can!"

We all watched Cameron Burr carefully uncap the discovery and pour it out on a piece of canvas.

Boyd cried, "Hey! How much is there?"

Sylvia Bevans, who had changed from the lime linen suit to baggy khaki pants, sensible boots, and a wide-brimmed sun hat, bent down to ask Cameron a question. Then she turned toward us. Her face was stern. And then, for the first time in my life, I saw Sylvia smile.

"Jewelry!" she cried. "Old bills! Gold coins!"

I exhaled and smoothed the tablecloth. *Well, finally*, I thought. *It's over.*

♦

"So don't you want to know what I told Leah?" Julian asked when we got home. His face was bright with mischief.

I pressed my lips together and unpacked the first box of dirty dishes and set them in the dishwasher in my brand-new beautiful kitchen. *You can't hold on to him any more than Leah could hold on to her grandfather's land. Or Bobby could be a young and slim model forever. Or you could keep André forever. You can't hold on to people. You can't hold on to anything.*

Tom's large hand clasped mine. He murmured, "Stop worrying so much."

Julian put his hand on my shoulder. "I told Leah," he said, "that I really appreciated her offer to move in with her. But that I already *had* my family here."

My eyes filled and I cursed them. The doorbell rang. "Oh, answer it, answer it!" I cried. "I can't deal with any more in one day."

Julian disappeared. I heard him open the front door and then argue with someone whose voice I did not recognize. Tom gave me a hug and I snuffled contentedly into the familiar warmth of his shoulder. We really are a family, I thought. An absolutely *terrific* family.

Julian reappeared in the doorway. His face was ashen.

"It's the county health inspector. Should I let him in?"

Index to the Recipes

♦

About the Author

DIANE MOTT DAVIDSON lives in Evergreen, Colorado, with her husband and three sons. She is the author of eight bestselling culinary mysteries, including *Dying for Chocolate, The Main Corpse,* and *The Grilling Season.*